T0149320

TEMPLAR'S TREASURE

A NOVEL

✝ ✝ ✝

JERRY WISER

TEMPLAR'S TREASURE
A NOVEL

iUniverse books may be ordered through booksellers or by contacting:

iUniverse
1663 Liberty Drive
Bloomington, IN 47403
www.iuniverse.com
844-349-9409

ISBN: 978-1-5320-8935-0 (sc)
ISBN: 978-1-5320-8936-7 (e)

Library of Congress Control Number: 2020906208

Print information available on the last page.

iUniverse rev. date: 05/06/2021

This Book is Dedicated

To My Many Friends at

FPC Pensacola

SYNOPSIS

During the thirteenth and fourteenth century, a band of warriors rose to prominence in Europe and Palestine. The lands of the Middle East were known as Outmemer. The men who dominated these lands were a group of warriors known as the Knights Templar, poor fellow soldiers of Christ. These knights gave up all wealth and nobility to follow the covenants of Christ.

The House of the Templar's, based in Paris, became a powerful economic force amassing great wealth by donations of money and property. They were the most skilled fighting units of the crusades in the Holy land. Through their acumen they also became financiers, bankers, merchants and seaman with their own fleet of merchant ships.

When the Holy land fell under the control of the Ottoman Empire, support for the order faded. King Philip IV of France was deeply in debt to the Templar order, a debt he could never repay. With the aid of Pope Clement V, they denounced the Templar's as Heretics, killed many while burning the leaders at the stake.

A dedicated order of Knights stole away in the night, taking a vast amount of treasure with them, a treasure that has been searched for yet never found to this day. Yet the myth of the vast hoard of hidden treasure remains a mystery. Meanwhile, in present day, a New York lawyer, hired to locate millions of dollars of ill gotten gains supposedly brought to Casablanca, Morocco from Florida by Scott Rothstein. A perpetrator of the fourth largest Ponzi scheme in history, a scheme that bilked innocent victims of $1.4 billion dollars.

Mark Radin, aside from being a prominent criminal attorney, was also a decorated Navy Seal with extensive combat experience in many clandestine and covert missions around the world.

> While in Casablanca, he becomes involved in the murder of a ruthless criminal who was attempting to steal an ancient document from a young messenger. The young courier was in the process of delivering this manuscript to a scholar of ancient history for translation. The writing was in an ancient dialect making it difficult to decipher. The young boy, in possession of the portfolio containing the manuscript, meets Mark in a deadly confrontation with the killer who is intent on seizing the manuscript. During the struggle to save the boy Mark is forced to kill the evil assassin. Because of this killing the pair must run for their lives, being pursued by police and members of the criminal gang.

Their journey takes them from Morocco to Egypt then Israel in search of someone with the knowledge to understand, than translate the papers in the leather case the young courier possesses.

The search to discover the contents of this archaic script sends Mark on a dangerous journey to determine the validity of the information contained in the mysterious papers. Following the trail of a loyal band of Templar's who traveled this way eight hundred years before. The journey leads to turkey where a treasure may be hidden away.

That is if the myth, the rumors of the hidden treasure are true! Only time would tell where the trail would lead.

CHAPTER 1 ✠ ✠ ✠

Would you live your day differently if you knew you would be dead by nightfall? Mark stepped out of the bathroom, a blue, terry towel wrapped around his waist. He smiled at Kat lying in the king-size bed in the Excelsior hotel in London.

"You look tempting with just that towel around your waist," Kat smiled, a look of lust evident in her pale-green eyes. "It's a shame it's so late or I would invite you to join me in this comfortable bed for another round of pleasure."

"I would love to join you," said Mark, gazing at the woman he adored, the partner he had spent the last twenty two months with in New York. "Let's put it on hold until tonight. I'll make it up to you for making you wait so long."

"Yea sure Mark. That's all I get. Promises, Promises."

Once they were dressed, Mark in a conservative navy blue business-suit, Katherine in her Intercontinental Airline uniform, they left their room taking the elevator to the lobby. They walked to the entrance where a line of black London cabs sat waiting. They kissed briefly.

"Remember, we are going to dinner with Chris tonight," reminded Kat.

"I know, Mark replied. "I'll meet you back at the hotel by 5."

"Good," Kat smiled. "You behave today. I'm off to Heathrow, to speak with my ground personnel. That will complete my last working day in London. Tomorrow, we can be tourists for the day before flying home to New York Sunday morning."

They kissed again. Mark getting into a unique London cab, a sturdy, black hackney. A vehicle only found on the streets in England. Catherine climbed into the back of a Jaguar limousine for the ride to one of the largest airports in the world – Heathrow. Mark settled into the rear seat of the cab thinking how lucky he was to be in London after a glorious week in Paris all expenses paid, with a beautiful woman he loved at his side. It was a fortunate happening. Mark had to attend an aviation conference in Paris while Catherine went to check on the hotels her flight crews used for layovers. Kat was Vice President of Intercontinental Airline, she worked her way up through the ranks having started as a stewardess at age 21. They were now in London, where she was engaged in her duties inspecting hotels and ground personnel under her guidance, while Mark was meeting with law firms he wanted to start an affiliation with. Today's meeting was with a firm he was trying to enlist as his United Kingdom representative. Mark thought back to the turn of events that made him one of the best known aviation plaintiffs' attorneys in the legal profession. The crash of an Intercontinental Boeing 757 in Maine in February nearly two years ago. A flight from Paris to NY on a bitter cold February night. His affiliation with Intercontinental airline was because of a lawyer, Christopher Marlow, who was InterContinental's in-house counsel. How that meeting had introduced him to Kat who was now his live-in partner, his current love. All leading to a high profile complicated and difficult trial that lasted three months A trial that Mark won for the plaintiffs resulting in the largest jury award in the history of aviation law. The trial made him a fifteen-minute celebrity; but also made him and his firm rich beyond belief!

"Here we are Webster House." Mark stood on the sidewalk, looking up at the many massive modern steel and glass buildings surrounding him.

"Not like the London of old mate," remarked the driver. Strange for stodgy London; but the old and the new co-exist well together, don't you think?"

Mark nodded his head. "Yes I do, it seems incongruous but they complement each other well."

It was 4:30 in the evening when Mark arrived back at the Grand Excelsior Hotel. The doorman held the door for Mark as he exited the cab.

"Welcome back Mr. Radin, Ms. Bennet has not returned yet."

"Thanks, Walter. I'll wait for her in the lounge."

Kat walked into the lounge, a big smile on her face. Mark stood kissing her on the cheek.

"Sit my love. I 'll get you a drink."

"Thanks Mark, I could use one. It's been a full day; but I'm done at last. My crew at the airport is excellent; I chose my people well. I also had a chance to speak with three flight crews, two arriving from the states, one departing for New York; they all seemed happy."

"How was your day?" Kat asked.

"Interesting," said Mark. "I met with three partners of the firm, Goodwood and Partners, except Goodwood is dead, has been for thirty some years; but the name lives on."

"So, did you make a deal?"

"Don't know yet, Kat. They told me in rather stuffy English: 'Mr. Radin, we will take your proposal under advisement. You will hear from Mr. Forsythe within two weeks. He is our Managing Partner.'"

"After lunch in their club, I spent the day talking with various members of the firm, then came back to wait for you."

"After we finish our drink let's go up to the room so I can get out of this uniform, shower, then get dressed for dinner. Chris said you will love the restaurant; it dates back to the 1800's. The atmosphere and food are renowned in London. Many important people go there to dine and be seen – politicians, celebrities, prominent dignitaries; we'll fit right in."

The telephone rang at 7:30. Mark picked-up the receiver.

"Hi Mark, its Chris. I'm in the lobby waiting for the two of you."

"Great, Chris. We'll be right down."

"Let's go Kat. Chris is waiting in the lobby."

"Do you think I need a coat, Mark?" she asked.

"No, Kat. I know its Friday October 13th in London, but we've been lucky. The weather has been balmy as the Brits would say; so you should be fine in that dress. By the way you look ravishing, a new outfit?"

"Keep that thought for later tonight buster. I bought this dress in Paris last week on Rue Saint Honoré. Thought I would break it out for tonight's big event."

"You choose well; it shows off your many assets and I do mean a-s-s ets."

"Don't get fresh" she laughed, kissing Mark's cheek. "Let's go."

They got into a black cab for the ride to the famous eatery, Mark on the left, Kat in the middle Chris on the right behind the driver.

"Overtons on Saint James," Chris told the driver.

"Aye, Governor. You'll love the place. Not many Yanks know of it, but it is a standard, been around forever; gets better with time. There are some of the best gentlemen's clubs nearby– Brooks, Carlton Club and Whites are three well-known ones. You'll also find several posh shops on the street, but they will be closed by the time you finish your dinner.

They entered Saint James Street, a one-way street. The restaurant is on the left-side of the roadway the cab driver said pulling up on the right-side directly across from the restaurant.

"No stopping on that side" informed the driver. "The street is too narrow for parking on both sides; we have to keep the lane open for passage. Please exit on the sidewalk; don't open the door on the street-side."

Chris got out first, followed by Kat, Mark sliding across got out last."

"You two go on," instructed Mark, "I'll pay the driver and join you inside."

The two Intercontinental employees both Vice Presidents and good friends, started across the street heading for the entrance to Overton's together. The restaurant, established in 1782, proclaimed a gold-painted sign over the front windows next to the wooden entrance door.

"That'll be six quid, Governor," said the driver, looking at Mark through his open window on the right-side of the cab.

Mark glanced up to see his two companions in the middle of the street when he noticed a man rushing down the sidewalk toward the restaurant. It was growing dark, the street lit by old-fashioned gas-lamps. The man was wearing a heavy overcoat that looked two sizes too large for his slender frame. He had a fedora pulled low on his head as he hurried along, head bowed, eyes looking at the ground. Mark began to hand the money to the driver when his brain flashed a warning to his subconscious mind. The message went something like this: *Why a heavy overcoat on a warm night, especially one too large? The hat pulled low hiding the face, the fast pace to get into the restaurant. Something isn't right,* Mark's mind shouted loudly. Had he not been engrossed in paying the driver, he would have realized the implication sooner. Mark looked up to see the man push in front of Chris then dart into the restaurant.

Chris, with Katherine by his side was just stepping onto the sidewalk when Mark screamed out: "Wait, don't go in, it's a bomb, a suicide bomber!"

There was a bright flash followed by thick black smoke as debris from the blast flew through the once peaceful night. Mark heard no sound, as the shock wave hit the cab, the concussion blowing Mark into the stone wall of the building behind him. A curtain fell over him, all went black.

He awoke in a bright room, the light hurt his eyes as he tried to get his bearings. He was groggy. He looked at his surroundings trying to determine where he was. He lay in a clean bed, lines and wires hooked-up to his body – a body swathed in white bandages. One arm was in a cast, one leg suspended from the overhead bed-frame by a rope and pulley. His left hand attached to a weird wire contraption. There were wires attached to various parts of his body feeding into a monitor, plastic oxygen tubes in his nostrils. He ran his right hand, his free hand, over his face and head, touching bandages on both cheeks forehead and scalp. He was a mess, he ached all over, but he was alive; the pain told him that. There was a buzzer near his hand. He grasped it depressing the red button. A nurse hurried into the room.

"Oh sir it's good to see you are awake at last. I was afraid we were going to lose you. The first three days, it was touch and go, you were barely hanging on to life."

Mark tried to speak but his voice was hoarse, raspy. His throat hurt from the effort.

"Don't speak, sir. Try to drink some water. The doctor will be in to speak with you shortly."

That was the beginning of the road to recovery for Mark. It was a slow process. He learned he was unconscious for seventeen days in a coma which helped him recover. He was confined to the hospital bed for three additional weeks before he was deemed fit to travel.

Roger Sherman, President of Intetcontinental Airline sent a chartered jet to fly Mark home to New York. Now he was going to his office for the first time after being away for over three months. It was February 24th of a new year, a year without Kat by his side.

After two months in New York, Mark said goodbye heading back to London. He had an unfinished job to do. He was intent on finding the perpetrators of the terrorist act that had killed 36 people, injuring scores more. Two of the dead were his lover and a good friend. Mark was one of the lucky survivors of the horrendous terror act. He spent seven months in London seeking revenge. But, that is another story, an intense story of payback.

Mark Radin walked into his law offices early in the morning just one day after his return to America. Mark had been in London for seven months to find the killers of his live-in lover and his close friend, both of whom were executives of Intercontinental Airline. They had been killed by a terrorist bomb in London, nearly a year ago. He had extracted his revenge.

As he walked toward his comfortable office, members of his firm nodded to him, said *Hello*, even clapped to see had had returned. On hearing the commotion, one of his partners walked into the hallway from his cushy office.

"Mark, it's good to see you after all this time away, you look great. Come into my office; we can talk there, I'll call Jim to join us."

"Thanks Dan. It's good to be home after all these months in Londonstan. Good to be back in familiar surroundings. Things still look the same here which is comforting to see."

"They are Mark. We've been keeping the firm moving along in your absence; nothing extraordinary but we are making a profit."

Jimmy Gitomer walked into Dan's office reaching out to grip Mark by both shoulders. "Good to have you back buddy. Was your trip a success?"

"Let's just say Mission accomplished, as President George Bush II said on the deck of the aircraft carrier after the invasion of Iraq."

"Good for you, now what?"

"If my office is still waiting, I'll go back to practicing law. Bring me up to date first."

Dan began. "We have a lot of new cases in the works. I've gotten six divorce cases since you were last here; two are really big ticket items, a couple of heavy hitters. Jim has a major criminal case working through the courts in Florida. You tell him, Jim."

"It's a criminal case in Miami, Dade County. It happened in Fort Lauderdale which is known as Frauderdale. It was a major Ponzi scheme. I'm representing six New Yorkers and a hedge fund that has lost millions to the scheme. The case broke while you were in the hospital in England last November. If I can get the clients' money back we should make about forty million dollars in fees." "That's a big payday Jim. How much money is involved?" The case involves over a billion dollars. My clients are in for slightly over 230 million. We miss Alexa, continued Dan. She's in Hollywood practicing entertainment law; seems to be happy in La La Land. She is doing really well seems to be happy surrounded by the rich and famous. She sent us a client a few months ago. A TV soap opera star here in New York, a palimony case." We owe her a referral fee.

"Thanks for the update guys. I'll go dust off my office and get settled in. I have to let people know I'm back in business." It's good to see you two have kept the firm going without me during my absence.

After two weeks of sitting looking at a blank computer screen, picking up then putting down legal briefs, Mark sat gazing out his window at Park Avenue. *What is wrong with me?* he wondered. *I just can't get back in the groove. I should be happy to be sitting here in New York City ready to practice law instead of brooding all day and night.* He was jarred from his solitude by the ringing of the telephone on his desk.

"You have a visitor, Mr. Radin."

"Who is it?" Mark asked."

"A Mr. Durkin," came the reply.

"Send him in."

Derrick walked into Mark's office, a big smile on his lined face. "Man it's good to see you in one piece buddy. You sure put on one hell of a show back in London-town. The boys in all the services, civilian as well as military are still talking about that night."

"Bring me up to date, Derrick. You probably know most of it by now."

"We rounded-up all eleven Muslim terror suspects you told us about. I'm told some are singing like canaries. They have all been put away where no one can reach them while they are being interrogated. You turned that butcher shop into a real butcher shop. Blood and body parts were all over the place. Same thing upstairs in your apartment. The body you left in your place was blown apart, not much left to identify. Forensics believes it was you, DNA was yours, so case closed."

"Good," said Mark. "That's how I planned it."

"The Brits want to give you a reward for your efforts, but since you are dead they can't do that. Your connection to the whole affair is over."

"No one will ever know what Amir Kahn did since he died in the explosion. His alter-ego, you Mark, walked away without a trace. You can have any reward Derrick. You were the one who brought in MI5 and the SAS."

"Yes Mark. There is talk of that already. A lesser amount than you would have received; but it will be substantial nonetheless. That's all well and good, but what next?"

"I guess you go back to being a PI, while I try to become a lawyer again."

"You don't sound happy Mark; not much enthusiasm in your voice."

"I'll tell you, Derrick, I can't seem to settle in to my old job. I sit here looking at the walls or out the window when I should be working but I can't get motivated. It's like I'm out of my body looking at me wondering what the hell I'm doing in this office impersonating an attorney. I used to think I was important, now I don't know. I'm not sure I belong here anymore Derrick, I've kind of lost my way."

"Just hang in there, mate. It will get better, trust me."

CHAPTER 2 ✚ ✚ ✚

Stacy came into Mark's office, a look of concern on her face.

"You wanted to see me, Mark?"

"Yes. I need someone to talk to, confidentially, just you and me. "What we discuss stays with us, like that Las Vegas commercial on TV. You know the one, what happens here stays here".

"I got it, Mark you can rely on me to keep your confidence secret. Now what's troubling you Mark."

"I'm kind of lost, Stacy," "with Kat gone just over a year now, I'm lost in space. Not interested in the firm or my work. My apartment is lonely. I don't want to date or even go out. I met an interesting woman on the flight back to the States, went out with her twice then broke it off. I'm not sure what to do."

"I know what you are going through Mark. When my husband, was killed in Afghanistan I was devastated, even years after. When I finally went back to work I would burst out crying over nothing. I didn't want to see anyone, not even my folks, who only meant well."

"So, what do you suggest Stacy? What do I do since I'm no good to anyone like this, not even to myself."

"Get away Mark. Break the routine, change your lifestyle. You don't need to come here every day. Nor do you want to stay in your apartment alone thinking of Kat. Look for a change of scenery, get a new prospective on life. Take some down time to sort things out. Go some place new where you can do some serious introspective personal thinking." "Maybe a deserted island in the South Pacific."

"Thanks Stacy, that's good advice, I'll take that thought under consideration." I don't think I have to go that far away.

Thanksgiving had come and gone, Christmas was just three weeks away. Normally this was the happiest time of year in New York for Mark, but not this year. Two years ago, it had been the best of times for Mark with Katherine by his side. The days shopping spree with the orphans. Spending New Year's Eve in his penthouse in the sky. Just the two of them snuggling by the warm fire. Kat cozy in his king size bed. This year life was cold and bleak. Even the sight of the giant blue spruce aglow in Rockefeller Center could not make Mark smile.

He walked into Dan's office on a cold, cloudy, grey, December morning in Manhattan. "Dan, I'm taking a leave of absence from the firm, from New York. I'm heading out of town for a while." I've been thinking of this for a few weeks. I think it will be best for the firm and me.

"What is it, Mark? Can I help?"

"No one can help me but me Dan. I've been seeing a therapist for almost two months now. According to him and some close friends, I need some time to rehabilitate, to get a fresh prospective on life. It seems my involvement with Kat, the burden of the ICA case and my vendetta in London seem to have affected me more than I realized. My buddy Derrick says it is like PTSD troops experience in battle."

"What is PTSD?" asked Dan.

"Post Traumatic Stress Disorder. Lots of GI's experienced it after Vietnam and Iraq. I would like to think I was tougher than that; who knows."

So, what are you going to do? You notice its winter in New York; cold, bitter cold, and gloomy." said Mark. It's very depressing.

I decided I'm going to head for warmer climes. Going to go to Miami where I can sit in the sun by the beach or pool, relax, get brown, swim in the ocean. Take a little time to think about my situation. I will try to come to terms with my life so I can come home to be a productive citizen again."

"Sounds nice," said Dan. "I'd like to join you, but someone has to stay to watch the store."

"You won't have to worry about me or my pay while I'm gone."

"Like hell," said Dan. "And I am sure Jim will agree. Your pay will be deposited into your Chase account each week. After all Mark, you are the founder of this firm."

"But Dan –"

"Don't interrupt me. If it wasn't for you, we wouldn't be sitting here like fat cats. It was your money that got us started. The ICA case was yours; that award alone could keep us afloat for ten years if we didn't get another case. Both Jim and I would be sitting in a dingy office eking out a paltry living, instead of earning two million dollars a year, plus a bonus. No Mark, I won't hear of it; you get your pay while on this sabbatical of yours." Just be sure to come back to us healthy and rearing to go. We need your inspiration and guidance, your our guiding light.

"Thanks Dan, I appreciate that."

"When are you going to fly south?"

"It's the tenth of December today. I'll leave on Friday the 14th. That way, I can take care of a few things before I leave."

Mark came into the office on the afternoon of the 13th to say goodbye to his partners and staff. Jim and Dan shook hands, wishing him well.

"Keep in touch, fella," said Dan. "By the way, I have a surprise for you. One of my old client's, is a big time car dealer in Florida, one of the biggest I'm told. He has twenty stores, just about every type of car conceivable – from the tiny smart car to Rolls Royce. I saved him millions on his divorce when we proved his wife was having an affair with one of the managers in a BMW store. He has a house, more like a mansion I'm told, over 7,000 square feet, on Biscayne Bay in the Gables. I spoke with him Tuesday after you told me you wanted to go south. It seems Mort is going to Saint Bart's in the Caribbean to spend the next three months in a more pedestrian 4,500 square foot villa. Of course, he will have his 88-foot Berrloti motor yacht docked in the harbor."

"That's a nice story Dan. But Mort didn't ask me along."

"Why would he want you when he has a 28 year-old Miss Tennessee beauty contestant with him? However, when I spoke with him, he offered me the use of his hacienda for up to three months. Here are the keys, address, and the code to the alarm system. He also has a six-car garage with six assorted vehicles in it. *Use what you want*, he told me when he hung up the telephone. Mi casa es su casa. Enjoy yourself, Mark. Come back when ready."

CHAPTER 3 ✛ ✛ ✛

The house was palatial. It had seven bedrooms, each with its own bathroom, a home theatre and fitness center. It had a gated entry with a driveway leading to the house set well back from the street. There was also the six-car garage with a bevy of sleek cars. Mark settled into one of the smaller guest bedrooms which was larger then master bedroom in his New York apartment. He spent the first six days outside sitting in a comfortable lounge chair looking out over the Olympic-size Infinity pool at Biscayne Bay. The Bay was a placid blue stretching off into the distance. Aside from the six cars in the garage, there were two jet ski's on floats, plus a 35-foot Riva Portofino runabout tied up to the sea-wall which stretched a good 200 feet on the bay. On the seventh day God rested, but Mark felt the need for some companionship. He wanted to be around people since he had spent the past seven days alone in Mort's gated compound, Mark's sanctuary. When he had arrived there were three pages of notes, instructions really, which were intended to make his stay more pleasant. One paragraph told him to take advantage of membership in a beach-club on Key Biscayne. Mark climbed into a sparkling Maserati Gran Turismo, a navy-blue convertible with deep brown leather seats. He fired it up and drove down the long drive, through the metal gate onto De Soto Boulevard. I drove by the Venetian isle Mansion and pool which was a major tourist attraction in Coral Gables.

Cruising over the Rickenbacker Causeway Bridge that connected Miami to Key Biscayne, Mark felt a sense of euphoria. The bay was a splendid sight spreading out on his right, the Atlantic Ocean on the left. He drove by the famous Sea World Seaquarium on the bay next to the

Oceanographic Institute of the University of Miami. After driving down the main street, Crandon Boulevard, he saw the sign for the Ocean Club which was directly on the ocean at the end of Beach Club Lane. A closed iron gate protected the members from the rest of the world. The sign on the pale yellow stone gate-house read: Members Only Private Club.

A uniformed guard stopped Mark at the entrance. "May I help you, sir?"

"Yes," replied Mark, handing him Mort's club membership card.

"You are Mr. Brewster's guest?" he inquired.

"Yes I'm his house guest. I will be staying at his hacienda for some weeks."

"Very well sir, continue to the club house, follow the drive, it will lead you there. Have a pleasant day."

Mark drove up to the front entrance of the impressive two story building. A valet came to greet him. The tanned attendant was dressed in a blue polo shirt, and khaki shorts, the uniform of the day.

"This is Mort's car right, I mean Mr. Brewster's car?" said the cheerful young man.

"Yes, it is," Mark replied. I thought I recognized the car, it's one of many he drives.

"What's your name, sir?"

"Mark Radin. Why?"

"Just so I can address you by name in the future. Go into the Clubhouse, look around. Have a good day, Mr. Radin."

Mark did have a good day. He sat relaxing on a lounge chair by the pool. There were four pools that Mark could see from his vantage point. A small pool for parents with kids set way off by itself, A big one for families, a bigger one yet for teens and young couples; then biggest for big people like Mark. It was quiet by the pool, lazy but nice. Mark went to the Beach Bar and Grill overlooking the sand beach, the ocean beyond beckoning the ex Navy Seal, the nearly empty pool just a few feet away. He had a delicious rear cheeseburger with a cold Ultra-Beer before going back to his lounge chair to soak up more sun. That evening, he walked to the parking area to retrieve the luxury convertible. It was nearing six o'clock. The sun was setting over the bay turning the sky a soft red, puff ball clouds floated in the otherwise clear sky.

"I'll have your car up right away, Mr. Radin."

The ride home with the roof down was a pleasure. Mark was relaxed, comfortable for the first time in months. He came to the club each day, arriving early before it got crowded. He swam laps in the big pool wearing his Speedo and goggles. After swimming laps he would change into a more modest boxer suit to lay on his lounge to soak-up the sun. He always sat in the same lounge chair each day. It was the day after Christmas. A pleasant sunny day in Miami, while it was a brisk 28 degrees in New York. Mark thought of Stacy and her advice to get out of the city. Aside from being an efficient legal assistant she was a smart confidant. He had just returned to his chair after lunch in the Beach Bar.

He lay back closing his eyes, mind wondering, just relaxing in the warm sun.

"Excuse me," a female voice intruded. "Could I use some of your lotion? I'm out."

Mark sat up to look at a tanned blond standing at the foot of his lounge chair, sun behind her; because of the glare he couldn't see her features well.

"I don't think you want to use this. It's Panama Jack 4; not much protection from the sun's rays. It's mostly oil; with this lotion you slow fry instead of broil."

"I would like to give it a try. I can see you've gotten a great tan using it."

"Here, be my guest."

She sat on the next lounge applying the oil to her legs, midriff, arms and face.

"Would you mind putting some on my back so I get an even tan. I can't reach back there."

Mark began applying oil to her smooth muscled back. "Ok, you're done," he said.

"Thanks. What's your name?" she asked.

"Mark. Mark Radin."

"Do you live here?"

"No, I'm from New York, just visiting."

"I love New York, especially at Christmas; but it is cold. Is that why you're here?" she asked."

"Partly," he replied. "I need some R&R as they say in the military, you know, rest and relaxation."

"Well, you are doing that. I have seen you sitting alone in the same place each day for a week now. Just sitting alone, not speaking with anyone. You're not gay are you?"

Mark laughed. It felt good to laugh, he thought. "No, I'm not gay. I don't know anyone here. I'm staying alone over in the Gables just trying to sort some things out."

"Well, you know me now she smiled. My name is Jennifer Hirsh. I live in Miami. Can I take you to dinner tonight?" she inquired. "It's a prerogative of women today to ask men out on a date, especially virile, good looking men." I like your style, Jen. I've always admired strong women.

"I may not be good company. I've been kind of a solitary figure for well over a year now."

"Then it's time you got out a bit. This is Miami at the height of the season. Everything is jumping; the city is crowded with tourist, give it a try you may like it."

"Ok, if your game." "But don't complain if I disappoint." "With your tanned body and looks, I doubt you will be a disappointment. Pick me up at my apartment. I live at 49 Brickell Drive; it's just off Tobacco Road; pick me up at 8. This is my telephone number in case you get cold feet and want to back out."

Mark thought with a name like Tobacco Road, the area would be run-down, shacks, shanties, like the back woods of Kentucky. But this Tobacco Road was the opposite. Large well kept houses, low stone walls for privacy, beautiful tropical landscapes; it was definitely a high-rent district. When he turned onto Brickell Drive, he got more of the same, except the single-family homes became high-rise apartments, one more modern than the next. He turned into the driveway to 49, a modern glass and steel building, rising into the Miami sky on the bank of upper Biscayne Bay.

"I am here to pick up Jennifer Hirsh," Mark told the doorman.

"Very well," Mr. Radin. "Miss Fried told me to expect you. I will let her know you are here."

She walked to the car smiling. Her blond hair pulled back into a long pony-tail showing off her tanned face with pale almost transparent- pale green eyes, full lips shiny with a red lip-gloss.

"Good to see you Mark. I was sure you would fink out on me."

"How could I disappoint someone as attractive as you?" That would be a crime of the first magnitude.

"Thanks Mark; that's a nice thing to say, gives me a warm feeling."

"I am out of practice Jennifer, but some things are coming back to me."

"She got into the Maserati sports car, the doorman closing the door for her.

"You keep trying to remember how a date goes, Mark. It could be a memorable night yet."

"I will try, where to?"

He pulled up in front of the Grill Room on Ocean Drive, in South Beach; a valet attendant taking the Maserati away since there was no street parking. The sidewalk was packed too overflowing with people trying to get into the restaurant dinner club.

A huge black bouncer blocking the door saw them. He waived. "Hi Jen, come on; I get you in."

The restaurant was more crowded than the sidewalk outside. A hostess in an almost-nothing dress with six-inch Stiletto's pushed her way toward us.

"Who is this sexy guy Jen? Where did you find him?

"He was sitting by the pool at the club alone and forlorn. I thought it my duty as a girl scout to rescue him."

"Good job, girl. He looks like a winner. The scar on his cheek only adds to his charm; bet it's a good story."

"I'll see if I can find out later," smiled Jen. I'll let you know Chrissy."

"Grab a drink at the bar. I'll get you a table soon; I'll come for you."

Jennifer squeezed up to the bar, pushing between two women, raising her slender arm to get the bartender's attention; a well endowed female bartender came to Jen. The woman's full raised breast glistened with a light sheen of perspiration. The huge pair being held in place by a skimpy halter top.

"If she isn't careful, those twins are going to jump out of that slim restraint," said Mark.

Jennifer laughed. "It's happened before. You should see the tips she got."

"I'm sure smiled Mark."

"What do you drink?" Jen asked.

"I'm not much of a drinker," Mark replied.

"Ok, I'll order for us. Dina – two Sex on the Beach. We can drink them now, then try it later."

They had an excellent dinner, finishing about 11 – the restaurant even more crowded now than when they had arrived.

"A band starts here in an hour. Want to stay?"

"No, replied Mark. "Let's get out of here; too crowded; too noisy."

After a walk on the sidewalk along the beach, they drove to Lincoln Road. Jennifer took him into Club Vibe, one of the hottest night-spots on Miami Beach. At midnight the party was in full swing. After an hour, Mark had had enough.

"Let's go, Jennifer. That is enough excitement for me for one night. That's all the socializing I can take at the moment."

He pulled the Maserati up to her apartment door. "I'm sorry, Jennifer. Maybe five years ago I could have handled that scene; but it's a bit much for me now." I'm still having trouble adjusting.

"No sweat, Mark. I had a good time anyway. You could be fun if you relaxed a little. Do you want to come up? I've got a great view of Miami Beach across the bay."

"Thanks, Jennifer; not tonight I'll take a rain check though."

She leaned over, kissing him on the lips. Not a passionate kiss, no tongue or open mouth, just a soft easy pressure of lips. "So you'll remember me," she said, then kissing the scar on his cheek. See you at the club tomorrow."

CHAPTER 4 ✠ ✠ ✠

The next day at the pool, Jennifer walked up to Mark where he sat in his chaise lounge.

"Hi fella, remember me, I'm the one who loves you. Getting some more rays I see." That's a great song Jen, performed by many of the best country singers, Cash, Haggerd and my all time favorite Willie. I'll remember.

"Yes Jennifer, it's good to see you this morning, did you sleep well. Not as well as I would have with you next to me. By the way, you look extremely sexy in that one-piece tank suit; shows off your assets extremely well. And, I do mean a-s-s-ets."

"Thank you, sir. But this body isn't doing that well. We've gone out three nights in a row now. I've invited you up to my apartment each time only to get a kiss and a goodnight. You are giving this girl an inferiority complex. I usually don't have to work this hard"

"Don't take it too personally. I told you I had some things to straighten out. I'm not quite there yet; almost, but not all the way. Any problem in this relationship is me, not you. I can guarantee most, if not all men would have taken you up on your offer."

"That's the point, Mark; I don't want most men. I have pretty high standards; it's you I'm after. So tell me, what's holding you back?"

"I don't like to talk about myself, Jennifer. Although we have been together most of the past four days, and I do like you, like your company, I am not ready to tell you my story – at least not yet. But I don't know all that much about you. So, why don't we start with you?"

She sat on the chair next to Mark.

"Sure" she said, "I'll tell you about me. Grew up in California; Santa

Barbara. Dad is a doctor, OB GYN, big-time doctor. After graduation from Santa Barbara High, I went to UCLA for four years; majored in Biochemistry. After graduation, I went to Vanderbilt Med School; it is one of the best in the US, definitely the best in the south, graduated ninth in my class."

"So, that means your a doctor?" asked Mark.

"Sure am," she replied. "I applied to Jackson Memorial to do my residency while taking courses to become a surgeon. I've been in Florida for four years. Finished my residency, then went to work in the Surgery O R. One of my teachers, Dr. Gelman, is a plastic reconstructive surgeon. He liked my work with a scalpel; asked if I wanted to train with him. I jumped at the chance since he is a well-known professional. I finish my training in eight months. August of 2012. I will be a full-fledged Licensed Plastic Surgeon when I complete my training."

"Now I know how you can afford that high-end apartment on the water plus this club."

"I hate to disillusion you Mark. The apartment I can afford with a little help from my Dad on occasion. I am a guest here at the Ocean Club much like you. I did some reconstructive surgery on a spoiled brat kid who wrecked his father's Lamborghini without wearing a seat-belt. It messed his face up pretty bad. The young man suffered broken cheekbones, eye-orbit, jaw, nose, plus numerous cuts. His father gave Gelman and me guest privileges for the work we did on his son. I've been off for two weeks. I'll be going back to work on January 4th. Fun and games almost over since it's the 29th today; New Year's Eve just two days away."

"That's a good story Jennifer. It's nice to be with a smart, accomplished, beautiful woman. You are a complete package all in one very attractive person. It also tells me why you are assertive. You are used to taking charge.

"Thanks again for letting me be me Mark.

. Most men run when they hear I'm a doctor. They get intimidated by my stature, my accomplishments. They head for the hills looking for a dumb blond, definitely not me. But let's get back to us. What are you doing New Year's Eve?"

"I have no plans. I told you I don't know anyone here in Miami. If you hadn't picked me up I would still be sitting here alone."

"I doubt it Mark. I am a woman, an observant one at that. I can point out four or five predatory females who would be coming for you. The cougar, across the pool would like to kill me for beating her to you." They would be circling like sharks around fresh meat, and you're the catch.

"From your time-table it looks like you are stuck with me for at least seven more nights, that is unless you find a better date" smiled Mark.

"I will keep you until I go back to work. Now what about New Year's Eve?" Jen asked again.

"I give up. What do you have in mind?"

"There are all sorts of wild parties on the beach New Year's Eve. Everything from LIV in the nightclub at the Fontainebleau Hotel to a dozen other hot-spots around town. But, from your reaction at Vibe the other night, I think they would be too overwhelming." "You would be uncomfortable, probably wouldn't last to midnight."

"You are right," said Mark."

"Then, we can stay here. The Palm Court has one of the most elegant affairs in Miami. People try everything to get an invite to this event. It's like trying to get into a gala at the White House. If you don't have a printed invitation you are not getting past the guard at the gate."

"That's it then," said Mark. "To make it official, Jennifer Hirsh, would you please be my date for New Year's Eve?"

A big smile lit her tanned face, showing her even, white teeth. "I thought you would never ask, sir. I would be happy to be yours on the last day of the old year, the first of the new."

"However, I don't have a tuxedo. I didn't bring one with me." I'm sure it will be a formal affair, tux and gowns required.

"No sweat, Mark. Let's see George the concierge. He'll order one for you. He will see it's delivered to you place. It will be there in time for our big date." "Where are you staying, Mark?"

"A small cottage, in the Gables," he replied.

"Just give him your measurements and the address of the cottage; he will see to the rest."

Mark picked Jennifer up at 8, New Year's Eve. He met her at the elevator in the lobby. She stepped out wearing a black sheath, floor-length strapless gown. With her tan complexion, blond hair combed out set off by her pale green eye's, she looked stunning, which is what Mark told her.

"You look very handsome yourself. I do think we make a nice-looking couple."

Mark opened the door for her.

"What's this?" asked Jennifer, "A new car?"

"Yes, it's a bit more formal for tonight. A Bentley GT coupe. I could have driven the Rolls Royce, but I thought we would be more comfortable in this – classy, but not pretentious."

She laughed heartily. "You keep surprising me, Mark."

The massive main building was awash in bright lights; well-dressed, beautiful people were filing into the lobby. I pulled the Bentley up to the front door. A valet opened the door for Jennifer, I walked around to join her. We walked into the Palm Court where a twelve-piece band was playing on a stage, a female singer crooning for the guests. Couples danced to the music swaying happily on the dance floor.

"I requested a table for the two of us by the window. I wanted to be alone with you, wanted to enjoy your company, rather than have to make small-talk with strangers."

"Thanks Mark. That was thoughtful of you; I appreciate the gesture. Who knows, this could turn out to be a memorable night yet, a night to remember."

"The room is elegant. I can see why people want to come here on New Year's Eve."

The couple ate a delicious dinner, sipped champagne, danced the hours away, the clock winding down toward midnight.

"Only twenty minutes to go, Mark 2011 coming to an end. Are you looking forward to the New Year?"

"Yes, very much so; I want to move on with my life." Now that the dishes had been cleared away they were holding hands, speaking quietly, absorbed with the closeness. A distinguished-looking man in a well-tailored tuxedo walked up to their table.

"Excuse me," he said. "I hope I am not interrupting, but I had to ask: Are you Mark Radin? The ICA Mark Radin."

"Let's just say my name is Mark Radin."

"Let me introduce myself. My name is Harris Becker. I am an attorney; firm of Becker, Fertel. Here is my business card. If it is not too much trouble, I would like to see you in my office on Monday the fourth of

January, That's the day we go back to work. The first Monday of the new year."

Mark looked at the card, then the man standing there. "I'm not in any trouble am I? Do I need an attorney?"

"No, no, Mark," laughed Becker. "I can call you Mark, can't I?"

"Of course Harris, we are all friends here, I think. This is my date, Ms. Jennifer Hirsh."

"You are very beautiful, Ms. Hirsh. Watch her closely Mark she is a keeper." Yes, we are all friends here, which is why I would like to see you on Monday morning, the 4th, about 10, if that is convenient."

Mark looked at Jennifer: "I will be off to work at 8 Monday morning; so you will be free of me."

"I will be at your office at 10, Harris." Mark looked at the address – 220 Alhambra Circle. It is at the end of Coral Way, also called the Miracle Mile. "Don't worry, I will find it."

"Good," said Harris. Happy New Year to you both." Enjoy the rest of your night.

"What was that about?" asked Jennifer, looking at Mark quizzically. "Are you some undercover celebrity or big-shot? He asked if you were that Mark Radin. What did he mean by that?"

"It is almost midnight; let's dance until then," replied Mark ignoring the question.

As the band-leader counted down 10-9-8, the band played *Old Long Signe*, the lights dimmed as the couple kissed. This time the kiss was passionate it lasted an eternity. Jennifer held Mark's head in her hands, slowly savoring his mouth, tongues touching, softly, slowly, exploring not urgently, sensually. People around were cheering, the celebration was in full swing. They continued to kiss, holding each other in a warm embrace.

"That was nice, Mark. I'll bet it didn't even hurt."

"No, it didn't," replied Mark. That is the first real kiss I have experienced in well over a year."

"See what you have been missing. You've wasted a week of that."

At 1:20, they made a toast with the last of the champagne.

"To health, happiness and success in the coming year," Jennifer smiled.

"I will drink to that. But I will add to pleasure in the coming days."

The valet pulled up with the Bentley, parking under the portico "Happy New Year, you two."

Mark handed him a 10-dollar bill.

"Thanks, Mark, Mr. Radin. Nice ride tonight- I mean the car," he smiled.

"I know what you mean," said Mark, sliding into the driver's seat.

As they crossed the Rickenbacker causeway into Miami Jennifer slid her hand onto Mark's thigh.

"We can turn right over the bridge toward my apartment, or left toward your cottage. I say go left."

Mark did not reply. When he came off the bridge, he put on his directional signal; it was blinking left.

CHAPTER 5 ✠ ✠ ✠

The car pulled up to the gate at the compound on the bay. Mark pushed the button on the dash. The gate began to swing open, lights coming on along the drive. He came to a stop before the imposing house. He opened the door for Jennifer helping her out of the car

"You fraud," she said. "This is your cottage? The damn place is as big as the White House."

"Not quite," replied Mark. "It's only 7,600 square feet under air. The White House is 56,000 square feet, 132 rooms and 35 bedrooms." I only have 7 bedrooms in my cottage.

She threw her arms around his neck, kissing him warmly again.

"I can't wait to find out what other secrets you are keeping from me."

It's a comfortable house once you get over the size, he told Jennifer. Beside the 7 bedrooms it has nine bathrooms, a media room, gym, and a six car garage with six cars parked inside. I am sleeping in one of the smaller bedrooms but I'll move to another if you prefer."

She had her shoes in her right hand. "You lead the way, Mark. If there is a bed with you in it that's where I want to be."

He took her hand, leading her to his room.

"Holy cow, this room is almost as big as my entire apartment. The bed is enormous. Do you think it will be big enough for the two of us?"

"You can have the left side, I'll take the right."

"Fat chance buster. I'll lead, you just follow. Are you going to tell me you haven't made love in over a year either?"

"No, I haven't."

"Good," she said smiling, this should be fun.

"It's actually more than a year."

"Oh God," she said. "Poor boy, were you in prison?"

"Something like that."

"Well Mark, I am told it is like riding a bike; you don't forget.

Mark began removing his tuxedo.

"Can you unzip me, please?" Mark pulled her zipper down while Jennifer held the bodice in her hands. When he finished, she turned, letting the dress fall around her ankles. Mark had been looking at Jennifer for over a week in various two-piece bathing suits or her one-piece Speedo. But he was not prepared for the woman standing naked before him. Since she had not been wearing any undergarments, no bra or panties, her lush body stood proud before him. She had a dark tan except for two narrow bands of white, the contrast was exciting. Her breasts were natural, just right for her body, not too large, firm, perky, the nipples inviting. Her stomach was flat, firm but what he liked best was the small, trimmed triangle of fuzzy blond hair between her legs. She was a picture to behold.

"Why are you standing there, with your pants still on? Never saw a naked woman before?" Standing with her hands on her hips, legs spread slightly she was a picture of feminine beauty.

"I have seen many naked women Jennifer - not meaning to brag or seem conceited, very many. But I must say, you are stunning your beauty is overwhelming."

"Let's hope I don't disappoint you. Now get undressed, then come join me in bed." Let's see if you remember how this goes.

Mark woke, looking at the clock on the nightstand – 8:20; that was late for him. He looked at the face on the pillow next to him. She was pretty in sleep, relaxed. He rose from the bed, walking into the bathroom. The sun was shining through the floor to ceiling glass window with its walled garden outside. *Another day in paradise*, he thought. After showering, he walked into the bedroom, where Jennifer sat, propped on a pillow, watching him.

"Good morning, Mark. How goes it this glorious morn?"

"Fine, Jennifer. I'm feeling good; thanks for asking."

"You were good last night,""I mean this morning, really."

"Told you if you relaxed it would all come back to you. Like riding a bike only better"

"You were delicious by the way. I knew you would be the first time I saw you at the pool." You performed even better than I anticipated."

"You made me wait longer than I expected, but you did not disappoint. Now drop your towel, and get back in bed with me," she said, as she threw off the blanket, revealing her inviting body.

Later, as they lay side by side, Mark reached out, taking Jennifer's hand in his.

"I want to thank you," he began. "I have been in a pretty bad way mentally for some months now. Today, for the first time I feel a little better about life, about myself. You have made a difference these last weeks. Most people would have bailed on me after our first date; so thanks for sticking it out."

A tear appeared in the corner of her eye, slowly running down her cheek. "That's nice, Mark. It's good to know that you didn't keep me around just to get laid."

"No, Jennifer, I am not complaining mind you, the sex was great – definitely in the top 20 or so. It is the fact that you were there for me, with me that makes a difference. Now enough of the sentimental stuff. What should we do today? Actually, for the next three days before you have to go to work. Then, I go to see Harris Becker about I know not what."

"Here is my suggestion," said Jennifer. "It looks like this cottage of yours has everything we could want or need. Let's camp-out by that large Infinity pool to get more Florida sun. It's only nineteen degrees in New York today. That way, we won't be too far from your bed in case we need a nap or a roll in the hay. I also have a surprise for you. Didn't want to tell you before in case you were done with me after you had your way. You would be surprised how many men say *Biff, bam thank you, mam*, then fly."

"I can't see that happening with you," said Mark.

"You would be surprised, Mark. Beside which I want to work at improving my ranking; it's hurtful to be mere 20th."

"Now, what is your surprise?" Mark asked.

"I have two tickets to the Orange Bowl game tonight. Ohio State is playing the University of Florida Gators for the national title. Want to go?"

"You're a winner, Jennifer. I love college football." I will enjoy the game even more with you by my side. I'm also looking forward to come home to enjoy our new found activity.

The three days flew by; Though they just lounged around the house they found great comfort from their shared companionship. Mark picked up the Sunday New York Times stopping in a local deli for bagels, lox, tuna and cheese, which they ate sitting on the patio under a large beach umbrella with cold Mimosa's to wash it down. As they lounged by the pool Mark told Jennifer about Kat. The love story that was shattered by an explosion in London, his months of recuperation leading to his trip to Florida. He conveniently left out any mention of his seven months in London to seek revenge for his lover's death, the payback he extracted on the killers. It felt cathartic to tell someone of his loss; especially someone who cared for him, who would be sympathetic to his plight. That Sunday, their last together, was consumed with love-making, separated by bouts of tenderness, just holding each other, speaking softly; dozing, then rousing to make love again.

"It is 6:00 a.m. Mark. You've got to take me home so I can dress to head off for work."

They walked to the elevator hand in hand, neither wanting to let go, to have their fairy tale adventure end. She looked into Marks eyes, "I am not sure when I will see you again. I will be busy all week. I know we, Dr. Gelman and me, have three operations scheduled. You have my number. If you want me, just call; if you don't call I want you to know I care about you deeply. You have been great — no, more than great. If I helped you move on from that horror you experienced, I am glad. Take two aspirin, than call me in the morning."

He kissed her soft mouth. "Thanks for putting up with me." Jennifer stood in the elevator as the doors closed between them. Mark was sure he saw a solitary tear run down her cheek.

CHAPTER 6 ✝ ✝ ✝

The Bentley pulled up in front of 220 Alhambra Drive. The building was a throw-back to Florida in the late 1920's. Designed in Mediterranean-Spanish architecture in the Mizner tradition. The buildings stone was a soft shade of brown with pink tones. After giving the Bentley to a parking attendant Mark walked toward the bank of elevators on the garage level.

"Get the ticket stamped," the attendant instructed. "That way you don't have to pay me twenty dollars."

"Thanks" said Mark pushing the button for the eighth floor. He stepped off into a large waiting-room where a middle-aged woman sat behind a dark wooden counter.

"Mark Radin to see Mr. Becker."

"Yes Mr. Radin. He is expecting you. Down the hallway on your right; Mr. Becker's office is the second door, on your left."

Mark looked into the first doorway as he walked by. A good-sized conference room, large glass topped table with eight chairs, more chairs available along the wall. The far facing wall was glass, floor to ceiling windows looking out to a terrace and the modern glass Bank of America office building across Alhambra Drive. Mark walked into Harris Becker's office. It was like a men's club, dark wood paneled walls, tile floors, a Persian rug with a colorful, multi-colored motif to brighten up the room covering the floor. Harris sat behind his large wooden desk; its top surprisingly clean of papers except for a legal pad, a few typed sheets of paper, and a maroon accordion file stuffed-to-bursting.

"Sit down Mark," Becker said, indicating an arm-chair before his desk.

"Thanks you Harris. You have a very pleasant office, very tastefully done."

"I know you are curious about why you are here; about what I could want of you. We will get to that in a few moments. First, let's take a little time to get acquainted, get comfortable with each other. Let me assure you we are not adversaries. To the contrary by the time this meeting is concluded I hope we will be associates working together."

"I didn't realize I was in the market for work," replied Mark. "I am here in Florida to take a break from my work. The routine was getting me down. I was not happy. No – that Isn't the right word. I was not content, not fulfilled by my work as I once was. I was missing the spark." That's why I came to Florida. I came to find my way in this cruel uncaring world.

"I am aware of some of what you say. I ask you to listen to me. Try not to interrupt; I know that can be hard being a lawyer and having an inquisitive mind; sometime reaching a conclusion even before the full premise is explained. Here is a legal pad and pen. Let me finish my dissertation before you interrupt. If you have questions jot them down so we can come back to them once I'm finished. Since I spoke with you last Thursday I have done some research into your background, whatever is public notice The more I read the more impressed I became. I am convinced as we sit here now that you are the right person for the job I have in mind. Let me ask you, are you familiar with the Scott Rothstein case?"

"The name is familiar," said Mark. "My partner, Jim Gitomer mentioned something about it. He is representing six or seven people, who lost money to a fraud perpetrated here in Florida. He told me it was a Ponzi scheme."

"Mark, it was no mere scheme, it is the largest such operation in Florida history. Rothstein ripped off people, so far about 300 we know of,to the tune of 1.4 billion dollars. That is the fourth largest Ponzi scheme in history. Bernie Madoff made off with 60 billion, by far the biggest of all con-artists. But his game went on for more than thirty years. Rothstein stole his 1.4 billion dollars in just four years. He is in jail now awaiting trial. When he is found guilty he will be going away for a long time, which is as it should be. However, there are probably fifteen or twenty more people who are going to be incarcerated because of their actions. Some few deservedly, others fringe players who are not necessarily guilty of a crime. But, this is Florida – a strange state both socially and legally. Rothstein's firm, RRA, Rothstein Rosenfeld and Adler, had 80 full-time lawyers and a total of 170 employees. There are going to be prison terms along with disbarment for some of them, fines for others. I am one of the five preeminent bankruptcy attorneys in the United States, number-one in Florida. So it was not surprising when Judge Handler nominated me as conservator of Rothstein's assets. I am to reclaim all his property, to dispose of it, gather the proceeds so the investors can get some money back. This is a daunting task Mark. To give you some idea of the monumental job involved, Scott had over twenty pieces of real estate in various names. Some are corporations, others in personal names, his wife Kim, various girlfriends, his parents and other people in many states. Some of these people are living some dead. I know what you are thinking – no big deal. Wrong, we are speaking of real estate worth upwards of 100 million dollars at face value when he bought them. That means they could be worth $150 million or more today. He owned over 100 watches at an average cost of $20,000 each; twelve cars ranging in price from $200,000 to $1.6 million each. The Bugatti is one of the most expensive cars in the world at $1.6 million; he owned two of them. Getting the picture?"

"Yes," replied Mark. "But I still don't see where I fit in."

"I am coming to that. When the house of cards began to tumble, our Orthodox Jewish fraud artist got on a private chartered jet to Morocco."

"Morocco," blurted Mark. "Why there?"

"Make a note," said Harris. "But I will tell you now. Rothstein was worried about getting caught, all smart criminals are. He needed an exit strategy in place if that day ever came. So back in 2007 he gave an assignment to three of his legal associates, his smartest associates. The assignment was: find a country a criminal can run to without fear of extradition to the United States or Israel."

"Why not Israel?"

"I asked you to make a note. Remember I told you Rothstein was an Orthodox Jew. He was afraid of Israel. If they got their hands on him he feared they would make a deal with America, their principle benefactor, to turn him over, to extradite him. You want to know what one of his clever associates came up with?"

"Morocco," said Mark.

"Yes, to Morocco. An Islamic country with little ties to the west - France mostly, but neither Israel or the United States. The story is vague at this point in time. Some say he left with many millions in a case to live in Morocco, in comfort for the remainder of his life."

"How many millions?"

Harris looked at the ceiling in exasperation, rolling his eyes. "The number varies somewhere between ten and twelve million dollars; the favored number is twelve million, no one knows for sure. Mark doubted that statement. Scott flew back to Florida the next day after speaking with his partners at RRA. Again, the story is cloudy. Some say he got a call from a Mafia Don since one of the New York hedge funds he got $120 million from is supposedly a front for Mafia money. Either come home or we will whack your wife, mother and father. I am not sure how he felt about his wife, but he was close to his parents; so he came home. The important item for you, Mark, is he came home with eight dollars in his pocket. That is on record at the Federal Courthouse. So, if he did go with a briefcase suitcase or duffle stuffed with money, the question is where is the money now? I want you to try and track it down if it exists."

"Mr. Becker, Harris, I appreciate your thinking of me, but I'm an attorney not a detective or private investigator. What your asking is a little outside my realm of expertise."

"I think you diminish your ability Mark. I have your military service record here; quite impressive. The combat experience, the awards; they speak volumes. I also spoke with Jim Gitomer this morning. He could not praise your analytical ability more. The cases you have won, your work ethic and insight. He also alluded to some sort of operation overseas recently; didn't have details but called it pay-back of some type. He thinks you were successful at whatever it was." Mark sat not speaking.

"Here is what I propose," continued Harris. "This file on my desk is much of the information on the Rothstein case. It is all the public records, along with some personal statements from witnesses and government investigators; very private. I suggest you spend the next week going over this material. Meet here in my office on Friday at 10; we will talk more then. If you are interested, I will make my pitch. If not, give me back that file. I will reimburse you for your time. Then, you can go back to doing whatever you are doing while I look for someone else to do what I need done. Does that meet with your approval?"

"Ok, Harris. I will look at the contents of this folder. I don't know if I can get through it all by Friday morning, but I will be back to you then."

At 10 on Friday morning Mark stepped off the elevator into the waiting room of the Becker law firm.

"Go right in," said the receptionist he is expecting you.

Harris stood as Mark entered the office, the bulky folder in his arms.

"How did you enjoy your reading assignment?" asked Harris, taking the file.

"Very interesting," said Mark. "That material is good background for a novel. In the hands of a talented author it could be a number 1 best seller on the New York Times book list."

"What about from a legal perspective?" asked Harris.

"There is no question about Rothstein; he's toast. Rosenfeld is going to get federal time, so is Adler. Scott's secretary, Debra Villegas, is going to get hit big-time, as are some of the attorneys who helped in various ways. The two banks are on the hook for big bucks due to their complicity." There is no doubt they were engaged in money laundering.

"You are right Mark. I have already begun proceedings against T.D. Bank."

"They will settle," said Mark. How much are you seeking from them?"

"$100 million," was the reply.

"Good number; they will cave. You will get 60 or 70 million dollars, without a fight."

"Now, let's get back to you," said Harris. "Will you come to work for me in a limited capacity?"

"Spell it out for me," said Mark.

"I want you to track down any money Rothstein sent off-shore. Morocco is a starting point but I would not rule out other havens for illegal money. Israel, Cyprus, who knows where else. Not Switzerland or the Caymans, he is too smart for those locals. Maybe twenty years ago, but not now. Rhodes, Hong Kong or Singapore could be strong possibilities. I want to get back any dirty money he tried to hide so he could live the good life in the future."

"If I say yes, what's in it for me?"

"I am the Court-appointed receiver," said Harris. I can compensate you in a reasonable way."

"Let's stop talking legalesse. What will my compensation be based on?"

"Ok. First, I will pay you a fee of $2,000 per day, while you are working on the case. That is for a seven-day week/twenty-four hours per day. One month in advance - $60,000 dollars. Second you can have $1,000 per day in expenses. That is to cover you for hotel, food, lodging, air, and any other expenses you may incur. You will surely have to go to Morocco, that is another $30,000. After the first thirty days, if you need more time to complete your search we will discuss the situation then. Is that satisfactory?"

"Almost," replied Mark. Make it an even $100,000 for the month. Here is a bank deposit slip to deposit the money into my account. I have a private investigator. We have worked together in the past. Put him on the payroll at $1,000 per day. I will need him to work with me here in Florida for 2 or 3 weeks I will cover his expenses. This is his bank information."

"Is that all?" asked Harris.

"One more important item. What happens if I recover some hidden funds, say, $1 million, $10 million, or even more. Do I get compensated above my base monthly pay?"

"I am not sure. I had not thought of that."

"I think you have, Harris. You tell me, you are the best bankruptcy lawyer in Florida. You already have an answer to this contingency. I think you are playing cat and mouse with me. Wanted to see if I thought of this, maybe you are just testing me. Did I pass? You are good Mark, I'll have to stay on my toes with you. So what type of commission or finder's fee can I expect if I find any money?"

"I could probably justify three percent, replied Harris"

"I was thinking ten percent," said Mark.

"Might be too much, Mark," Real Estate agents only get 6 percent. True Harris but personal injury attorneys get 33 percent.

"Just think, $10 million would net you $1 million, $20 million would be $2 million.

"Harris, I'm very good at math. The teachers actually taught us in the public schools I attended in Paterson New Jersey. If I bring you a sum like that for your clients, do you think anyone would complain? I think three percent is fair Mark. You want ten percent. I am told you are a tough negotiator and I want you on this case – you and your private investigator side-kick. So I say 7 percent to save time; it's the proverbial split." Can we agree on 7 and move on.

"Consider it done," said Mark. I am on the payroll beginning now. There is one more thing I want."

"Not more money," said Harris.

"No, no more money. I want access to RRA offices - Scott Rothstein's, in particular. There are some people I intend to talk with. If I am sitting in Scott's office, in his chair, it may give me a psychological edge, unnerve them; get them to talk more freely."

"Smart," said Harris, smiling. "I knew I had the right man for this job. Let me get you the keys you will need to get in, plus a letter from me you can show anyone who challenges you."

CHAPTER 7 ✛ ✛ ✛

Mark spent the weekend drawing up a list of people to summon to the law firm. He wanted to speak to them all. With Rothstein in jail, Mark knew the other parties involved would be represented by high-priced attorneys who would advise their clients not to speak to anyone about the case. He knew the short list of people would grow even shorter. Early on Monday morning he was waiting for the arriving Jet Blue flight from LaGuardia. He stood in the terminal at Miami International Airport waiting for the passengers to enter the terminal. Derrick walked into the waiting area like a pit-bull looking for someone to attack. He walked up to Mark "Here I am, as you instructed. What is going on down here, what do you need me for?"

"Yes, it is good to see you too Derrick," Mark smiled. "Let's go, I will explain everything in the car."

"That's the whole story," Mark concluded. I have got to find some missing money. I felt I would need your help here in Florida. So I got you put on the case for $1,000 per day. You have to admit, it's nicer in Florida than freezing your ass off in New York."

"I do admit that, Mark. So thanks for the work; also for thinking of me. I'm sure you could have gotten local talent cheaper."

"I know I could, Derrick. But I trust you to watch my back. Also, I will have less questions to answer with you."

When Mark pulled up to the gate leading to the palatial cottage Derrick let out a low whistle. "Holy cow, Mark. This is some spread. Are you staying here?"

"Yes, have been for three weeks now. Come into the office. We can go over my plan there."

As they sat in the office, Mark explained. "Here is a list of twelve people I want to talk to. The first three are musts. I will contact Debra Villegas myself. She is the most important. Next is Jeffrey Drier he was a close confidant of Rothstein's. The others are Rothstein's law partners, plus some lawyers in the firm. I don't have much hope of speaking with them, but we have to try. Kim Rothstein is the perp's wife. See if she will meet for lunch, casual – maybe on the beach at a nice restaurant, or in Bal Harbor. Get me Debra Villegas' telephone number or address. I will contact her personally."

It was an hour later when Derrick came back into the office.

"Debra's number has been disconnected. But I got her address, a house in Weston."

They pulled up to the house in the Bentley.

"Nice house," said Derrick. "Trimmed lawn; nice quiet street. Let's go talk to the lady."

Mark knocked on the door, which was opened by a burly man with a bleached blond crew-cut. He was wearing a tight black tee-shirt and faded jeans, a skull and cross bones on the shirt, a swastika tattoo on his beefy bicep.

"What do you want?" he asked gruffly. "Whatever you're selling, we ain't buying; so beat it."

Derrick went to move, opening his mouth to say something, when Mark reached out gripping his arm.

"My name is Mark Radin. I am an attorney here to speak with Debra."

"Well, Mr. Attorney, maybe you don't hear too good. I said we don't want none of what your sellin so hit the road."

"You don't look like Debra Villegas to me. Why not let her tell me to leave."

"I'm tired of talking. Now get out of here before I break your face!"

"For the last time, tell Ms. Villegas I'd like to see her."

"That's it," he snarled, cocking his arm to swing at Mark. Derrick grabbed the arm, pulling the big man out of the doorway, bending his arm back painfully.

"Ow, Ow," the man cried, sinking to his knees to relieve the pressure on his shoulder joint.

A woman walked to the door. "What's all the commotion out here? Basel, what are you doing on the ground?"

"I'm afraid he was a bad boy, Miss. I'm just teaching him some manners," replied Derrick with a smile.

"Are you Debra Villegas?" asked Mark.

"Yes I am."

"Can we come in to speak with you for a moment? I am an attorney, here is my card. If you want us to leave after I tell you why I'm here, we will go quietly. I promise."

She hesitated a moment. "Ok, come in, and let my bodyguard up."

"Some bodyguard," said Derrick with a sneer.

"I'm here because of the Rothstein case," began Mark.

"Isn't everybody. That's why my lawyer put that big palooka here in my house, to keep people away."

"The reason I am here," Mark continued, "is because I believe you have some information that could be vital for me. I think we could be mutually beneficial to each other. In order to protect you, I would like you to call your attorney to tell him of my request; see what he has to say."

She spoke on the telephone for a few minutes. "Alright Howard, I'll tell him."

"My attorney, Howard Lerner, doesn't want me to say anything to you now. He wants to meet in his office tomorrow morning at 9:30. Just the three of us."

"That's fine, Debra. I'll see you at Mr. Lerner's office in the morning. Let's go, Derrick."

As they walked to the door, Derrick turned to Basel, who sat rubbing his shoulder. "Boy oh," he said. "You should find another line of work, you're a lousy bodyguard."

CHAPTER 8 ✚ ✚ ✚

Mark was shown into Howard Lerner's office in the Omni Tropical Building in downtown Miami on Miami Avenue. The information-board in the lobby listed his office number with just his name, which meant he was in practice by his lonesome; probably an ex-District Attorney now in private practice, making a living but not charging large fees.

"Good morning, Mr. Radin. What can we do for you," said Howard.

"I've been retained by Harris Becker, the receiver in the Rothstein fraud case. You know him?" the firm name is Becker-Fertel in Coral Gables.

"I know of him, Mr. Radin."

"Call me Mark, Howard."

"As I said, I know of him; a powerful lawyer. He has political contacts up to the Governor, legal contacts to the State Supreme Court and beyond nationally. If you are working for him that tells me a lot."

"I want to speak with your client, open and in-depth. I need to pick her brain regarding certain matters at RRA. I have no axe to grind, no affiliation with the District Attorney, the government, or any agency involved in this case, like the FBI, IRS, DEA – none of them. That means anything I learn from Debra stays with me. I am bound by attorney-client privilege to retain any information; I cannot be made to divulge it."

"That is true," said Howard. But you are not her attorney, I am.

"That's easily rectified," said Mark. "Hire me as your associate Howard. Don't worry, I will come cheap."

"Won't there be a potential conflict of interest if you represent Debra?"

"I don't see any." "I am doing what I was hired to do. You are her counsel of record. I am just assisting you on some legal technicalities. I think you will be asking me to resign in thirty days or less, at which time I will most likely be out of the country."

Howard continued. "Debra told me the two of you would both be gaining from this interplay. I see you getting information from her. But, what does she get?"

"I am going to be blunt, I prefer to call it realistic. There is going to be a lot of collateral damage in this case. A lot of people are going to get hurt. Rothstein was the prime mover but he snared a lot of people in his web. I have been studying the particulars of his scheme for a week now, twelve hours per day or more. There are at least a dozen lawyers who are going to lose their license to practice law. Most of them are going to be taking government-paid vacations of from two to six years. I think your client, if what I have read is accurate, is going to be offered a plea deal; but she is going away also."

Debra began to sob.

"I'm not trying to be cruel or intimidating, but it is a fact. The Feds are going to take your possessions, anything that you bought or acquired by gift or whatever, while employed by RRA. I am sure Howard told you all this already, Debra."

Howard shook his head in the affirmative.

"When you get out of prison in five or more years, you will have nothing – no house, no $125,000 car that Scott paid for; no $250,000 dollar a year job; nothing. So, in exchange for what I want, I will see that a separate trust fund is established for you in your name Debra. It will be secure from government seizure. If you want, I will even have my financial advisor in New York monitor it so it increased by 5 or 7 percent per year."

"How much are we talking about, Mark?" asked Howard.

"I was thinking about $500,000, Howard. That will be Debra's to keep for speaking with me, whether the information is helpful or not. However, she must be truthful in what she tells me. She must tell me everything. No half stories or holding back information. If I find out she lied or did not give me all she knows, then no deal."

"Will you put that in writing?

"You draw it up, Howard. I will sign it," said Mark.

The document was signed by Mark, than notarized by Howard's Legal Assistant.

Standing outside the modern glass office building, Mark asked: "Can I buy you lunch, Debra? We can get to know each other before we begin our walk down memory lane."

They had lunch at the Harbor Restaurant, looking at the cruise ships tied to their piers in the Miami cut. Mark walked Debra to her car, a 2009 Maserati convertible that had been a gift from Scott.

"Where are we going to meet?" she asked.

"What time did you go to work at RRA?" Mark asked.

"I was in at 8:30. Scott liked to be in at 7:30 or 8."

"A man after my own heart," said Mark. "I like to be in my office between 7 or 7:30. So let's meet at your old office at 8:30."

"But those offices have been locked since November 12th." The Feds threw everyone out and took possession of the place.

"What you say is true, but I have magic powers. I will meet you in the lobby at 8:30."

CHAPTER 9

Debra walked into the lobby of Las Olas City Center at exactly 8:30. Mark was waiting for her, Derrick at his side.

"Who is this?" she demanded. "I thought it was going to be just you and me. I am not talking in front of anyone else."

"This is a good friend of mine he's a private investigator working for me. You saw him at your house 2 days ago. He will not be involved with us. You and I will be working in the separate offices you shared with Scott while Derrick will be speaking with other employees of the firm in an outer office. Is that satisfactory?"

"Yes, just so long as you are the only one I speak with."

The elevator let them off on the eleventh floor.

"God, it is quiet," said Debra. "Scott had seventy lawyers working for him, plus another 100 or more employees. These offices were a beehive of activity. Now, it's like a morgue, eerie."

"Let's go to your office Debra; lead the way."

Debra led Mark down a long hallway, offices on both sides.

"Derrick, take off and go to work," instructed Mark. "You know what to do."

They walked up to a blank wall, a heavy locked door with a magnetic key-pad on the wall. A light was blinking red on the pad mounted on the right side of the door.

"Our offices were inside this door, Scotts and mine. No one could enter without the key-card, which only we had. Anyone else who wanted to come in had to be buzzed-in. That closed-circuit camera Debra said, pointing over the door, would show us who was out here. Then Scott would decide if they should be allowed to enter."

"Seems like a strange procedure for a law firm. Usually, the senior partner is available to any of the staff at any time."

"Yes, well Scot had his own rules and habits."

"Sounds like he may have been paranoid," said Mark.

"He was definitely secretive. He changed when his financial business took off. What do we do now?" asked Debra. Mark pulled a plastic card from his pocket – a card with tiny electronic chips in it. Holding it up to the scanner, the red light turned to green as the door clicked open.

"We go in," said Mark.

They stood in a large vestibule, at least twelve by fifteen feet, with three doorways leading off the vestibule.

"The closed door on the left is a file room, just for Scott's private business, both investment company files and his special legal work. That work involved the sale of Structured Settlements. Scott came up with the idea himself; developed it; then sold it to hundreds of people. It was brilliant. I even believed it was real."

They looked into Debra's office.

"Very nice, cozy, and conveniently close to your boss. Let's sit in Scott's office to get started."

Rothstein's office was large, very large, only fitting for someone of his size and importance. Two walls of windows, one looked east toward the Inter-Coastal waterway in the distance. While the south-facing wall gave an excellent view of the New River with the Broward county jail across the water. Mark sat in Scott's comfortable, high-backed executive chair, indicating a seat for Debra across the desk. The walls were covered with pictures, plenty of politicians and celebrities. Mark recognized Senator John McCain, Governor Charlie Christ and Jeb Bush.

"Let's begin," said Mark. "Give me some background so I can form an idea of your relationship with the mighty Mr. Rothstein, how he worked, what he did and where you fit in"

"I met Scott when I was a student at Nova Southeastern University. I was taking law courses so I could get a better job. I was divorced, a single mom making $26,000 a year and going nowhere. Scott was one of my professors. I went to school two nights a week from 6 until 8:30. One night after class, he came up to me.

"Do you understanding my lectures, the course work?" he asked.

"Yes, I am following along." It's all very interesting, new to me but interesting.

"Good, if you have any questions or problems, come see me. I will be glad to help you."

A few weeks later, we were analyzing a case I couldn't comprehend, something about insider trading. After class, I stopped Scott to ask for an explanation.

"Let's get some coffee; we can discuss it then." Coffee led to a room at the Riverside Hotel just down the street from his office on Las Olas. The hotel was a client of Scott's. They kept a room available for him when he got someone like me to have sex with. When the school year ended he offered me a job in his firm – Paralegal, $40,000 per year with sex as a perk. I worked as a Paralegal for three years. The sex diminished as he found other willing partners to share his bed. One day in 2004, he asked me into his office; not this one, we didn't have this set up then.

"I'm starting an investment company," he said. "It has nothing to do with the legal practice of RRA. Rothstein Rosenfeld Adler. The legal work will go on, but I am going to let my partners run that with my help, my oversight. I'm going to concentrate more on investments, namely Structured Settlements."

"That's sounds fine," I replied. "But what do you want with me? I don't know anything about, ah . . . Structured Settlements."

"You don't have to. That is an investment vehicle I came up with all by myself. I believe it will make me rich. What I want is someone smart, someone I can trust, someone loyal, who will listen to me, then following orders." I want you by my side to help me with whatever I need.

"I should have run then"

"But," – he continued – I am going to have a new office constructed – private, secure, just for the two of us. You are going to be my CFO - Chief Financial Officer, starting with a salary of $125,000 per year, plus a company car."

"I was flabbergasted. $125,000 a year, more than twice my current salary, a new car to replace the crummy Ford Escort I was driving. How could I say no?"

"You will be my strong, right-hand," he continued.

"I'm in," I said.

Everything was great. We worked as a team. Whatever he needed done, I did. Or, I made others do. Money began to roll in daily – first, thousands, then hundreds of thousands and finally, millions. I had to keep track of the money, deposits, withdrawals, write checks to investors for any profits when settlements closed. It was exciting, intoxicating, dealing in these sums. As our bank balances grew, so did my salary. By 2008, I was up to $175,000 a year. My Honda Accord was sold – replaced by a Maserati Gran Turismo, at a cost of $100,000. Next, Scott bought me a house, in his name of course but for me to live in. He made one other purchase for himself – a new wife. She was pretty, blond, Jewish – Kimberly Wendle. Now that I am getting married, our sexual encounters are over. Then, he gave me my last raise to $250,000. All was grand, until the walls come crashing down on December 1st, 2009, just six weeks ago."

"Thats an Interesting story. Now, I have to give you some background so you understand why I am here and what I need from you. Your mentor ran the fourth largest ponzi scheme in history. He bilked investors out of 1.4 billion dollars. Needless to say he will be spending the balance of his life in prison, as will many others from the RRA firm. Unfortunately, from what you have told me you are going to get a Federal vacation also. The Federal Court is interested in getting as much of the 1.4 billion dollars back to return to the investors. Some of that money and property belonged to Scott, Kim, the firm along with individuals who will be indicted. Their property will be seized, than sold. The proceeds of these sales will be collected by the Court-appointed receiver, put into a trust account to be divided, than distributed by the receiver. Do you follow me so far?"

"Yes," said Debra. This has been explained to me by Howard. The government will take my house in Weston, plus my car."

"Correct, they have already taken Scott's twelve cars worth about eleven million dollars, his 100 watches and his wife's jewelry. There are liens on his many millions worth of real estate here in Florida; that is all obvious. The receiver is handling the collection and sale of those items. I have been retained to find, than repossess funds that no one knows about.

That is no one but Scott Rothstein and his Chief Financial Officer, you Debra."

"I don't know what you are referring to," replied Debra.

"Don't lie to me, Mark said in a stern voice. "You are going to be near 50 by the time you get out of Federal prison. The $500,000 I promised you is going to look damn good. I told you in front of Howard, if you lie or are not forthcoming, no money. So make up your mind, cooperate or we can say goodbye, it's your call. Either way, you are going to prison. Do you want a nest egg when you get out?"

She began to sob.

"I want to know about Morocco. Rumors are Scott flew from Fort Lauderdale Executive Airport to Casablanca with no luggage. But, he had a carry-on bag full of money."

"It's true," she said. "He was leaving the country for good. Back in 2006, he began to bring in a great deal of money, sometimes seven or eight million dollars a week. When he saw the flow of money, two things happened. He began to skim some off the top for himself. He installed a mega safe in our file room next to my office. By 2007, we would have between five million to twenty million dollars in that safe, at any time. The second thing he did was ask Adler, his partner, to send the brightest associate to see him. When the young man was seated right here where I am sitting, Scott tells Steve: *I have an assignment for you. Find a country that has no extradition treaty with the United States or Israel. Give me the answer in two days.* Two days later, Steve is back: *There are two countries Mr. Rothstein Cyprus and Morocco. Here is the brief I wrote for you.*

The next week, Scott calls me into his office, "Call Lieutenant Sorkin. Tell him I am going to need Dick for a week, a special assignment."

"Who is Sorkin and Dick?" asked Mark.

"I'll explain," continued Debra. "At this time, Scott had half the Fort Lauderdale Police force working for him. They were a security detail at his house 24 hours a day. They would escort his wife Kim where ever she wanted to go. Some were always in the lobby in plain clothes, even in our offices here. They would run errands for him. He was like the Chief of Police, who by the way, picked up a bonus once a month. Sorkin was Chief of Detectives, also on Scott's payroll. Dick Lake was a detective. He worked for Sorkin, who would assign him to do anything, any job at any time for Scott. So, when Scott asked for Dick for a week, Sorkin would make up a bullshit story to cover his ass. Dick was doing surveillance, working undercover, whatever. When Scott heard Morocco was a safe haven he contacted a law firm in Casablanca - Yousef Daoud, a single-lawyer firm established in 2003. After several telephone calls Scott sent a $100,000 retainer to Daoud to form a new Moroccan corporation, Sunshine or Shady Inc. Papers were sent to open a bank account in a small, local bank, First Arabian National Bank. Daoud was the registered agent for the corporation. Scott's brother was the Director and President as well as signatory on the bank account. The only problem is, Scott's brother was dead – killed in a car crash eight years ago. Scott signed his brother's signature.

CHAPTER 10 ✠ ✠ ✠

Lieutenant Sorkin sent Detective Dick Lake to Scott's office for the special assignment. Scott told Lake "You're going on a five-day vacation Dick, all expenses paid by me. You are going to deliver a case to a courier for me."

"Sure," said Lake, "Where to, New York?"

"No not the big city to somewhere further and more exotic. Got your passport?"

"Sure I do, Mr Rothstein."

"You are going to Morocco. Flying from Miami to Madrid on Iberia, then on to Casablanca on Air Moroc. That night I put three million dollars in a briefcase." Scott locked it, then sent the key by overnight mail to Daoud's office on Mers Sultan, in Casablanca.

Six days later, Dick was back in Scott's office. I was sitting with Scott. "How did it go Dick?" asked Scott.

"Piece of cake," replied Lake. "I did exactly what you said. A guy met me at the hotel on the second day; he gave me an American dollar-bill with the numbers you told me. I gave him the case. He just got up and left, never said a word. Here is his picture, and another one shows him walking off with the case. He never knew I had a pin-camera in my baseball cap."

"Once a detective, always a detective, right Dick."

"Just wanted to cover my ass, boss."

"Scott got a copy of a deposit slip from Yousef Daoud showing $3,500,000 was sitting in First Arabian National Bank in Casablanca, Morocco. The money was in Scott's personal account. Dick made two more trips to Casablanca, one in November of 2007, the next in July of 2008. On those two trips the briefcases held five million dollars. I know, because I packed them while Scott watched smoking a big fat cigar. After I finished stuffing the case Scott would seal and lock them sending the key to Douad."

"You're telling me you had $13.5 million in this Moroccan bank."

"Yes, that is what I am telling you."

"Now, for the $64,000 dollar question, what happened when Scott flew the coop. It's rumored he had a case full of money when he left but came back a few days later with eight dollars in his pocket?"

"The day before he left he told me he didn't think he could hold things together any longer. I asked him what he meant by that. *The law firm is doing fine I said. Not the firm,* he replied. *"I have been robbing money from everyone. There are no Structured Settlements. I have been selling air. Now, I have no more money to give to the investors; especially the three, big hedge funds.* Scott had convinced three hedge funds to invest 100 million each - two were New York funds, one was a Miami, Florida fund. They wanted their investments back, but he didn't have the cash to give them."

How much cash do you have in the safe, Debra? Scott asked. Just over seventeen million dollars, I replied. *Go to Altman's Luggage Store in the Galleria Mall. Get me a sample case, a strong one, nice brown leather. Bring it in tomorrow morning.*

"The next afternoon, November 9th, we packed the sample case with most of the money in the safe - $17,400,000 went into that salesman's case. When we finished, there was $117,000 left on the shelf."

I am going out of town for a few days on business. Take $100,000 to my house, give it to Kimmy. You take $10,000, leave $7,000 in the safe.

"Debra, are you telling me there is 30.9 million dollars in the bank in Morocco?"

"No, I am telling you there is $13,500,000 in the bank. I am not sure where the sample case with 17.4 million dollars is. It went to Morocco with Scott but never came back; it could be anywhere."

"Thanks, Debra. You definitely earned your $500,000."

CHAPTER 11 ✝ ✝ ✝

Derrick pushed the buzzer outside the inner-sanctum where Debra sat with Mark in Scott Rothstein's opulent office.

"What do we do now?" asked Mark.

"If you want to let him in, push the button in the right arm of the chair. The door will open. If you want to leave without being seen just get up and leave. There is a doorway to a private elevator in the file room, takes you to the parking garage under the building. You could disappear from there."

"Convenient, but all this undercover stuff is a bit unusual for the head of a law firm who should be available to his staff at all times," said Mark, he pushed the button by his right hand opening the door.

Derrick entered the office, "Wow, this is some pretty set up."

"Yes Derrick, it sure is. What do you have for me?"

"Spoke to a dozen lawyers of the firm, including the two partners. No one will speak with us. They each have attorney representation. Speak to them, they say. I tried, got the same answer from each attorney – no comment. Spoke to Kimberly Rothstein. She had no reservations about speaking with you. Name a time and place."

"I have a job for you Derrick. There is a Detective on the Fort Lauderdale police force who was a hired gun for Rothstein. He was Rothstein's personal gofer, made more money a year here than he did on the police payroll. Work him over; you do not have to be polite. Get me everything you can from him, especially about three trips to Casablanca."

The three people kept at it for the entire week. Mark had lunch with Kim Rothstein, Scott's wife. He got no useful information from her. She claimed she was in the dark about his investment scheme. Mark believed her. He and Debra covered more of the inner workings of Scott's legal settlement sale. An interesting fact was the investment of $120 million by a New York hedge fund, a fund which was reputed to have ties to the New York Mob – the Mafia. If that was true, Rothstein was sailing in deep water without knowing it.

Derrick came to Mark after speaking with Dick Lake. "The guy's a real low-life. He did all sorts of favors for Rothstein, some of which were plain illegal. I had to threaten him with a variety of crimes he committed from money laundering to embezzlement, fraud, using his office to commit acts that could send him away for years. He finally caved in, gave me the info you want. He went to Casablanca three times in two years, each time with a locked briefcase; claims he didn't know what it contained but he had to show off. Tells me he's a detective, a smart detective. Since the cases didn't make any noise, whatever was in them had to be soft. He thinks he was carrying money out of the country; lots of money because the cases were heavy."

Derrick put four pictures on the desk. "He took these pictures of the guy he met in a bar or hotel in Casablanca. The same guy he gave the cases to each time. He wanted to cover his ass if there was a foul-up. You know, like someone says *I never handed the cases over.* The pictures are grainy, taken with a small Sony spy-camera; but you can make out the features of the face. In this one, you can see his back with the briefcase in his right hand, as he walks away."

"Good job, Derrick."

Mark called Harris from Rothstein's fancy desk phone. "We should meet," said Mark. "I have information for you." Mark was sitting in the throne chair in Rothstein's office gazing out at the splendid view on a sunny Saturday afternoon, an afternoon he should be at the ocean club with the sexy Jennifer lying next to him.

"Good said Harris snapping Mark back to the present. How about brunch tomorrow? Sunday brunch at the Biltmore Hotel. It's a tradition, dating back to 1926; say 11 o'clock." Fine, replied Mark, see you at the hotel at 11.

Mark walked into the Biltmore Hotel on a gorgeous Sunday morning of the third week in January. It was a grand, old hotel. Built in the

Magnificent Mizner architecture, all pink and shiny having just gone through another renovation at a cost of many millions. The dining room was elegant, twenty foot high ceilings with gold frescos reminding Mark of the Sistine Chapel in the Vatican in Rome. The champagne brunch was world renowned, at $85 per person it should be. Harris was seated at a table looking out at the gigantic Olympic-size pool already crowded with people.

"Sit and join me," said Harris, smiling up at his legal bloodhound. When Mark was seated, a glass of champagne in front of him, Harris said, "Did you know Johnny Weissmuller worked here once as a lifeguard? That was before he became famous as Tarzan in the movies."

"This is a very impressive building. Glad you invited me since I probably would never get another chance to see it." Mark spoke while they ate.

"From all I have learned this week, it seems you are correct Harris. Rothstein has a cache of money somewhere in Morocco. Most likely, more than you think. Some is in a bank account in Casablanca, deposited over a two-year time period. The money he flew off with could be anywhere. We have no way of telling where it went after he landed. I want to go to Casablanca, try to find and claim the money. There is money in an account deposited in a Moroccan bank that I know of. I will have to search for the money he took with him in November."

"When do you intend to leave?"

"As soon as possible, probably on Tuesday. I will spend today and tomorrow getting things in order, assembling items I want to take with me."

"Good," said Harris. "You have my blessing. I will have some documents drawn-up tomorrow at my law firm; give you power of attorney to act for the receiver of claims, me, plus some government authority just in case you need some additional leverage. You are still on retainer including expenses. I will have an envelope with $5,000, in cash to help you on your way.

CHAPTER 12 ✛ ✛ ✛

The Air Moroc flight landed smoothly on the runway of Mohammed V International Airport in Casablanca. Mark got into a white Mercedes cab for the forty-minute ride into the city, a city made famous by the movie Casablanca, starring Humphrey Bogart and Ingrid Bergman in the 1940's. Casablanca is the largest city in Morocco, with a population of three million, the international center of the country. He checked into the modern Sofitel Tour Blanche. All Mark wanted was a hot shower and a good night sleep, since he had been flying over 16 hours. He wanted to be fresh to start in the morning.

The next morning Mark approached the concierge who gave him directions to the Arabian National Bank of Morocco. "It is a ten-minute walk from the hotel sir. The day is pleasant, 58 degrees and sunny, ideal for a stroll."

"Thank you," said Mark, as he set out to find the bank with 13 million dollars in it vaults. The boulevards in the business section of town were wide, busy with both pedestrian and vehicular traffic at 9 a.m.; what you would expect in any large, cosmopolitan city. What he did not expect was the sight looking at him at 28 Rue Sid Belyout. He stood looking at a large stone building, a building whose sign had been removed from the facade leaving a shadow in the stone which was barely discernible. But if you looked closely you could detect the impression of the name, Arabian National Bank. The bank was shuttered. The windows were dirty, soot-stained. The doors locked, a chain across the handles held in place by a massive lock. A sign in the glass-door announced "Closed," in English – "Fermé," in French. *Now what*, he thought, standing dejectedly, looking at the locked doors. He saw a sign further down the street, Banque De Moroc. He entered the large marble lobby of the bank, saw a sign, Manager, above a doorway of a glass-enclosed office to the side of the banking floor. Mark walked to the open doorway.

"Excuse me," he said. "Do you have a moment?"

The manager looked up, seeing a well-dressed American standing in the doorway, he stood to greet him. "But of course, Monsieur. How can I be of service? I am Clyde Murco, Manager of Banque Moroc."

"I had some business to conduct with Arabian National Bank, but was surprised to see they are closed, Fermé."

"Yes, it was a surprise to the entire banking community. No warning; just one day two months ago, they closed their doors never to open again."

"Do you know what happened?" asked Mark.

"I am sorry, no Monsieur. There are many rumors of course; none good or complimentary – all dark stories of corruption, fraud, the usual stories when this happens, but no known facts. You could check with the Central Banking Commission. They may be able to tell you more."

"Thank you," said Mark walking into the street, where he stood pondering his next move. Then, it came to him. He recalled something Debra had said while they were going over details of the Moroccan venture while sitting in Rothstein's opulent office. The local lawyer who had formed the corporation for Scoot had an office here in Casablanca. His name was Yousef Daoud. The concierge at the hotel gave Mark a map with directions to the Law Office of Daoud PA, at 61 Mers Sultan.

"Take a cab," the concierge suggested, for two reasons. "It is to far to walk. Also, that section of Casablanca is not the best, not the safest if you know what I mean."

Mark handed the man fifty dirhams, about six dollars US.

"Thank you."

The office was on the fifth floor of a brick building located on a narrow street, just off Boulevard Hassarei where more modern office buildings stood side-by-side. Mark entered the small lobby staffed by an old Arab wearing a fez. This caused Mark to think back to the office of his partner Dan, on that eventful day they met in New York; the feeling became even stronger as he entered the office of Yousef Daoud, Attorney.

Black letters on a smoked-glass panel of the door did not lend an air of executive status. An older woman, hair askew, sat at a battered steel desk.

"Yes," she inquired briskly.

Mark handed her a business card. "I would like to see Mr. Daoud," he said.

She looked at the card, do you have an appointment. No Mark replied looking around the shabby office. I don't see many people waiting to see Mr Daoud. "Moment Si vous plait," She said standing to enter another office. No intercom thought Mark. Returning immediately she said "Entre," pointing to the open doorway to the inner office.

Mr. Daoud was a short swarthy man with a heavy five o'clock shadow at 11 in the morning. "Mr. Radin, how can I help you today?"

"I am here in Morocco on a rather delicate matter Mr. Daoud. A most important affair in America that leads me here to Morocco."

"What is this matter, Mr. Radin? How can I be of help?"

"I must say, your English is very good, Mr. Daoud."

He smiled. "Yes, I went to school in America for three years, Nova Southeastern Law School in Florida; I graduated in 1999. I stayed for two years practicing law in West Palm Beach before I decided I missed Casablanca. So I returned to open my practice here in 2003."

Now it fell into place. Rothstein graduated Nova in 1988. They probably knew each other there, which is why he was contacted in 2005 to open Sunshine Shady Corporation, a fitting name in light of current events.

"Now, what is this matter you have come to me about?" he asked.

"I am here in Morocco to locate a large sum of money that was deposited over a period of years. It seems this money was derived from a business plan that was illegal, a Ponzi scheme. You are familiar with that term?"

"Yes, I am," he replied.

"This plan was developed by a fellow Nova lawyer in Fort Lauderdale, an attorney named Scott Rothstein. Did you know him?"

Mr. Daoud seemed to be uncomfortable, squirming in his seat, little beads of perspiration above his upper-lip. "Go on," he said, without answering the question.

"Mr. Rothstein had made deposits totaling in the millions of dollars to a corporate account in the Arabian National Bank. I went to the address of the bank this morning. It is closed. I came to you to seek your advice since you were the attorney of record for Mister Rothstein's corporation. How do I find the missing millions Attorney Daoud, can you help me?"

"How am I supposed to know about millions of dollars? I am a lawyer, not a banker."

"I see," said Mark. "You want to play the innocent with me; fine. But do not think I believe you." Mark opened his briefcase, putting a folder of papers on Daoud's desk. "These are incorporation papers, prepared by you for Scott, who picked the name, it has proved very accurate. These documents are signed and notarized at this address. The President is David Rothstein, Scott's brother. Scott's dead brother. He died in a car crash in Connecticut in 2004. The year before he signed these papers; notarized by the way. I believe in the legal profession. We call that fraud."

"What do you want with me?" asked Yousef now clearly uncomfortable.

"I want your help, Mark continued in a calm soothing voice. I am not going to cause you any trouble. If you cooperate, give me the information I need to complete my task, we will part as friends. I may even be able to compensate you for your Time and effort." Mark's tone changed, becoming more sinister. "If, on the other hand, you try to mislead me in my efforts, hinder me in any way, I will see you suffer grave consequences here, and in America, where I believe you are a member of the Florida Bar."

"Come back tomorrow morning at 9. I will try to have information for you then." Said a shaken Daoud.

The two men shook hands, looking coldly at each other. Mark walked from the office, wiping his hand on a tissue. Yousef's palms were damp with sweat.

CHAPTER 13 ✝ ✝ ✝

Mark took the same seat as yesterday across from a clean-shaved Yousef Daoud.

"I made all arrangements here in Casablanca," he began. I was aware the incorporator was in fact Scott, not his dead brother. We were good friends. He was a professor in many of my classes in Nova. We became close friends during my time in Florida. I agreed to help him when he reached out to me some years later. I set up the corporation, made deposits into the Arabian bank on four occasions in 2007 and 2008. "I thought there were only three deposits said Mark.

"Yes, there were three cases, 3,500,000 in the first, 5,000,000 in the second, and 5,000,000 a third time. I received a cache of money myself when I traveled to Florida on vacation with Scoot. I deposited the amount when I returned to Casablanca sending a deposit slip to Scott for 7 million dollars."

Mark put a picture on the table. "Do you know this man?"

"Yes, I do. He works for me. He met the American who brought the cases to Morocco on three separate occasions. My courier then brought them to me."

"Where is this money now?"

"When I was made aware of the problems at the Arabian National Bank I withdrew the money in bank checks. I had my courier, the man in the picture, take the money to a new account in a bank in Rabet, Banque Al-Wafi. The money is there in the name of Sunshine Shady Corporation"

"That means the $13.5 million is safe at this moment. Yes he nodded.

You mentioned a fourth deposit." You said you brought the money back yourself.

"Yes, that's correct. I went to Florida in December 2008. Scott and I spent five days together, like old times in Florida – plenty of sun, plenty of sex, a little business. Scott has many lovely ladies at his beck and call. They are all young voluptuous nymphs who are eager to please a man of Scott's stature. We sailed to the Bahamas with four of these lovelies on a 75 foot motor yacht. It was a glorious trip, a riotous bacchanal, an orgy of pleasure. When it was time for me to fly home Scott had a driver take me to Miami International Airport. It was his Detective, the one who came to Casablanca with the cases of money. Before I left his office, Scott had his efficient financial officer gave me another briefcase; this one with seven million dollars to deposit on my return. Scott embraced me warmly before I left him. Watch over my money Youssef, I'm afraid I will need it one day soon." I did a fast calculation that meant there was twenty million five hundred thousand dollars in Arabian National Bank that should now be safe in the new bank in Rabat.

"I want to know what happened when Scott came here on November 5th. Did you meet him?"

"Of course I did. He was in a panic when he arrived. He told me everything he had done for these last five years had fallen apart. His clients were screaming for their money, money he no longer had. Hundreds of people were going to be hurt financially because of his actions, his lies and the illegal things he had done. "He told me he was leaving that all behind along with everyone - his partners, staff, even his wife. He had enough money to live on comfortably for the rest of his life. The money he had secreted away over the years already deposited in Morocco, plus what he had brought with him."

"Did you know, did you see what he had brought?"

"no not then, but the next day. Something happened overnight. He got a telephone call that changed his plans. He called me early in the morning. *"Come to my hotel immediately; it is urgent."* He was pacing in his room when I arrived, tears, running down his cheeks. *"I have to go back to Florida. I have no choice. If I don't return, my mother, father and wife will be killed. Then someone will come to find me here, or wherever I run to. We won't be seeing each other again Yousef. I am going to be taking a Federal vacation, a long one.*" He wiped his eyes. *"Take care of this case for me,"* he said, handing me a large leather sample-case, a very heavy large sample-case. *"If I can get word to you, I will. Otherwise, just hold it until someone comes for it. I am sure someone will come to you eventually. Goodbye."*

"That was the last time I spoke with him. A private jet picked him up that night. You know the rest."

"What was in the sample-case?"

"It contained $17,400,000."

"Where is the money now?"

"It is in the bank in Rabat, in Rothstein's account. I had my courier bring it to the bank president to deposit into the Sunshine Shady account." That was enough of an incentive for Mark.

The two men were on the express train to Rabat the next morning.

"It is only an hour to Rabat," said Yousef. "We will arrive at the main station by 9:30. The bank is not far; ten minutes by cab.

Upon entering the bank Yousef told the Receptionist, "We are here to see Tarif Abu Alhamim, the President of the bank." After a brief conversation on the intercom in Arabic, she said, "Follow me, please." The two men followed her down a short hallway to a door marked *Private*, which she opened showing them into a large, dark, wood-paneled office.

A tall slender man in a well-cut European suit walked from behind his desk extending his hand. "Please call me Tarif," he said. "What can I do for you?"

We all sat waiting for someone to speak. Mark allowed ten seconds of silence to fill the room before he began in a hushed tone. "I am an attorney in Morocco on a very delicate matter of grave concern to the Federal government in the Southern District of Florida. It is a delicate matter since it involves a large sum of money, a very large sum which was transported from America to Morocco clandestinely. I will tell you this money was secretly removed from America illegally. The money I am referring to is now sitting in a bank in Morocco Mr. Tarif Abu Alhamim." Mark used his formal name to push home the importance of the matter. As a matter of fact I beleive the money is in Banque Wafi, your bank Mr. Alhamim.

"That is all very interesting, Mr. Radin. If that is the case, have the American government make a formal request to the Moroccan Banking

Authority. They will assist your agency to retrieve these funds. They will give me a Court Order which I will be obliged to comply with."

Mark had expected that answer from this dapper banker.

with more determination in his voice mark continued. "However, if you recall, I said this matter is delicate, sensitive. The money is part of an illegal business enterprise, one that totals in the billions of dollars. The money we are speaking of is illegally gotten gains from a corrupt scheme. If we are forced to go through Government channels, it will become public knowledge. Many people, including you, Tarif, will be brought in for questioning. Your bank will be implicated since we are speaking of more than thirty five million dollars, more than half in cash. We are speaking of American dollars Tarif. Packages of hundred dollar bills which you received from a stranger; no questions asked. You, your employees, and the bank will be under scrutiny, suspicion, maybe even sanctions, who knows. You could even lose your license to operate as a bank. I am sure you know what happened to Arabian National Bank in Casablanca."

"I only know they closed," said Tarif.

"Yes, but my friend sitting next to me is Mr. Daoud, a prominent attorney in Casablanca, he can tell you why they closed." Yousef looked at Mark, surprise on his face. Before he could say anything Mark continued: "They were involved in illegal money transactions. In America, we call it money laundering, taking dirty money, cleaning it by running it through various corporate accounts; then using it to buy consumables on the legitimate market. Big ticket items like real estate, commercial or industrial, transportation, like steamships or a trucking company, items with a high price. My associate, Mr. Daoud, is working with the Banking Commission which is investigating this incident and any others that come to their attention. That is how this inquisitive legal mind determined you were the recipient of 17 million 400 thousand US dollars in cash on or about November 10th or 11th of last year. We are here to help you remove this stigma from your association with known criminals."

"I don't know what you are talking about Mr. Radin. I suggest you go to the proper authorities with your claim, your unfounded accusations." Tarif stood, signifying the meeting was over. Yousef rose also while Mark remained sitting.

"Please sit Tarif, I am not finished. I have a few more items to cover. If you are of the same mind when I am done Mr. Daoud and I will indeed go straight to the Banking Commission as you suggest. Mr. Daoud will file a formal complaint, already prepared and in my briefcase resting by my foot. The complaint will be against Arabian National Bank and Mr. Tarif Abu Alhamim, of Banque Wafi.The charges are for fraud, deceitful banking practices, aiding and abetting in the commission of crimes involving money laundering, conspiracy, embezzlement in the sum of $200,000, associating with known criminals, plus any more charges Mr. Daoud and I can discover in the course of our investigation."

"This is preposterous," sputtered Mr. Abu Alhamim angrily, but he sat down.

Mark took the picture of the courier from him briefcase laying it on Tarif's desk. "Do you recognize this man?" Tarif just looked at the picture saying nothing. "He met you to hand over the case which contained $17,400,000. He will testify to this under oath. Mr. Daoud has his sworn statement. A deposit was made in the amount of 17 million 200,000 dollars which leaves $200,000 unaccounted for. Since you received the case personally the money had to disappear between you taking possession of the funds and the deposit. I am sure with that amount of cash more than one teller was involved in the counting of the money. I'm sure they will testify that the amount deposited was 17.2 million dollars. It could just be a clerical error with so much cash involved. That is a very nice suit Tarif – looks European, French is my guess. Been to Paris lately? I do love good clothing myself. Did your personal checking account increase by a substantial sum after November 10th or did you make many smaller deposits – spread them out over time until your flight to Paris?" Tarif poured water into a glass from a pitcher, resting on the credenza behind his desk, his hand shacking ever so slightly

"No thanks," said Mark. "I don't want any; I'm fine." None had been offered. Mark saw Tarif's hand shake as he drank. "Furthermore, you received an official cashers check - probably more than one –drawn on Arabian National Bank, a bank under investigation for illegal banking practices. A bank now closed whose officers may be facing criminal charges. That is what attorney Daoud will determine in an investigation that has brought him here to your bank. The checks were from a corporate account, which you deposited into a corporate account with a different name.

A similar name, but different. Technically another banking violation, another crime. Do you wish me to continue?" asked Mark.

"Maybe I should reconsider my thinking on the subject. What precisely do you want?" asked Tarif.

Mark now took out copies of the documents Harris Becker had given him, placing them in front of the banker. "As you can see, I have been appointed agent of the US Federal Court in Florida. Official Agent of the Receiver of Claims in the Matter of Rothstein and the firm RRA, in the Southern District of Florida. I have the authority to find, seize or transfer any funds connected to this case. Now consider what I tell you for your and your banks well being. I request you have a wire transfer prepared in the amount of – he turned to Yousef, who answered $37 million 700 thousand dollars. It should have been 37.9; but 37.7 will be sufficient. We will come back to the 200 thousand dollars shortly. Make a wire transfer for that amount, 37.7 is the figure we can agree upon. I request the wire transfer go to Bank of America, Coral Gables, Florida for payment to the law firm mentioned, wiring instructions are written out." Mark put that sheet on Tarif's desk, picking up the letters from Harris with the picture of the courier.

Tarif called his secretary on the intercom. "Please have our Controller, Mr. Amwani, come to my office at once." When the man entered the office Tarif spoke with him in French. The man shook his head said, "Tout de suite – at once."

While they waited for the Controller's return, Mark continued speaking. "You are doing the correct thing, Tarif. Your association with my good friend and legal counsel Mr. Daoud, can only help you in the future. He is in-line for appointment to the Board of Bank Examiners. Some bank is going to buy the assets of the closed Arabian National Bank. You might think what a move like that could do for you. Imagine a branch in Casablanca." Yousef was looking at Mark with a questioning gaze on his face; where was all this coming from, he wondered.

Amwani came into the office carrying a check in one hand, papers in the other. He placed both on Tarif's desk. Tarif handed Mark the papers. He read them, handing them to Yousef to read.

"That leaves $200,000 yet to be distributed. What would you like me to do with that?" asked the banker.

"First," said Mark. "What is the normal bank fee for a 37 million dollar wire transfer?" Tarif took his desk calculator, punching in numbers. "The fee would be $35,400."

"Please take that amount for the bank fee. For your considerable help in this matter, I am giving you the sum of $50,000 which you took from the cash that was handed to you. I'm not accusing you of any wrong doing. As gentlemen lets attribute it to an oversight on the part of the bank. However you will now have a written document signed by me on behalf of the court attesting to its authenticity. That way, you can sleep peaceful at night. If my math is correct that leaves a balance of 114,600. That is correct said the banker in a more subdued tone then when they first entered his office. Please have an official bank check made out to the law firm of Yousef Daoud PA for that sum. It was 2:30 when the three men stood in the bankers office shaking hands like old friends. Mark left with Yousef to catch the train to Casablanca. The train arrived at Casa Voyageurs, the main station in Casablanca at 4:30 that evening. A bank check for 114,600 dollars secure in Mark's inside jacket pocket.

"I must go to my office," said Daoud. "I have some unfinished work to attend to."

"Very well," replied Mark. I will be at your office at 10 in the morning to finish our business. Tonight, I will relax; see a bit of Casablanca act like a tourist." We did a good day's work today attorney Daoud, thank you for your help. Until tomorrow

"Very well, I will see you at 10," said Yousef, hurrying away. Mark watched as he disappeared into the crowd of travelers.

After a hot shower, Mark dressed for an evening on the town. He wore officers pink slacks, a pale blue open-neck shirt with a powder blue sport jacket. He slipped his feet into a pair of Cole Haan burgundy loafers, no socks. It was just past 7, when he walked to the concierge desk in the lobby. "Can you suggest someplace to eat?" Mark asked.

"The best restaurants to eat in are on the Boulevard De La Corniche, about twenty minutes out of town on the water, the Atlantic Ocean. The restaurant at the Villa Blanca Hotel is beautiful, romantic, with excellent food, French or Moroccan."

"But alas, I am alone," replied Mark.

"One place you should see while you are in town is Rick's Café."

"That Rick's Café?" asked Mark.

"No, no. smiled the concierge, This Rick's is a new venture owned by an American woman, an ex-diplomat in the American Embassy. It is a copy of Rick's from the movie *Casablanca*, but bigger, brighter, more brash. A piano player who plays the same songs; it is an experience not to be missed."

"Thank you for your suggestion, you convinced me Francoise; I will go to check it out." Mark handed the man a fifty Dirham bill.

Mark exited the cab on a bustling street in front of a brightly lit building. He could hear the music coming from speakers mounted outside on the street. Two speakers overhead attracted attention immediately. There were two movie posters mounted on the front of the white building, one on each side of the swinging bar-room doors. They showed Ingrid and Bogy from scenes in the film. Talk about nostalgia. He pushed through the door into a large white room, bright lights shining on a dance floor where a few couples moved to the music. A spot light was centered on a white baby grand piano in the middle of the dining room next to a dance floor. Many tables with white table cloths surrounded the room. Mark smiled, it was the perfect setting for Liberace. There was a long polished bar at the rear of the room, a wall of mirrors behind the bar. Though Mark was not a big drinker, he walked to the bar thinking he could survey the room while nursing a drink.

The barista came to him, as soon as he was seated. "What can I get you, sir?" she asked, speaking English with a thick French accent.

"I don't know," replied Mark. "Do you have any suggestions?"

"We have a drink that we invented. Now, it has gotten around town; every bar is taking credit for its invention. I have seen it done many ways but I still think our way is the best."

"What is it?" asked Mark.

"It is called the Porn Star Cocktail or Porn Star Martini. I will make you one; I guarantee you will love it. If not I will exchange it for anything you want."

"Go for it," said Mark.

She took a martini glass, filled it with ice and water.

"That's it," said Mark. "That's My kind of drink."

"I'm just chilling the glass" she laughed, as she went about mixing the ingredients in a tall shaker, then putting the chrome cover on shaking it well. She poured the contents into the martini glass filling it to the brim. The drink had a soft orange glow to it. Next to the Martini glass, she poured a tall shot glass of Prosecco. "Sip this first, then the drink."

Mark did as instructed. The drink tasted wonderful – not to strong, a bit sweet with a hint of orange. "That is very good," said Mark. "My compliments to you young lady the drink is exceptional."

A female voice down the bar asked: "Are you one, or do you want one?"

Mark turned to the voice. A woman sitting three stools away was smiling at him. She was an extremely attractive woman.

"I must answer no to both questions I'm afraid. I'm not one; nor do I want one. I prefer my women to be real, to savor a passionate moment in private; not to perform for a camera. That type of act should be for them alone. If I recall, making love is a special act done with someone you care for."

"A very well spoken reply sir. I mean no disrespect with my question. Do you mind if I join you?"

"Stay where you are," said Mark. "I'll join you." Mark moved next to the woman, sizing her up as he moved his seat. She was exquisite–long black hair, red lips which accented her tawny complexion. Aside from her lipstick, he doubted she wore any other make-up. She appeared to be about thirty, give or take a few years.

"So, you like your Porn Star," she smiled.

"For a drink, it is delicious. I am not much of a drinker, but I could get used to these."

The barista smiled, as she set the glass down in front of Mark. "Go easy with this drink. There is plenty of vodka in it; the alcohol is disguised by some of the other ingredients; but it can jump-up and bite you."

The piano player began to sing the theme from the movie *Casablanca*, As Time Goes By.

"They are setting the mood," Mark said, looking into the woman's eyes, which were a clear aqua, almost transparent. She has a beautiful face, her features were delicate. "They would play that song at Rick's," he said to her. She laughed a throaty laugh that he found sensual. Yes they play it about twelve times a night, maybe twice an hour. "Will you join me with a drink?" asked Mark, seeing her glass was empty. Rick's slowly filled with people. The noise level increased, the piano played on. "I have had enough of Rick's," said Mark. "Would you care to join me for dinner?"

"What do you have in mind?" she asked pointedly.

"The concierge at my hotel suggested Daphne's at Villa Blanca Hotel on the Corniche."

"An excellent choice," she said. "It is one of the better French restaurants in Casablanca. I would be happy to go to dinner with you. However, I want to be clear so as not to lead you on or mislead you. I will join you for dinner only. I am not going to your hotel with you afterward. Since you met me in a bar, bought me a drink, and are taking me to dinner, this is what men call a pick-up. If you are looking for someone to bed you may want to ask someone else to dinner. I will understand.""You are direct in your approach; I will say that. But how do you know I even want to make love with you? After all, we just met."

"Exactly, that is my point. I am not a prude, nor am I a virgin. However, I believe if I am to engage in the intimate act of intercourse there must be a reason, a purpose, a feeling between two people. My mother told me the most precious gift I can give a man is my body. I should respect it, not abuse the power of it.

"There is a saying that relates to sex," she continued. "A woman needs a reason, a man needs a place. I treat the intimate act of love making as something special. That means I must get to know you, to like you, to feel a kinship with you before I lay down to open my legs; before I allow you to see me with all my vulnerability."

Mark looked at this beautiful woman with newfound admiration. He had had many brief encounters with women, many one-night stands. He knew the ones that meant something were relationships where a meaningful sense of sharing was achieved. "I understand your thinking. I both agree with and approve your rational. Let's just enjoy each other's company for the remainder of the evening. I choose you to accompany me to dinner."

They sat with dessert on the veranda overlooking the ocean, waves rolling slowly onto the rocky shore. Mark looked at Angelique in the dim light of the candle burning on the table. The conversation during dinner had been stimulating. "You are a remarkable woman. Not only are you beautiful, but intelligent as well."

"I told you, Mark, my father was French, my mother Moroccan. Jean

Pierre, my father, spent thirty-five years in the French Foreign Legion, retired at age 51 as a sergeant-major – the highest, non-commissioned officer rank. He met my mother here in Casablanca when he was on a ten-day's rest from the fighting in neighboring Algeria. I was born in 1980. He came to live with my mother when he was discharged after thirty-five years of service with a military pension in 1981. The Moroccan military was trying to build an army at this time and needed competent officers. They hired him in 1987 to establish a training program for new recruits. They gave him the rank of colonel, a substantial salary, with a voice in the Elite Military Staff Corp. When I was nineteen he sent me to Paris to study at the Sorbonne. I went on a full scholarship because of his military service of thirty-five years. The French tend to look after their own people. He had many political and military friends in high places. After graduation, I entered Science Po, the premiere political and economic college in France, where I received a Master's Degree in Urban Administration. I came home to Morocco in 2004."

"Very impressive," said Mark. "You father sounds like a fascinating man. I would like to meet him."

"Maybe you shall one day," said Angelique. "Now, it is time to go – almost midnight."

"May I see you home?" asked Mark.

"Just walk me to a cab. You have to go back into the city. I will go on by myself."

"Can I see you for dinner tomorrow night?"

"Yes. We can meet for cocktails at 7 at Rick's." You can have another porn star. If it's ok I will settle with you.

"Then I will take you to the best restaurant in Casablanca," she said, while Mark opened the door of the cab for Angelique.

She turned before entering the cab, kissing Mark first on one cheek, then the other. "Bonne soirre," she said. "Thanks for a pleasant evening. You must tell me the story of the scar on your cheek. I'm sure it is an interesting story."

CHAPTER 14 ✠ ✠ ✠

Mark walked into the Law Office of Daoud PA at 10 a.m. Yousef came to lead him into his office.

"We have some important matters to attend to today," began Mark. "First, here is the check for 114,600 made out to your firm. I want you to prepare a retainer letter from your firm to the firm Becker Fertel, in Miami, Florida. The retainer fee is $50,000, which you will have in your bank when you deposit this check."

"To what do I owe this?" asked Yousef in surprise.

"To me," replied Mark. "It is for your help in bringing this matter to a quick satisfactory conclusion."

"That is very kind, Mark. I don't know what to say; how to thank you for this unexpected gesture."

"It is no idol move on my part. I spoke to Mr. Becker, in Florida last night at 1 a.m. our time, 6 p.m. in Florida. I explained what happened yesterday. He was overjoyed to learn thirty seven million dollars would be in his account tomorrow, a major sum to add to the money being accumulated to reimburse the victims of Scott Rothstein's fraud. You are being retained by Mr. Becker's firm and by Jacobs Gitomer Radin PA, a New York law firm – my law firm, which is retaining you for an additional 50 thousand, that's a total of 100,000 thousand dollars. What about the balance, the 14 thousand. Keep it in your bank until I decide. However, if you are going to represent these two prestigious firms you will need new offices, – offices that better show your success, your newfound prominence in the close-knit legal faction of Casablanca. Letters are already going out to many organizations here in Morocco, attesting to your legal skills. By next week, your career is going to be much changed due to the efforts of your new partners."

"How do I do this?" asked Yousef.

"Come, I will show you where to start. The rest will be up to you." The two men walked a few blocks from depressed to stately. They walked to the Bulivard Mohammid V, a broad avenue much like Park Avenue in Manhattan. The street was lined with modern glass office buildings rising thirty stories into the sky – high for Morocco.

"That is Tower Center, one block away. It is the most prestigious buildings in the city," said Yousef. "It is actually twin towers."

"What about that building," said Mark, pointing at a building of about 20 stories, modern, bright, all shiny glass and metal. "The Adona Anfa, a 22 story office building, very nice address, – 555 Blvd Mohammid V. That is going to be your new home. Come with me."

Mark asked the uniformed attendant in the lobby: "Where is the leasing office, please?"

"Room 202, Sir, on the second floor." A woman came to greet the two men as they entered the leasing office. She was smartly but conservatively dressed.

"We would like to rent office space for my friend, a law firm, about 1,200 square feet," said Mark.

"We are normally 100 percent occupied," she replied. "However, an office on the 18th floor just became available. An import-export company moved to the port to be closer to their shipments. It's not even on our list yet, but I can show you the space; it is 1,450 square feet."

The offices were ideal. The view from the 18th floor was breath taking. Mark let Yousef negotiate a price with three months free rent to allow for moving in and setting up a new office.

"Move in on the 10th of March. Prepare the lease, I will sign it tomorrow," said Yousef, a broad smile on his face.

CHAPTER 15 ✠ ✠ ✠

The two men stood on the corner of the wide boulevard, cars and buses whizzing by.

"I must get back to my office," said Yousef. "I have a client coming at 2:30. I must prepare."

"Fine," replied Mark. "It's a lovely day. I will get a bit of sightseeing in; get a feel for the largest city in Morocco."

"Catch a cab," instructed Yousef. "Tell the driver to take you to the Souk. You will get your full of Morocco in an hour."

Mark exited the red petit cab at the corner of the entrance to the Souk, the main bazaar in the city. It was a gigantic outdoor market. The teeming market was a combination street-fair, flea market and food emporium. A person could find anything they wanted in the long, narrow alleys, which were crammed with natives as well as tourists pushing along shoulder-to-shoulder. After an hour of wandering through the maze of stalls with vendors yelling for attention, Mark had had enough. He spied an exit into a narrow street leading away from the crowded market. There were a few people walking on the roadway which was comparatively empty of vehicles. He began walking away from the crammed market place enjoying the relative quiet. After traveling a few blocks he saw a row of umbrellas lining the sidewalk, one said *Sabrett. I doubt they would have Sabrett hot dogs here in Morocco; yet, you never know.* He walked toward that umbrella determined to find out since he loved hot dogs– the sign over the doorway read Café Rahal. Mark took a seat under the umbrella at a round-table, sitting in a wicker chair. He ordered a cool bottle of *Flag Speciale*, the local Moroccan beer, but no Sabrett hot dogs. Mark relaxed watching people walk by, drinking his cold beer from a frosted mug. He was just beginning to get comfortable looking forward to his encounter with the lovely Angelique when he heard a loud bellow, a raucous yell shattering the air. A small boy darted around the corner to Mark's left running hard being followed a second later by a brute of a man running after him. The man was yelling in Arabic – "Tawaquf, tawaquf. Stop, stop!" But the boy kept running, a leather bag suspended by a strap hanging from the boy's shoulder bouncing as he ran. The man was gaining on the boy, who stumbled almost falling but quickly regained his balance running even harder. They had almost reached the spot where Mark was sitting, now alert, body ready to spring. Mark sat on the edge of his chair gazing at the strange scene before him. The man reached out with his left hand, clutching the boy's shoulder in a firm grip. The young boy screamed out as the large man threw the boy to the ground. He lay on his back looking up at the man who had to be at least 6'4.The man raised his right arm high above his head. Mark could see a knife clutched in the man's right hand, a knife with a wicked-looking steel blade – a blade at least eight inches long. Mark was out of his wicker chair in an instant rushing to the middle of the road where the hulk of a man stood over the cowering boy. Mark came up behind the man, as the hand clutching the knife reached its apex. The brute was ready to lower the blade in a death blow into the cringing frightened young boy. Mark grabbed the man's wrist with his two hands, pulling back with all his might. Startled, the man was pulled backward off balance. He quickly regained his balance turning to the right in the direction he was being pulled, while lashing-out with his left hand at whom ever had the temerity to interfere with his mission. The blow caught Mark in his right side, knocking the air from his lungs, causing his grip to slacken. Mark hung onto the big man's Wrist determined not let the hand with the knife free. The giant grabbed Mark by the throat with his left hand, lifting him up so only Mark's toes touched the ground. *The man is a brute. He is squeezing the life out of me with one hand. This fight will be over quickly*, thought Mark, as strobe-lights began to flicker in his vision. *The man is too strong for me; I must end this now.*

A thought flashed through Mark's mind:

"You must finish any fight in ten seconds, no more than fifteen seconds, or you die."

"How do you do that?" Mark had asked. In Isreal we have developed a technique called Krav maga. It is taught to all commandos, paratroopers or elite forces."

Pishal was an Israeli frogman sent to train with SEAL Team 4 in Little Creek Virginia – Mark's SEAL Team. We were training Philip, Pishal, and his buddy Avi in advance SEAL training when they took three hours to train us in Krav Maga, which was hand-to-hand combat with the emphasis on killing your opponent and killing him quickly.

"Thank you," Philip said Mark, as he recalled the brutality of the training.

Lowering his head to his chest caused the pressure on his neck to relax slightly, just enough to draw a breath, clear the flashing lights from his brain. He drew back his right hand, stiffening his fingers as his arm shot forward. There was a howl of pain from the big aggressor who reached for his face. Mark's fingers had sunk into the man's left eye up to the middle joints of his two fingers. Once standing on firm ground Mark delivered three quick kicks to his assailants groin, causing the attacker to drop to his knees He was holding his groin with one hand, while blood poured from his blank eye socket. Mark drove the heel of his foot into the man's face causing him to fall onto his back in the street, the knife clattering to the ground next to him. Mark bent, picking up the wicked-looking knife, plunging it into the man's exposed throat. The blade met no resistance, as Mark moved it left then right. A gusher of blood splashed from the wound covering Mark's right hand and lower arm, the carotid artery was severed. Mark left the knife sticking in the man's neck; it was buried to the hilt. It took Mark more than fifteen seconds, but he was sure the Israeli's would be proud. Mark turned to the boy sitting on the ground; a horrified expression on his face.

"Do you speak English," Mark demanded.

"Yes," replied a quivering voice.

"Good. Get on your feet. We must leave here at once." Mark took the boy's hand. "Let's go, now!" They began to run down the street away from the crowd gathering around the dead body lying in the road; a pool of blood forming around the head and shoulders in a dark, almost black puddle. After running hard for two blocks, they slowed to a brisk walk.

"We need a main street, boy. We need to hail a cab. Can you get us out of here?"

"Yes," replied the boy. "Boulevard Des Far is this way." The boy brought them to a broad heavily traveled avenue – the sign in Arabic and English – Boulevard Forces Armees Royal Blvd Des Far. Mark waived down a red cab petit. "Ave Froch," he told the driver. That was a street one block away from Daoud's office, which is where they were going. Two Police cars, red lights flashing, sped by in the opposite direction. The young boy looked at Mark holding the large leather case to his chest with both small hands. It was nearly 5 o'clock, when the two walked into Yousef's office.

"What happened to you?" Yousef asked. "Are you hurt? You have blood on you. Who is the waif with you, a street beggar, where did you find him?"

"Too many questions at once, Yousef. Could I have some water first; for my young friend also."

Yousef came back into the office, carrying two bottles of water. "Now, tell me what happened." Mark related the entire chain of events just as they had unfolded. "You killed a man," Yousef exclaimed in horror. "You, an American, a visitor in my country. Do you know what will happen to you he demanded?"

"Yes," replied Mark.

"I will go to the Police with you. You tell them what happened. There will be many witnesses; it was self-defense.""I saved this boy's life. They will surely let me go."

"No, my friend; they will not. There will be an investigation, then a judicial hearing to decide if you are to be tried for the crime of murder. This will take better than eighteen months, maybe two years. Criminal law moves slowly in Morocco. During this time you will sit in jail. The Judge won't let you out since you are American, a flight risk. Once you are in America you are free, since we have no extradition treaty with America. That means you will sit in Ait Melloul Prison for at least two years." Yousef shook his head in dismay.

"What do you suggest I do, counselor?"

"I suggest you run. Get out of Morocco while I hire an excellent criminal attorney to represent you. He will argue the self-defense theory. If and when he is successful, you can return to receive a pardon."

"That sounds fine," said Mark. "But, how do I run? I am sure all points of exit from the city are already being watched – airports, train stations, buses, everything. I don't know my way around your country. Where do I go?"

The young boy sat quietly, listening to the conversation.

"Stay here. I will see what I can arrange," said Yousef, walking into the next office. Mark sat, looking at the young boy, obviously still frightened. He was sitting hunched over, knees pulled up protectively, ill at ease. Mark smiled at him, speaking quietly, reassuringly. "You don't have to worry now, son. You are safe with me. I won't let anything or anyone hurt you." The young boy made no sound. He just sat staring at Mark, his arms crossed over the leather case he held to his chest.

"What is your name?" asked Mark, trying to get the boy to talk, to relax.

"I am called Hakim," was the reply in a low, hesitant tone.

"Where do you live? Where are your parents?"

"I am an orphan – no mother, no father. I slept in the house of the Rabbi; he is dead. Now I have no place to go."

"Tell me what happened today. Why was that man chasing you, trying to kill you?"

"For this case, I think," said the boy, clutching the dark-brown leather pouch even tighter."

"Tell me," urged Mark.

"My keeper, rabbi Benjamin Levy called me to his study. Hakim, he instructed, take this case, handing it to me. Take it to Dr. Professor Hayim Abbas. His address is written on this paper. Protect the case well; it is extremely valuable. Tell the Professor: rabbi Levy sent it to him; he will know what must be done with it. When you have delivered the pouch, come back to me. As I turned to go, the door flew open. Then this giant came rushing into the room, knocking me to the floor with a blow to my head. I lay frozen, as he advanced to the desk where the rabbi sat, grabbing him by the neck."

Mark unconsciously raised his hands to his neck, remembering the strength of the brute's hands. "It's alright, Hakim; go on."

"I watched as he choked the rabbi. *Tell me where the journal is! he demanded.* But the rabbi just looked him in the face. The rabbi's eyes were bulging. He said something I could not hear, than spit in the man's face. It enraged the man even more. He took out a long knife, the one you stuck in the man's throat. He took the knife, stabbing it into the Rabbi's chest. That's when I got up running from the house. I think after he had killed the old man, he turned to get me. But by that time I was running for my life. I could hear him screaming after me. I just ran faster. I may have gotten away, but I slipped and fell, which allowed the giant to close on me. As I rounded the corner I knew he was close. I could hear his feet striking the pavement, his breath rasping, as he ran until he reached out grabbing my shoulder, squeezing hard. I turned, looking at him, hatred on his face. *I am going to die like my protector rabbi Levy, I will die with a knife stabbed into my body.* Then you appeared. You saved my life. For that I am grateful, but still frightened."

"I promise you, Hakim, no harm will come to you, if I can prevent it. Where were you taking this case?"

"To this address." Hakim handed Mark a slip of paper, as Yousef came into the office.

"I have someone coming. He will be here shortly, Mark. He will know what to do."

CHAPTER 16 ✚ ✚ ✚

The man who came through the door was a visage of death. He could have had a sign around his neck, saying: Don't fuck with me or prepare to die. It was his appearance. He looked sinister. It was the set of his mouth, the lines in his face. He was a picture in black, from his black hair to his black shoes, suit and crew-neck shirt – all black; even his eyes were dark. Then, it dawned on Mark this was the man in the picture. Yousef had called him the courier; obviously, he was more than just a delivery-boy.

"Shalom," the man said in a deep, husky voice. "What has transpired today? Tell me everything; leave no details out." If I am to help you I must know all the facts.

After Mark finished his narrative he had Hakim tell his story. The man just stood listening, not interrupting; a serious frown on his face. When they had finished, he spoke.

"This is very serious, even more serious than I anticipated. The man you killed today is evil. He is an enforcer for a ruthless gang of cut-throats - a criminal organization based in Casablanca. They have tentacles stretching throughout Morocco and beyond. You must be a proficient opponent to have bested Rachman. Until now, no one has lived when he came for them. A light of apprehension, or possibly concern or respect, possibly all three shone in the man's dark eyes. Yousef is correct in his assessment of your situation. You cannot get arrested or turn yourself in. You would not be seen again for at least two years, if ever. People have a way of dying in our prisons. If the Police don't kill you, the Vorani Gang will. I am sure they are looking for you already, both you and your young friend. They didn't send Rachman to find the boy with the case because he was a Boy Scout. He came to get that case by whatever means necessary. Give me the address Hakim was given, also the key to your hotel room. I will be back in a few hour's, no one goes out until I return. Understand."

Mark shook his head in agreement.

"Good," said the man.

"Wait," said Mark. "What is your name?"

"Call me Nazim," he said, leaving the room.

Nearly three hours past when Nazim walked into the office, two large shopping bags in his hand. "Both of you take off your clothes, I brought you new ones. I will speak while you change. The Police were already at your hotel Mark, which is why I had to get you new clothes. That means they know who you are. They will have an alert out for your arrest. Since you killed a man in a violent confrontation you will be considered armed and dangerous. The Police were also at the home of Doctor Professor Hayim Abbas. I mingled with the crowd gathered outside asking questions. Someone entered the Professor's house, killed him, than ransacked the premises searching for something. No one, including the Police know what the intruder was after, or if he found it." But we know they were looking for that leather case in young Hakims grasp.

Mark was sure they hadn't found what they were after, so they killed the professor. That makes 2 dead plus the killer Nazim called Rachman. He was also sure the item everyone was searching for was resting on the floor, in the pouch Hakim had put there in order to change. Mark stood in his new cloths, beige jeans, a denim shirt over a white t-shirt, Nike sneakers, a baseball cap, hoody-sweatshirt, sunglasses. All fit very well. He looked at Hakim who was similarly dressed.

"Based on what I have seen, we have to leave Casablanca within the next few hours."

"That is fine for you to say Nazim. But I have very little money, no Passport or idea how to leave Casablanca or where to go."

"I will take care of those problems" said Nazim confidently. He produced another bag. "Some food," he said. "Eat now since I don't know when our next opportunity will be. I will try not to be too long, maybe one and a half or two hours at most. Be ready to go when I return." He left the office carrying a shopping bag, filled with the old clothes to be discarded.

"I will get you some money," said Yousef, writing a check for 14,600 dollars. "Accept the money over my retainer," he told Mark.

"Where can you cash a check at this hour? It is after 8 already, no banks will be open late at night."

"Have no fear, Mark. I will return with cash for you."

Yousef was back first, a smile on his face, a brown paper-bag in his hand. He emptied the bag on his desk. The three looked at the large pile of paper bank notes laying there.

"I got 12,500 dollars for you, only 3,200 dollars American. I am afraid you have 7,300 is Moroccan Dirham plus 2,000 Euros. Because of the hour, the Halualh sensed an emergency of some type; so he demanded a premium from me to accept my check, 2,100 dollars was his fee; I didn't argue."

Shortly after Nazim returned. "Let's go," he said. "Your ride is waiting."

To Yousef, Nazim said, "I will be back in two days. We can settle accounts then."

"Now we must move, time will not wait. We have to leave Casa at once. The city is crawling with gendarmes all looking for you." We stepped into the street where a black Audi A8 sat at the curb. Nazim walked to the driver's door while I held the rear door for Hakim. I slid into the passenger's seat next to Nazim, who accelerated away from the curb.

"Where are we going?" I asked.

"A small port on the north coast on the Mediterranean; it is called Tenabes. You will be able to get a boat there to take you out of the country; no questions asked. The port is home to smugglers and pirates." I have already called to alert a boat captain of your dire situation.

"Great," replied Mark. "How did you get this car? Or, do I dare ask?"

"I borrowed it for a few days at the airport. A man parked it, than took a carry-on bag from the trunk wheeling it into the terminal. He walked up to the Lufthansa desk to get a boarding pass. I followed close behind.

When he left the counter, I asked the attendant: "My friend just checked in, is he going to Germany?"

"Yes," she replied. He is on the 9 o'clock flight to Stuttgart, coming back on the 4th of February, one week from today."

"When he returns, his car will be in the same space or in close proximity to it. There will be a few more miles on the odometer; but he won't notice."

Mark looked on Hakim in the back seat, his eyes were closed; he seemed to be sleeping. After fifteen minutes of silence, Mark asked Nazim, "What do you think is going on with this young lad and his case? Did you look at the contents of the case?" Nazim asked.

"Yes, I did. It is a large bundle of papers, possibly a manuscript of some type. Maybe a diary; I couldn't tell. Why?" asked Nazim. "It is in a language I couldn't understand. I showed it to Yousef. He was as mystified as me. "Never saw anything like it," he said. "Which is as I thought," replied Nazim. "It all fits together."

"What does," asked Mark.

"Please try to follow me. rabbi Ben Levy is a noted Jewish historian and linguist. He came to Morocco from Israel where he taught ancient Judaic history at Bethlehem University which is predominantly Christian and Muslim. Yet, this Jew taught there until 1967. During the Yom Kippur War, the Israeli military closed the University. That is when Benjamin Levy came to Morocco. He began to teach in Casablanca at a small seminary he opened to educate the poor, the illiterate. The Mayor of Casablanca gave him a post on the education committee. Many world scholars came seeking his counsel since he was a renowned historian. He had even been up for a Nobel Prize in ancient history. He did not win the award, but it brought him much attention and acclaim,"

"So, someone comes upon this rose journal of yours, continued Nazim... not mine," protested Mark.

"It is yours now – yours and Hakim's, since everyone else who came into contact with it is dead. Let me continue. So someone in a far off land somewhere discovers this journal. They study it, but cannot decipher the meaning. Then this person remembers a man, a renowned rabbi, who studied ancient history, religion, ancient languages'– maybe this wise man can translate these pages. But it is a long way from where the document is to the rabbi in Morocco – a very long way."

"How far?" asked Mark. "Where are we talking about?"

Nazim cast a stern look in Mark's direction, even in the darkness Mark could sense his impatience. "I'm sorry," said Mark. "Continue."

"So, a messenger is sent to find the rabbi in Casablanca, an easy task since everyone knows of him. The hard part was getting to Casablanca.

I believe this young messenger walked most the way, either from Iraq, Turkey, or possably Syria."

"How do you know this?"

"Because three days ago, the body of a young man – possibly a Turk or Kurd – was found in a garbage dump outside town in the squalid section of Casablanca called Duar Skat. His body was covered with bruises, fingers broken, burn-marks on his arms and torso. In a word, he had been tortured before he was killed. You can be sure he told his captures what they wished to know before he died."

"Now let's assume this young man, according to the coroner he was in his early twenties. Let's say he was the one who carried the parcel to the rabbi. The rabbi fed him, bathed him, gave him some food and money then sent him on his way. How or why he was taken is of little import. The fact is he ended up in the Vorani Gang's hands. Once they had the information from him, they sent Rachman to get the package from the rabbi; you know the rest. But, I will fill in some more for you. The rabbi could not understand the pages either; but he thought of his friend the Professor. They spoke by phone; the rabbi telling him about a fascinating document that had come into his possession. He could make out some words, but the language was something he had never seen before. Maybe you will have more luck than I had. You were always smarter than me. After all, you won my Nobel Prize. They, the killers, sent another emissary of death to the Professor's house to see if he had received the document. That is why his house was ransacked; the assailant was looking for it." The professor was killed so he wouldn't talk.

Mark sat quietly, thinking. "How much further do we have to go?" he asked.

"The trip is about three hundred miles. I have been driving slowly since I do not want to attract attention. Also, these inland roads are not the best; it will be about a 6½ to 7 hour ride. We should reach the port by 5 a.m." Mark sat quietly, thinking of what Nazim had told him.

CHAPTER 17 ✠ ✠ ✠

The sky was beginning to lighten when Nazim brought the car to a halt at the head of a cement pier jutting out into the water. They sat overlooking a harbor filled with many boats.

"We're here," said Nazim. "Tenabes – home to the best smuggling fleet in the world."

Mark roused himself; he must have dozed off. Now, he was wide awake, just as he had reacted over many years ago serving as a Navy SEAL. He was ready for survival, the moment his eyes opened.

"Take the boy, walk down this pier. You will see a sleek, black hulled boat. The name on the transom is *Macher*. The Captain's name is Alon; tell him I sent you. Take this paper. There are two names on it, both are renowned world scholars – one lives outside Cairo, the other in the old section of Jerusalem. Alon can help you find them. Good luck, Chayei Olam." With that, Nazim drove away into the early morning haze leaving Mark standing on the wharf looking at the boats in the harbor. The sky lightened more going from black to grey. The false dawn was the term used in the Navy for the period between black of night and budding daylight. This was just the illusion of light, not bright but not the deep black of night. Mark took Hakim by the hand. "Let's go find our ride out of Morocco little prince," he told the young boy, holding him by the hand walking down the ramp to the long pier.

CHAPTER 18 ✠ ✠ ✠

The name on the transom of the boat said, *Macher* in bright gold letters against the black hull. There was no gangway leading aboard the boat, just an opening in the guard-rail for an entry-way. Mark knew from experience you never board a boat without the owner's permission. Even in the Navy you saluted the officer of the deck and requested permission to come aboard. The two stood still in the breaking dawn while Mark tried to decide what to do next. He did not want to call out possibly alerting others to his presence.

A soft voice from the dark asked: "Are you going to stand there like a statue or are you going to come aboard?"

"I request your permission to board." Mark spoke in the direction the sound had come from, since he still could not see anyone. Mark stepped across the space from the dock to the boat deck helping Hakim after him. The boy stood still clutching the pouch the rabbi had put in his care holding onto Marks pants leg for support.

A man stood in the shadow of the bridge where he had been waiting. He walked up to Mark. "My name is Alon. I have been expecting you. Come join me in the galley; we can talk there." Mark followed Alon to a hatch where a ladder led down into the boat. The space was warm, bright, illuminated by an overhead light, a space-heater hissed, giving off just enough warmth to take the chill out of the morning air.

"Welcome to my humble boat," said Alon. "Sit at the table. I will give you food and drink; you must be hungry." Over the food, a glass of tea, English-style before them, Alon asked: "What do you have in mind now?"

"Do you know our circumstances?" asked Mark.

"Some, but I am sure you can fill me in. I only spoke with your benefactor briefly. He did not want to say much on the telephone. So please tell me what I need to know." Mark told the story again from the time Hakim rounded the corner to the present, including the ride in the borrowed car with Nazim driving from Casablanca.

"Nazim dropped us at the head of the pier, telling me to find the black boat; unless there is another one, you must be it."

"There are no other black boats in Tenabes, or possible the entire Mediterranean. As for your friend Nazim, you are lucky to have him; he is a most skilled operator. I understand why you are here. What do you want to do now? Where do you wish to go?"

"Any place out of Morocco first. Then, I need to find someone who can translate the papers my young companion has been given. Papers that have already caused three deaths I am sure of, and another that Nazam told me about on our night road-trip. I want to tell you, Alon, I do not think the four dead will be the final tally. I have a feeling more deaths are coming."

"Do I have a choice of options at this point?" asked Mark. No was the reply. "Then we have a deal," said Mark, as he extended his hand.

"Help me cast off; it's getting light. I don't want anyone to see you. Keep the sunglasses on with your hood up." The boat passed the light at the end of the jetty as they moved into a slight chop entering the Mediterranean Sea. Mark let his eyes travel over the boat. Now it was light, the sun coming up in the east over an endless blue sea. The land receded into the distance. "I will turn east about ten miles off-shore," said Alon standing at the helm.

"From what I can see, this is a very nice seaworthy craft, Alon. I would guess about eighty five feet?"

"92 feet, actually; it is not just nice, it is exceptional. It was a German naval patrol boat for twelve years. They built new ones to replace these in 2007. The surplus boats, this was one, were put up for sale. I bought it with my saved funds. Brought it to a ship-yard in Italy where I made some changes. I customized it to my tastes. It has two Mercedes Benz twelve-cylinder diesel engines; top speed is 49 knots. I installed larger fuel tanks, now I can cruise comfortably at 19 knots. I have a range of 3,800 nautical miles. That means I can cross the Atlantic. The boats hull is fiberglass, Kevlar reinforced so it can take a pounding in heavy seas. The bridge is an express bridge, low slung like an old E-Boat or Pt. Boat from WWII. You may get a little wet in rough seas but it makes the boat cut through the air and water better. I also enlarged the forward cargo compartment for my smuggling activities. The compartment is a good forty five feet of open space with seven feet of head room, useful in my kind of work. I will take you on a tour of the vessel when we are at anchor."

After a light lunch, Alon told Mark: "You take the helm. Just keep us on a heading of ninety degrees due-east; wake me in three hours." Mark sat at the helm station, wheel in hand. It had been a long time since he had the helm of a powerful vessel like this. He had to admit it felt good with the breeze on his face, the sun warm on his back. White sea-birds screeching, as they followed in the boats wake.

At 4, Mark told Hakim to go wake the Captain. "Also, put your leather pouch away. You don't have to keep in on your shoulder while we are at sea; it can't go anywhere."

"Well, let's see how you have done," said Alon, walking up to look at the compass, than glancing at the GPS and electronic map computer.

"I see you have all the latest electronic gadgets on the bridge," remarked Mark.

"In my kind of work, it is imperative I stay abreast of those trying to catch me. Actually, I must keep ahead. Therefore, I learn all there is about new digital items as soon as they reach the market. I then add them to my array when I can."

"It is very impressive," said Mark, like the flight cockpit of a jet liner.

"Since you are now my first mate, I'm happy to see we are dead on course – exactly where I want to be. Now, we turn toward shore."

"Why?" asked Mark I want to go east to Egypt, we can't be there already.

"It is called business my friend. We must make some money to pay our way since I am sure you don't have enough to fill my tanks. I timed our trip so we come in at dusk. We will load our cargo in the dark."

"Where are we going?" asked Mark.

"A small inlet in Algeria, not even a harbor, more a cove called Ed Americ. Are you familiar with firearms? Can you handle an automatic rifle?" asked Alon.

"I am quite capable of using just about any weapon known to man. I've had plenty of training at Uncle Sam's expense."

"Good to know. When we dock, I will go ashore to transact business. I will supervise loading of our cargo in the hold. Your job is to cover my ass. These are dangerous people we will be dealing with. They would not hesitate to kill me, then steal my *Macher*; so stay alert.

The sun was already dropping below the horizon, as Alon eased the boat slowly toward the approaching shore. Mark sat next to Alon; Hakim holding the rail on the side of the cockpit. He stood gazing forward into the gathering gloom. There was a short wooden pier – about sixty feet long - jutting out from a sandy beach. Alon put the throttles to neutral, allowing the boat to glide into the shadows alongside the pier. The boat bumped gentle on the rubber tires acting as fenders hanging over the side of the dock to protect the boats hull. Alon reached into a compartment built into the side of the cockpit; turning to Mark, an automatic AK47 combat rifle in his hand. "I'm going to meet our friends on the shore; take this. You said you know how to use it."

"Yes," said Mark. It looks like an AK47." I'm familiar with it, an excellent weapon at short range.

"Very good," said Alon. "But this is the AK74, a newer version of the 47; but basically, the same weapon." It fires the 5.56 x 45 NATO Rounds in a thirty bullet clip. Here are two more clips. I don't anticipate any problems; I've dealt with this group before. But I like to be prepared – like a Boy Scout. Keep your eyes open. If there is trouble, waste them; keep me alive."

"Got it," said Mark. as Alon turned climbing to the rickety dock walking toward the long bow of the black boat. He turned back to face me.

"Remember," he said pointedly, "There are probably two or three men in the dunes with guns pointed at us, stay alert."

"Nice," said Mark. He counted seven men standing around a truck parked in the dirt at the head of the pier. Alon talked to one of the men, handing him a canvas duffle bag which the man opened, looking inside. He then turned to the men speaking to them in a low voice waving his hands in the air. The rear door of the truck opened. One man climbed into the back while four men walk to the bow of the boat with Alon. The men took off their shoes climbing onto the foredeck. Alon pushed a button to open a hatch in the deck. Mark could hear the low whine of an electric motor. Two men dropped out of sight, Alon right behind them, as the others began to unload the truck. Two men carried the bundles from the truck to the boat, passing them up to the men on deck who then passed them through the hatch to the men in the hull. Alon was showing the men how to stack the bundles in orderly rows. Soon, it was a smooth chain in motion. One man handing the packages from the truck to the two men on the ground, who walked to the boat where they handed the bundles to the men on deck. They in turn passed the bundles below; while the two men walked back to the truck for more. The packages looked to be about three feet high by two feet wide. They were covered in burlap, two yellow straps securing the bundles. They appeared heavy but not overly so, since one man was carrying the bundle without too much difficulty. Maybe fifty pounds, Mark estimated. He kept his eyes fixed into the darkness looking for any movement. As the last bundle was passed through the hatch, the men ashore stood waiting for the two on the boat to return. The men climbed into the back of the now empty van. The leader waved to Alon, closed the doors, walked to the passenger door and got into the truck which promptly drove off into the darkness without turning on his lights.

A good night's work," said Alon, joining me at the helm station. He started the twin diesel engines which came to life emitting a pleasant growl. "Let's get out of here." I always feel safer at sea.

CHAPTER 19 ✚ ✚ ✚

The boat was moving across the flat surface at a leisurely twelve knots.

"Why so slow, Captain?" asked Mark. "You said the *Macher* could cruise at nineteen knots."

"We are heading for this spot said Alon, pointing his finger to the map display on one of the computer screens on the electronic console. "Abu Heshaith," just over the border into Egypt. That is where we unload our cargo. I don't want to arrive before 2 o'clock tonight so I'm going at a leisurely pace. It will also conserve some fuel. Let me put the boat on auto-pilot. I have some things to show you below. Hakim, come here boy; you take the helm,sit in the pilot's seat. If you see anything, a boat, plane, anything at all call us at once; understand."

"Yes, Captain," replied Hakim, saluting. He would be in charge of the boat.

"Good boy," said Alon. "Come Mark."

When they were standing in the engine room, below the rear deck, a big smile on Alon's face, he asked, what do you think of my engine room Mark?"

Mark was impressed at his surroundings. The room was large, spotless, bright lights illuminating the room. Gun metal diamond plate steel decks, two generators, a water distillation unit with gleaming gauges and two massive diesel engines humming away in a steady throb sitting side by side separated by a wide walk way. A very impressive engine room Alon, nicer than many ships I've served on.

"Yes it's all very nice as it should be; but I want to show you some special features I've added. Come here. Do you see this button?"

"No," said Mark I don't see a button.

"Good, you're not supposed to; it looks like a normal chrome rivet. Now push it."

Mark did as he was told, then stepped back in surprise as a panel slid open to reveal a compartment – a compartment that was really a weapon armory. "My God," exclaimed Mark. "You could start a small war with this arsenal."

"You exaggerate my friend. These weapons are for defensive purposes only." I have two shotguns, twelve-gauge tactical weapons. One is a Remington Model 870 Marine-type pump action, it holds six slugs in the magazine plus one in the chamber. The other is a Mossberg 500 ATP. It holds five in the magazine, one in the chamber. They are both loaded with double ought buck shot. The Mossberg has two pistol grips, no stock; it is a lethal gun, a tactical weapon. The shotgun is a deadly gun at close quarters. There are two American Colt M16 assault rifles, 2 HK 416 machine guns and my favorite an Israli Galil AR sniper rifle. Then there is an America M79 grenade launcher of Viet Nam era fame. It fires a mortar shell that explodes on impact. In addition I have six handguns, four automatics, two revolvers. I even have two suppressors for them. The cabinets below hold all the loaded mags for the automatic weapons, along with boxes of bullets and shotgun shells."

"Most impressive Alon, that's a varied assortment of firearms." There's a gun in this compartment for any contingence. I told you I like to be prepared for any situation we can confront Mark.

"To close the bulkhead, just press the rivet again," which Mark did.

"Keep this our secret." said Alon. "You and I are the only ones who know about my secret gun compartment. Oh, and your friend Nasim knows since he helped design it."

CHAPTER 20 ✠ ✠ ✠

At exactly 2 a.m. the boat ghosted slowly, silently, over the water toward the black shore. A red light flashed from the beach – one – two – one.

"That's our party calling us in. They are telling us the coast is clear. Not to worry here. These people want me to keep coming back. Just stand by the cockpit holding your gun so they can see it. Keep alert, look mean. Come on Hakim, you can be my assistant."

Alon had a parley with two men, one of whom was carrying a Samsonite-type piece of hard luggage which he handed to Alon. Alon gave it to Hakim as he whispered in the boy's ear. Hakim struggled to carry the bag back to the boat. Once aboard he walked to Mark who was standing in the cockpit near the helm station.

"The Captain say you watch this for him said Hakim setting the bag down next to Mark."

The unloading began using four men to shuttle the burlap covered bales from the forward compartment to the men on shore. Another group on shore began to stow the bales into the waiting transport. Mark couldn't believe the scene. There were three wooden carts pulled by two donkeys each. A camel stood with an odd contraption over its back into which his handler placed four bales, two on each side. As soon as the bales were in place, the man and camel began to walk away into the dark night. Each of the three wooden carts were loaded with sixteen bales. Alon had told Mark the bales weighed 60 pounds each which meant each wagon contained 960 pounds of Hashish. They moved off into the darkness as soon as they were loaded, a brown tarpaulin covering the loads. That left two white Ford closed vans, each of which was stuffed full of the remaining drugs,

30 bales weighing 60 pounds each, 1,800 pounds per van. It was 4:20 in the early morning before the off-loading was complete.

"We are going now said Alon. That's what I call a profitable night's work. We are going a few miles off shore where we will drop anchor, grab a snack, than catch a few hours' sleep. We will take turns – one sleeps while the other keeps watch. I sleep first," said Alon. "Wake me at 8 a.m. The sun will be well up into the sky by then. I will get us underway for Alexandria, about six hours away at cruising speed. You can go ashore to find the old scholar then."

They moved into the large port of Alexandria at 2:30 on a hot sunny afternoon. Alex as the city was known is a very busy port. Large merchant freighters were steaming in and out of the harbor while numerous cruise ships sat docked at the cruise terminals nearest town gleaming bright in the afternoon sun.

"How do we play this?" asked Mark.

"I will put you ashore at the outlying pier away from the eyes of the constabulary. Take this passport with you. You will need it to get back into the restricted port facility.

"Whose passport is it?" asked Mark.

"It doesn't matter. This is Egypt. Put a twenty Euro-note on the picture page, they will pass you through with no questions asked. When you leave the port catch a cab to this address. I pulled it up on Google. When you return, take a water taxi out to the boat. I will be tied up to one of these floating buoys we are passing now. Hakim and I will be waiting for you to return. Good luck."

The ride to Giza, where Ahmed Orabi lived was 111 miles from Alexandria. Mark judged it would take at least two to three hours to cover that distance depending on road conditions and traffic. He passed through the gates from the port without every attracting a glance He walked into the heat and smells of the city of Alexandria,. Both were overwhelming. Mark stood looking at the line of waiting cabs until he spotted the one he wanted. It was a Toyota FJ Cruiser, yellow, covered in dust with a lot of dents around the body. A youngish-looking driver stood leaning against the fender. Mark walked up to him asking: "Do you know who Ayrton Senna is?"

"Of course," came the reply. You mean was. He is dead now, killed in a crash in San Marino Italy. "He was one of the greatest Formula 1 drivers ever. If he had not died tragically he would have beaten Shumacher. The noise around them made the man shout in order to be heard."

"You're my driver," said Mark. "Can you get me to Giza in under three hours?"

"Climb into my Ferrari" he laughed; we'll see how good I am." The car pulled up in front of the Professor's house in two hours and eighteen minutes. Record time I think the driver smiled. Mark handed the driver, whose name was Shawak, 50 Euros.

"Wait for me. I have to go back to Cairo but I don't know how long I will be – maybe an hour, maybe three. Here is another 10 Euros; get something to eat, then wait right here for me to return."

The house looked old, as did most buildings in Giza. The pyramids of Giza were only a short distance away, their peaks visible in the distance. Mark knocked on the carved wooden door. He stood in the late afternoon heat waiting patiently. After a minute he banged again, harder this time, then waited some more. Finally the door was opened by a frail old man who looked truly ancient. Although Mark had been told the scholar was only 82 he looked much older. He was stooped with scraggly grey hair, a brown wrinkled face. The man looked at Mark with grey rummy eyes.

"Yes, what do you want? Why are you here banging on my door?" he asked in a high pitched raspy voice. It was obvious the old professor smoked too much, probably harsh Turkish tobacco.

"I was sent to you by rabbi Benjamin Levy in Casablanca. He told me you may be able to help me with a project."

"What type of project" the old man asked rudely. Mark opened the leather pouch he had hanging from his shoulder removing one page of the manuscript, handing it to the old man who squinted at it, then looked agitated.

"Where did you get this?" he demanded.

"It's a long story," replied Mark.

"Come in then young man and tell me." Mark followed, as the man shuffled across the floor sliding his feet over the tiles as if they were too heavy to lift. He wore a traditional Arab robe, a black loose-fitting dish-dasha. A small crocheted white skull-cap covered his bushy grey hair. He led Mark into a study whose walls were covered with diplomas and pictures of excavation sites; some showed people at the various sites. "Please sit the old man said, indicating a chair before his desk as he settled behind the desk; the single sheet of paper lying in front of him. He took a magnifying glass from his desk drawer and began to study the paper intently; there was no sound in the room to disturb him. Mark sat quietly, patiently waiting for the professor to finish.

He looked up at Mark speaking slowly. "You have presented me with a dilemma. This paper is in quite good condition for its age. I would guess it was produced in Italy, around 1300. The Chinese invented paper. The process came to the Muslim world first over the silk-road, then to Europe many hundreds of years later. The words on this page are a combination of at least three, maybe four languages; very difficult to decipher. I see some Turkish, Hebrew, and even Sanskrit, possibly a European influence also – French or Spanish, even some Latin. It would take months to transcribe the many pages you have, and even then I could not be sure I had it right. What did rabbi Levy say?"

"He gave up," said Mark. He was convinced it was more than he could do. He suggested I find you. *My friend and colleague, Professor Orabi can help you. He is the foremost scholar in all of Egypt, possibly the Middle East. He has been a Professor of Ancient Civilizations for over 54 years, Head of the Antiquities Department at Al Azhar University – a university dating back to 975 AD; it is the chief center of Islamic learning in the world. Ahmed is on the Board of Senior Scholars; they run the University.*"

"Do you want a drink my guest? Some Tea or water?"

"Yes, water please," said Mark. Ahmed left the room saying I will be back shortly. It was eighteen minutes until he returned carrying a glass of water in a frail hand. Mark had waited impatiently wondering what took so long to fetch a glass of water. Did the old man have to go to an oasis to get water.

"Let me examine a few more pages, please." After almost an hour of silence while the Professor looked at each sheet carefully, he passed the pages to Mark, who put them into the leather case. "May I see the case?" Ahmed asked, reaching for it. "An interesting case – the impression embossed into the leather is unique."

"Yes," agreed Mark. He had looked at it many times before, but it meant nothing to him.

"I am sorry I could not be of more help to you after your long trip. I suggest you go to Jerusalem. Find Rabbi Ben Simon in the Old City. Tell him I sent you for his help. If he cannot translate your document, no one can. He has collaborated with me in the past, a brilliant man. A few years my senior, but his mind is still sharp; his knowledge is encyclopedic. Find him, I am sure he can help you. Good luck on your trip. Be careful on your boat; sea voyages can be dangerous, even deadly."

The trip back to the port was even faster. Traffic was light at this late hour as my race-car driver tried to impress me with his skill. I gave Shawaz 100 Euros since he waited over three hours for me to finish my business with the Professor.

"Goodbye friend. I leave for other ports now."

"Shalom Aleichem. Go with God." Thank you for this treasure you have bestowed on me,160 Euros is a goodly sum.

It was dark when Mark walked up to the guard at the entrance gate to the port. "Passport," The guard demanded in a stern voice. The man wore a military uniform, a pistol in a white holster at his hip. He opened the passport looking at the picture, then my face, then the 20 Euro-Note. He looked at my face again, a grave expression on his face, a frown wrinkled his forehead.

This is it, Mark thought. *I am going to jail.* The guard pocketed the bill handing back the passport, a smile on his face. He nodded his head for me to go on. The old American saying: Money talks. Mark could make out the boat tied to a buoy about a half mile from the pier. The water-taxi moved slowly across the smooth oily surface of the inner harbor toward the black hulled boat which lay dark bobbing gently. *Strange*, thought Mark as they got closer; no lights showing on the boat, not even running lights. *Guess Alon wants to keep a low profile.* Mark jumped onto *Macher* walking toward the pilot station. "Alon, Mark called out. "Hakim, where is everyone?"

A man stepped out from the shadow of the bridge structure, a gun in his hand pointing at Marks chest. "Come with me," he commanded in a deep voice. "Please do not do anything foolish. My two companions have your Captain and the boy tied up below. They will die immediately if you resist." He was a big man holding a large revolver in his hand. He waved the gun toward the hatch leading to the cabin below. Mark climbed down the ladder to the salon, the gun pressed into his back. Hakim sat on a bunk, hands tied behind his back, a cloth tied around his mouth. The boy's eyes were large with fear. Alon sat next to Hakim tied the same way.

"Sit down," said the leader pushing Mark onto a chair across from the bunk. "Listen carefully you two. I want you to start the boat then head out to sea. My friends will not hurt you, not until we are twelve miles from shore. Once we cross the 12 mile limit we will be in international waters. Then we intend to kill the three of you, dump you at sea and take this boat for ourselves along with that leather case you have on your shoulder. I want the two of you to walk onto the bridge, cut loose from the buoy then head straight out into the Mediterranean. Do you both understand me?"

Mark said, "Yes." Alon just shook his head, since he had a gag in his mouth. The boat was soon underway, Alon at the controls, Mark standing nearby; while the killers stood on the rear deck watching them closely.

"Fatim, stand on the port side. Keep your weapon on them. If they make any sudden or strange moves, shoot them all. Ali, stay by the back of the boat to starboard, keep your weapon on them, same instructions. I'll sit on the stern jump seat to keep a close eye on them also. You have about an hour to live, enjoy it. The night is beautiful." A shame it is your last night on earth or should I say on the water.

After about twenty minutes, the leader called out: "Hakim. Come here boy, I have something for you to do before you die. The man stood, unzipped his fly, taking his penis in his hand. He had put his revolver in a shoulder holster at his left arm pit. He took his left hand, pushing Hakim's head toward his exposed penis. "Make believe it's a lollypop boy. Take it in your mouth; suck it." He held Hakim's head in one hand holding his nose with the other thus causing the boy to open his mouth to breath.

"Stop," said Mark, taking a step toward the man. "Leave the boy alone."

"Stand still or you both die now! Get ready to shoot Fatim!" Fatim raised the AK47 to his shoulder. Mark stopped looking at the leader with fire in his eyes.

"Don't do anything stupid," said Alon. "We must get out of this; I need you alive."

The man had forced his penis into Hakim's mouth when he let out a loud cry. Hakim had clamped his jaws down on the man's shaft. The killer had Hakim's head in his hands, – now, because of the pain or anger, maybe both, he twisted the boy's head in a brutal turn. Both Mark and Alon heard the loud snap. Hakim fell to the deck, head flopping to the side – neck broken. He was dead before his body hit the deck.

"You shouldn't have done that said Mark through clinched teeth. You shouldn't have hurt the boy. When I kill you it will be slowly. I will be sure you suffer." What is your name, I want to say it as I kill you.

The man laughed through his pain. "No American, it is you who will die, slow or fast it is no matter to me. But to make you happy my name is Omar, I am the angel of death. All I care about is the 20,000 dollars I was promised along with this boat. Both will be mine in twenty more minutes."

"Where are we?" he yelled at Alon, as he zipped his pants, grimacing in pain with Hakim lying dead on the deck.

"We are at the nine mile point now, three more to go." Mark looked at the computer display. They had just crossed the twelve-mile limit; they were sailing in international waters. Suddenly the boat began to surge, engines backfiring as they slowed, rpm's dropping. One engine stopped abruptly while the other continued to struggle. The engine continued to backfire. Black smoke poured from the exhaust, the engine was missing badly. Alon turned to the leader. "There must be water in the fuel or the fuel-pump is clogged. I must send my mate to the engine room to see if he can fix the pump while I shut down both engines."

The three men looked at each other. Finally, the leader spoke: "Ok go, but no funny business or you die here; fuck twelve miles."

"Go Mark," said Alon. "Fix the engine." Mark went into the engine room locking the door behind him. He pushed the button opening the wall to the armory. He looked at the array of weapons stacked there, which to take he wondered. He reached in removing the Remington 870 Magnum Marine shotgun. He also put a revolver into his waistband, a 357 S&W magnum. He walked to the forward hatch which let him enter the galley. Working his way forward he passed through another hatch to the forward double cabin. Opening another hatch in the bulkhead Mark entered the empty pitch black forward cargo hold. He turned on his small pen-light in order to see the emergency hatch that opened to the deck above in the bow of the boat. Mark lay still on deck for a moment to catch his breath and to let his eyes adjust to the darkness around him. He heard Alon trying in vain to start the engines. They just continued to whine and backfire struggling to start. Mark realized Alon had pulled the choke on both engines to the limit. This allowed fuel to flood the engines causing them to choke on the excessive amount of fuel being forced into the cylinders. Mark began to make his way aft on the port side of the boat. He paused when he reached the open aft deck using the deckhouse for cover. He leaned against the side to assess the situation before he made his move. The men were where he had left them. The man Fatim stood on the port side near the rear edge of the deck. The second man, Mark thought his name was Ali was still on the far side of the after deck, while the leader, Omar, was sitting in the middle of the aft deck in the swivel chair. Mark went over the moves in his mind one last time playing out what he would do, than what he could expect would happen. He knelt on one knee aiming at the Ali's chest. The man stood at the aft end of the deck thirty feet away. Mark squeezed the trigger. There was a loud explosion then a thud as the three double ought buckshot slugs impacted Ali's chest. The force of the impact pushed his body backward throwing him over the side into the water. Mark stepped away from the cockpit structure, turning to the left where Fatim was raising his AK47 to his shoulder.

"Wrong," thought Mark, "You should have fired from the waist." He pulled the trigger again, another loud bang. The slugs, each bigger then a marble, hit Fatim in the face literally blowing his head away, his body crumpling to the deck, blood running into the gunnels. The third man, the leader Omar, who had snapped Hakim's neck, was rising from the chair where he had been resting. He was trying to clear his pistol from the leather shoulder holster but he was moving in slow motion. Mark aimed for Omar's right shoulder at the point where the upper arm met the body – the rotor joint. The pistol was in the man's hand clear of the holster when Mark fired. The powerful slugs tore into his body only twenty feet away. A twelve-gauge slug from a shotgun is deadly at close range; the large pieces of lead impacted the body at the exact spot Mark aimed for ripping the arm away from the shoulder. The severed arm fell to the deck, pistol still clutched in the detached hand. The man fell to his knees – left hand clutching the shoulder where the arm should have been. Blood was running between his fingers as he cried in pain. Mark handed the shotgun to Alon, who stood watching as Mark walked up to the wounded man who lay moaning on the hard deck.

"I told you you would die slowly and in great pain," said Mark. He kicked the man in the face pushing him onto his back. The man struggled to get to his feet, crying in pain as he stood upright swaying unsteadily. Mark put his foot on the severed arm opening the fingers to retrieve the lethal looking revolver.

"I'll kill you," screamed Omar, as he tried to lunge for Mark. He was reaching out with his good left hand covered in blood. Mark raised the pistol firing one shot into Omar's left knee. The big man toppled to the deck where he lay screaming, blood running onto the deck from his shoulder.

Mark knelt next to the man. "Where should I shoot you next?" he asked. "I know – the other knee." With that, he placed the gun on the knee-cap and pulled the trigger. The man's leg jumped to a strange angle as he continued to moan; now sobbing deeply. "Who sent you to kill us?" asked Mark. "Who is giving you 20,000 dollars and my friend's boat? Tell me. If you do, I will kill you quickly. Otherwise, I will keep this up for hours."

"I have nothing to tell you, you American pig."

"Very well," said Mark standing, stomping down hard on the man's shattered knee. Omar howled in pain, tears ran down his face.

When he stopped screaming from the pain, he cried: "It was the Professor. Orabi. He is giving the money to us – a reward for bringing him the leather case, the one with the embossing."

"Your reward now will be death. But first, I have one more thing to do.

"Watch him Alon. Don't let him go anywhere, I'll be right back." Mark came back on deck carrying a knife in his right hand. It was a wicked-looking knife with a long, slightly curved, shiny, stainless steel blade, a Micarta handle.

"Where did you get that?" asked Alon.

"In Casablanca, in the souk; I love knifes. They kill well, silently. It is a Japanese Katana made by a master maker. This blade is called a Kiku, named for the maker." Mark knelt over the dying man who did not have long to live. His blood was running out quickly onto the teak deck.

"Now, my friend," said Mark with sarcasm and loathing in his voice. "It is time to pay you back for the dead boy. Do you remember what you were doing when you killed him? You were holding your prick in your right hand. Since you don't have a right hand I will hold your member for you." Mark unzipped the man's pants, reaching in he pulled Omar's penis out. Holding it in his left hand with one swift stroke of the blade he cut the penis free of the body. The knife was exceptionally sharp. The man screamed in agony, mouth open wide in pain and disbelief over what had just happened. Mark jammed the severed penis into the dying leaders open mouth. He grabbed the man by the collar of his shirt, pulling him to the side of the boat, pushing him over.

"Good knife," said Mark. "Worth the 150 dollars it cost me."

CHAPTER 21 ✠ ✠ ✠

The boat was underway moving slowly over the calm water, no lights showing, no white waves to mark their path. Alon was only making five knots as the boat closed onto the shore of the harbor.

"What now my first mate? Do we go to Israel?"

"Yes, but not yet. I have a call to make in Giza first."

"I was afraid you were going to say that."

"The Professor must know more than he told me," said Mark. "Maybe he could not understand all that he read, but obviously he knows these papers are important, valuable. If he does not get them tonight he will send others after us. He knows where I am going next, he'll send men to find me. I must go to him for two reasons. First, to find out what he knows but didn't tell me. Second is to kill him. I must keep him silent to keep our secret. Also I will take revenge for poor Hakim."

"How will you do this?" asked Alon.

"I will swim to shore from the boat so no one sees me. I will steal a car, drive to Giza to confront the professor. I know how to get there and where he lives. After I get what I want from him I will kill him, drive back to the port, then swim out to the boat. It is almost midnight. The round-trip with the interrogation will take me five to six hours. I want to be back before 6 a.m. wait for me here and don't let anyone on board. I want to take one of your revolvers with a suppressor."

"Take the 686 S&W 357 Magnum; it has a red-laser sight, a six-shot cylinder, fires 357 hollow-points, a deadly combination at close range. With the silencer in place all you'll hear is a low pop. Thanks Alon. When I return in the morning I will swim out to you.

Move slowly down the beach about three hundred yards from shore. I will be waiting at a spot out there for you to come for me. Wait a half a mile off-shore. I will flash you using the red-laser sight. When you see it, come to get me. I will be swimming out to you. Leave a line trailing astern; I will grab it as you go by, that way you won't have to stop to pick me up. Once I have the line head out to sea at about ten knots. When you clear the harbor, stop and pull me aboard." Mark went over the side naked, a plastic bag with his clothes, knife, and gun trailing behind him. The bag pulled along by a string attached to a belt around his waist. Once on shore he dressed placing the gun in his waist band the knife in a scabbard on his belt. He walked into the dark deserted streets near the port looking for a vehicle to steal. After searching for 10 minutes he found a parked pick-up truck with a door unlocked. He hot-wired the truck in 60 seconds and was on his way to Giza to meet professor Orabi.

CHAPTER 22

It was two thirty when Mark walked up to the house he had been at only seven hours ago. In that time, four people had died. Now there was going to be one more. Mark tried the handle. The door swung open. The Professor was waiting for his assassins to return. Mark removed the revolver from his waist, gripping it firmly in his hand as he attached the silencer. He slammed the door it made a loud crash in the silent night. Mark walked boldly across the tile floor, heels clicking so Orabi would hear him coming.

"Ah Omar you're back at last. I am here in the study with your boss. Come join us."

Mark walked into the room, gun up, ready to fire. There were three men in the room - two men standing by the far wall, the Professor sitting at his desk still dressed in his robe. Mark didn't hesitate; he shot the body guard in the forehead just above his nose. He then swung the gun to his right, where the smaller man struggled to get his gun from his belt-holster. Mark shot him in the face, just below the right eye. Mark was aiming for the forehead, but the swinging movement plus the weight of the silencer on the end of the barrel, pulled the gun down. It didn't make much difference with a 357 hollow-point bullet, a large part of the back of the man's skull disintegrated in a spray of blood and bone.

"Now Professor Orabi I think it is time for us to continue our discussion from earlier today."

"You're going to kill me?" asked the Professor.

"I think that is obvious," said Mark. "You hired people to kill me. Now I have come to pay you back for your treachery. It is payback time as we say in America. But first, there are things I want to know. You understood what I gave you to read didn't you?"

"Not all," replied the Professor. "I could only make out a few words, phrases, not sentences. This document is a journal of some type, written around 1309. The writer is a man who I believe to be a Templar. A Knight Templar of France around the time of the fall of the Templar's. This document may have to do with the lost treasure that was hidden, than smuggled out of France before King Louis the Fourth could find it."

"That's why you tried to kill me? For the papers, so you could steal the treasure of the Templar's?"

In part," replied the Professor. "Not for the treasure alone, but for the find; it would be fantastic, a spectacular discovery. I would be revered, immortalized, one of the greatest historical discoveries of all time. The amount of money would be vast, but the fame would be greater." Thank you for that information professor, I must go now." Mark, walked over to the two dead bodies lying on the floor. He took the gun from the dead man's hand. Turning back to Orabi, Mark raised the gun. "Sorry Professor. I gave you two thousand American dollars for your time; also, to keep our secret, which you promised you would do. You lied to me." Mark pulled the trigger once, shooting the Professor in the forehead. He wiped the handle of the gun on the Professor's black abaya, then put the gun back into the hand of the dead body-guard. Mark walked from the house into the night, his work in Giza complete.

CHAPTER 23 ✝ ✝ ✝

He sat at the water's edge, the night still black but not for much longer. It was almost six o'clock. Day would arrive within the hour. He had taken off his clothes, stuffed them into the plastic bag tied to the belt around his waist. He aimed the laser out to sea, flashing it on and off for thirty seconds. He put the gun into the bag, closing it tight, and then waded into the cold water beginning to swim out to sea. *Hope Alon is there*, thought Mark. If not, this *is going to be a long swim.* He had been moving through the water for ten minutes when he heard the sound of a boat approaching. He stopped swimming looking toward the sound; a dark shape was moving slowly in his direction. Mark raised his right hand above his head so Alon could see him in the dark. Mark was transported back fifteen years, to the time he was a Navy SEAL. How many times had he done this same thing in waters around the world? It was déjà vu all over again. Here he was still risking his life, still in danger, would it ever end? He could see the boat clearly as it moved by slowly. A line trailing over the stern leaving a slight wake as it moved through the water. Mark reached for the line, grasping it in both hands, and then looping it around one arm as the boat pulled him along. Day was breaking now, the sky lightening. Mark could see Alon at the helm looking back at him being pulled through the water. After what seemed like an eternity Alon stopped the boat. He ran to the stern pulling Mark to the boarding ladder helping him aboard.

"I'm tired Alon, cold, help me below. Alon wrapped him in a blanket, helping him into the galley below, where the heater hissed warming the cabin. I have a cup of hot tea with a shot of bourbon in it on the table for you. Drink it, it will warm you.

"Did you accomplish your task?" asked Alon.

Mark sipped the warm tea. "If you mean did I kill the Professor, the answer is yes."

"Did he tell you anything before he died?"

"Again, the answer is yes. What we have here in the leather case has something to do with the Templar's. All I know is they were a group of Knights from Europe – France, I think. They fought in the Holy Land; that is about my complete knowledge of them."

"Thanks for computers," said Alon. "I think you and I are going to become Templar experts over the next few hours. Where do you want to go now, Mark?"

"Set a course for Israel. I've got to find a rabbi in Jerusalem. I hope he will be able to help me, since he is my last, best hope." I am very familiar with the coast of Israel.

"There is a deserted beach at a cove just south of Yavne. I've done some trading there in the past. You mean smuggling asked Mark. Whatever, I prefer to call it trading. I'll put you ashore there; you will have to find transportation to Jerusalem, to the Old City on your own."

Mark sat in the passenger seat of an old Ford rack-truck. The truck was driving down a black-top two-lane road toward Jerusalem, which Mark could see rising in the distance. The truck was full of vegetables, watermelons and other farm produce. Zev, the driver, was taking his cargo to the Bazaar inside the gates of the Old City. "The address you gave me is not in the Old City. It is inside the city walls but it is in the Sheikh Jarah. That is a wealthy Arab section of Jerusalem. There are a smattering of Jews throughout that section; but it is predominantly home to wealthy Arabs. I will let you off by Nablus Road; you can walk to the address you want from there. Mark walked toward the address he had been given following Zev's directions. He marveled at the wide clean streets with large stately homes set back from the road. The houses were well cared for, trimmed grass, old trees stood on the front lawns. This was not at all like the cramped, crowded pictures he had seen of Jerusalem. An Arab man in robes, a thawb, and a traditional head-shawl, a ghutrah, walked toward him.

"Excuse me sir, do you speak English?"

"I do," replied the man.

"I am looking for this address," Mark said, showing the man the wrinkled slip of paper.

"Oh yes," came the reply. "The home of the old Jew. The revered Hebrew Scholar. The old rabbi's house is just around the corner. You will see it on the left side of the street." Mark stood looking at the large manor house. He wondered how a Jewish rabbi could afford such a splendid house in an Arab section of Jerusalem. He stood before a carved wooden front-door waiting for someone to answer his knock. The door opened to reveal a young man in his twenties, dressed in Western clothing. The man looked fit, muscular, like someone who worked out regularly.

"May I help you?" the man asked.

"I am here to see rabbi Talal ben Aksimon," said Mark.

"He is in his study at this time of day. He is not seeing any visitors," said the young man.

"Tell the rabbi I have come a long way on an important matter. I was sent from Cairo by an associate of the rabbi's, Professor Orabi. Tell him I must see him, I am sure he will agree to see me."

The young man was back quickly. "Follow me, please," he instructed, turning back into the house. They walked down a long corridor to an open door. The office Mark entered was bright, cheerful with large windows letting in sunlight from the rear of the house. The rabbi looked much younger than Mark expected. He looked to be in his late sixties, maybe seventy. He was dressed in a black suit with a crisp, white shirt. The man looked fit although Orabi said the rabbi was older than Orabi's 82 years.

"You tell me Professor Orabi sent you. When did you see him?

"I left him the day before yesterday at about two in the morning."

"Is he well?" asked the rabbi. After all, we are getting older. Let's see, he would be 83 now, since I am 85, slightly older by a few years.

"No," replied Mark. "He is not well. As a matter of fact, he is dead."

"Oh my," said the rabbi. "A Heart attack?"

"No," replied Mark. "It was most likely the results of lead poisoning. How horrid," said the old rabbi.

"Yet, he sent you to me. For what purpose?" asked the rabbi.

Mark opened the Israeli IDF backpack he had purchased from Zev to place the leather case in so as not to be so conspicuous. The IDF military pack was commonplace in the streets of Israel. He removed the leather case, placing it on the rabbi's desk.

"He sent me because of the manuscript in this case. However, before you read it, I must tell you the contents of this case have caused the death of many people, some of which you may know or be familiar with. Rabbi Levy and Professor bin Zakour, in Morocco, where this journey began for me. After rabbi Levy's death, I took these papers to Professor Orabi, in Cairo for help with the translation. He claimed he could not understand the writings; he sent me to find you. He claimed you were more learned in this area. He said if you couldn't help me no one could."

"He was being kind. He has an enormous grasp of ancient works. He was Professor Emeritus of the University in Cairo, possibly the oldest university in the world. He was famous for his work, some of his discoveries. I was fortunate to work with him on a few of his findings. You say you were with him when he died?"

"Yes, I was.

"Yet, you are here now. Didn't the authorities come? Wouldn't they have questioned you? Detained you? Tell me; be honest, young man. If you want me to help you, tell me the truth."

Mark told the rabbi about the Professor's deception, his treachery. "So, I returned to his home late in the night to learn the reason for his deceit. He confessed he understood a small part of the first page; how he wanted the work for himself. It will cement my place in history, the greatest discovery of my long career, possibly the greatest discovery of all time." That's what he told me before he died.

That is an inspiring story, young man. Can I see the document now?"

"No rabbi not yet. I must get your answer, your promise to these questions first. Your life may depend upon your answers."

"Very well," said the rabbi. "Ask."

What you read, what you discover cannot be shared with anyone. You and I will be the only ones with this knowledge. You will carry it with you to your grave. I will pay you for your time, your effort, but, the information is for me alone."

"I will agree with your conditions," said rabbi Talal ben Aksimon. "But tell me young man, did you kill, Orabi?"

Mark hesitated only a second. "Yes I did," he replied. "I shot him for three reasons. He caused the boy who carried these papers to die; he tried to have me killed also. He lied to me about not being able to read the pages, and then tried to get them for himself. Also, I know if he lived, he would send people to find me again; so I shot him."

"I am sure you would shoot me also," said the rabbi."

"Old man no harm will come to you if you agree to keep your word. It is my wish you outlive Moses."

Rabbi ben Aksimon laughed. "I have no desire to live to be 121. I will agree to your terms since I have no desire to die any sooner than God has planned for me. Now, show me the document."

Mark opened the leather case removing ten pages of script, handing them to the rabbi/professor. "Start with these," said Mark.

"Fine. I will call my assistant who is my adopted son to show you to the bathroom. You look as if you could use a shower. I will begin to work on these pages until you return."

When Mark stepped from the shower, there were clean clothes hanging on a hook on the bathroom door. He walked downstairs to the rabbi's study, where the rabbi sat with the papers Mark had given him, a note pad next to him. Pen in hand, he made notes as he read the script moving the finger on his left hand along the line. Rabbi Talal looked up when Mark entered the room.

"Sit down young man. This much I can tell you now. The pages you've given me are written in a strange script, a combination of many languages. Old languages, not just old, I think ancient some of which do not exist anymore."

"Can you translate it?" asked Mark eagerly.

"I do not think I can give an exact literal translation. I will get you an outline, a plot or theme, maybe more; but I can't promise. Also, it will be very slow for me to get through all these pages," he said, indicating the pile of papers on his desk. "It will take me weeks, possibly a month or more. In order to do a thorough job will take time. I can tell you translating this entire document will be a daunting task. It is a very difficult job you have given me. If it were a museum or government organization that offered me this work, I would ask for a minimum of six months to complete my work." And I would charge accordingly. You want me to do it in 4 weeks.

"Can you tell me anything at all?" asked Mark. "I think you may know something already."

"What did Orabi tell you before you kill – erh . . . terminated his time on earth?"

The rabbi might be old, thought Mark, but his mind was still sharp. Mark looked the old man in the eye. "The Professor believed the pages have to do with the Knights Templar movement. He thought there may be some information about the lost Templar's treasure."

The professor nodded. "He may have been correct. These papers were written, I think dictated to a scribe, who put the words to paper. An underling, not a knight; but an apprentice whose job it was to keep records. It was someone not from Europe, where most of the Knights were from, but a person who was with the Knights in a cleric's capacity. I believe this scribe, there may have been more than one, was a native from the Middle East. Possibly a captured Bedouin or an Iraqi pressed into service for the Templar's. I strongly suggest you go to one of the universities to study the history of the Templar's – how they came into being, their rise to prominence and power, then their sudden dramatic fall from grace. I taught at Hebrew University for forty-five years, retired when I was 75. I still hold a chair in the Ancient History Department, which is why I have this house."

"I meant to ask you about that, rabbi. What are you doing in this splendid house in a Muslim section of Jerusalem?"

"The house is a perk to me for my service at Hebrew University. I also taught at the Hebrew Yeshiva called King David School. I taught many youngsters, who today as grown men are in all branches of Israeli government, including our military and intelligence services. They remember me with favor. They take care of me in my older years; since they know if there is ever a problem they need help with, a problem that is in my area of expertise, they can call on me for help like you have. As for me living in a Muslim neighborhood, how much do you know of Israel – the country, the history, the people?"

Mark shrugged his shoulders, shaking his head. "Not a great deal."

"Are you a *goy*?" asked the rabbi.

"No," replied Mark. "I am Jewish. I was Bar Mitzvah at thirteen, but then drifted from religion. I observe the holy days, also Passover; but that is about it."

"Then let me give you a brief lesson in Jewish history of the Holy Land. Eretz Israel."

CHAPTER 24 ✚ ✚ ✚

"This land is sacred to the Jewish people. It is the land of our forefathers going back almost 6,000 years. For all that time, the Jewish people have had a presence here. At times a prominent presence other times under foreign rule – the Romans, Greeks, Ottomans. But we persevered, always coming to claim our birthright. Then one day Mohamed the false prophet came with a new religion called Islam; a religion given to him by his one God, Allah. A religion told to him by angels who delivered the word directly to Mohamed in spoken form. This prophet would then recite what he heard – since he could neither read nor write. He would repeat the word of Allah to these faithful scribes who put the words to paper. These were the words of God as transmitted only to Mohamed. He was called a great prophet. But on close examination, what Mohamed received over 21 years seems very much like the Jewish bible. As a matter of fact, if a paper like this Quran was given to me by one of my students, I would fail him, accuse him of plagiarism. But this religion is accepted by the Arab, the Islamist as the true teaching of Mohamed. It spread throughout the Middle East, but it caused no problem in Israel. Why? Because the Israeli Arab and Jew are a similar people, Semitic people. These people work and live side-by-side as good neighbors. The origin of the Semitic people included Syrians, Babylonians, Hebrews and Arabs. Even our religions are similar, as they should be since they are Jewish ideas slightly embellished. As I grew up many of my friends were Arabs. We lived together then, sharing meals, homes, ideas. Life was good, hard but good until the end of the first Great War. The British and French came with their laws, new rules - a different culture than ours. They created countries on paper changing the map of the region and the world forever. Lebanon here, Jordan there, Palestine squeezed into this area by the sea. But we still co-existed until the second Great War. At the end of that conflict in 1945, there came the Great Flood; not water, people. They came by the thousands, then tens of thousands. Who were these people? Where did they come from? They were Jews; yes, much like you. Not religious, not Semitic in the true sense. They were European Jews, mostly Eastern European. These people had strange ideas, strange customs. They also came with engrained prejudices. Who were these Arabs living among us? They were inferior to the new immigrants who treated them poorly. They were pushed into ghettos, like the ghettos these same people had escaped from. Instead of being sympathetic, they were cruel. By 1948, there was open antagonism between the two groups. The new Jew was not like the old Jew, not like me. We had Arab friends, brothers, love and compassion for each other. We lived in harmony. No, the new Jew was full of himself. He wanted his new country to be an image of Poland or Russian. A country where there were no Arabs, no Quran, no mosques. They didn't understand or accept their Arab neighbor. So there was no understanding or compassion for your fellow man, your Arab counterpart. Because of that attitude, we have suffered 62 years of war, ill-will, terror and death. That is why I choose to stay with my Arab friends. They know me as a Sabra – a person who would bring back the early days of the twentieth century, when we were all brothers; all one people. But alas those times never be again. The injustice, the hate is too ingrained to return to that time. Now, it is for younger men, men smarter than me to find a just solution to the animus between our people." The rabbi paused. "Enough of this talk. I hope you understand why I live in the Arab part of the city where I am accepted and looked up to. Now, what do you intend to do?" asked the rabbi. What will you do to occupy your time while I work to complete this herculean task you have given me.

"I will leave you to your work, at least for the four weeks you requested. I will study at the Jewish National University Library since there is much I must learn. I may travel some, but I will return to you at the designated time. Please remember my edict: No one must know what you are doing, it must remain our secret."

"Very well," remarked the old Jew. If you wish to stay in a dorm-room on the campus of the University, ask for Gershon Alta. He is Dean of

Students. Tell him I sent you. He will take care of you." With that, the old rabbi shooed Mark out of his study, putting on his glasses, pulling the sheets of paper closer; so he could begin the tedious job of translating the text.

CHAPTER 25 ✚ ✚ ✚

Mark hitched a ride to the coast to meet Alon at the boat in the secluded cove. The sinister black hull bobbed up and down on the gentle waves moving slowly toward the Israeli shore. Alon stood on the fore deck waiting for Marks return.

"I have to remain in Jerusalem for the next four weeks while the professor translates the work I brought him." I will be living on the campus of Hebrew University while I do research on the Templar's. I will study their order to gain an insight to their existence and downfall.

"Fine," replied Alon. "I will head out to sea; it will give me time to make contact with some Arabs in Lebanon. I will be waiting for you four weeks from today. Friday night at 5 p.m., at this spot." Mark climbed from the boat, turned stood on the shore as Alon moved out into the calm, blue Mediterranean.

The next four weeks were long and tedious for Mark. He spent twelve hours a day, each day, in the National Library on the campus of Hebrew University. He poured over volumes of history of the Knights Templar. He learned their existence was intertwined with that of Palestine and France. There were many books, old as well as modern, detailing the existence of this storied group of men. His day reminded him of his time in law school in New York where he spent long hours studying in the library as well as the tombs. The tombs were small, cloistered rooms in the basement of the law school. Small cubicles where he and other students poured over legal treaties, trying to absorb years and years of legal precedents. He had seen the Dean the rabbi had sent him to. At the mere mention of the Talah's name, the Dean had proved most accommodating, giving Mark a room in a male dorm close to the library. It is yours to use as long as need be. Here is a meal ticket for the cafeteria, you can eat there with other students. I'm sure you will find the food filling.

As the sun rose on the fifth day of the forth week, Mark packed his few belongings into the Israeli Army knapsack, slung it over his shoulder, then set off walking to the professor's house in the affluent Arab section of Jerusalem. The stately house sat behind a trimmed green lawn. The large house was an impressive sight, an oasis in the middle of the Arab hoard. Mark proceeded up the paved walkway to the front door. He knocked. The door was opened by the rabbi's assistant, Amir Zakari. The young man greeted him a sullen look on his face. "Come this way," Zakari said in a curt tone, eyes downcast not looking at the professor's guest. He led Mark along the hallway to the rabbi's study. You may go in; the rabbi is waiting for you. The study was filled with sunshine; the room was bright, warm with a comfortable feeling. The rabbi stood at his desk, a broad smile lighting his face.

"Come here, my American friend. I wish to hug you for bringing me this fascinating work. Now sit, so we can begin."

"You have finished?" asked Mark.

"It was a difficult task you put before me. I only completed the text at two this morning, fascinating, truly remarkable; it does much to bring certain matters into focus about the demise of the Templar's. A footnote, if you like, from the mouth of one who was part of the history of betrayal that befell this band of warriors. What you have entrusted to me is the most important document I have come across in my long life time. A document I must keep secret because of my promise to you. So, shall we begin?" asked the rabbi.

"Yes," replied Mark, removing the IDF knapsack from his back, setting it alongside the closed door of the office.

"You may call me Talal," or professor since my studies have brought back memories of my days teaching at the university. "We are alone in this office together for at least the next six hours. So my scholar, tell me what have you learned in the month you were studying. Tell me what you now know of the Knights Templar's, since you knew very little four weeks ago."

"Well, began Mark, I have spent many long days going over dozens of books, treatises, articles, even information on the computer; all I could find."

"Very good," said Talal, but what have you learned from all this effort? Tell me."

"The Knights Templar, or the Templar's, as they were known, were a medieval military order of men, which was started right here in Jerusalem by nine French Knights, around 1120. The order was formed to protect pilgrims who were coming to the Holy Land to pray. These pilgrims were being attacked by highwaymen, robbed and murdered by renegades, who then stole the money and possessions from these faithful travelers. Oft time killing them, leaving the bodies by the side of the road for others to see. A French Knight named Hugues De Payens petitioned the Ruler of Jerusalem to create a monastic order of knights to protect these pilgrims on their journey. The mission was approved. The Knight requested a place for his men to live. He wanted a headquarters so his band of knights could operate effectively. The space given them was on the Temple Mount, in the Al Aqsa Mosque, a holy site to the Muslim, as well as the Jew and Christian. The space he was given was in the stables below the Temple of Solomon. For this reason, the nine Knights took the name Poor Fellow Soldiers of Christ, the Temple of Solomon. Thus, Knights of the Temple. The order of the temple; thus, Templar's."

"How did they live? How did they survive?" asked the Rabbi.

"In the beginning, they lived on donations from the wealthy. But when they were officially recognized by the King of France, as their reputation grew, the donations became larger and more frequent. But the real impetus for the organization was the edict of Pope Innocent, which gave them official status in the Church of Christ in Rome. This official edict by the church exempted the order from local laws. This meant they could do whatever they wanted – pay no taxes, open travel to any country. *This meant they could go where ever they wished. Do whatever they deemed necessary.* There was no higher authority than the Pope, which made the Templar's equal to or above Kings, governments, everything. Though they were formidable fighters, only a small portion of the members of the organization were fighting knights. As the order grew, there were merchants, farmers, tradesmen, even mariners since they had their own fleet of ships for commerce throughout Europe and the Middle East. With their accumulated wealth, they owned vineyards, built castles, even started the first international banking system in the world, operating with letters of credit. It was the banking system, along with losses in battle that led to their demise."

"How so?" asked the rabbi keenly listening to the story being told to him.

"They acquired so much wealth that noble men would come to them for loans," continued Mark. "These loans were to be repaid with interest thus making the order even wealthier. One of those that borrowed money from the Templar's treasury was King Philip the IV, Philip the fair – King of France. He owed so much money to the Templar's he was not able to meet the interest payments. The order of the temple asked for security for the loans – jewels, deeds to property other security - which only made the King angrier. The King had helped Pope Clement to the leadership of the church, which made the Pope indebted to the French King. It seems Clement was a weak Pope, afraid of the King's power. He feared the King would force him from his position as head of the church. So when Philip came to him with a plan to discredit the Templar's order, Clement went along with the King to save his own position. King Philip the fair, felt if he could dissolve the Templar's he would be free of his debt, which he would never be able to pay. The King prepared his troops to move against the Knights in Paris at dawn on the morning of October 13th, 1307, a Friday. The myth of Friday the 13th being an unlucky day stems from the acts carried out by the Kings troops on that fateful day. The King's army attacked many Templar buildings that dawn morning. The most significant were three sites in Paris – the Knight's residence, the treasury and the headquarters. They arrested the Grand Master, along with 149 knights and sergeants. The chief exchequer of the treasury and banking system, along with many of the functionaries of the order. Over one hundred of those captured were killed in the streets of Paris, either by burning at the stake or beheaded with their own swords. Master De Moray, the Grand Master, was imprisoned, along with other high-ranking knights. They were tortured until they confessed to crimes against the King and the church, The crimes they confessed to were heresy, homosexuality usury, and a long list of other made-up charges. Pope Clement voiced no disapproval of the King's actions, which spelled the end of the Templar's.

The one edict the Pope did announce was the confiscation of all Templar property, wherever it existed in the world. This led to the loss of all real and personal property that had been accumulated by the order."

"Very good," replied professor ben Aksimon, a twinkle in his eye. "I see you have researched the Templar's thoroughly. Now, with the knowledge you have gained as background, I can reveal what I have gleaned from the manuscript you have entrusted to me. This story has been written in the first-person by a Knight Templar. His name is Guy de Vaux. He was a Knight with sixteen years service when he wrote this manuscript. Before that, he was a cadet for three years from age fifteen till his initiation into the order at eighteen. He was in Lars on the morning of October 13. Guy de Vaux had served in many parts of the world including the Holy Lands, and other locations in Outremer, including Syria and Turkey. These locations become important in his narrative. He fought at Acre, but somehow escaped before its fall to the Mamelukes. He also fought at Tortosa, the final battle of the Templar's in the Holy Land. They were pushed into the sea, never to have a presence in the Middle East again. Are you ready for the story of Guy de Vaux and the end of the Templar's?" The end of the poor fellow solders of Christ.

"Yes," said Mark. "Please tell me what Guy de Vaux wrote."

CHAPTER 26

"Translated, this is the story I have for you, a fascinating tale of courage and determination."

My name is Guy de Vaux. I have been a Knight Templar for sixteen years of faithful service in Palestine, as well as several cities in Outremer. After the fall of Tortosa in Syria, the survivors were taken by boat from there to Cyprus. Cyprus was a Templar stronghold at that time. I was one of the few survivors to escape the onslaught. I remained in the fortress at Gastria for 5 long months waiting for passage back to France. Upon my arrival in France I was assigned to a post at Fort de Arsenal outside Paris. After my service in the Middle East my present duty proved dull and unfulfilling. After four months of boredom I was called to the Temple headquarters in Paris to meet with the Seneschal of the high order. Upon my arrival I was escorted to the chamber of Andre de Morbard. He was a Seneschal, an officer ranking just under the Grand Master. His chamber was dark, foreboding; the room smelled musty. The officer was a big man dressed in a brown monks robe, a red cross emblazoned on his chest. The red cross was the emblem of our monastic order. The imperial leader sat behind a large table covered with papers, diagrams and maps.

"Brother Guy," he began. "I hope you are well after your journey over the sea." "I am quite well Seneschal Morbard; a bit bored by my present duty, but well nonetheless." "That is why I summoned you to me today. I have an important post for you if you will take it."

My spirit rose at these words. "What is it you wish of me my lord?"

"There are rumblings about our order now that we are no longer fighting in the holy lands. We have lost all of Palestine to Saladin and the Saracens."

"Though we are still wealthy, the wealthiest order in the world; it seems those who oppose us, of which there are many, see no need for our existence any longer. I fear, as does the Grand Master, there will be trouble for us in the days ahead; Our problems will continue grow, there for we must prepare. We have nine fortified positions in France today, from the north in Rheims to the south coast at the Port of Bayonne, then East to the Italian border at Manton. Bayonne is our main port on the Mediterranean Sea. The Grand Master has decided we shall establish another fortified keep in southeastern France away from prying eyes. The location we have chosen is a deserted fortress in the Village of Lurs. It is a mountainous area, well away from major population centers; ideal for what we have in mind. There is an old fortress there already that is high on the hill overlooking the village and all the Durance valley. What we propose is to send you with fifteen knights, ten sergeants along with 120 workers to rebuild the fortress by strengthening the walls and adding additional vaults underground. You must enlarge what exists while adding more space for storage. Why do I need so much underground storage space for so small a fighting force? Because, continued the Seneschal, Grand Master DeMoray wishes to send a portion of the Templar's accumulated wealth out of Paris for safekeeping. Although the great bulk will remain here in Paris in our treasury, a goodly portion will be sent to this new fort in Lurs. This will be done in a clandestine manner without anyone's knowledge, if that is possible. We have already sent a small portion to Cyprus although our position there seems tenuous at best. That is a subject for a later date. However, the fortress you will command will have a substantial amount of Templar treasure for safekeeping. You will be responsible for this wealth. It will be your responsibility to command the garrison and safe guard our property. What say you, Brother Guy?"

I hesitated only a moment. An adventure, any adventure was better than sitting idle on the outskirts of Paris watching the grass grow. Although I foresaw my job as a babysitter to a large amount of treasure, I would be providing an important service for my order. I would also be in command of a force of knights, infantry and support staff. "I accept the post," I replied. "But you must give me the details of your plan."

"Thank you for taking on this important assignment for your order. The Grand Master will be delighted to hear the news. He chose you himself. This is what you will do."

CHAPTER 27 ✠ ✠ ✠

It was 520 kilometers from Paris to Lurs, a distance of 300 miles through the French countryside, a ten-day ride for my fifteen knights. The sergeants and industry workmen were coming in wagons with their tools. I did not expect to see them for another two weeks since they could only cover twelve to fifteen miles per day. When we arrived we found the fortress deserted, but in fairly good condition. We knights had six squires to share between us. They were put to work preparing our quarters. I sent Sir Groth de Charneau with four knights to inspect the battlements; while I took two brothers with me to inspect the underground vaults. We walked from one large cavern to the next, torches held aloft to light our way. There were three large vaults with one small vault off each large one.

"The space seems adequate," said one of the knights.

"It would seem so," I replied. "Yet, I think we shall build another twelve small rooms, four to the side of each large vault."

"Why do we need so much space for so small a party of men?" another of my trusted knights asked.

"We will have more men sent to us once we are prepared for them. The Grand Master gave me my orders in Paris. He told me to enlarge the Vaults and that is what we shall do. I met with Brother Sir Geoffrey Bonhomme upon my return to my room; a room my squire had chosen for me. He had chosen well.

The room was bright and airy, on the second floor of the castle with a view of the front gate and the countryside outside the walls. What did you find brother?"

"The walls are sound, said Geoffrey. "Some of the battlements need repair. The front gate must be reinforced; the wood is rotten. Also, the main look-out tower is crumbling in places. Stone must be quarried to replace the old."

"Very well. When the sergeants arrive with the infantry, I will give you forty men to begin your repairs. I will put the other seventy to work in the basement. The remainder will work on the stables and kitchen. It took three months to complete the work. I planned to make the castle into a fortress my men could defend, at the same time enlarging the vaults to hold the treasure we would be receiving from Paris. I dispatched a rider, a sergeant at arms, with my handwritten note addressed to Andre de Morbard Seneschal of the Knights Templar Paris. The memo read, "The castle is ready to receive your cargo. I am awaiting shipment". The first wagons arrived five weeks later accompanied by the sergeant who had taken the letter. Men opened the newly-repaired, massive wooden gates, allowing the eight wagons in the convoy to enter the large courtyard in front of the castle proper. The leader of the wagon-train walked up to me.

"Sir Guy," he said. "I am Oliver de la Roche. I saw you once at acre in the Holy Land." "It is good to see you are alive and well. It is always a pleasant surprise to see survivors of that battle since we lost so many of our knights on that holy ground."

"Yes," I replied, I agree. "What have you brought me?"

"I have eight wagons, six with a special cargo of I know not what, however I was assured you would know what to do with the cargo." "The last two wagons hold provisions for the castle. We will unload, then rest the night before heading back to Paris." "There is another wagon-train coming to you; it left three days after us; it should reach you in three more days." "I was told to inform you a similar wagon-train will arrive each week for the next five weeks." That means you will be getting a total of 56 wagons.

"Thank you, Brother Oliver. Have your men eat, and then rest so you can start back for Paris tomorrow."

The provisions were taken to the galley store-room, while I put the rest of the men to work transporting the wooden crates from the wagons into the three vaults we prepared in the underground of the castle. Each wagon carried sixteen wooden boxes, weighing 100 pounds each. They contained ten bars of gold weighing ten pounds each. This first shipment consisted of 96 boxes, which equaled 9,600 pounds of gold. With the wagons arriving in three days plus another five trains at one-week intervals, I could expect 576 more boxes, which means I would have 67,200 pounds of gold in my underground vaults.

"You realize, said the old rabbi, at today's price that would amount to some 120 million dollars." But I digress; let me continue with de Vaux's story.

It was September 15 when the seventh wagon-train arrived, again led by Oliver de la Roche. He dismounted his war horse walking up to me where I stood on the steps of the castle.

"This is the seventh shipment of crates, as I told you. However, I was instructed to inform you there will be one last delivery for you of other merchandise. It will consist of 24 wagons, 20 will be carrying goods for your vaults; the remainder will bring blankets, comforters, and heavy clothing – capes, coats with hoods, some with fur since winter is fast approaching. Your fort is near the Alps, which means you can expect snow and freezing temperatures to be arriving soon."

"I know Brother. I have had my men cutting timber to supply wood for our fireplaces, along with peat to burn and cook with. You can see the stores growing behind the castle; we will weather the winter just fine."

A rider on horseback came to our gates two weeks after Oliver had departed for Paris with his empty wagons. The temperature had begun to drop during the night, causing the rider and his horse to breathe mist into the chill air.

"Sir Guy," he began. "I rode ahead to tell you our train of 28 wagons will be at your gates in the morning. The men will be cold and tired it has been a long journey. We would like to lie over for three days to rest the horses and men. Can you accommodate us for that time?"

"Fear not Brother. I will have the cooks prepare food for your weary men. The horses will be cared for either in our stables or the pasture outside the walls. However I was told there would be 24 wagons in the train not 28."

"I don't know about that Brother Knight. I can assure you there are 28 wagons."

It was a big task to unload the heavily packed wagons. But my men, with the help of the Waggoner's, moved all the chests from the wagons into the castle courtyard. I only allowed my men to move the crates below ground into the vaults which were now crammed to over flowing with hundreds of crates and chests of various sizes. In examining the new shipment, I was amazed to see the chests were full of jewels, silver trays and utensils, jewel-encrusted statuary, items too numerous to mention. This shipment was not like prior ones that contained boxes of uniform size. The array of valuable artifacts dazzled the eye, even in the dim light of the separate chambers off the 3 large vaults. I had my men place the precious chests in the small rooms I had constructed on each side of the main chambers. My castle now held a King's ransom of treasure. I signed the chit as receipt for this last delivery, as I had for the seven previous ones. I handed the chit to the Knight to bring to the Grand Master in Paris. Before they left the castle, my Brother Knight came to me.

"I am instructed to tell you an additional compliment of men is coming to reinforce your assembly. There will be 32 crossbow-men, 20 infantry-men, 12 plow-horses, with three grooms to add to the stable, there may also be some additional wagons of goods."

I was happy to know our garrison was to be strengthened, but it would also mean more mouths to feed. The castle had a set routine of watch-keepers, cooks preparing our meals, grooms caring for our horses, plus our fighting knights. I would take my Knights into the countryside on regular excursions to keep them fit for duty or battle, should the need arise.

Two years passed quickly, seasons changing; but duty always the same. I would send men on rotation to Paris for a month of rest during the year. In summer, we would go to the azure shore of the Mediterranean to swim and frolic in the surf. All in all it was a good duty. We kept a watchful eye on our treasure trove around the clock.

In May of 1309, a dispatch rider came from Paris to fetch me.

"You are wanted by the Grand Marshall at once, said the rider. If you supply me a fresh horse, I will accompany you on your trip to Paris." We rode hard for five days, keeping on even after dark. We pushed our horses hard covering fifty miles a day. After 6 days sitting in the saddle we came to the Village of Anton. A light shone above the door of an inn ahead.

"We will stop here," I commanded. "Get a hot meal, some needed rest, then continue to Paris at sun-up." "We should arrive by early afternoon. Besides, the horses need rest also; we have pushed them hard over the last 6 days in order to cover at least fifty miles per day."

The next day, I rode into the Templar's magnificent walled property in the center of Paris. The grounds lay beside the Seine not far from the cathedral of Notre Dame on Ill de Cite. I noticed French troops standing across from the main gate of the Templar's compound. A contingent of twelve armed men in royal blue uniforms, some with lances, all with swords at their side. The troop stood at attention watched over by a stout officer who watched intently as we entered the citadel. Three squires and two grooms were waiting at the entrance to the Grand Master's Residence which was set to the right of the main staff building.

The grooms took the horses, while a squire said: "Please follow me to the Masters quarters. He has been expecting you." As I entered the chamber, I saw three men were present. Two I recognized, one was my Seneschal who had sent me on my mission to the castle at Lurs; the older man seated at a sturdy desk was Jacques de Molay, the Grand Master, head of the Templar's order.

"Please sit Brother Guy," instructed the Seneschal. "It was good of you to respond so quickly. You must have ridden night and day."

I smiled in reply. "Only half the night, my Lord, the horses were tired, they needed rest"

Jacques de Molay spoke, his voice deep with emotion. "It is of grave importance I called you here," he began. "Since you have been away from Paris nearly three years now, you have no knowledge of what is going on, the current state of affairs of our once proud order."

I could see the troubled look in the eyes of the three men. De Molay looked much older than I last saw him – as if he were carrying a great weight on his shoulders.

"We are besieged on all fronts, I'm afraid. The King of France, King Philip, who is no longer fair, is seeking to dissolve our order." "He has Pope Clements ear; so we are being squeezed from two sides." "They want us to band with the Hospilitiers, give up our identity to join their ranks." "Neither of us wants that." "However, if we defy the King, I fear there will be grave consequences." "The King seeks our wealth, while the Pope just wants to please the King so he can keep his seat as the leader of the Christian world in Avignon." "King is spreading false rumors about us." "He is calling us everything from a band of homosexuals to anti-Christ."

"We know it is not true, but the stories are believed by many; since it is being repeated by countless noblemen as well as commoners."

"What would you have me do?" I asked.

"I brought you here to tell you personally of the dangers we face. It word gets out that you have a portion of the Templar wealth in the fortress in Lurs, the King will set his army on you." "Nothing is more important to him than our money, lands, business, banking ventures and our fleet of merchant vessels." "Therefore, you must put a plan in place to protect that small part of our treasure in your care."

Small part, I wondered. *What wealth must we have if that enormous amount in my vaults was only a small part?* "I understand," I replied. "I will return to my fortress to devise a plan with my trusted knights. I won't let you down brethren. I will do my duty to you and the order."

"Very good Brother Guy. Rest and eat. This is Marshal Rupert Didier. He is a trusted member of my inner circle. If a catastrophe were to befall us, as I fear it will, he will come to you with instructions; heed them as if they come from me directly since they will be from my mouth to Rupert's ear."

CHAPTER 28 ✛ ✛ ✛

I set out for the fortress at Lurs with two companions riding by my side, a long-bowmen and a squire. The bowman wore a black mantel with a red cross. The squire, who was a fledgling knight, wore a brown frock. I was dressed in my white mantel with red-cross on my chest, the insignia of a Knight Templar. "We will ride hard my fellows. I want to return to the keep as quickly as possible. There is much work to be done."

"Ride on, Sir Knight. We will keep pace," said the squire, a stout lad of sixteen. The Master had told me the young squire had been in training for two years and was due to face initiation next year. I could see he was a proficient horseman a Saracen scimitar at his side. I would have to ask him about that blade. We raised the castle on the evening of the fifth day, having covered the 320 miles by riding well into the night. We slept on the hard ground but five hours before rising well before dawn to continue our journey. The men of the castle were gathered in the courtyard awaiting my return. My second in command, Geoffrey De Cherney, met me, a groom took the reins of my horse.

"Treat him kindly," he is spent after that forced ride.

"What have you to say to us?" asked Lourant De Beaumen sitting tall in the saddle on his magnificent jet black war horse.

I addressed the assembled men. "I bring sad, no, troubling tidings from the Grand Master. Many factions throughout France are joining in opposition to our order. Chief among them is the King of France, Philip IV, Philip the Fair and Pope Clement V. They are appealing to the Hospitiliers to minimize our order and, I fear, to destroy us. We must prepare our castle for attack, which means stockpiling provisions, weapons and horses in the event the worst happens. I will meet with my trusted officers and sergeants in the morning. We will issue orders then. Now I must rest."

At the meeting in the enormous conference hall the next day, I was joined by my fifteen knights and four sergeants. The head groom who was in charge of the stables and all the livestock and horses, the kitchen master, along with my new squire.

"This is what I have concluded," I told the assembled group. "If our order is attacked, it will begin in Paris. That is where the Grand Master resides with his deputies, Seneschals, marshals, and commanders." "It is also the seat of the treasury presided over by the Lord of the Exchequer, who is the financial head of the order loyal to the grand master." "Although we are some distance from Paris, also little known outside the temple, I think our importance and location will be disclosed sooner than later."

A knight rose from his seat. "Why do you believe that, Brother Guy? We have kept a low visible presence here; we are far from the mainstream of civilization."

That is true Brother Pierre," I continued. "But too many people know of our existence. Think of the many wagons we received, the drivers, grooms and workmen who came here. They know of our existence, our location. I'm sure they speculated about their cargo, the reason they had protection from knights, bowmen and infantry. Think of these laborers drinking in a tavern, telling their companions of a magnificent castle near the Alps, a secluded fortress that received many crates of valuables." They would be speculating about the contents of those crates.

Laurent De Beaume stood to his full height, an imposing knight in his mantel, sword at his hip, standing 6'4". "If there was a spy or traitor among the many people who came to us in the six months of receiving wagons, the King's court could already know of our existence, also our number and capabilities. I believe Brother Guy is correct." "We must prepare as if they know, or will shortly know after they make a move against our order."

"What do you propose we do, Commander Guy?" asked Laurent, as he took his seat.

"We must start to assemble wagons along with draft horses or oxen to pull them." "I mean to try to save the treasure or as much of it as we can move." "I want to prevent it from falling into the hands of the King, the

Pope, or any others that mean to take it from us". "With this in mind, I want the grooms-men, with infantry escort, to go into the countryside near or far to acquire sturdy wagons. It took 84 wagons to carry the treasure to us. I will need at least 95 wagons to carry the treasure, provisions for my men and feed for the horses. I intend to remove it all from the reach of the French King."

Another knight stood; it was Robert de Lille. "Where can we go that is out of the reach of King Philip?"

I looked at the men before me. Good men, all stout, loyal men, who would fight and die with me if necessary. I didn't answer at once, silence hung in the air like a heavy weight. When I spoke, I uttered just one word. "Outremer." A murmur passed through the chamber.

Then Ode de Vandrie stood his sword in his up-raised right hand. "Brilliant," he exclaimed. "I'm with you Guy." With that, the entire ensemble of men rose cheering and clapping. When the chamber was still once more I spoke again. "I don't know how much time we have – weeks or months – so we must begin preparations immediately. If anyone has suggestions, complaints, or just wants to talk, I will be available anytime day or night. Do not hesitate to seek me out no matter how silly or trivial your thoughts. Remember, our lives will depend upon it.

CHAPTER 29

The summer months sped by while Guy De Vaux's garrison worked tirelessly making preparations to move from the castle that had been their home these past 3 years. All the treasure from the vaults and chambers below was brought up into the council chamber and ante-rooms on the ground floor where a guard stood watch over it around the clock. Wagons were being assembled in the massive courtyard before the main building. The men worked to grease the axils, reinforce the beds or rails, while repairing or replacing wheels. The grooms saw to the draft horses that were being added to the stables. They would need at least two animals for every wagon. There were eighteen large oxen that would also be used for hauling, while the fifteen knights would require at least two horses each on the journey to the coast. The cooks were drying and smoking game to bring for the trek to feed the men since they could not march on empty stomachs.

Toward the end of August, Guy De Vaux called another meeting in the field outside the walls. The castle keep was a bee-hive of activity. "You have done well, my brethren. I am proud of what we have accomplished." A loud cheer went up from the assembled men. "I am going to take a party of six troops on an expedition to the coast. I want to check the route we will follow when we leave our sanctuary. We will need places of rest along the way. I will look for a suitable harbor in which to transfer our cargo aboard sailing ships in preparation for our sea voyage."

"Where are we sailing to, Brother? I know you said Outremer – but where, exactly?" asked a knight. Outremer means a land across the sea.

"What land I haven't decided yet," I lied; I knew exactly where we were sailing to, but I didn't want anyone else to know until we arrived. "I want Robert de Lille and Sir Geoffrey De Cherney to ride with me, plus my bowman, Simon Percivel. You will come also Sergeant Bermond. Pick another man from the rank to join us."

"I will take Squire Allman as my aide." The young lad smiled up at me. "Thank you, Master Guy," he said in a strong voice, his hand on the hilt of his blade.

"While I am gone, Laurent, you will be in charge. Begin to load the wagons, cover the cargo with tarpaulins. Tie them down securely so the precious treasure will be hidden from prying eyes. Continue your search for more wagons. If necessary, send a rider to Metz, or Lyon, to find more. Do not go to Avignon or Paris. I don't want to alert the French garrison there, or the Pope. They will be curious, maybe ask questions or pry into our purpose. We have 49 today; we need at least 38 more by the time I return. I estimate it will be three to four weeks until we return."

Everything will be ready on your return," replied Gil Laurent.

"Those going with me draw rations from the kitchen, bring a bed-roll since we will be sleeping outdoors most nights. Meet me at the stable in one hour's time."

CHAPTER 30 ✠ ✠ ✠

The small contingent of men rode out of the castle, heading south on the hard packed dirt-road toward the Cote d'Azur, the warm Mediterranean Sea. After eight days of riding, the last two along the coast, they came to a small village nestled above a beautiful natural harbor with two curved stone jetties - one on the east, one on the west of a sheltered bay. An open mouth to the sea lay between the stone arms. "This is perfect," I said aloud.

"Yes, an excellent port," said Sergeant Jeremy Bermand. "This harbor can hold at least ten large Templar vessels comfortably, maybe more."

"You're right," joined in Robert de Lille. "All we would need is a pier to load the ships. We can't move everything from shore to the ships by boat or barge."

"Come," I said. "Let's ride into the village to see where we are." People came into the street upon seeing the horsemen enter the village. It wasn't often knights of the Temple came this way.

"Where are we?" I called out. "What is this place?"

A man strode up to my horse. "This is Giens, a village of 800 souls - men, women and children."

"Do ships ever come to your harbor?" I asked.

"Yes, but not often. They come for water, or to escape a storm. The harbor is well-protected you see."

"Are you the head of this village, the master or mayor?"

"Yes, I am both," was his reply.

"My men and I would like some food, a warm meal with some ale if it is available. We would also like to speak with you about a project I have in mind." After a meal of beef stew in broth, bread, and ale, the men spoke for hours. "I did most of the talking with the Mayor, Hugo by name," who had his Deputy Mayor join us. "Coincidentally, my deputies name is Hugolin," said Hugo.

After settling our affairs, coming to a price for the work I wanted done, we went to sleep on a bed of straw in a large warm barn. I woke the men as day was dawning in the east. It was a glorious sight, the sun – a large orange ball climbing above a dark horizon, turning the sea a brilliant emerald-blue-green. "Here are my instructions, listen well. You, Robert, take our Sergeant as a companion. Ride west to the port of Marseille. I'm sure you will find some of the Templar fleet at anchor in the port. Commander at least five ships, more if you can then set sail for Giens at once. Try to have one warship, plus whatever cargo vessels you can get. If the captains give you any problem, tell them you are acting on orders from the Grand Master. Tell them Sir Guy de Vaux takes full responsibility for this order. Here is my badge to show your authority. You men board the lead vessel, the one in command, than set sail to the harbor of Giens. If we are not here when you arrive, anchor; wait for our return." "Meanwhile, Sir Geoffrey, you will remain in the Village with my bowmen Percival, to ensure my instructions are being followed". "I am giving you this pouch full of gold sovereigns give them to the mayor to distribute as the work progresses." "Be sure the work keeps moving along since we are on a short time table." "While you are doing your duty, my squire and I will ride to the castle to assemble the caravan." "We will not be ready to march until the end of October, which means we should arrive in the village about 19th or 20th of November." "I estimate the trip will take three to four weeks with loaded wagons, foot soldiers, grooms herding cattle for food along the way." I expect it to be an arduous journey under difficult conditions but we will persevere.

"Very well Sir Guy. I will do my duty here," said Geoffrey, nodding.

"You can count on me" said Robert de Lille. "Come Sergeant, we ride."

Gerard Allman, my squire, and I mounted our chargers. I looked down at the mayor. "When my men arrive in a few months' time, your village will gain much wealth in livestock, wagons and supplies. You will get this from me only if the chores I gave you are complete. If not, I will burn your village, eat your livestock then take the children and comely maidens to sea with me. My fleet will arrive in your harbor within a month." I nodded to the two men staying behind. Follow their orders; they are now in charge in my stead. Putting the spurs to my mount we rode north on the road toward Lyon, my squire behind me on his trusty mare.

CHAPTER 31 ✦ ✦ ✦

I stood on the castle porch watching the activity all around me. Most of the wagons were loaded, ready to move, while some few waited for cargo to be placed on them. One of our knights explained: "Laurent found those four-wheeled land schooners in a vineyard in Bordeaux. The wine-master was reluctant to lose them so Gil de Foresta made a shrewd deal. He took a driver for each wagon from the vineyard, promising they would return with the wagons as soon as we are done with them. When the wine-master saw the gold coins de Foresta was handing him, any reluctance he had vanished. They only arrived here three days ago. They will be loaded by tomorrow night. They will hold the equivalent of three; two-wheel carts each, but will need six horses to pull because of the weight." Those five schooners are equivalent to fifteen wagons.

"Good Laurent, see to the loading. It is already October 15. I want to be ready to move by the 18th."

The next afternoon, as I walked from the stables after talking to the master groom about the horses and livestock under his care, a cry went up from a guard on the battlement tower. "Rider approaching at a gallop," he yelled. "It is a Templar; open the gate." The knight thundered into the courtyard pulling hard on the reigns to stop the charging horse. The wild eyed beast reared up on his hind legs, front legs pawing the air. I rush toward the man as he settled his steed then climbed from the saddle. The horse shook his head, eyes wide, white foam dripped from his mouth, his body slick, wet with lather. As I came closer I recognized the knight who had dismounted. It was the third person who had been in the Grand Master's chamber four months ago. I searched my memory for his name, but it escaped me. "Marshall," I began. "What brings you here in such haste?"

"We must speak privately, Sir Guy. But first, get me a groom to see to my horse."

"My squire is here behind me. He will take charge of your beast."

"You," the rider said, addressing Gerard. "This is my favorite Palfrey. He is an Arabian pure breed, four-years old. His mother gave birth to him when she was eight. I brought the stallion to France from the Holy Land when I returned. Take care of him."

"Now we must talk, it is urgent," Rupert confided in me. "Lead the way to your chamber." Once in my study with the door closed, Rupert seemed to relax; actually, he seemed to deflate.

"I am exhausted," he began. "Not only from the exertion of the ride, 320 miles in just over four days, that takes a toll on horse and man; but it is the burden of the events of four days ago that is weighing on me."

"Tell me brother, what has happened?"

"It is just as the Grand Master, Jacque de Molay, predicted when you were in his chamber six months ago. King Philip, with Pope Clements help, has attacked the order of the temple. But they didn't just attack us; they have destroyed all we have accomplished over 200 years. We are annihilated, finished as an effective, prosperous organization."

"Tell me what transpired so we can plan accordingly," asked a curious Guy De Vaux.

CHAPTER 32 ✚ ✚ ✚

It was early Friday morning, October 13ᵗʰ Rupert began. "I was in the courtyard doing my morning exercise, which I do each day to keep my body and mind in top condition. I heard a loud commotion at the gate of our compound.I watched as a large group of French troops of the royal regiment stormed the grounds attacking the guards killing them all. Once into the courtyard they swarmed toward the main building. I ran unseen to the stables, hiding in the tack-room where I had a clear view of the action. We were taken by surprise and greatly outnumbered as more and more troops filed into the courtyard. Our brothers were herded from the buildings, many still in their night-clothes. They were shackled or tied together. If they resisted, they were cut down by sword or lance. "Finally de Molay, the Seneschal, along with three marshals were taken from the headquarters building in chains then marched away flanked by armed guards, an officer leading the way." "I watched all through the day while my brother knights were made to kneel in the courtyard, their heads chopped from their bodies." "Many died by their own swords, while the French troops stood cheering and laughing." "Once night fell I discarded my white mantel, put on a groom's brown frock, saddled my palfrey and walked out of the stable into the countryside." "The Streets were now empty except for the many dead bodies of my fellow knights lying where they fell." "My squire came upon me in the street. I told him to take two of my Desti's from the stable then follow my path to Aups, then on to your fort at Lurs." "If he was able to leave Paris, he will be here in a few days."

"This is horrible. The most dreadful news I could imagine Rupert, worse than the Grand Master feared." "For the King to act against the order with such impunity he must have the Pope under his control." "We are finished, a mere footnote in history." "With the preparations I've made, we may still be able to save ourselves before the King's men arrive."

"How much time do you think we have Rupert?"

"If someone speaks to save themselves from torture, it will take the king a few days to mount a force of men able to attack this castle. Such a force would move slowly to save their strength for an impending battle." "By my estimate, the earliest a regiment would be able to move against you would be tomorrow. If I am correct that gives us a week before they arrive at your gates. I will give the order now to begin our march to the coast at first light. We have eighty two wagons to start down the road. Over 250 men on foot between our infantry and support staff; then there is the herd of cattle, sheep, goats and horses. We will be moving slowly. Come, I have to alert the men." I assembled all the people on the parade ground advising them of our difficult situation. "We march at first light.' "I will address all hands at 5:00 a.m. before we set out for the coast." My trusted knights gave orders to the cooks, grooms, and staff to make preparations for the arduous march.

I did not sleep that night. My mind was full of conflicting thoughts thinking of last-minute details, the fate of the Grand Master, the death of the order I had devoted twenty years of my life to. What will become of us now I wondered?

CHAPTER 33 ✦ ✦ ✦

It was dark as I stood on top of a wagon to speak with all the men gathered round. A chill was in the air, mist hung above the fields. I first told the assemblage of the events that had transpired in Paris. Relating the sad tale as told to me by Rupert. There were angry shouts, calls for revenge, some even demanding we ride to Paris at once to save our brothers. I let this banter go on for a few minutes, than raised my voice demanding silence. When the noise subsided, I spoke in a loud, stern voice that carried over the assembly.

"Hear me now, for I am your new Master." "No," I corrected. "Not you're Master – your your leader." "I have thought all night on this matter." "Our present position and what we must do to survive." "Thankfully, we have prepared well over these past months so we are ready to move at once." "I tell you now, the order of the temple is dead, if not today then very soon." "Hundreds of our brothers in Paris have been slaughtered in the streets." "At this moment, the King's troops have been dispatched to take control of our nine strongholds around France." "I fear the French army, at least a regiment of seasoned troops, is setting out to attack this castle as we speak." "Templers are being rounded up where ever they are found, then either killed or imprisoned. They are tortured to confess to crimes against the church and crown." "They will then be killed based on the confessions tortured from them." "The same fate awaits us if we are captured." "With this in mind, I now resign my place as a Knight of the poor fellow soldiers of Christ." "I remove my white mantle with the red-cross for the last time." I pulled the mantle over my head, throwing it to the ground. "I renounce my vows made at my initiation. I unburden myself from the vows to God and the order of the Temple of Solomon."

There were cries from the crowd: "Blasphemy; traitor; heathen," and worse could be heard.

"Stop and listen," I yelled. "I do not denounce God, just my vow of chastity, poverty, humility. What I propose is not so different from before." "I denounce the vow of poverty since we must now earn our way in the world." "We were taken care of by the order of the Temple. An order that controlled all the wealth, which meant we as individuals were impoverished; but not our order." "We lived as good men true; without the succor of women. We had new recruits join us continually, so there was no need for us to seek women to fornicate." "That life is over for us, and by us, I mean you standing with me now." "We will need sons and daughters to carry on our lineage." "We must earn our keep in order to survive." "We will need a place of our own in order to live a fruitful existence." "What I envision is a group of independent knights and helpers living by the same rules of obedience, duty, loyalty and humility as before." "But dependent on each other, not an order with rules to govern all our acts." "The rule of the temple is dead, as dead as the temple that is no more." "From this moment forward we are now a free union of knights." "Our governing principle is the ten commandments of Moses. We march as free men owing allegiance to no master, just our brothers, those standing next to us now."

A cheer began in the crowd, growing louder, stronger as more voices picked it up until everyone was screaming loudly. I raised my arms over my head: "Silence," I commanded. "Throw off your mantle knights. Mount your horses or wagons; take a step forward. I will lead the way into the future; follow me to a better life." I rode out to the road, wagons following behind in a long line, people and live stock strung out behind.

Rupert Didier would remain in the castle waiting for his squire along with any other stragglers who might come along. "I will join you in a few days," he said, grasping my arm.

I rode at the rear of the column, young squire Allman at my side. Now that the sun was up the caravan was a magnificent sight. 82 carriages stretching over a mile from head to tail watched over by my knights, now dressed in black tunics – similar to the uniform of our grooms, cooks or workers; we made a merry band. That first day, we only covered eight miles when we stopped for the night. I gathered my knights, sergeants, the chief groom and master chef to me.

"The first days March was satisfactory, but not good enough" I began. "We must cover more ground each day, a minimum of twelve miles so we can reach the port in twenty four days." "In order to achieve this goal, I want our walking infantry to place two men on each wagon so they can ride." "Knights, take up positions throughout the train to keep the wagons moving." "Cook, I want you to take your party ahead of the column." "Set up your mess depot at least twelve miles in advance of the wagons, fifteen miles would be better. Look for a good field so the people can rest comfortably through the night." "When we reach you, we will stop for the night." "If any wagons break down, leave them." "Off-load the cargo onto other wagons, distribute the load but keep moving." "Now see to the men, feed them, have them get a good night sleep, we move again at first light." For the next 24 days, we made good progress through the French countryside. When we lay down to sleep on the hard ground on that 24th night since leaving the castle at Lurs I could smell the sea on the night breeze.

CHAPTER 34 ✚ ✚ ✚

The next morning I crested a small rise, my squire at my side. I was greeted by a splendid sight spreading before me. "It's the blue Mediterranean," Gerard exclaimed. "By the Lord God we made it."

"Yes," I replied, "We have. Ride back to inform Laurent to keep the wagons moving until we are at the village green in Geins. You can join me there."

"Yes, Sir Guy" Allman replied, wheeling his horse around to find my deputy. I rode downhill toward the village gazing at the harbor where seven ships lay at anchor. They were a magnificent sight to behold bobbing peacefully on gentle waves rippling across the surface of the water. Tall masts with white, furled sails reaching toward the soft puff ball clouds floating across a clear blue sky. My chest swelled with pride at the sight. A Templar ensign was flying from the mast head of a large warship. When I neared the water's edge I saw my welcome party waiting for me – Robert de Lille and Geoffrey de Charney – still wearing the white mantle with red-cross of the Knights Templar's. Simon Percival, bowman, and Sergeant Bermond standing to one side.

"It's good to see you, my liege," said de Lille. "We have been waiting for your arrival with great anticipation. But why are you dressed in black? Where is your knight's garb?"

"I will explain to you in due course. We have more important matters to see to first. There will be 82 wagons of various sizes arriving over the next several hours. You, Sir Geoffrey, with the sergeant's help, place them across the field in an orderly rank so we can bring each to the pier to unload in good order. Robert see to the men. I trust you have made accommodations for them."

"I have," said Robert de Lille. "I will see to them when ready."

"Good. Now show me the pier you had built." Hugo, the Mayor of Giens joined us as we walked to the loading pier which jutted some eighty feet into the water from the shore line.

"I trust this will be sufficient, your honor," said the Mayor. "We did the best we could under the circumstances; it was a difficult project."

"I'm sure it was, Mayor. Let's walk to the end of your pier so I can see how sturdy it is." As we walked out onto the pier the Mayor told me the story of its construction.

"There are stones, large boulders, gravel, everything solid we could find to lay a foundation. Then a layer of flat stones were placed on top to make the upper bed which was then covered with trimmed logs for the top surface. We cut trees in the forest then hauled them to the head of the dock to be cut into planks."

"There," he said, pointing to a stand of trees about a mile away." There is what remains of our forest.The dock felt firm, unyielding beneath my feet as I walked to the end. I stood looking at the ships envisioning the loading procedure.

"We can bring a vessel-nose in to the shore alongside the dock. That way at least sixty or 70 feet will be tied to the pier. The ship can send a cargo net on a boom over the side to be filled with cargo then hoisted aboard. It will take time, but it can be done."

"You have done well, Mayor. Your village will be rewarded for your work. However, you have more to do. I want forty of your strongest men to work on the dock and aboard the ships to help stow the cargo."

"Very good, my lord. You shall have them."

That evening, over an excellent meal of roasted beef from six slaughtered cattle, the men sat resting around campfires to ward off the chilly night air. Three nights later Marshall Rupert Didier came to me accompanied by two knights and a squire.

"These three men joined me at Lurs Sir Guy. They came from Paris by way of Lyon with news of the evil King's actions against our order. I wish to have them tell you their tale directly."

"Precede," said Rupert, turning to the three men standing in the flickering light of the fire.

"My name is Fabien Le Blanc, Knight Templar stationed at residence, in Taillevent, thirty miles east of Paris. We were overrun by French troops on the morning of October 14. I was held captive in Paris in a dungeon in Le Timbre. There were many other knights in cells near me. Each day men were taken from their cells never to return. I was told on the 8th day of my captivity they had been executed. I saw for myself on that day some weeks ago. I was taken from my cell to Place de la Concorde where I stood with other disgraced Knights. A row of gallows had been erected in the square. Men were hanging by the neck, swaying in the breeze, all Templar's, some still in the knights garb. In the center of the plaza five stakes had been driven into the ground. I watched as four men were tied to these stakes, wood piled around their feet and legs. I gave a start when I recognized the Grand Master, the Seneschal, next to him, Robespierre, the head priest along with Commander Montclair, leader of our military units. I stood in horror as each fire was lit, the flames burning fiercely. I stood watching the four men burn to death. No one spoke or uttered a sound, except for de Molay. He yelled defiantly at his captors: "Let evil swiftly befall those who have wrongfully condemned us. God will avenge us. God knows who is wrong and who has sinned." I stood with three other knights, tears streaming down our cheeks as our leader and our order died before my eyes. We stood in mortified silence as a tall figure wearing a black cloak and hood approached us.

"I am Guillaume De Negaret," the man began. "I am Chief counselor to Philip King of France."

Rupert interrupted, "The man is evil. I met him once in the King's chambers. He is ruthless in pursuit of power. Death and torture are his playmates."

"I am releasing you four knights to tell the world what you observed here this day. The champion of the Templar's has perished, and with him the order of the Temple of Solomon has perished as well. Go from here to Lyon, Metz, Avignon, even to Cyprus, with that message. The Templar's are no more. Go now, before I change my mind and have my troops behead you." We turned and ran from this evil presence.

"You are safe with us, Fabien Le Blanc. Thank you for your words; it strengthens our resolve to see that the wicked King Philip doesn't get his hand on our precious cargo."

The next morning I was rowed from shore in a captain's barge to attend a meeting aboard the flag-ship of the fleet. I had instructed the admiral to have the captains of the cargo vessels in attendance so I could explain my plan to all at the same time. I climbed aboard the warship marveling at her size. The crew stood on the fore deck on parade in pressed uniforms. Gun captains stood at their stations next to a row of cannons lining the deck. Robert de Lille at my side along with Rupert Didier, who asked to join us out of deference to the dead Grand Master. We followed an officer to the raised structure on the aft deck of this grand vessel.

The admiral was waiting in his sea-cabin sitting resplendent in a blue naval uniform with gold-braid on shoulder boards as befitting of his rank. An aide de camp stood beside him, while six naval officers stood in a row to his left. "Welcome to my Man of War," said the admiral. "Please join my captains with me at the conference table. We are anxious to hear the details of your planned expedition." After many hours of discussion, we had reached a consensus. "So," said the admiral, "Let me go over the plan to be sure each person knows his assignment. We will load your cargo of trade goods aboard four of my merchant vessels at your improvised pier. A cargo vessel will carry your live stock, it can carry ninety horses, also your cavalry officers, feed for the animals, along with your grooms. The sixth merchant ship will carry your infantry, archers, sergeants, along with your knights. While you, your squire, Mr. Rupert Didier your aide, will travel on my man-of-war, is that correct?"

"Yes it is," I replied. "However, I will want three archers with me, two crossbow-men and my longbow-man."

"Very well. Then after we are loaded we set sail for Cyprus?"

"That is the plan, admiral."

Although Cyprus wasn't out final destination, it's what I led everyone to believe. I would give the admiral additional information when we were sitting snug in the harbor of Limassol. "Remember, I also want six carriages lashed to the hulls of the six merchant ships, three to a side – a total of thirty-six wagons in all for my cargo when we reach our destination. They will have wagons available in Cyprus said the aide Why take yours along?"

"Yes, I agree they may have wagons, however, I want to be sure transportation is available."

"I believe Transport would be available where we are going but I see no problem if you wish to bring some of your own," continued the admiral. "Our journey should take us about twelve to fourteen days, if the winds hold true. At this time of year they blow from the west, which is favorable to our voyage." If we get a mistral wind it will push us Eastward at a good clip.

"Fine, then take my party ashore so I can supervise to loading; we can begin at once."

It took twelve days to load the cargo, men working round the clock. Another two days to load the horses since they had to be raised onto the ship's deck in a sling, one animal at a time. Finally, on the morning of December 20th, we were ready to set out to sea.

CHAPTER 35 ✛ ✛ ✛

On the last night ashore, one of my knights, Sir William Harcourt of England, came to me. I was sitting in my temporary shelter with Master Didier round a fire since the nights were cool in late December, even on the coast of France.

"A word, Sir Guy," he began.

"By all means William, what can I do for you?"

"You instructed us to renounce our vows to the Temple. At your instructions we are now living as free men, just knights, no longer Templar's. Yes William, that is correct. I would like to know, that is to be certain I am no longer constrained by our vow of chastity."

"That is correct, Will," I replied.

"Then Sir Guy, I would like to bring a lass from this village with me on our journey."

"What," I exclaimed, surprised by Will's request. "Bring a female on this trip to the Holy... I mean to Cyprus with us."

"Yes, William continued. "I have been here near two months now. This woman and I have become close. We desire each other. She wants to stay with me since her choices in Giens are few." She would like to join me on this journey.

"Let me think on this William. Come back to me in an hour, I will have an answer for you then." The idea had merit. Where we were going we would need females to form a true community. We would also require children if we were to have our society grow and survive. I pondered the implications of the idea over in my mind. William returned in an hour as directed.

"First, tell me truthfully William, have you lain with this woman?"

"No, Sir Guy, I have not."

"She would have to be segregated on the ship, kept to herself can she do that?"

"Yes, Sir Guy. She has two close friends who wish to come along also."

"Bring the three women to me at once so we may speak."

After a ten-minute conversation, I was assured the three were chaste. They agreed to follow my instructions and expressed a true desired to come with us seeking a new life. I sent word to the admiral asking permission to bring three females on our voyage. He replied it was highly unusual, but the Navy had transported women to and from the Holy Land in the past. He would find suitable accommodations for them on his warship. We set out to sea on a bright cool Christmas morning in late December. The Mediterranean was calm as we cleared the harbor breakwater, the majestic war ship leading the way, the small convoy following in line. The entire village had turned out to see us off. They stood lining the shore, cheering and waving, sorry to see us leave but happy for the bounty we left behind in the form of 39 wagons, horses, cattle, and assorted equipment. The voyage proved to be uneventful. On the morning of the 14th day at sea a look-out in the rigging called down: "Land Ho." Everyone crowded the rail watching the small dark shape on the horizon grow larger as the seven ships sailed toward port. The harbor was crowded with vessels of all types flying flags from many countries. There were small fishing vessels, passenger boats, and large commercial cargo vessels with barges shuttling from boats to shore then back again. Everyone gazed at our seven-vessel convoy since we were flying French flags. The warship also displayed the Templar pennant from the tallest mast. I had asked the admiral to take it down in order to hide our identity but he refused to heed my advice.

"I am still employed by the House of the Temple until I am told otherwise," he insisted.

"I tried said Rupert Didier, but he wouldn't listen to me or anyone else. He is a stubborn man." Too many years at sea giving orders not taking them.

"We must make preparations to off-load my ships," said Admiral Villars.

"Not yet, sir," I replied. "We are going on from here." I have another destination in mind.

"But you told me in France we were going to Cyprus. We have arrived. Now you tell me you wish to go further."

"Yes, that is what I propose. We can provision here, fresh food and water. Then sail to the port of Famagusta on the East side of the island. From there I wish to sail a few days more to the coast of Turkey. I wish to go ashore at Mersin, do you know it."

"I do," replied the Villars. I have been there on two prior occasions. "Templar Knights were stationed there when they fled from Syria." I led an evacuation of exhausted troops. I brought two groups of men to safety on Cypress.

"Yes, I know, since I was one of the knights who escaped the Sultan's army. We retreated to the port of Mersin in disarray to await ships to carry us from the Islamic hoard that was bearing down on us. Now, I wish to return."

"It seems like madness, man. But if you insist, I will take you there. We will rest here for two days to allow the men to go ashore. We will leave with the tide at sun-up on January 18th. A new year in a new land for you and your people."

On the morning of the 18th of January, we set sail for Turkey. The captains of the cargo vessels were instructed told to hold position off the stern of the lead warship. They were told to follow where the Admiral sailed, to stay in tight formation behind the war ship. They were not told the name of the new destination. Standing on the bridge with Admiral Villars, his executive officer at his side, a telescope in his hand, we watched Cyprus slide by on our port-side. We were sailing about eight miles from land. The officer brought my attention to a large map resting on the navigation table.

"We are going to stay close to Cyprus until we reach the point at Andreas. We will turn north for Mersin once clear of the last outcrop of land. The Caliph has a fleet of warships here at Latakia on the Syrian coast which will only be about forty miles distant from us. I would just as soon avoid any conflict with them." "Has there been trouble with them in the past I asked?"

"They usually only attack small unarmed merchant vessels. The Syrian crew then sail the captured ship into port in Syria for the cargo. They are ruthless in that they kill all aboard the captured ship. I doubt they would attempt to come for us since my ship is too powerful for them with my 24 cannons, but we must keep alert lest they try for one of the merchant vessels; especially if one lags behind or drifts out of position."

It was four in the afternoon when we rounded the narrow tip of Cypress referred to as the horn. The sun was slipping slowly toward the horizon in the clear blue sky casting a golden radiance onto the water. Suddenly a shout from the crow's nest startled all on the deck below. "Sailing ships on the horizon coming toward us." The crew of the warship sprang to quarters to the beat of a drummer boy. The Admiral and First Officer marched to the helm-station where I stood at the side of the helmsman. The First Officer had a telescope to his eye, surveying the scene. He was standing on a ladder at the side of the Captain's sea cabin to get a better view.

"Well man, what do you see," demanded the Admiral.

"It seems there is a small boat, looks like a Dhow moving fast with lateen sails full. They are being pursued by three dhows, a larger vessel lagging behind. The command vessel is either a Barijah or a Boum. I can see archers and marines on her main deck."

The Admiral didn't hesitate, "Helmsman – rudder hard to starboard. We are going to the aid of the fleeing Dhow." The Admiral looked me in the eye, "A Templar always helps the underdog. Signal the six ships behind to hold their present course stay in close formation. I will return to them shortly."

I turned to Rupert, "Have my bowmen come to me at once." When they arrived I explained the situation. "Crossbowmen into the rigging, fire upon the three pursuing Dhows when they come into range. You Simon, take your long bow into the bow, shoot at any target you have. Go with him Rupert; take a few quivers of arrows. Go quickly!"

As we neared the fleeing boat we could see warriors holding shields aloft to protect the passengers from the missiles being fired at them by their pursuers. The boat was caught by one of the three pursuing Dhows. Grappling lines were thrown across the water allowing the boats to be pulled together. Fierce fighting broke out on deck. A boarding ramp was passed between the two boats. Armed men tried to board the fleeing vessel; both had come to a stop in the water. As we bore down on the boats, sails billowing loose in the wind, the pursuing two Dhows, seeing the warships armed crew manning the rails, turned tail heading back toward the larger Barijah for protection. Alexander standing in the bow let fly with arrows from his long bow. Two men on the fleeing boat fell to the deck, arrows protruding from their bodies.

"Long boat over," yelled the Admiral. Two boats were swinging outboard on davits, which began lowering them to the water below.

"I'm going," I yelled, running to one of the boats as it lowered away. Leaping from the rail I landed with a thud on the deck of the boat. A second later a body fell upon me knocking the wind from my lungs.

"Sorry, Sir came a weak reply." It was my squire, Gerard Allman.

"What are you doing, boy," I demanded. Are you trying to kill me? No sir I'm just doing my duty Sir. I must go where you go. I am here to protect you. Lead on I will follow."

"Very well, draw your weapon. We shall be in a fight soon, please don't stab me by mistake." The long boat flew over the water, eight men rowing, four per side keeping a steady cadence as the Helmsman yelled: "Stroke men Stroke faster."

Six of us stood in the bow of the craft, swords in hand. Four Marines from the ships' crew, me with a Scimitar in my right hand, the sheath made of hard-wood in my left. I turned to Gerard, standing just behind me. He carried a heavy-bladed falcon he had taken from a marine aboard ship. The lethal weapon in his firm grip.

"Are you ready, Lad?"

"You lead, my Liege. I will be by your side." The boats closed the distance to the embattled Dhow rapidly.

"Boat oars!" yelled the Helmsman, holding a firm grip on the tiller. The rowers shipped the dripping oars into the boat. The long-boat collided with the port-side of the Dhow. Sailors in the long boat grabbed the gunnels of the embattled Dhow holding the two boats together.

"Let's go men!" I screamed, jumping to the deck of the embattled boat, follow me. I quickly appraised the fighting being waged on the deck of the vessel. The wooden deck was running red with blood. Two crossing platforms had been passed across the gap from the Arab-manned Dhow to this one. Men were trying to cross over to capture the boat I had jumped aboard.

"You men!" I yelled at the four ships' Marines, "Stop the boarding party at the forward bridge! I will stop this one!"

The armed marines turned running forward, broad swords in hand, while I ran to the aft boarding platform; Gerard coming behind me. It was chaos on deck. Men stood fighting bravely to prevent the opposing crew from gaining control of this boat. A group of Arab assassins were struggling to cross the aft bridge between the two boats. Two men, one with a severe arm-wound dripping blood, stood gamely trying to stop the horde from boarding. I pushed my way to the front standing at the foot of the boarding plank. I swung my sword at a man standing above me on the platform. The steel tempered blade hummed cutting into the man's leg. It severed the limb at the knee. The now one-legged man fell backward, knocking the man behind him onto his back blocking the crossing. I jumped onto the plank kicking the one-legged assassin over the side into the water. The man who had been knocked on his back was trying to regain his feet. I stabbed my sword into his chest, quickly withdrawing the blade. Blood began to spurt from the wound, the man screamed in agony. I kicked him in the face, pressing forward to confront the next man in line. He lunged at me raising a two-handed long sword above his head. I stepped forward, thrusting my blade into his exposed throat pushing the point up to the hilt causing the man to fall backward to the deck of the boat behind him. His body falling back into a group of warriors standing on the deck below. I followed the body into the crowd swinging my blade left and right, connecting with bodies who staggered back from the mad-man covered in blood screaming like a banshee. I was soon joined by my squire, his falcon dripping red with blood. Two of the warriors from the Dhow were standing beside me. The four of us made a formidable force as we pressed forward dropping the Arabs who confronted us. Our attack gave the men at the forward crossing-point enough momentum to surge ahead. We now had what remained of the attackers caught between our two groups. Soon, none of the Arab pirates were left standing. The boat was ours. A cheer went up from the survivors of the battle. I turned to the marine officer from the ship's company: "Clean this boat. Throw the dead over the side, wash the deck clean. I'm going to find the Commander of the other Dhow." One of the wounded warriors told me to follow him, which I did, crossing back over the bloody boarding plank between the two vessels still tied together. He led me to a forward cabin where two young, strapping warriors stood guard before the door.

"Let us pass," said the man at my side. The guards stepped away. He led me into the cabin where an older man sat on a pillow, a bloody bandage wrapped around his head.

"Come, sit with me," he instructed, indicating a cushion next to him. "I would rise," "But as you can see, I was wounded slightly during the fight. I've lost some blood and am still a bit dizzy. If not for you joining the battle, I might be dead by now. I wish to thank you and your men for coming to our rescue. What is the cause of this fight, I demanded."

"I came to your aid because you were alone, being pursued by four of more vessels. Tell me why you were being pursued. What is the cause of this?"

"As you can see, we are Jews. We were trying to escape from Jaffe, where the Saracen horde turned on us suddenly after years of living side-by-side in peace. There was a huge battle; it lasted two days. But the outcome was inevitable since we were vastly outnumbered. All our men were killed, except for the handful you see on this boat. When I realized all was lost, I gathered the survivors to my side. We fought our way to the pier where this Dhow was tied; I loaded my passengers and the few troops aboard, cut the mooring lines and set out to sea. We had a good head-start on our enemies. But they rallied quickly, and then set out after us. My men are competent but not expert sailors. The Arab pursuers were slowly gaining on us. That is, when you came to our aid. Thanks be to God."

I'm not sure that's who the old man should be thanking, but I kept my mouth shut.

"Where were you going?"

"We were trying to reach Rhodes. There is a settlement of Jews there. We would seek their protection."

"A long trip for men who are not accomplished sailors."

"Yes, but we were desperate to escape. The danger on the water is less than what we are running from."

With that, a figure burst through a door at the rear of the cabin. I was startled by the sudden movement, my hand involuntarily going to the sword at my side.

"Hold," said the old man. "It's Princess Shana."

I stood in wonder looking at the woman standing before me, a long curved blade in her right hand. "Who are you?" she demanded in a stern voice. I stood looking at her in the dim light of the cabin. The woman was tall, about 5 feet 7 or 8 with dark hair, almost black, reaching to her shoulders. Her complexion was dark also – olive, with big brown eyes in a beautiful face, accented by high cheekbones and full lush lips.

I asked: "Who are you, she demanded "Have you lost your tongue?"

"No, I said recovering my wits. It's just I am surprised to see a woman on-board a ship; especially one that has been in a fierce battle."

"It is me the battle has been fought over," she said. "The Saracens want me as a symbol of their dominance over the Jews of the Holy Land. Jews who are now all dead or captured. I am Princess Shoshana. My husband was the leader of our tribe, the last Jews in the Holy Land living in Jaffe. He was a great leader and a great man, which proved to be his downfall."

"How so?" I asked.

"Because of his wisdom and charm, his charisma, people flocked to Jaffe to join him. His fame began to spread throughout Palestine until Salah ad Din, the Saracens King, began to worry this upstart Hebrew scholar would become his rival. Salah could not allow that to happen; so he sent his army to crush Abraham, kill him, me, our son David, along with all his followers. The Saracens attacked at sun-up. They killed Abraham first. That is when Mordechai took me to the port,to this boat to escape. If not for him and his men I would either be dead or in Salhadins chambers to sexually amuse him. Now, I ask again, who are you?"

"My name is Guy De Vaux. I am a knight, late of France, now a mercenary traveling to Turkey, to the port of Mersin on the Turkish coast. I had planned on arriving there at first light, but this little side adventure will throw off my schedule."

"What is the purpose of your trip to Turkey, may I ask?"

"I have some 300 people with me along with six ships of trade goods. I am taking us there to live. I intend to establish a base in an area some thirty miles inland to form a community; a home where we may sustain ourselves to live in peace and comfort for the remainder of our days."

"Sir Knight, unless I am mistaken, from your bearing and knowledge of this area along with your fighting prowess, I detect a Knight Templar in my presence. Please step outside for a moment while I confer with my Commander in private."

While I was waiting on deck, I instructed Gaspar, the naval officer from the Picard, to return to his ship and come back with six qualified sailors to man the two Dhows we now had in my possession. In the meantime, the able-bodied men were cleaning the two boats, dumping the dead overboard, throwing buckets of water onto the decks, scrubbing them clean of the blood and gore of the battle. The scuppers ran red, as the bloody water washed into the blue sea. Weapons were being collected into a pile amid ship. The door to the cabin was opened by a Hebrew guard. "Please come in, my liege," he said.

The defiant princess stood in the middle of the cabin, hands on hips, head thrust defiantly forward. "My good knight, what do you think of this boat with my people joining your party on this trek to Turkey?"

I was taken by surprise. It's one thing to rescue this group of Hebrews from Jaffe, another to become responsible for them. I told Princess Shoshana of my concerns

"We are capable of taking care of ourselves," she replied defiantly, "You will not be responsible for our safety."

I smiled. "Meaning no disrespect Princess, but I'm afraid if my men had not intervened when we did your entire party would be dead, or worse by now." That took the wind from her sails, as a blush of crimson colored her cheeks.

"Yes, you are right Brave Knight. But we would still like to go with you to Turkey. We need a new home, since we have been chased from Palestine."

"If I allow you to join us, you will be under my direction, You and your people must obey my commands without protest or argument." I addressed the wounded leader. Mordechai do you understand my edict. "Do I have your word on this?"

The old man looked at his Princess, who nodded slightly. "Very well," he said. "Me and my depleted troops will obey your orders."

"Princess, how many people do you have with you?"

"There are nine in my party – my son of three years, myself, and seven servants – all women. I had twelve warriors at my side when we left Jaffe. There are seven left alive; five were slaughtered in the fighting on deck."

"We will set sail as soon as the seamen arrive from the warship. The sun is already setting. We will be sailing in the dark." I sailed on the captured Dhow with my squire, Simon Percival the long bowman, plus two cross-bowmen." The boat was manned by three sailors from the Picard. The captured dhow had 4 seamen and 2 Hebrew warriors aboard. We followed the red stern-light of the warship; the six cargo vessels hugging our wake. At three in the afternoon of the next day we sailed into a quiet natural outer harbor. It was more a large bay, about a mile wide. To enter the protected inner harbor required a ninety-degree turn through a narrow cut of land. This passage led to a wide body of water capable of accommodating the warship and the six cargo vessels. Since the opening to the inner harbor was no more than 100 yards wide, the harbor could easily be defended against intruders. Admiral Villars designated each ship to an anchorage separated by a comfortable space. He then positioned his flagship just inside the narrow entrance, thus blocking the harbor so no ship could enter or exit past him. I ran the captured Dhow to a quay on the beach tying the craft to shore. The captured dhow with the seamen from the Picard docked behind the Dhow of Princess Shoshana; both boats made secure, watched over by the Hebrews. We stepped ashore in Turkey, our new home. A large crowd gathered on the beach to observe us, but no one came near. The long boat from the Picard came ashore, the Admiral standing proudly in the bow. He looked resplendent dressed in his navy uniform, gold-braided coat, an officer's dress-sword at his side. We discussed plans for off-loading the cargo. First ship to unload would be the livestock vessel, then each of the cargo vessels. I walked to the crowd of people, Rupert Didier, Robert de Lille and my squire, Gerard Allman, joining me. Once I had explained my purpose with the aid of a Turkmen who spoke French, promising both money, the captured weapons and the two Dhows as payment for labor, plus the loan of draft horses to pull our wagons we set to work. The men began loading the thirty-six wagons we had brought from France. I estimated it would take five days to travel to the castle at Gulek, 33 miles from the port of Icel, where we were now secure. I broke our squadron down taking fifty infantry - most of the grooms and ten knights to travel with the wagons. I left the remainder in the port with the ships to guard the balance of our cargo. I also left the Princess with her entourage aboard the ship to await our return in what

I estimated would be two weeks. The trip to the castle was slow due to the conditions of the road, plus the heavy load the horses were pulling in the thirty six wagons. We made about seven miles per day at a slow pace, but a pace necessary to preserve the horses' strength since the path to the castle from the valley floor was steep and dangerous. On the fifth day, we caught sight of the fortress rising into the sky above the valley floor on which we approached. A mist hugged the ground in the early morning chill which only added to the mystic since the castle seemed to rise into the sky from the mist.

"It is magnificent," said Gerard at my shoulder, "So high in the sky."

"Yes," I replied. "Over 860 feet up the steep, narrow trail; built that way to withstand any siege. The only way up is the one narrow ramp with steep drops on either side. No formidable force can attack up that steep incline. They would be cut down, decimated to a man. We will have to unload half of each wagon so the animals can climb the ramp to the castle; it will mean more trips, but the climb is so steep they could not manage with a full load." It took four days to transport all the treasure up the steep grade to the castle grounds. The men had to assist the horses by pulling on ropes tied to the wagons or pushing from behind. By the time all the freight had been transported up the ramp, both men and horses were exhausted. I gave them a day of rest. Then we prepared to go back to the port of Icel for another load. I took the 36 wagons with a drivers and one man riding along as a guard, 72 men, me and my squire on our chargers and one knight, Fabien de la Blanc. He would ride at the end of our column to be sure there were no stragglers. I left the remainder to guard our cargo and prepare the fort for the arrival of the others. We made excellent time on the return trip arriving at the port after a four-day journey. The wagons were loaded with the remaining crates. The troops were marching in line behind the wagons. The Princess and her people came next riding in a large passenger carriage, not grand but functional. I bid goodbye to Admiral Villars who had come ashore to see me off.

"Have a safe journey, Admiral. May you always have a favorable wind at your back."

"And you, Sir Guy. Be careful in this land of the heathen Saracens; a safe stay for you and your people. I hope we cross paths in the future." We clasped in a manly embrace. Our goodbyes said I signaled the caravan to move out. Both the Admiral and I sensed we would never see each other on this side again. We were like two ships passing in the night. The journey to our new home was uneventful but tiring. After two weeks of work, everything was stacked in the outer courtyard of the mighty fortress high in the sky. There were ample quarters for all my people. The Hebrews were given a suite of rooms on the second level of the main building overlooking the courtyard. From our vantage point high on the plateau we had an unimpeded view of the surrounding countryside. In the distance I could see a grey river curving through a valley of green, lush vegetation. With Robert de Lille and the Grand Master's advisor, Rupert Didier, at my side, I pointed to the fertile valley.

"What think you of that land by the river? I believe it would make an ideal location for a village to be built. I believe a community could flourish there."

"What do you have in mind?" asked De Lille.

"If we are to remain in this land of the Turkmen, we must have a life for our people. A place we can live, prosper, grow a family, have an economy in order to survive. We must have more than just this gated keep for our people."

"I see what you mean," said Didier. "What would you have us do?"

"Take a troop of men, 25 or 30. Mix them – knights, sergeants, grooms, cooks. Ride to the valley, walk the land, test the water, see if it will be able to sustain buildings, stables, fields for cultivation. Find a place where our 400 or more can live a happy, full existence." Take two Hebrews with you. I want to include them in the process.

"I will select the people," said De Lille. "We will set out within the hour."

While they were gone my men worked on storing the treasure in the chambers of the castle. I conclude my discourse with these final words. It has been nine years since our escape from France. We have prospered in our new home. The castle is a strong sanctuary overlooking the vast countryside. The people flourish, men, women, children, happy families. We have an economy which provides for our needs. There are fertile farms, pastures for our animals, we continue to multiply. Some of the men have taken Turkish women as wives or companions. There are children growing in our midst. I have used three scribes to write this treatise, which

I hope will be understandable to the reader. The purpose, my purpose in recording this narrative is to assure whom ever comes to possess this work will understand that I have devoted my life to protecting that which belonged to the Temple, the wealth that was accumulated over 200 years. It is safe in its hiding place away from the evil clutches of the King of France and the false Church of Rome and Avignon. It is safe in purgatory and accessible only through water. Guy de Vaux, 1318.

"There you have it," said the rabbi, professor handing Mark two bundles. One the original transcript in its Arabic, Hebrew, Hittite script the other the written English translation. "There are no other copies," continued the rabbi. "I have destroyed all my notes. You now hold all that the brave knight transcribed some 700 years ago."

"Thank you for your effort. I am grateful for your work on my behalf," said Mark, reaching into his jacket pocket, removing a large wad of bills.

"There is no need for that, my son," said the rabbi. "My reward was in reading the story, in learning the journey and travels of those brave men. My greater pleasure would be in making it public to the world, to the Hebrew University library for others to share."

"That may come to pass someday," said Mark, "Just without any reference to the treasure. We shall see what time holds in store." Mark place 5,000 dollars American on the old man's desk. "Till we meet again," said Mark, picking up the papers, placing them into the leather pouch which he slung over his shoulder. "I'm off. Stay well, old wise man. I hope I live to see you again." Mark was two blocks from the house when he realized he had left his IDF backpack by the Rabbi's office door. In his elation at having the transcript in his possession, he had forgotten the Israeli Military backpack with his personal belongings. Not of much value, just some clothes and personal items but he decided to go back to get them. He walked to the front door of the stately house knocking gently. No one answered. *Strange*, he thought, since he knew the Rabbi's adopted son and assistant was at home. He knocked again, but still no one came to the door. Mark tried the door which opened silently to his touch. He stepped into the foyer standing quietly, listening before he moved. He could hear voices down the hall coming from the rabbi's study; Mark walked that way. When he came closer he could hear the sound of Zakari voice. The adopted son's voice was raised in anger. "Listen to me carefully old man. If you don't give me what I want, I will kill you since you will be of no use to me or my cause. I know you have been working on a translation having to do with the Templar's and their treasury. I have reported that information to my Hamas handlers in Ramallah. We want to claim the treasure for our own. The vast wealth will fund our war, our intifada against Israel, against Zionism, death to the Jew. We will wipe the land clean of Zionism; reclaim the country of Palestine for Islam. Give me the information I want or you will die by my hand."

"What has happened to you, Zakari? I took you into my house when you were an orphan, a poor waif of 10. I raised you as my son. I taught you English, Hebrew, had you bar mitzvah as a Jewish man. What happened to you? Where did I fail?"

"I'll tell you, old man. I am an Arab. I will always be an Arab who believes in Islam, the Quran, the true prophet Mohammed, all praise onto him and the one true god, Allah. I listened to you but laughed inside. You are not my father; you are just an old, stupid man. I played you as a musician plays a violin; and now I mean to collect my reward for the thirteen years I suffered under your roof." I never trusted you or the other Jews who came to you. I reported everything I learned to my faithful leaders in Gaza.

Mark eased up to the open doorway of the rabbi's study. Taking the pouch from his shoulder, he placed it gently onto the floor at his feet.

"Enough of this talk," said Zakari in an agitated voice. Give me what I want and I will leave. I will let you live out your useless life. If you defy me you will die now."

"My heart is sad, my son. Better I had died before I came to know such treachery. My years of caring for you, of hope for your future, for a better life, a peaceful existence. You have shattered my belief in goodness, kindness."

"Enough of this foolishness, yelled Zakari. "Give me what I demand or die, you old fool of a Jew."

Mark moved quickly. He stepped into the room behind Zakari, threw his left arm around the young man's neck, gripping his left wrist with his right hand pulling back sharply then leaning backward raising Zakari's feet from the floor, the man's slim body supported by Mark's chest and stomach. One shot went into the ceiling before the gun clattered to the floor. The young man's hands clawed at Mark's arms and hands in a vain attempt to release the strangle-hold clamped tightly around his neck. His feet kicked hard, hands clutched, as the choke-hold strangled the breath from the struggling man's body. After less than a minute the flopping ceased, the arms fell limp but Mark didn't release the pressure being applied to the windpipe. Another thirty seconds, finally Mark loosened his grip allowing the body of the now dead Arab to fall to the floor. There were tears in the old rabbi's eyes.

"Thank you my friend," he muttered in a weak, quivering voice. "I know you did what had to be done. Yet, it is most hurtful to me."

"I'm sorry rabbi. I saw no other way. He was a fanatic. A fanatic with a gun. If I didn't kill him, he would have killed us both."

"Yes, my Son. You are right. Now, you must go. Go at once. I will take care of our problem."

Mark slung his knapsack onto one shoulder. The leather pouch with the strap onto the other. The Old man's voice came to him as he walked down the hall. He heard the rabbi' speak into the phone: *This is Hok,* he said. *I need a cleaning crew at my cave, come at once.*

It was with a troubled heart Mark made his way to the sea to meet Alon. He felt bad over the killing of Zakari; although he knew it had to be done. It was the look of anguish on the rabbi's face that tugged at his heart. A man the rabbi had taken in as a child, raised, nurtured to be a man of faith, a good, kind caring individual. To see him as an angry brutal killer caused the old man insurmountable grief. He had loved the boy who was now a dead man lying on the floor of his study. He was a dead Arab fanatic, a blossoming terrorist. Yet Mark, someone the old rabbi knew for only one month, had killed this person the rabbi loved in front of his eyes. Mark could only hope the rabbi held no ill-will toward him. After all, as Mark said: *I had no choice.* The boat waited in the same place it had been a month ago, Alon standing at the bow of the sleek craft. He waved when he saw Mark approach the beach.

"I left the rubber dingy for you, row out to me."

Mark climbed onto the deck of the boat, the IDF backpack in his hand.

"Let's pull the dingy aboard. Help me," said Alon. "Then, we'll get underway."

"Where are we going" Mark asked, as the boat moved north through the calm Mediterranean – the coast of Israel slowly moving by on the starboard side.

"Let me tell you about my month alone first," said Alon. "It's been interesting, but the time seemed to move in slow motion. When I left you, I took a trip up the coast to Lebanon, a small coastal port called Hanikna. I met some Hezbollah leaders there. You know Hezbollah is in close kinship with Hamas in Gaza. Two terrorist organizations pledged to kill all Jews and make Israel Arab again. Hezbollah has access to all sorts of military weapons due to its close ties with Assad Basher, President of Syria. Hezbollah has thousands of warriors who are fighting alongside Bashers' troops in his fight against the rebels in their bloody civil war. Syria has close ties with Russia and Iran. Both those countries supply Hezbollah with every type military weapon they want. Some of these items end up in Hezbollah's arsenal in Lebanon. Meanwhile, Hamas is a distant poor relative. They are cut-off by Egypt and Israel, who impose strict embargos on any movement of arms into Gaza. This sets up a perfect scenario for me. I pick up the banned items in Lebanon; get paid by Hezbollah to transport them to Gaza, where Hamas pays me again upon delivery."

"I see," said Mark. "But doesn't it bother you to be dealing with Arab extremists who want to destroy Israel, to kill all Jews, your brothers and sisters, of which you are one."

"I'm just doing a job, I provide a service. I have no political affiliations. I'm a freelance entrepreneur Mark. Besides, if I don't do it someone else will. Anyway, I went to meet with Tawfiq Kakuda, who agreed to get the items the people in Gaza need; but it took much longer than we anticipated. Tawfiq had to contact his counterpart in Syria. That person had to assemble the supplies, locate transport to move it all into Lebanon, to the port where I sat waiting for more than two weeks. We didn't finish loading until yesterday afternoon. Because of the delay I had no time to make delivery before I had to come for you."

Are you telling me we are now carrying a load of weapons in the forward hold?"

"That's what I'm telling you," replied Alon. "Enough weapons to supply a small army. You should see what's down there. I could probably get upwards of 20 million dollars or Euros for that load on the open market. The Africans would kill for it."

"What are you getting for the delivery?"

"A mere pittance. Hezbollah paid me $150,000 to deliver the cargo. Hamas is paying me $250,000 upon delivery. I charge Hamas more since I don't like them very much. Also, they are the ones using the weapons to kill Jews and Egyptians."

"Then why are we heading north toward Lebanon instead of south to Gaza to unload this devils hoard?"

"Are you crazy, Mark? I wouldn't go near Gaza with this load. All the coast is under surveillance by Israeli ships, planes, and drones. The Israeli government knows of my illegal activities with drugs, whiskey, other nefarious items but not guns. It they caught me doing anything like this, they would blow me out of the water."

"Then how are we going to get rid of your cargo, and the sooner the better."

"Well Mark, first we're going up the coast to the port of Caesarea. A small port and city of only about 4,500 people. The port has had a tumultuous history, changed hands a dozen times over the years. Its only about twelve miles from Haifa, just 24 miles north of Tel Aviv. We'll be there by 7:30, where we'll spend the night. I'll buy us dinner in town, a good restaurant I know. I'll go in while you watch my boat and cargo. After a good meal we'll get a night's sleep then leave for our destination in the morning."

"And where would that be?" Mark asked.

"Rhodes," came the reply. "The beautiful island of Rhodes, Greece. Ever been?"

"No," said Mark.

"You'll love it, a true gem of an island. A quaint old city, beautiful beaches, excellent restaurants and lovely women walking around, some near naked. We will meet an old tramp steamer in the harbor where we will transfer our cargo. But enough talk for now. I'll fill you in with the details on the way to Rhodes. We're coming up to Caesarea. You take us into the pier. I'll get off and go for our dinner. Pull out and wait until I come back."

Alon was gone a little over two hours. I saw a car pull onto the pier, headlights blinking. I moved the boat back to the pier. Alon came aboard carrying a large cardboard box in his arms, a small plastic cooler gripped in his hand.

"That looks heavy," said Mark.

"I have food enough for the week. Really it is just for dinner, but it is enough for two or three nights. Take us out to the buoy. We can tie-up there until morning. Now let's go below and eat."

When Alon set the food on the table, I was amazed at the enormous amount.

"What the hell is all this?" Mark asked.

"I'll explain," said Alon. "The restaurant is run by an American ex pat. A Texan. A big Texan, about 6'4" add at least another inch for the crazy cowboy boots he wears. He says something about Lucchese Boots being the best boots in the world. They cost him 1,000 dollars a pair, orders them on-line. His name is big Al. I don't know if that's his real name, but that's what he goes by. He opened the place about 20 years ago; calls it the Texas Road House. People come from all over to eat there."

"If this food is any indication, I can see why. These steaks must weigh two pounds each," said Mark.

"Actually this one weighs 3 pounds,special for me. He has one-pounders, two-pounders and a larger one at 3½ pounds. They can naturally feed more than one person. I think a whole family could feed on a steak this size. Let's you and me split one, save the other for tomorrow. We have garlic mashed potatoes, cauliflower, and Heinz baked beans, plus two six-packs of Lone Star Beer."

"What's a spread like this cost?" asked Mark.

"For me it costs nothing."

"Nothing," Mark said startled. "In New York, you'd be looking at $250 or more for this feast."

"Let me explain. About twelve years ago, Nazim and I were having dinner in the Road House when some Lebanese thugs' barrged into the restaurant armed to the teeth. They landed on the beach in a rubber zodiac sailing down over the boarder. They rush into the restaurant shooting with automatic rifles. Five customers and two waiters were shot dead before we opened up with our Uzis. We killed all five terrorists. Since that day, Big Al calls us Maveth – death in Hebrew; he refuses to take my money. So enjoy your free dinner."

As we ate, Alon said, "You heard about my adventures over the past four weeks; now, tell me yours."

While enjoying one of the best steaks I could remember, I told my story. My studies at Hebrew University, the translation by rabbi Talal ben Aksimon, the fatal encounter with his adopted son. I explained the translation, which I had in the leather pouch, the translation that had almost caused the rabbi's death.

"Some story Mark. You've got mine beat by a mile, and you managed to kill another person. I think I will have to call you Dr. Maveth."

"Not so funny Alon. I had to do it, but I feel terrible for Talal."

"How much do you know of the rabbi, Mark?"

"Not very much. He is a brilliant man that I can tell you. He is old but very sharp and spry for his age. I like him. More than that, I trust him. He seems like a righteous, honorable human being."

"Would you like to know more about him?"

"You know him?" Mark asked.

"Very well for all my 51 years actually. He is my father's cousin. I always called him my uncle. His story, his life has been an interesting one full of conflicts, despair and regrets."

"It sounds like life," Mark interrupted. "Everyone is subject to doubt and disappointment."

"He had a normal childhood. In the 1930's in Palestine, as it was called then, Arab and Jew lived side-by-side in peace. He had many Arab friends while growing up. They went to school together, played together, ate or slept in each other's houses. Tal had an older brother; I think five years older, who watched out for him during their formative years. Talal's father was a school teacher in his village school in Ayot, a village only a few miles west of Jerusalem. The political climate began to change after the end of the Second World War. Thousands of Jews of European extraction, mostly from Eastern Europe, flooded into Israel. These were secular Jews. They had no concept of the Levant. They didn't know the history, culture or close assimilation of Arab and Jew, both Semitic people. The new Jewish settler, with some arrogance, began to put rules in place restricting Arab movements and quality of life. This caused tremendous resentment. After all, Palestine was their homeland also. The Arab people felt the policy should be live and let live. In the meantime, in order to protect the Jewish people from the British, who were ruling Israel after the war, the Jews formed a political party that was a semi-military force, the Haganah. It was meant to work with the British, who were in control of Palestine under the British mandate. The British Governor made it very hard on the Jewish people while siding with the Arabs. Haganah tried to be diplomatic in its workings with the British. This was not to the liking of more militant Israelis. Because of the friction two new groups were born. Actually there were many small splinter groups but it was these two that came to the fore in military operations. One was the Irgun, which had many members who fought for the Brits during WW II in Italy. It was called the Jewish Brigade of the British Army. Many of these Jewish soldiers had distinguished combat records. The other group was the Palmach. The Palmach was even more deadly than the Irgun. Its members meant to oppose the British military by constant pressure and armed attacks on the British troops stationed in Israel. The Palmach also filled a role in protecting Jewish citizens from attacks or harassment by extreme Arab groups. There were many gangs rebelling against the Jewish settlers. The Arabs would ambush people, kill indiscriminately, burn houses buses or cars. I give you this as background information because of what follows. One day in March 1946, while Talal's father and older brother were coming home to supper from school they were surrounded and abducted by a blood thirsty gang of Arab men. Its estimated there were about twelve Arabs armed with knives, at least a few had guns. The two Jews were marched into an open field where they were tortured then killed. Talal's father was beheaded, the brother castrated. The teen age boy went wild with rage. He couldn't understand how Arabs, his friends, could kill a good man like his father. A teacher a man who gave his life to teaching Arab and Jew alike. In his grief and anguish, Talal found hate for those who had committed the heinous crime. It didn't take him long to find a release for his rage. He was seventeen years-old when he joined the Palmach to avenge the death of the father and brother he loved. He decided his brother's life was worth that of 50 Arabs, his father's at least 100. That was his goal. Kill 150 Arabs for his brother and father, a fitting revenge for their deaths. Nothing less would do.

"Did he do that?" asked Mark. "Kill 150 Arabs."

"No one knows for sure but the old man himself. It is known he was a prodigious fighter, who killed many Arabs. Then the war of Independence started in 1948. The Palmach was brought under control of the Haganah. Three divisions were formed; military order was instilled. The Palmach became part of the Israeli Army. One of the divisions was called Harel Brigade, under the command of a leader named Yitzhak Rabin, who later became Prime Minister. The Harel Brigade fought in and around Jerusalem until the Arabs capitulated. I'm told Tal distinguished himself in combat many times. Now, with the war ended, Israel independent, a sovereign country, some semblance of order returned."

"Yes," said Mark. "Some degree of peace but still sporadic fighting - much unrest, much dissension."

"You know," said Alon. "This country of Palestine, Israel – whatever name – it's still the same land. This land has been at war for over 5,000 years. Every century through the ages, dozens of countries have fought here. The land is saturated with blood from many tribes, sects, groups. It may be the way of the world. Maybe it's God's plan that the Holy Land will always be conflicted. But I digress. It seems that after the War of Independence, Tal had had enough. Enough blood shed, fighting, death and misery. He decided he would kill no more unless in self-defense. First, he went to college for a degree, philosophy, I think. While studying, he found many varied ideas, from Plato to Karl Marx. He studied them all: Kant, Nietzsche, Sartre, Descartes, Spinoza, you name them. Then while sitting in a lecture one day, he had, what do you call it, an epa- epith."

"The word is: epiphany," said Mark.

"Yes, that's it," that's the word. "He had a sudden realization of what his life should be. He would dedicate it to the betterment of mankind. He would become a holy man. Since he was a Jew that meant a rabbi. He was 19 when the war ended, 23 when he got his degree in Philosophy from Hebrew University. At 24, he enrolled in Masorti Yeshiva in Jerusalem. It takes four to six years to graduate yeshiva and be ordained a rabbi; he did it in three, almost unheard of. It's not called graduation. In the yeshiva you are a Semicha, one authorized to teach. A rabbi is a teacher of the Torah. The term rabbi means master or great one. So at 27 years of age, Talal ben Aksimon was a Ha Ran, a Master, a leader of men. He didn't want to find a temple, a synagogue to lead. He felt he would be tied down with the same congregant's week-to-week. He wanted to be like Jesus walking among the masses, dispensing knowledge to any who would listen. It didn't feel right or fit his perception of things to do otherwise. He needed an informal atmosphere, not a restrictive one."

"What did he do?" Mark asked impatiently.

"He went to the Army, to an officer he had served under, whom now – eight years later – had moved up in the chain of command. He asked Yigal Allon, an officer from Tal's old Palmach unit, to get him a commission as a military chaplain. He was given a commission in the IDF, where he began speaking with the rank and file troop. Men who had religious principles, honored society and God, but were asked, no ordered to kill. Tal was only too familiar with these contradictories – he had lived them. So now, he tried to help the young solders, only eight or ten years younger than himself, to handle these contradictions. In 1956, he went to the front-line in the Suez War, marching through the Sinai with the front line troops – his minions. I understand he saved many lives - both spiritually and physically – tending wounded as they died, while ministering to their souls. By '61, he was done with the Army and being a rabbi. He went back to school to study."

"What now?" asked Mark.

"Your name it," continued Alon. "He studied Ancient religion, societies of thousand years past. He studied in Iraq, Iran, Syria, even Pakistan and Egypt. During his travels his reputation grew along with his knowledge. By 1974 he was being asked to lecture in colleges and universities around the world. Because of his expertise he associated with other learned scholars in other universities in foreign countries. There was a vast informal network of professors throughout the Middle East who would meet regularly to talk, to share information and Talal was one of them. They had to be careful where he was concerned since he was a Jew. He was a heathen to the masses of people in the Middle East, but not to his scholarly brothers. They loved him for his ideas, his forward-thinking, his love for his fellow man, but mostly for his sharp mind and grasp of reality. He returned to Israel in 1976. He was offered a professorship in Humanities at Hebrew University, his old college, his Alma Mater. Within two years he was the most popular professor on campus. People were signing up for his courses a semester in advance. I understand students were coming from other colleges in other countries to attend his classes. They came from Damascus, Cairo, Baghdad, Teheran he was becoming one of the best known academic minds in the world. He claims he owes it all to his father. A wise man who taught young waifs in elementary school. This was your friend Tal. I was 19 when I enrolled in Hebrew University. I came from a small town in the Galilee. I took a course in my uncle's class in my freshman year, Humanities 101; I was fascinated. He brought the subject to life, made you want to study, learning became fun. In my sophomore year I took two more courses taught by him, Ancient History and the Crusades. In my junior year he was teaching a course in Comparative Religion, teaching about the three main religions in the world – Christianity, Islam and Judaism. It was fascinating stuff, things no one thinks about, much less espouses. During these three years I had formed a friendship with another student whose name was Yaakov Yellin. We took many of the same courses together. We began to study together, and in our junior year moved into a dorm-room together. We became inseparable friends. Sometime near the middle of our senior year we passed a question to our scholarly professor. This was a profound question about the Iranian Ayatollahs regime and their relations with America and Israel."

"My bright students," said the professor. "That is a deep and perplexing question, one that will need hours of conversation to answer adequately."

"So what do you propose?" asked Yaakov.

"Come to my home for dinner tonight. We will discuss your question then."

"My friend and I were elated. A private dinner with the most eminent professor in the University, in all Israel, all the Middle East, maybe even the world. Remember, we were still impressionable 20 year-olds. We arrived at his campus house at 7 for dinner. There was a black; American Chrysler New Yorker parked on the street in front of the house, two men sitting in the front seat. We knocked on the door which was opened by a young woman."

"You must be Alon and Yaakov. Come in, they are waiting for you."

I looked at Yaakov. "They I asked?"

"He must have brought company for protection," Yaakov said.

The girl laughed. "No, just an old friend who comes to eat with the professor periodically. Come, I'll bring you into the dining room."

Two men sat at a table set for four. The professor and another gentleman dressed in a dark suit, open-necked dress white shirt.

"Come gentlemen, sit. This is a friend of mine," said the professor. "This is Alon and Yaakov, two of my erudite students with some important questions for me. Let's eat while we talk."

"I noticed Talal didn't introduce his other guest, no name, nothing. The young women served us. Her name was Hanna. The professor called her Hannapescal. We drank three bottles of good Israeli red wine from the Negev, one that had been on the table when we arrived, plus two Yaakov brought as a house gift. At 9:30, the man stood at his place.

"Thank you for inviting me Hok." He then turned to address us: "I understand from my friend Hok, you will finish University in four months. If you want a job after graduation just tell the Hok, he knows how to reach me."

It was less than two weeks until graduation, May 12, 1988, when there was a knock on our dorm room door. Yaakov opened the door wearing a black t-shirt with black jeans, his usual attire.

"Hello," he said in surprise. "What are you doing here?"

I looked up from my bed to see Professor Aksimon standing at our door. I jumped up. "Please come in Professor. It's a bit messy, please sit at my desk."

'"No, no. I don't mean to disturb you. But you graduate in two weeks, then it is off to who knows where. I wanted to ask if you had given any thought to my friend's offer made at my house months ago. You remember, he offered you a job upon graduation."

"We thought about it but haven't come to a decision. We don't even know what he is offering."

"He called me this morning," continued Tal. "He would very much like to talk to you both, explain things to you personally."

I looked at Yaakov. "What do you say brother?"

He shrugged his shoulders, "Why not. After all he is a friend of the professor's, the Hok.

"Oh, so you remember," smiled Talal. "Here is his address on this card. Go there at 10 in the morning. He will be glad to see you. Give him my regards." With that, he smiled, shook our hands then left.

CHAPTER 36

"We couldn't afford a cab," continued Alon. "So we took a bus, and then walked five city blocks to the address 1866 Alfasel."

"Kind of out of the way, don't you think Yaakov?"

"Yes, definitely not the high-rent district."

The buildings were plain grey stone, five or six stories high, one looking just like its neighbor on either side.

"This is it," I said. "Let's go in; you know, nothing ventured nothing gained."

The lobby was vast, high ceilings, stone floors with a desk in the center of the vestibule where an old man wearing a yarmulke sat waiting. "Can I help you?" he asked in a cracking voice.

"Yes," replied Yaakov. "We are here to see Israel Ballin."

"Ah, you must be Alon and Yaakov, he is expecting you. Walk down the corridor behind me to the end. Knock; I'll let him know you are coming."

Yaakov knocked loudly on the door. A muffled voice called out: "Come in."

He walked around his desk to greet us, right hand extended. "Welcome," he said. "Welcome to my humble office. Come in, sit please. Can I offer you tea, coffee, water, anything?"

"I was surprised to hear Yaakov ask for tea, some cream and sugar, please; definitely out of character for my friend. The door opened to admit a young woman carrying a tray. It was the same young woman who had served us in the Professor's house some months ago."

"Hello again," I said. She just smiled and left.

"So you remember Anna," said Ballin.

"Look Israel, or Mr. Ballin," Yaakov said. "How do we address you? What do you want to be called?"

"Anything you want is fine by me. My usual title is Director. You can call me that if you wish."

"Director of what?" asked Yaakov.

"Let me ask you young man, are you always like this?"

"Like what," replied Yaakov defiantly.

"Well direct, bordering on rude."

"He is always very to the point, Mr. Director; impatient, aggressive, but not rude."

"Just Director Alon; no Mister."

"Yes sir."

"Now, let me answer your question. Do you know where you are?"

"Sure. 1866 Alfasel Street," said Yaakov.

"Yes, but do you know what this building is? What goes on here?"

"No, we both answered."

"That's good; that is how it should be. This building is Headquarters to a branch of Mossad. Are you familiar with that term, Mossad?"

"Just in a vague way, I responded. It's like the American CIA."

"Yes, to a degree but more complex than that. It's like the CIA, FBI, NAS and Homeland Security rolled into one organization. There are six departments in Mossad, each with its own area of expertise and responsibility. This building is home to the Third Department. I am its Director."

"We sat looking at the man in silence, waiting to hear what he would say next. After ten seconds of silence, he began again."

"I want you both to apply for entry into Mossad as new recruits. If you do, you will begin a six-month training course, a course you must pass to move on to one of the six departments. I will claim you for mine; you will then belong to me." At that point your real training will begin.

"What Department are you Director of, Director?" asked Yaakov.

"I run the Third Department, Special Ops. We do the dirty work that must be done to keep Israel safe. To insure Israel will survive."

"Special Operations," said Yaakov. "You mean undercover work, assassinations, kidnappings, things like that."

"Yes, the Director smiled. "Things like that. The pay is adequate, the hours varied, travel is a bonus, well sometime. I can promise you the work is interesting. You won't be bored."

"How many people are in your Department?"

"I can't tell you. It's not that I don't know; I do; but that's secret. Let's just say more than one less than 200. We're very selective."

"Why us?" asked Yaakov.

"Well first, you dress the part young man, always in black. You are either an undertaker, a gangster or killer."

Yaakov colored slightly.

"It's because of your uncle," Ballin continued. He recommended the two of you. He said you would make excellent agents, smart, inquisitive, but also cool in stressful situations. He feels you are imaginative and can adapt quickly to changing situations. After spending 3 hours at dinner with you, I agreed. That is why you are sitting with me this morning. So now to the close, what do you have to say regarding my offer,?"

We looked at each other.

"When do you want to know by?" asked Yaakov.

"When is graduation?" the director asked.

"May 22nd, Friday; ten days away."

"Then how about May 25th Monday, Is that sufficient?"

"Yes," I said. "But what does the Professor have to do with Mossad?"

"Ah, said the Director. What I tell you now I tell you this in strict confidence. Forget what I say when you walk out my door. Consider this your first test because if I ever hear you have mentioned this to anyone I'll have one of my agents terminate you. Or better yet I may do it myself. I recruited Hok in 1980, like I'm recruiting you now. Someone brought him to my attention, I don't remember who; it's not important only the results are. Here was this renowned person becoming famous even then. Think about it; he spoke who knows how many languages, both ancient and modern. The man had been to every country in the Middle East, some in Asia and Europe. He was greeted everywhere by governments, scholars, academics. He knew politics, philosophy, psychology and people. He is a true humanist. I sat thinking for only a few seconds before I realized what an asset this man could be if only he would be. Aside from everything else, the Hok is a true patriot. He is a man of the world, but he loves Israel.

Especially the Israel he knew as a boy, as a young man growing up. An Israel that was but will never be again. He was an active member of Special Operations for twelve years serving in various capacities. Then he became a Sayanim. Do you know that word, do you know what a Sayanim is.?"

"No, we both replied."

"It's like a sleeper. Someone who is there for you when you need him or his special talent, but is otherwise not there. That's what our Rabbi is today, and I love him. No, we all love him. You have no idea what that man has accomplished for his country over the years. So that's it, I'm finished with my spiel. Go back to campus, think about my proposal. Let me know by the 25th. Shalom."

"So on the 25th of May, we called Director Ballin, Yaakov said two words, we're in."

"Take a week to enjoy yourselve's, then report to this address on Monday, June 1 at 8 a.m. It is our training facility at Herzilya. You will meet your new instructor at the Midrasha, the training academy. His name is Sampson Hecker He'll be expecting you. The address was an army depot, really a commando training facility, and Sampson was a British block of granite."

"Ok Ladies. Your ass is now mine until you graduate or quit. Alon, Yaakov, which is which?" he asked.

"I'm Alon."

"Then the visage in black must be Yaakov."

"No," he answered defiantly.

"What do you mean no?"

"There are only two of you. So you must be Yaakov."

"That is not my name, not any longer." From this moment on I disavow that name.

"What are you talking about man? Don't make my job any harder than it already is or I'll break you in two."

"I never liked the name Yaakov, too ethnic, makes me sound like a weak Jew which I'm not. Since today is the first day of a new time in my life I get to choose my name, not my father or mother."

"So my brave new warrior," Sampson smirked, hand on hips, lips parted revealing white teeth. "What is your new numen?"

"My name henceforth is Nazim. Nothing more; just Nazim."

"Very well," said Sampson. "I'll make a note. Yaakov is no more; he is now Nazim. Let's go to work."

"That night in our room, more like a cell, two beds, a wooden desk and one chair. I looked at my old friend sitting across from me. This was a man I'd been with for four years, someone I knew well."

"What's gotten into you, Yaak?" I asked. He glared at me.

"I told you, no more Yaakov, from this day forth it's Nazim."

"Alright alright what's with this new name?"

"Open your eyes Alon. See the reality of our situation, a situation we have chosen for ourselves. From this day on we are training to become killers. For a just cause hopefully, but killers nonetheless. That means in a year we will be trained assassins. Do you know anything about the assassins, Alon?"

"Just what you said, Nazim. Assassins are assassins."

"Yes Alon, but I'm talking about 'the assassins.' The Medieval Nazari Islamills. The group from Persia and Syria that existed in the 11th Century, are you familiar with them?"

"No, I don't think I ever heard about them."

"Neither did I until one day Professor Talal and I were speaking of the Crusades and ancient warriors. He told me about a group of fighters called the assassins. They were deadly killers led by a man named Sabbah. He called his men Fidain Nazari, which means faithful killers. These men were a patient, cold and calculating band. Obedient to their leader to death. They killed with many weapons, but preferred the knife. Many of the killings were carried out in broad day-light to intimidate people. The assassins never harmed innocents or civilians. Their targets were always ruthless leaders, rulers or people whose elimination would reduce aggression or violence in the world."

"Noble principles," I affirmed.

"Yes, and one of the most ruthless and efficient assassins was named Nazim. Now, I pick up his mantle. I will be the best assassin in all Mossad that I promise you here and now."

"Nazim, I think your heart is as black as the clothes you choose to wear."

Nazim smiled at me. "We are going to be like the Ninja from Japan, or the Sicari. The dagger-man of ancient Israel, look them up."

"I won't bore or trouble you with our exploits of the following years," Alon continued. Just let me say true to our illustrious recruiter, Director Ballin, we lived varied, exciting and dangerous lives. After four years, we were both transferred to a special branch within our special branch, the Kiddon. There were only 49 people in this ultra-elite special unit. It consisted of a group of expert assassins, the best of the best led by a fearless, imaginative leader. A leader who had been a member of Israel's special forces before being picked for his post. One bright, sunny morning at the beginning of September, Nazim and I were on a morning run just to stay sharp. It was only 8:30 on a day that was quickly turning hot. We ran down a narrow dirt road intending to run about ten or twelve miles on a summer day that promised to become a scorcher by noon. We were just getting into a rhythm after covering about a mile over rough ground when both our beepers went off simultaneously. A small red light and a buzz coming from a tiny plastic box half the size of a pack of cigarettes which we carried at our waist at all times."

"His Master's voice," said Nazim, slowing to a walk, sweat dripping from my brow and nose.

"What did you do now?" I asked.

"I don't know. Should we go find out?"

"I guess we'd better; or someone will come looking for us."

"We walked into Ori's office dripping sweat having run hard to get back quickly knowing we weren't going to get ten miles in today."

"You look good," Ori said smiling. "Keeping in shape; excellent since you will need to be to complete this easy mission I have for you. Donna – bring two towels for my prize fighters," he yelled to his assistant, an attractive female agent on loan from the collection department. She walked into the room with two towels, handing one to each of us.

"Ok," Ori said. "Tell my best operators what you told me an hour ago. Sit my boys. this will take a little time. The collections department, known as Department 1, which was the largest of the 6 departments of Mossad with about 280 employees was responsible for gathering information which could be critical to Israel's safety from around the world. They have agents everywhere, it's rumored even in the North Pole. The agents who worked under cover overseas were referred to as Katsa, a Hebrew word that means a collection officer. We received a coded message from an agent in Jordan she began. It came from a small village named Karak, a village just a few miles from the West Bank of Israel. The agent is in the Daivdean Unit in the West Bank."

"I know it," said Nazim. "The counter-intelligence unit."

"Yes," said Donna. "This is what he relayed to us before he was discovered and caught. We think he is dead. There is a meeting being planned to take place in the Gaza Strip between nine or ten high-ranking Arab leaders. Two are coming from Lebanon through Syria into Jordan, where they will join up with two more in Karak. We have the names of the four, their profiles are in our data-base, they are all very bad actors. The Lebanese are Hezbollah, the other two al Qaeda. There are three Hamas members in Gaza who will be joining the others. This bad-boy conference is to take place in Gaza. One Fatah militant from Arafat's band of killers by the name of Imed Mugahni will also be present to represent Arafat. The meeting is due to take place sixteen days from now in a small village in the Gaza Strip."

"Do you have the name of this village?" asked Nazim.

"Yes. Abasan Al Kaleria. It is a small village near the larger city of Khan Yuniz."

"Great," said Nazim I know of it, a dangerous area of Gaza. "Now what?"

"Thanks," Donna said. "Ori, I can take it from here. Let me know if you get any more Intel."

"When she was gone, Ori turned to us."

"There it is, boys. I'm giving this one to you."

"I just sat back, trying to stop from laughing since I knew what was coming."

"What!" yelled Nazim. Just what the hell are you giving us? An invitation to die in Gaza?"

"Ori was only slightly shocked by this outburst; he knew Nazim's temperament after all our years together. He'd been working with us for nine years now. It was like being in a cage with a lion, an angry temperamental lion. You had to know how to tame him, quiet him down, then get him to do what you wanted. Very tricky, difficult, but Ori was good at his job, that's why he sat at his desk."

"Nazim, it is a mission. Some missions are more difficult than others but we always find a way to accomplish them. Now tell me, what is bothering you?"

"A lot of things about this one, and we haven't even scratched the surface yet."

"Let me give you my thoughts first continued Ori in a calm conciliatory tone. We have sixteen days before this meeting is to take place. That gives us plenty of time to work out the details. I'm sure we can come up with a plan that will satisfy you.

"For the next two weeks, the three of us spent ten hours a day going over maps, reports, air recon photos to remove any doubts that might exist. But as minus -3 day dawned, while the pressure mounted, neither Nazim nor I felt the usual confidence or enthusiasm we normally experienced as jump-off for a mission approached. Then it got worse. The word came down from above said Ori during our morning briefing."It's going to be a seven-man mission. Nazim, you're the head-master, you lead. Alon, your second in command. You will have five men in your detail for a total of seven."

"Not bad odds, only about 20 or 25-to-1," said Nazim.

"How do you figure that?" asked Ori.

"Come on man don't take me for a fool. You told us there will be nine or ten bad guys, real bad guys. Is that right?"

"Yes," replied Ori.

"These men are from at least four different political and ethnically diverse groups. Am I right again?"

"Yes."

"Do you think they trust each other since each wants to be top-dog, and dog-eat-dog as the saying goes."

"What are you getting at Nazim spit it out?"

What I'm telling you is this. Each of those leaders will bring his own bodyguards for protection – probably 10 or 12 men, a squad of fierce killers dedicated to keep their boss alive. Ten leaders, 12 men each equal 120 armed killers. Now Arafat called for the meeting right? If anything happened to any of these men while in his area of control he would be held responsible. I'm right again so you need not answer; I think Arafat will send troops loyal to him to stand guard over the entire encampment; maybe another 40 or 50 heavily-armed well trained fighters under competent leadership. I think I'm up to 200 or more fighting men. And you propose to send seven men into that hornet's nest?"

"Actually six men and one woman," replied Ori.

"Nazim was on his feet in an instant pointing a finger at our commander. He spoke slowly, leaning forward, voice low, muscles taut, the position I knew to be his most lethal."

"Listen to me carefully Ori, If you think I'm going on a suicide mission with that girl you're crazy."

"Nazim, that girl, as you call her, is a vetted member of our team. She's been in the field before and proved her worth. She performed well in combat conditions and is highly regarded by her peers."

Those missions were easy compared to what you are proposing here. I'm not being a chauvinist or knocking women. But in reality they are not equal in strength or capability in hand-to-hand combat, which this could turn into."

"You talk to him, Alon."

"No Ori, you choose him leader; let him lead."

Ori tried again. "She can run like a deer."

"A doe," said Nazim.

"She is an excellent marksman, a qualified sniper. Most importantly she wants to go. She volunteered for the mission. The brass wants her to go. Do you know what that means, Nazim?"

"Yes," he replied. "It means she goes."

"Exactly. Now, let's get down to the actual operation. Your team will board a fishing trawler at a dilapidated pier in a desolate part of the harbor away from prying eyes. You will board,2 days from today at three in the afternoon on the 8th of September. Six men, one woman and one rubber inflatable.

"A naval vessel?" I asked.

"No, a real fishing trawler with a civilian crew. The captain of boat is lending it to us for this operation. Mossad is paying him for the use of the boat and crew. The officer in charge will be a qualified Israeli naval officer who will stand next to the captain directing his every move. The trawler will set out down the coast sailing about four miles off shore to a point here," said Ori, placing his finger on a large map of Gaza. "Al Mawasi is a small fishing village on the coast. The naval officer in charge will put your boat over the side at 9 p.m. It's supposed to be a dark night, no moon. You will land about two miles south of Al Mawasi on a deserted sandy beach. We're giving you an hour to reach shore so you should be on the beach by 10. Your target is due east in-land about nine miles. The village of Abasan Al Kabira. That's where the meeting is being held. Sink your boat when you reach shore. Then –"

"Hold it, if we sink the boat how are we coming out," demanded Nazim.

"I'll explain, let me go on. We estimate it will take you four hours to cover the nine miles in the dark. You don't know the terrain, so I'm allowing four hours. I've added another hour to get into position to carry out the actual attack. You strike at 3 a.m. Hopefully, they will all be asleep by then. At 3:15, a helicopter will land at this spot marked with a red *X*. It will wait for you until you arrive then fly you home."

"Wait one minute," I said, looking at the map. "That spot looks to be about a mile further east of the village. That means after we attack, after all the troops are awake and fighting mad, since we have now killed their bosses, we have to advance another mile to reach our ride home."

"That's about it," said Ori.

"I must tell you Major, that's about the most fucked up plan I've ever seen. Some arm-chair tactician dreamed this up. I don't think it has a chance of working." Ori glared at Nazim a cold look in his eye.

"But you will make it work, Nazim. After all you are the deadliest of all warriors."

"I will do it Major, for you I will do it. But I want you to know I have put my ass on the line many times in the past. It has been snapped at more than once. Someday it's bound to get bitten. I just hope it's not this time."

CHAPTER 37

We spent the next day going over our plan of infiltration, attack and exit with the five members of our team. Each team member was given an abbreviated name to go by. Nazim was Naz and I was Alon like my name. Benjamin was Bet. Gorden was Gordo and Kafir was Kaf. These three were all veterans. Each with six years or more in Kiddon, they were hardened combat troops. Elliot was the younger member. He had been a para in a secret commando operation into Gaza two years ago, where he had distinguished himself in battle. The story is he saved two wounded comrades, carrying them to a waiting helicopter, then lay down cover fire until the chopper was loaded and lifted off. Because of that action, he was asked to join special ops. This was his first deployment with Kaddan. Naz was going to keep him close. Elliot got the name Pie. Then there was our lone female, Miriam which was easy, Mem for M. On Tuesday morning, September 8th, we met at the armory at 11 o'clock to pick weapons and our equipment for the night incursion.

"Listen up," I said. "The six of us are taking Colt M16 A4 automatic rifles, the latest model M16 courtesy of our uncle in America. That way we all carry the same ammo."

"What about him?" asked Miriam, pointing to Nazim.

"He's the leader; he takes anything he wants. If anyone wants a second weapon, pick what you like." The four men chose to take only their M16's.

"You," I said to Mem. "I was told you are an excellent marksman. Is that correct?"

"Yes, I even went to sniper school, qualified as a marksman." "I Scored 98 out of 100."

"Good, then get a Galatz sniper rifle with a night scope and a few ten-shot mags. You'll carry it on your back keep the M16 handy as your primary weapon. Who knows, the Galatz might prove useful."

"Yair – I said to the young armory sergeant handing out the equipment. "Let me have my marching gear."

"Coming right up, Alon." I turned to see Miriam struggling to put a large back-pack over her shoulders.

"What the hell are you doing girl?" I asked.

"Getting my gear on," she replied.

"Look you beauty, we are going out for about sixteen hours, we should be back here by 5 in the morning. You don't need all that make-up and cream. Just essentials, bare essentials; drop that rucksack now."

"Here you are, Alon," said Yair. "You're special battle vest?"

"Do you have a spare, like I asked you?"

"Actually I made two more, exactly like yours."

"Get me one, Yair. Fit it onto this trooper, next to me."

"What am I wearing?" asked Miriam.

"It's light weight battle vest. You will find it comfortable and practical. It fits snug. I designed it myself a few years ago. I call it a combat vest. Five pouches in front for spare thirty-round ammo magazines, 150 rounds. Mine has fourteen loops for shotgun shells since I'm strapping a Mossberg 590 twelve-gauge to my back. The gun holds nine shells. I have fourteen to reload. These two pockets on the side are for First Aid kits; I carry two kits, that way I have enough bandages to treat a wounded comrade. And last, two net bags, one on each side at my hips for plastic water bottles. You must stay hydrated in the field to fight effectively. Metal canteens are bulky, make noise when you run, and in my experience the water always tastes awful, metallic. I slung the shotgun onto the flat back of my vest."

"Here's your Jericho 941," said Yair, handing me my IWI Jerhico 45 caliber pistol in a dark leather shoulder holster.

"Alright team, let's move out to the van I ordered, time to head to the docks for our little sea voyage." Nazim led the way into the bright sunshine where a black van sat waiting, rear barn doors open, a female driver standing smiling at us.

"Watch your step up," she said, offering a hand where needed.

Miriam came walking up to the van, a steel pot helmet in her hand.

"Now what girl, you can't wear that tonight. It's only good to cook in or shit in, which do you intend to use it for?"

She turned red and stuttered. "But my head."

"You can't possibly wear that thing where we're going. We will be running about ten miles to reach the camp. A helmet will jump all over your head. The beak will bruise you, maybe even break your nose. When it comes time to shoot it will fall over your eyes and blind you. It will be a big distraction. Give it to this lovely lady at the door. If you want something for your head, get a wool beanie or a doo-rag!"

"A what?"

"Just forget it; here put this Keffiyeh around your neck."

"It's too warm for that Alon."

"Then tie it around your waist for now. It will be cold in the desert tonight. Trust me, it will come in handy for many reasons."

She looked around; everyone had a Keffiyeh in some color or design. My Shemagh was black and white checkered pattern like the Palestinian militants wore. Mem's was olive, brown and black. Nazim's, of course, was pure black, just like the black SAS combat-gear he was wearing down to the black boots which he stuffed with sand-paper to dull the shine. We climbed into the back of the closed van taking our place on the hard metal benches down each side, I continued telling Mem about some other uses for a Shemagh.

"There are a hundred uses I'm sure, but consider just these half-dozen – protection from dust or sun a towel, sling, wrap for warmth, a pillow, a weapon, rope, emergency bandage. A scarf for warmth"

"Ok, ok, I get it; enough."

The van stopped with a lurch, motor shut down, all was quiet. The barn doors swung open, our driver standing at the opening. Time to move on she chided, hope you enjoyed the ride.

"I had my Oakley wrap-around sunglasses on since I know I would be blind stepping from the dark truck into bright sunlight. I took two steps when a body slammed into my back pushing me forward. I struggled to remain upright."

"Sorry," Mem said. "I couldn't see you."

"It's alright, you walk ahead of me I'll feel safer that way."

We were at a deserted end of a harbor. Derelict boats lay scattered on land and in the water. Some partial sunk or resting on the bottom in the brackish stagnant water. We walked down the pier to an old rusting fishing boat tied to the crumbling cement pier. A boarding gang-way connecting the boat to the dock. We started walking to the boat, Mem walking in front of me, the others coming behind. Climbing up to the deck above I looked up, my head even with Miriam's lush rounded backside. *Damn, that's a nice ass*, I thought, looking at her as a woman for the first time. I felt myself getting hard thinking about her lush body. I was wondering what I could do with that body in the right circumstance. *Down boy*, I thought, *You have more important things to concentrate on.* Two men were standing on deck at the top of the gangway awaiting our arrival. One was a grizzled old fisherman with a trimmed grey beard, a greasy sea-cap perched on his head. Next to him stood a young man of maybe 20 in a smart blue naval uniform, white officer's cap with a shiny black bill. *New*, I thought, *just out of the box.* An Arab seaman came over in response to the Captain's call. They spoke in Hebrew.

"Take these people below to the main cabin ordered the captain." The seaman led the five troops away as Nazim walked up to join us.

"I am the Captain of this boat. My name is Golam. This is my boat, The Pequod, like in Moby Dick." Don't call me Ahab, captain will do fine.

"Shit," I said to Nazim. "I hope we don't have the same fate as the Pequod."

Nazim looked at the pale young naval officer standing meekly next to weathered captain. "Don't tell me you are our guide; please tell me it can't be."

"Ensign David Dovar Sir, Israeli Navy; you're pilot and guide for tonight."

"Good God, Ensign. How old are you? How long have you been an ensign?"

"I'm 20, Sir. Graduated from the naval academy two months ago."

"Have you ever been on an incursion?" asked Nazim. "A combat mission, anything except a summer sail?"

"No Sir," he said, trying to stand straighter; my first mission Sir and I'm ready."

Nazim just shook his head.

"Nothing will go wrong, Sir. I've been briefed thoroughly. I know what to do. I know what is expected of me, I'm ready sir. I will put you ashore in the exact spot. I have it in my hand-held GPS."

Nazim put his hand to his head, pulling off his black beret. "God help us," he muttered under his breath.

"I'm going to speak with the Captain in the pilot house Alon. You get the troops settled in. I'll be down to join you shortly." There were 3 double decked bunks in the forward compartment, five bodies already resting in them, one empty for me. A top bunk conveniently above Mem.

At 2:30, Ori came into the compartment with Nazim. "Ok troops, this is the big one," said the Major. I just want to wish you all good luck. You are being led by the best warrior in all of Israel. Follow his lead, he will bring you safely home to me for breakfast at 5 on the base – steak, eggs and champagne." I'm buying. That got a laugh from the team, the last laugh that day. They turned to go back on deck. I heard the engines start, the boat began to shudder preparing to get underway.

"I'm going on deck to watch Israel drift away I said. I like to remember how beautiful it is."

"I'll join you if you don't mind Alon," said Mem, sliding from her bunk.

"Come on then, but promise not to knock me overboard."

As the land receded on the horizon a cool breeze began to blow over the deck, I turned to go below.

"See if you can take a nap," Miriam, it's going to be a long night. I climbed into my bunk pulling my Keffiyeh over my eyes so I could get some sleep."

Nazim woke me at 8:10; I'd slept for three hours.

"Let's get ready number 2; we go over the side in fifty minutes."

I checked each man to be sure they had everything and were ready to go into Gaza, into the jaws of death. On deck, we inflated the seven-man black rubber raft. Pei-Elliot and Beit attached the small, twenty horsepower outboard engine to the motor plate mounted on the rear of the raft. We had about three miles to motor to reach the beach. The motor would take us to a point about 700 yards from shore; we would paddle the rest of the way. We dropped the rubber boat over the starboard side of the trawl, the seaward side, keeping two lines attached to cleats on the deck of the Pequod. My underwater watch ticked toward 9:00 when I heard a loud commotion on the bridge.

"Stay put," I said to the troops. "I'll be right back."

Nazim was growling at the young naval ensign. "What do you mean your GPS isn't working? You told me you would put me right on the debarkation spot."

The young Ensign was almost in tears. "I don't know what happened," he cried. "I checked the program a half hour ago, it was working fine. It says to go in sixty seconds. I say go," ordered the frightened seaman.

"No," said the Captain, "It is too soon. Another twenty minutes at least. I have been sailing this coast over forty years. I can smell Al Mawasi from my deck, we are not there yet. I will tell you when it's time to go. I am in charge of this mission, yelled the ensign. I order you to go now." He was screaming at Nazim, not a good move on his part.

"If you're wrong you little shit, I promise you I'll come to find you and cut your prick off. That is if you have one you poor excuse for an INF officer!"

"Let's go, Alon."

"Wait," implored captain Golam. "Too soon, another fifteen minutes until we pass the fishing village, listen to me, wait." But we were gone over the side into the inflatable, the motor purring quietly. We cast off the lines making for shore four miles away. The Pequod slowly becoming a dark shape sailing off into the black night. After 15 minutes Pei shut down the motor, releasing the bolts holding the motor in place, letting the outboard engine slide beneath the dark surface of the sea. "It's job done."

Six of us paddled, three to a side while Nazim sat at the stern, black grease-paint on his face guiding us to shore. Suddenly, Bet held up his hand. "Wait" he said, listen."

Kaf whispered, "I don't hear anything, just waves crashing on shore."

"That's right, waves colliding with a rocky shore. But the water is pretty calm. If it was rushing onto a sandy beach, you wouldn't hear anything, maybe just a hiss. That's water breaking on rocks. I'm a sailor; I know the different sounds of the sea."

"Shit," said Nazim. "We must be in the wrong place. Let's move ahead slowly."

We paddled ahead at a slow pace the entire crew alert, everything black around us. Suddenly there was a burst of white water hitting rocks, white spray flying into the night air. A giant wave picked the boat up pushing us forward toward the danger ahead. The boat was out of control. The on rushing wave flung the small rubber raft high into the air.

"Hang on," I yelled, throwing my oar away and grabbing one of the straps on the rubber-bladder. The boat continued to rise as it rushed forward, then came crashing down onto some jagged boulders. People were thrown from the boat as another surging wave washed over me throwing me into the pounding surf.

"Sink it, Alon" yelled Nazim. He was trying to stay afloat while cradling his sixteen-pound Negev machine-gun in his arms. I pulled my knife from the scabbard on my chest web belt stabbing holes into the inflated rubber bladder I heard the compressed air escaping with a loud hiss. *Time to go*, I said to myself, waves cascading over me. Climbing over the rocks I slid down into the still water in the sheltered cove. It was calm on the inside; the rocks were acting as a breakwater protecting the beach. I swam toward shore about a hundred yards away. When my feet touched bottom I stood upright walking onto the sand to see six wet half drowned rats laying there looking up at me.

"Well that was fun," I said. "Is everyone alright, anyone hurt?"

"No bad injuries," answered Mem, I checked. Pei has a badly bruised ankle; I think Bet has one or two broken fingers and a sprained wrist. Kaf is taping them for him. Where are we Nazim, I asked?"

"I think we are about a mile north of Al Mawasi instead of three miles south of it. That old sea captain was right. We should have listened to him instead of that inexperienced Boy Scout. If we walk inland about a mile then turn south-east on an angle we should be able to make up about two of those four miles. That means we'll have eleven miles to go instead of nine. We can still make it on time but this will put us closer to Khan Yunis which is a big city, a fortified city that is the birthplace of Abufadi."

"Who the hell is that?" asked Gordo.

"He is a former leader of Fatah, second in command to Arafat. He is also the commander of the Fatah Hawks. When Hamas took over Gaza after Arafat died in '04, Abufadi merged his men into Hamas. They are now part of the Al Aqsa Brigade, Arafat's special royal troops. He's at the meeting tonight, that why it's here in Gaza."

"That's great. So there could be a large contingent of Al Aqsa troops in Khan Yunis. A permanent fortress or base of operation for the fighters."

"I'd bet on it," said Nazim. "We must move fast and silently to avoid detection."

We moved out at a slow jog. Even though Elliot tried not to show it, I could tell his ankle was bothering him because of the way he hobbled along. I trotted up next to him.

"Pei, give me your M16. I'm going to give it to Naz since he lost his machine gun in the water. Sixteen pounds of gun and another twelve pounds of ammo was too much weight for him to hold onto; he almost drowned. When we get near our objective, I'll give you my rifle. I've got my trusty Jewish shotgun on my back, a twelve-gauge Mossberg."

We both laughed at that. I ran up to Nazim keeping pace with him.

"You look naked without your Negev machine gun so I brought you an M16. Here's five mags in this sling, don't drop them."

"Thanks, Alon. I hated to lose that machine gun, cuts down our fire power."

"We'll be fine Nazim. It's 11:30 now, about six miles to go."

At 2:45 we stopped behind a low sand dune to catch our breath. We had been moving at a slow steady trot for the better part of three hours. We could see faint light in the darkness about half-mile ahead.

"That's it, men," said Nazim. "I want you to spread out in a line, twenty yards between each of you. I'm going to be on the left flank, Alon at the end on the right, everyone else between us."

We stopped 100 yards from our target. I could hardly see the building in the dark. It appeared to be a low cinder-block building, no lights showing, all was deathly quiet. The scene was eerie, the building sitting like a deserted tomb. There should be some light some movement in the compound. With 200 hundred or more enemy fighters only 300 feet away you would expect to see a few guards about. Nazim issued his final instructions. No one opens fire until I do instructed Nazim. When the shooting starts we charge in from this side. Don't stop for anything. Keep going to the block house. Kill anyone moving, than continue on to the pick-up point. It's a mile further on for the dust off, lets all meet their safe, got it." There were six muttered ayes that would turn into *oy's* shortly. Spread out, once in position we move in. We walked forward in a ragged line. I could just make Mem out about twenty yards to my left. The line was slowly closing on the compound. All was still as a deserted cemetery. I felt tense, something wasn't right, I could sense it. We were 30 yards from the blockhouse advancing slowly when the black night was shattered by a brilliant white light. There was a loud whoosh- bang. An illumination flair climbed into the pitch-black sky turning night into day. I looked to my left to see Gordo frozen in place, outlined by the flare floating slowly back to earth. He had set off a trip-mine sending the flare blasting into the sky.

"Down, down," I yelled, as I dropped to the dirt.

Gordo's body jerked as bullets ripped into him, knocking him backward to the desert sand.

I yelled to Miriam: "When the flare goes out, get up and run to me; stay low but move fast."

The white light drifted slowly to earth, sputtered, then went out. All was dark again. We would have to move fast before another flare was fired. Everyone's night-vision was fucked from that bright light. Mem ran to me. I was glad to see she was calm, in control, a determined look on her face.

"We've got to get out of here fast, stay with me." We began to run back toward the beach ten miles away. I took off in a hard sprint moving to my left in a diagonal line away from the center where we had been. After running hard for ten minutes I slowed my pace to a fast walk. We were now moving due west toward the beach some 9 miles away.

"Why did you run off to the left? You're running away from our troops."

"Exactly," I replied. "Those Islamic fuckers are going to be coming after us. They don't know who is out here or how many. They are going to move straight ahead. That's where they saw us. I don't want to be there. I want a pocket between us. You stay close to me. We'll try to move to the right to hook-up with the others when we get closer to shore. Nazim and I have worked together for twelve years. We know how to look out for ourselves and the others under our command. Give me your M16, you take your Galatz off your back; it's your primary weapon now."

We were just getting ready to move again when there was a loud explosion behind us, a red fire-ball climbing up into the black sky.

"What was that?" Miriam asked."I'm afraid that's big bird, our ride home; probably hit by a ground-to-air missile. Either a Russian SA7 grail or an American Stinger. The bad guys have a lot of them. Let's move Mem, I want to get us home. Is a steady trot ok with you?"

"Lead on, Alon. I'll follow." We were making good time, probably about ten-minute miles, a pace I could keep up for hours.

"You're doing good girl. You ok?"

"I told you I could run. Had to be fast to stay ahead of all the boys who wanted to have sex with me."

"We're coming up to Khan Yunis. See those lights to the north, that's the big Arab city. Only about three miles to go to reach the beach."

The night erupted into a bright flash of light about a hundred yards to our right, a few hundred yards further ahead of where we knelt in the sand.

"Down," I said, pushing her flat.

"What now," she asked a touch of panic in her voice

"A machine gun mounted on a truck or half-track. They must be shooting at the others. Let's keep moving. Go ahead of me but keep low."

We moved up parallel to the truck which was now just a hundred yards away. There was intermittent gun-fire being returned from the darkness. That must be Nazim with the rest of our troops.

"That machine gun has our guys pinned down. They're definitely outgunned. They won't be able to move and more towel-heads are going to be coming up fast from behind. The sound of the gun fire and the tracer rounds will lead the way. Here's what we're going to do. You set up here with your sniper rifle. Count to sixty after I start to move out, then show me how good they taught you in sniper school. I want you to hit the three gunners in the back of that truck." You can see their silhouettes against the sky.

"What are you going to be doing?"

"I'm going to crawl up to the truck and toss a grenade or two into it.

"Where are you going to get a grenade from?"

"From my cargo pants pockets."

"You didn't tell me you had grenades."

"Can't tell you all my secrets girl. We don't know each other that well yet."

"Do you have others?"

"Only three. Remember, count to sixty before you start to shoot, give me time to get in position."

"By the way, talking about getting to know each other better I want to tell you I'd like to make love to you when we get back to civilization."

"Where the hell did that come from at a time like this" she asked a smirk on her dirty face. Tell you what Alon, "If you get that machine gun, I'll think about it. Are you any good?" At what, knocking out the gun or making love. How about both she said.

"Guess we'll have to find out. Start counting; shoot straight, don't hit me."

I held the Mossberg shotgun in my left hand as I ran toward the truck counting as I ran. When I reached 55, I dropped to the sand, the truck only thirty feet away. The machine gun was still firing short deadly bursts. The gunners were looking into the distance away from me. Tracer flashes streaked across the sand. Suddenly the gunner threw his hands into the air, his body crumpled out of sight to the floor of the truck. One of the troops looked off to the right firing his AK47 into the dark. He disappeared from sight, shot through the head. The last man grabbed the gun turning it toward Miriam when his head dissolved in a spray of blood and bone, three shots, three dead Arabs. Not bad girl. I pulled the pin on a phosphorous grenade tossing it into the bed of the truck. There was a loud pop, than a bright white flash as hot phosphorous burning at 5,000 degrees began to consume the truck. I was caught in the fires glow so I turned running back toward Miriam. Something was wrong. I could make out the silhouettes of three men in black robes, white scarves around their heads. They were standing where I'd, left Miriam. They were looking down at a fourth man on his knees, right arm rising and falling.

"No," I yelled, running hard toward them, firing the automatic shot gun in rapid bursts. One man went down, then another. I surged forward, a mad man running in the dark screaming like a rabid wolf. The third Arab raised his weapon, an old revolver firing in my direction. His shots went wide, his aim erratic. My slugs ripped into his body sending him sprawling in the sand. I squeezed the trigger aiming at the kneeling man. Click, click, out of ammunition. He watched me coming at him, frozen in place by my wild screams. He was too frightened to move. He was knelling over Miriam, gripping a bloody knife in his hand. I reversed the gun in my hands as I ran. Holding it by the barrel I raised it over my shoulder like a baseball bat. Thank god for my Oakley tactical combat gloves. I could feel the heat from the hot barrel burn into my palms. I swung the rifle butt at the man's head with all my strength. The stock broke on impact splitting the man's face open from scalp to chin. He fell over backward, dead. I knelt next to Miriam.

"Hold on girl. I'll patch you up and get you home."

"Too late Alon. That Arab cocksucker got me. I didn't hear them come up behind me. I blocked everything out; I was concentrating on the shot."

"Stay with me, Mem. Hang on." I'll get you home girl, after all we have a date to keep.

"Too late, Alon. I'm done for, finished, kaput. I would have liked to see if you were any good in the sack though." The air slipped past her full lips in a rush, her body went slack she lay silent in my arms.

I stood over her dead body for a few seconds looking at her beautiful face in the glow of the burning truck. Goodbye girl. I took off running again. There wasn't much time to waste. That burning truck would draw those sand-jockeys likes moths to a flame. I could hear someone moaning low as I closed the distance to where I thought the men were.

"Don't shoot, it's Alon" I whispered, as I moved closer.

Nazim sat on the ground, his back resting against two backpacks. Kaf was whimpering softly, holding his stomach with both hands.

"The SOB on the machine gun got me Alon." The bullet tore me open. I'm done. Dying in Gaza.""Has a ring to it, should be a song he laughed, than slumped over dead.

"There are four of us left. We have to move quickly. More of the sand ants are coming this way; they know where we are now." The burning truck will guide them to us.

"We've got a problem," said Pei. We're the only two who can move fast. Nazim took a bullet to the chest. Bet had his foot blown away at the ankle. He can't walk much let run."

"Nazim, can you move," I demanded.

"Some broken ribs, Alon. Having trouble breathing, but no frothy blood; so my lungs are ok, probably just bruised. Only one hole, so the bullet's still in there somewhere. I can move, but it will be slow going."

"Alright, here is what we'll do. Elliot, help get a sling ready. I'll carry Bet on my back. I'll put a tourniquet and pressure-bandage on his leg. You patch Nazim's chest wound; wrap it with a bandage. Then take Kaf's

Keffiyeh, wrap it around Nazim's body. Make it as tight as you can, but hurry. We're running out of time."

Elliot helped get Bet onto my back then helped me to my feet. The military grade web-belts holding Bet tight against my body. We started off running as quickly as we could which wasn't very fast. Elliot was supporting Nazim, as they struggled along at an agonizingly slow pace. We managed to cover another mile, now less than two to go to reach the shore. Would our luck hold? There was the loud thump, thump, thump of a light machine gun behind me. I pitched over onto my face, a weight pushing me down into the sand.

"Elliot - help me!" I yelled. He dropped Nazim who cried out in pain and came rushing to my side.

"Roll us over. Bet is dead! Shot in the back. His body saved me but the impact knocked me over. "Help get me out of this harness."

I had been carrying the Jerico pistol in my hand with Bet on my back.

"Leave Bet I cried he's dead, pick up Nazim. I'll take his left side, you on the right. We'll carry him along between us."

Our pursuers were still shooting wildly but they didn't have us as targets. They were either too far behind, or it was too dark to get a clear shot at us. But some determined troops kept firing into the dark in our direction. Nazim was breathing hard taking short wheezy gulps.

"I'm hurting bad guys," he gasped in a weak voice. Please stop.

"Hang tough, my friend, we'll make it yet."

Elliot let out a loud cry, stumbled and fell to the ground. He lay holding his side. "Will you look at this, I'm hit." Blood was seeping through his fingers. A lucky shot in the dark got me. Can you believe this shit.

"How bad," I demanded.

"Bad enough. I can't move my legs. They are fucked up. Both legs are numb, I can't walk. Time for you to get Nazim out of here."

"I'm not leaving you, Elliot."

"Be practical Alon. You can't carry us both. I'm in worse shape than Nazim. I'm done. I've seen enough people die in my short life. I know what it looks like. Now I know what it feels like. I can tell you I'm finished. You go, I'll cover you. I'll try to hold them up to give you time to reach the beach. Leave me any extra ammo you have then go." I realized Elliot made sense.

"Ok Elliot we'll go. Here are two fragmentation grenades, my last two."

I grabbed Nazim under the arms lifting him to his feet. "Hold onto me," I commanded, hold tight. I got a grip on his web-belt with my right hand, the pistol still in my left. I began to run pulling Nazim along with me. I heard the sound of three-round suppressed bursts of gun fire behind me. Elliot was firing three-round burst to conserve ammunition. He was concentrating his fire on individual targets. I could distinguish the bark of the AK47's shooting back at him. I forged ahead, one foot after the other now running on remote control like a robot. My breath was coming in harsh gasps as I struggled to keep going. It was difficult pulling my bother along at my side. *How much longer could I keep this pace up*, I wondered. A grenade exploded behind us.

"They must be getting close to Elliot if he threw a grenade," said Nazim, his words slurred as he tried to speak and breath

A few seconds later, a second blast; both grenades gone. Soon, more gun fire for a few seconds, then silence.

"They got him. Now it's only us. A real cluster fuck. Five of my people dead, maybe me to. I don't feel to good my savior. Maybe you should just leave me here and save yourself. Keep moving Nazim I see the water. Come on, try to help me." I won't leave you to the fanatics dead or alive. We go home together or die here together but I won't leave you.

When we reached the shore I lowered Nazim onto some rocks at the water's edge. I took a plastic bottle of Ein Gedi mineral water from the Galilee out of the net pouch at my side. I handed it to my wounded leader: "Drink this Nazim," I said. After he had his full I finished what was left.

"What now?" he asked in a weak voice, I'm in no shape to swim home if that's what you have in mind.

"We're not out of danger yet Nazim nor do I expect you to swim. Hell man you can hardly walk. I think we're about a mile north of that fishing village Captain Golam told us about. I'm going to walk there, find a small boat to steal, and then come back for you. It's almost 5:30; it will be light in another hour or so. That means I'll have to move fast. You take my pistol I won't need it. This will have to be a stealth run; don't want to attract any eyes. "Hell in our condition, some Arab kids could kick our ass. Just stay hidden here in these rocks until I come for you."

With that I set off running again. A dog barked when I approached the small fishing village. Everyone was asleep. It was still dark. No boats were going out into the calm Mediterranean this morning, maybe it was a holiday. Many small boots bobbed gently on the calm breaking swells. I looked the boats over slowly. I zeroed in on a white plastic hulled center console Mako 214 with a 150 HP Yamaha outboard hanging on the stern. The boat was a 21 foot American boat, a plastic hulled craft. The boat was a perfect size for the two of us. I waded out to the boat in the shallow warm water, cut the anchor-line and began to pull the boat back toward Nazim. Walking in the shallow water, the line over my shoulder, the boat bobbing behind me as I moved to find Nazim. I could tell my battery was winding down as I moved along in the knee deep water. It had been a difficult 9 hours. I'd run twenty miles since we started at nine last night. I lost Mem, carried Bet about a mile on my back, than dragged Nazim almost two miles through the desert sand. Now here I was pulling this 21 foot boat through the water tugging on the line behind me. I remembered the old Navy Seal saying.

"You know it Mark; you're an ex-Seal."

"Which one, Alon? There are a few."

"The only easy day is yesterday."

"Very true," said Mark.

"Well, I thought of that as I pulled the boat along; it kept me moving. Thank God the water was calm, the bottom flat and sandy, I'm not sure I would have made it otherwise. Nazim saw me coming and walked out into the water to meet me, pistol gripped in one hand, the other pressed against his chest. He fell twice before I could reach him, once going completely underwater for about ten seconds; I thought he'd drowned. I hauled him into the boat by his collar. He shook water from his hair rubbing his eyes, a weak smile on his drawn face.

"That felt good; woke me up a little. I was fading out waiting for you to come back. I thought you forgot about your wounded brother."

"Hold on Nazim, I'm going to get us out of here." The engine started with the first push of the Start button - a beautiful sound as the Yamaha roared to life. I pushed the throttle forward. The boat surged ahead like a Formula 1 racecar at the start of a race. We were heading straight out to sea. I guessed we were going about 25 knots. The boat skimmed over the surface of the nearly flat sea hardly bouncing leaving Gaza in our wake as the sun rose in the east.

"A half-hour at this speed should put us 10-12 miles from shore. I'll turn north then head for Israeli waters."

I turned north slowing the boat to a more pedestrian speed. I put a bungee-cord on the throttle arm to hold us on course and went to examine Nazim. He was lying in the bottom of the boat in a small puddle of water. His complexion was grey, lips a little blue his breathing ragged. He was taking shallow breaths of air, his chest barely moving, his eyes were closed. I'm no doctor although I've seen my share of wounded and dying men. I've ministered to some who died in my arms. Nazim didn't look good to me. He looked like he was going to check out unless I got him medical help soon. I shook him awake, taking the last bottle of water from my combat vest I handed it to him.

"Drink some more" I ordered, holding his head as he swallowed a few pitiful gulps. I pulled an MRE package from a pouch on the front of my vest opening it to see what surprises were inside. I made a big deal of it for his benefit, but since I had packed it myself, I knew what I had. Israel MRE's are called Manot Kra, basically the same as MRE's from all militaries of the world. Not a gourmet meal but food to sustain you.

"Here Nazim, some Loof on a cracker."

"Ugh, Spam Jewish Spam."

"Try to eat a little; its protein, you need some energy."

"What else do you have?" he asked, after just a few pitiful bites.

"I opened a can of sliced oranges in natural juice. Eat this, it will help you."

"That's all, enough already. I think you're trying to finish what the fucking Arabs couldn't

"Just take a few bites of the candy-bar. It is really a soldier fuel-bar, a quick energizer." He took one feeble bite I took what was left and finished it.

"Now let me look at your wound," I said unwrapping the bloody bandage. The hole in his chest was a gaping wound. Blood began to flow when I pulled away the old, crusting gauze. I took some sea water on my scarf wiping the wound gently. "I'm going to sprinkle sulfur powder on the open wound, then put a new pressure bandage over the entry hole and tape it in place. I'm going to give you a shot of morphine Nazim, It will ease the pain and put you out for a while, give you some relief." I jabbed the ampoule into his thigh then watched as his eyes flutter, than close.

I went back to the Yamaha, cranked the handle and felt the surge as the prop spun wildly, the boat surged forward bouncing gently on the choppy sea. "Another two hours like this and I'll see the skyline of Tel Aviv." After 10 minutes skimming over the blue Mediterranean sea the motor began to miss. It would sputter then catch and run for a few more seconds only to sputter and choke again. "What the fuck," I said aloud. It's like we're out of gas. I checked the fuel gauge; it read 1/2 tank so that wasn't the problem. Then it dawned on me, water in the fuel. Either condensation build-up or the gas was contaminated. Either way, we were in big trouble since there was no place to pull in to refuel. I cranked back on the throttle, the boat moved in small spurts until the motor gasped, emitted a loud backfire, than died completely. We were drifting alone on a smooth emerald sea under a cloudless, azure blue sky. A large fiery orange ball beat down on us, hardly a breeze blowing. *Hell, I could be the old man on the sea*, I thought. I surely felt old, old and tired. I had to hang on for Nazim or he will surly die. I must save him somehow. My clouded mind thought of the rhyme of the ancient mariner. becalmed at sea with a dead albatross. I had Nazim, and God knows he was almost dead. Water, water everywhere and not a drop to drink. I'd been dozing under the intense heat of the sun while the boat bobbed gently on a calm sea. The sun beating down unmercifully, body sweaty, my mind wondering. I was hallucinating, drifting in and out of consciousness. We were at least ten miles from shore which meant I didn't have to worry about washing up into the midst of the angry people of Gaza. I was groggy with fatigue, dehydration, my mind wondering. I thought I heard a low buzzing in the distance. *Bees*, I thought; but no there can't be bee's way out on the sea, not out here ten miles from land. There were no bees on the water. My brain slowly engaged struggling to emerge from the fog of a numb stupor. Could it be a plane, the sound of a prop-plane? The sound grew louder. I sat up to search the sky. Nothing, just a spotless Blue expanse looking back at me, yet the noise continued to grow louder. I saw nothing as I searched the sky. The sound of an engine increased to a steady roar, growing louder, coming closer. Then I saw it. A dark blue-grey dot against a blue sky flying low over the water coming straight at me. I stood in the small cockpit of the boat waving my arms frantically. The plane flew over my head no more than 200 feet above us. The pilot pulled up in an inverted loop climbing into the sky, then noising over coming down in a shallow dive. He pulled up just above the surface of the calm sea throttling back to cruise slowly by my port side no more than fifty feet above the sparkling surface. The plane had an Israeli star painted on its side, a T6 Texan Tandem Seat basic trainer, student pilot in front, instructor sitting in the rear cockpit. It was a world war two American trainer, another gift from our adapted country. He went around once more, this time, waging his wings as he flew by. I could see both men in their helmets, goggles over their eyes. The instructor sitting behind the student pilot, canopy open. As he flew by he gave me a thumbs-up, than climbed into the sky. They receded to a dot, than they were gone. At least someone knows we were out here now. We'll just have to wait to see who shows up. Two hours passed slowly before I saw a speck on the distant horizon. Was it real or my imagination? I was still in a semi -trance from the heat and lack of water. The merciless sun beating down on us. I could only imagine the condition of Nazim who was in much worse shape than me. I searched the horizon for the dot. Was it wishful thinking, an illusion, or was something out there. I checked Nazim. He was still unconscious, breathing in shallow, wheezy breaths, his color like old parchment. I didn't know how much longer he could hold on. He had been shot about 4 last night, this morning really, almost ten hours ago. I knew the bullet was still in him since there was only an entry wound. Where was that bullet? What was it doing? The speck continued to grow in the distance. I whipped the sweat from my eyes so I could watch the grey hull of a warship growing larger bearing down on us. The ship passed me port-side to port-side at high speed, made a sweeping turn, losing speed as it came along side. The ship slowed, engines reversed to allow the ship come to a full stop. It drifted beside our small boat. The crew on deck dropped a boarding ladder over the side. Three sailors ran down the ladder; two held boat hooks the third seaman had a tactical medical bag in his hand. The boat hooks grabbed the small Mako fore and aft holding us firm to the side of the ship, the medic jumped aboard.

"What do we have here?" he asked.

"One wounded, bad, shot eleven hours ago now."

The sailor looked at Nazim closely. He put a stethoscope to Nazim's chest, checked his pulse, raised his eyelids looking into red unseeing eyes, than he turned to me. "We've got to get him into my sick bay at once. This poor guy is barely alive. I'm not even sure I can help him. He needs a trauma unit in a hospital, some real doctors, surgeons not a medical corpsman like me."

Once we were aboard, the ship got underway at full speed, leaving the small boat adrift in our wake. Nazim was hustled below on a stretcher, the corpsman following close behind. I was relieved of my Jericho pistol by three sailors armed with Uzis all pointed at me. They were navy commandos similar to American marines. The three keeping a close eye on me, guns pointed at my chest. They didn't know what or who they had standing before them. One said: "I'll take your pistol, holding out his hand."

"Do you have any other weapons?" another one asked.

"Yes, my knife; but I'll keep that. If I reach for it, you can shoot me."

"Don't worry, I will," replied the third man. "Now up to the bridge, the Captain wants to speak with you." The bridge on the third level was spotless. There were four people at work stations; the captain standing next to a navigation table at the rear of compartment.

"Come in fella," said the Captain. "Join me here at the table, that way we will be out of the way. It's where I usually stay so my crew can carry on with the real job of running the ship. By the way, before we start, I've got a helicopter coming for your friend. They're about twenty miles out. My hospital mate said if we don't get him to an emergency room fast, like at once, you'll have to plant him when we reach port."

The helicopter landed on the helipad on the aft deck of the ship. It touched down for less than twenty seconds. The stretcher was shoved in, the corpsman jumped aboard to minister to Nazim on the flight to shore. They swopped into the air dipped the nose speeding north no more than a hundred feet above the surface. The waves were picking up as a strong wind began to blow from the west off the coast of Africa.

"So," began the Captain "Anything you care to tell me. I'm sure you've got a fascinating tale to tell." I looked at the man who had rescued us. He was tall, about my height. He had a tanned unlined face, sandy hair under a navy blue baseball cap that said captain in gold letters

"I'm not sure how much I'm at liberty to say Captain." Before we start could I have some water, cold water please, I'm parched. I drank 2 bottles of that clear cold nectar before I was ready to talk. Thanks captain, that's better. I can talk to you now.

"Call me Eric," he replied. "Let me tell you the little I know. Then you can fill me in with any details if you want. I set sail at 4:30 this morning. My mission was to sail south to the Sinai line with Gaza then back again. All we were told was to keep our eyes open to find an elite group of Mossad commandos. I'd just finished one roundtrip and was starting back when we got an urgent message saying an air force training flight had spotted a boat adrift in the water. That is what we were told to look for. A boat adrift with one person standing in the cockpit. Seems a special ops mission went south big-time. We were searching for any survivors who may have escaped. The brass was hoping the raiding team was able to make it out like they went in, by water. We were told to be on the lookout for a team of seven troops. That's about all I know."

"You know a hell of a lot, Eric; more than you should really."

"Care to enlighten me more. I'll keep whatever you say to myself." It isn't often I get to meet a real life Mossad elite Special Forces member."

"Let's just say you are looking at the seven team members of the raiding party, me and my badly wounded friend." We are all that remains of our fighting unit.

"You mean five of your team are still in Gaza?"

"Yes, five KIA lying dead in the sand in Gaza. They won't be coming home. The Arab butchers have their bodies. The bodies are probably hanging from lamp posts being mutilated. One of the 5 was a woman. You can only imagine what her body is experiencing. My partner and I were lucky to make it out of that trap alive."

"From the little I know of your organization that means this was a major fuck up. Either that or your leader sucked."

"Well Eric, the body on the helicopter is the head honcho, I was Tanto second in command. All I'll say is we, he and I, have been doing this for a while. It is not our first rodeo. We've done this sort of thing many times before and we are good at what we do." No not good, we are the best our service has. We do not fuck up. We don't make mistakes that get our comrades killed.

Eric colored slightly. "I meant no disrespect, Alon." None taken Eric.

"But that means the operation must have been a cluster-fuck. So you'd better watch your ass. Be aware people above you don't like to have stains on them. You and your friend are likely to be made the scapegoats in this disaster." With five dead operators it is an unmitigated disaster.

"Thanks for your advice Eric. I was thinking the same thing while I was floating on that boat. Talking about boats, and yes I am trying to change the subject, this is one beautiful ship. Aside from the fact you just saved me and my brother it is a sleek vessel. I'll bet its fast. What is it?"

"It's German, actually. Israel got four of them two years ago as a gift from the German government. They called it partial repatriation for the Holocaust."

"Seems fair to me," I said. "Four Corvettes for six million Jewish lives; that's about 1.5 million lives per vessel. Aside from that, they are really excellent ships, said the proud captain. My ship is 294' feet long, it can do 32 knots at flank speed, has a crew of 119 men and officers. But best of all, it's my command – my first full-fledged command. I'm proud to be its captain."

We docked in Tel Aviv 75 minutes later at the naval pier in the secure harbor. We shook hands on the bridge wing of Eric's ship. Eric looked into my eyes, putting his left hand on my shoulder. "Remember what I told you Alon, watch your back. They are going to be out to get you."

"Who are they" I asked.

"You'll know when you see them. Keep your eyes open."

"Why do you think that, Eric?"

"Look down at the dock, at the foot of the ladder, what do you see." A long black Chrysler 300 sat waiting on the pier; a driver standing by the door, another man by the passenger door. Two other men carrying Uzis were waiting at the foot of the ladder. All four men were dressed in crisp military combat fatigues, side-arms at their hips.

"Not the reception you'd expect after what you've just gone through, right."

"Thanks again, Eric. I owe you."

The guard on the deck handed me my pistol and holster.

"Good luck sir" he said, snapping a salute. I walked down the ladder to the dock facing the two men waiting for me.

"I'll take that," the bigger one said, pointing at the weapon in my hand. "The knife also; I'm told you're deadly with it."

"What if I say no?"

"My friend behind you will shoot you in the back. Resisting arrest, trying to escape; I've got a whole list of excuses to use."

"Does that mean I'm under arrest?"

"Let's just say you're in protective custody, detention not arrest. We're here to protect you"

I handed over my weapon. Protect me from who I asked.

"You never can tell who has it in for you. Just be careful, since you obviously pissed someone off.

Get in the back, you sit in the middle over the hump cause that's what you'll be getting. Humped big time so get used to it."

The car took off driving out of the port. Two armed men sitting in front, a big guard on either side of me, making it a tight fit in the back. The car had dark tinted windows making it impossible to see my surroundings outside. The car accelerated leaving the city behind.

"Where are we going fellows?" I asked.

"The Ritz," the guard on my left snickered, the other said nothing. Where ever we were going, it wasn't to Tel Aviv since we'd already been driving 45 minutes. They should have taken my watch. Finally after another thirty minutes driving at eighty miles per hour the car came to a halt.

"Out," said the big guard. We are at the Ritz, your new quarters." I stood on a dirt driveway in front of a two-story grey cinderblock building. It was bigger than any single family house but smaller than an apartment building. It reminded me of a secure military bunker. There was nothing else in sight. Just empty flat land as far as the eye could see. *Shit*, I thought. *We could be on Mars, in the Sinai desert, or even in Syria or Jordan.* It finally dawned on me, Eric was right. Where ever I was I was in some deep doo-doo.

"Let's go check out your new accommodations," the guard said leading the way to the front door. The second guard poked me in the back with his gun, "move asshole." I didn't say anything but vowed to at least break this guy's nose if I ever got a chance. A solid steel door opened to the touch of a button on a key-pad set into a steel frame next to the door. Two more men, military personnel by their dress and stature, although I still hadn't been able to identify the branch, stood waiting inside the door.

"He's all yours Mitch. Take good care of him. These are his personal effects," he said, handing over my gear. The two men turned going to the car leaving me with my new minders.

"Follow me, asshole," one said rudely walking to a flight of stairs leading to the second floor. "Your room," he said, opening another steel door. The room was sparsely furnished, a tiny window high up on the wall the only source of outside light. The window was to small and too high to think of escaping through.

"Is there a shortage of wood I asked looking at the steel door of my room?"

"Don't be a smart ass. We're going to be together for a while so behave and things will be fine. Get out of line and you will regret it I promise."

"How do I know where the line is?"

"When I hit you with this club you'll know you crossed it."

I fixed him with a cold stare. "You raise that toothpick to hit me and you will die. My face will be the last thing you will ever see. Call me Mr. Lights Out, understand."

He turned pale looking at the hatred in my eyes. "I'm a Mossad killer, an assassin, not quite as deadly as my companion who is being repaired in a hospital somewhere. (I didn't add, I hope.)"

"You walk light, I will too. I'll come for you when it's time for dinner."

"Forget dinner. I ate on the ship, much more friendly reception. I'm going to take a shower, then go to sleep. Get me some clean clothes for morning. These should be burned."

CHAPTER 38 ✤ ✤ ✤

I was kept alone in that building in the middle of nowhere for three weeks. Just me and about twelve minders who took turns watching me. There was a cook who was pretty good. The food was basic, but there was plenty of it. I was let out twice a day for about an hour each time. I'd go out at 7 in the morning for an hour of physical exercise then another hour in the evening before dinner for a run. I was determined to stay in good condition both mentally and physically. I kept asking about Nazim, but never got an answer. Either they didn't know or weren't telling me. During my third week, one of the more friendly minders came to my room carrying half a dozen legal pads, plus a box with pens and pencils.

"Start writing a detailed account of your recent exploits."

"What for?" I asked. "Who wants it?"

"I don't know. Your narrative maybe a script for a movie. If it's really a good drama it will be picked up by Spielberg, if its Fantasy, George Lucas could end up with it, so take your pick."

It took me four days of writing to finish the account of the disaster in the desert as I remembered it. When I was satisfied it was complete I gave it to the guard who left with my epic tale. I never found out where those papers wound up. The next week, my fourth in captivity, the fun began in earnest. After breakfast on a Tuesday morning, I was told to smarten up; visitors would be coming to see me shortly. I was taken to secure a room on the first floor. It was a small room with office furniture. The room reminded me of a conference room in a boutique law firm. There was a table, six arm chairs, but no windows. The room seemed small, confining, the only light came from fluorescent fixtures on the ceiling. Two men in civilian clothes were sitting on one side of the table, an empty chair across from the two men. One of the men pointed to the chair, "Sit Alon. We've come to talk to you about the disaster in Gaza last month. We want to hear the details from you. I tell you before we start we are making a recording of this session,so act and speak appropriately."

"Before I say anything, I want to know who you are and what the recording is for."

The other man spoke for the first time in a low, well- modulated voice. He spoke slowly, carefully. "Our names are not important. We work for the IDF. The Special Investigations Department, Internal Affairs section. We investigate matters that may have criminal implications. Matters that could border on illegal, criminal, possibly even treasonous."

"And you're investigating me?"

"Just an investigation," he replied. "No charges. We just want to know the facts of the night of September 9th, 9-9-99." Just tell us what happened in your own words. Do I have the right to remain silent? You know the right against self incrimination. Are you saying you did something wrong that needs to be kept hidden? Not at all but it seems there are people who are suggesting that my team fucked up which is not the case. Then tell us your story and let us decide.

"Convenient how those numbers work out." 9-9-99. we spoke for almost six hours with a lunch break at 1. They used up ten spools of digital tape before we finished at 4 o'clock.

"Thank you for your cooperation, Alon." Then they left me sitting alone and were gone.

The next morning at breakfast, another guard came to me. "Alon, more company this morning, same routine as yesterday; so get ready."

I was brought to the same room as the day before. This time, three people in military uniform were waiting for me. One was Army, An IDF Paratroop Major. He had the jump badge and ribbons pinned to his chest to show he was a combat veteran. The second was a Navy SEAL Commando, the third an Air Force Captain. The three officers made an impressive group. "We are sorry to bother you the Seal commando said politely. But we must debrief you on your last mission. What we learn could help in further operations, maybe save some troops lives." I felt a bit more at ease with these men, Yesterday had been an interrogation. This was friendlier, relaxed – a conversation between professionals. We spoke all day. Before lunch, the four of us took a walk around the grounds, had a light lunch on the patio, than went back to work. We were still at it when dinner time approached.

"Do you mind if we join you for dinner?" asked the Para Major.

"Not at all," I replied. "It will be the first time I've had company for dinner in over a month."

After dinner, we retired to the interrogation room to continued discussing the ill fated mission. The seal commando, a Lieutenant, looked at me pointedly. "You've made it clear both you and the leader," he looked at his pad, "Nazim, thought this was an ill-conceived mission. You say 'the leader asked it be aborted more than once.' Do you think that underlying feeling could have contributed toward its failure? You know what I mean. Not enough conviction it could succeed. It could cause doubt or hesitancy when deciding to make a crucial decision at the proper time. His uncertainty could have influenced the others under your joint command." It could have contributed to the failure of the mission.

"Gentlemen," I said, "I can see by the ribbons on your chests we are all combatants. Warriors who have been in battles, seen people die, survived in desperate situations. Once a decision is made, a plan formulated, we must move ahead with a clear focus and determination. We, and by we I mean the entire team of 7 troops were battle tested warriors. We were dedicated to achieving success. Nazim is the best of the best. His record of achievements speaks for itself. He is the most dedicated leader you will ever find. I always felt privileged to serve with him, to fight by his side, to be his second in command." Once we accept a mission we see it through to completion. We have never failed to succeed. Until now pointed out the Para major. Yes, until now I agreed.

"Let me ask you," said the Aviator, gold pilot wings on his chest above a helo-badge with a combat star. "Would you have done anything different?"

I looked at each man in turn. "That's an interesting question Daniel. I've thought about that for five weeks now. I can tell you something smells rotten here. I'm no great tactician, but I want to propose a military problem to you. I've got an army paratrooper, a navy seal and a fly-boy. Let me pose a tactical military problem to you. We have a high priority target deep in Indian country, hostile terrain swarming with well-trained enemy combat troops. An exceptional concentration of well trained combat troops loaded for bear. These troops are guarding a building with high ranking military and government officials planning future actions against you. How do you attack this objective successfully to eliminate the people and the threat they pose?"

The paratrooper spoke first. "Maybe a large scale air assault. Twenty choppers with eight men in each. But if we were facing overwhelming odds as you indicate, the assault would probably fail."

"Yes major it would, just like my group of seven failed. Anyone have another idea?"

The seal Lieutenant shook his head. "I don't see a solution."

Daniel was silent for a few seconds. I knew he would think of the obvious solution. He finally spoke. "There is only one way to achieve success with the action as you described it" Three pair of eyes turned toward him.

"What is that, Daniel" the Seal asked?

"A strategic air strike. We have a central target which is easy to identify, easy to approach, easy to hit; not a difficult problem at all. Send two Phantom F4's loaded with two 500 pound bombs under each wing. Send a Wessel night fighter in first to light up the target with a laser beam. The laser would guide the bombs right to the target. Then fly around letting go with air-to-ground missiles doing as much damage death and destruction to the troops on the ground as possible. After that fly home to a cold beer or warm breakfast."

I smiled. "Exactly my thought," I said.

"Then why send seven men to achieve a mission that was doomed from the start?" asked the IDF Major.

"I will tell you," I said. "But you can't quote me on it. I will deny I ever said it. Do I have your word as fellow officers, as brothers in arms?"

They each said: "Yes."

"Alright then this is my theory, my opinion alone. An opinion I have formed over five weeks being locked away with nothing to do but ponder my situation. We weren't supposed to succeed. We were sent to deliver a message to the Arab leaders. We were sent on a one-way suicide mission. No one was supposed to survive to tell the tale. We were the proverbial sacrificial lambs sent to the slaughter house to die as heroes. Unfortunately,

I fucked that up by living. That is the reason I'm sitting here in isolation today." I'm not sure where my leader Nazim is or if he's even alive.

"What was the message you were delivering.?" asked the navy seal.

"Simple. We know who you are and where you are. We could have killed you all if that was our intent, but we didn't. We let you live hoping you would see the light. See the way toward peace, toward moderation in your attitude. If you don't change your ways we will kill you the next time." There was silence around the table. Then the air force Major stood the others with him.

"Let me walk you out, gentlemen; and thank you for coming."

"No Alon," said the Major. "Thank you for your candid narrative. It's been a most enlightening day."

We walked to the waiting car, an armed minder walking behind me. Daniel gripped my arm "A moment please Alon,I have a question for you. A helicopter was sent to pick you and your people up after the raid. That chopper was one of mine, from my squadron. I was a jet jockey, shot down over Syria in '98. I was captured and held prisoner for three months until agents from Mossad, dressed as Arab shepherds came to rescue me. We crossed out of Syria into Israel at the Galilee. I couldn't fly jets anymore due to my injuries so they gave me command of a helicopter-squadron. My brother was the pilot of the chopper that came to take you home. Any idea what happened to it?"

"Yes," I replied. I was running for my life, another trooper next to me. It was 3:15 we'd been running since 3. She grabbed my arm at the sound of a huge explosion in the sky behind us. What was that she asked looking back. I turned to see a huge fireball in the sky, bright red flame, billowing black smoke slowly fading out as the blazing wreck settled to the ground. The camel jockeys scored a direct hit with a ground-to-air missile. Maybe a Stinger or a Russian Verba. Whatever it was, the bird went down in the desert. Sorry Daniel."

"Thank you Alon. It helps to know my brother is not a captive in Arab hands."

CHAPTER 39 ✦ ✦ ✦

"Do I have any more company today" I asked the nasty head-master the next morning.

"No, you have a rest day today. But tomorrow will be your big day. Some old friends are coming to visit."

"What friends?" I asked, since I didn't have many at this point in time.

"It's a surprise, you will see tomorrow."

The next morning I was seated at the table in the sterile room when the door behind me opened. Three men in suits and ties walked into the room to take their seats at the table across from me. One sneered at me the other two just sat stone faced contemplating me with contempt.

It was my old recruiter, director Israel Ballin. Next to him stood my immediate boss Ori, the third person was head of the Collections Department, a man I knew by sight but had never met – Ezra Nehori. No one spoke they just stood looking at me as if I were a ghost. A strange apparition that had come to life to haunt them. I could see it in their eyes. They wished I were not there, better dead then sitting before them. My three best friends, my protectors were here to crucify me. Finally director Ballin spoke: "Alon, I should have known you would fuck things up royally, and you have. I told Ori to send others to lead this operation. Anyone, but not you or your black hearted partner Nazim; but no, he wouldn't listen to me. It's time to get rid of them he insisted. So we send the best, that way no one could question our commitment to succeed."

I looked at Ballin, then Ori. "I thought you two were my friends, my boss and my director. It seems my theory was on point, you sold us out.

You sent us all on a one-way trip to die. It was your job to protect us. Instead you sentenced us to die in the desert.

"Just you, Nazim and Miriam," said Ori, The three of you were a thorn in my side. "This was my chance to get rid of you two since your continued success was a mild threat to me. Minor but still an irritant – like an itch you can't scratch. *I felt you or your black hearted friend were after my job.*

"And Miriam," I asked feeling my blood rise. *I'd like to reach across the table and grab you by the throat to squeeze the life out of you.*

"She was forced on me. I saw this as a way to show equality for women and get rid of her at the same time." I never wanted a woman in my elite outfit.

"So you sent her to die, all seven of us."

"Yes, unfortunately that's true. The others were just collateral damage. The four others were of no real consequence in the bigger picture. They were just cannon fodder. As the saying goes, war is hell."

"Please let's concentrate on the current problem, shall we, directed Nehori.

"Yes," continued Ballin. "The problem is you and Nazim. You are both too dumb or too lucky to die with the others. Although, for all practical purposes you are both dead already. Now, we just have to make it a fact, a reality."

"What do you mean?" I asked puzzled by Ballin's remark.

"The word was released two days after the raid – seven elite special forces troops died in a failed secret mission in Gaza. Pictures, names, and short bios on all seven team members were given to the papers, television stations and social media. So you see Alon, as far as the world is concerned, you've been dead for over a month now."

"What about Nazim?"

"Unfortunately, he's alive also. He has been mending in a private, a very private medical facility" said Ori. A private and secluded medical care facility in the Golan near Banias, you know the area. It is near Mount Hermon National Park. We have a secure facility there to care for special operatives away from prying eyes"

"So he's alive," I said, relief surging through me.

"Yes," continued Ballin, unfortunately he is alive. It would have been more convenient if he had succumbed to his injuries. "He was close to death when he arrived by helicopter at the secure medical facility. I'm told he was in a terminal state when the doctors got him. He had three shattered ribs, a collapsed lung and a 30-caliber bullet resting against his heart. The doctors are mystified why it didn't continue on into the heart."

"Probably too black and hard," I smiled.

"Anyway, doctors dedicated to saving lives worked franticly to save this black hearted pawn. He was in a coma for over two weeks. I'm told he is stronger now. The medical staff are thrilled their critically wounded patient survived the trauma. Obviously we do not share their triumph. Black heart will be able to travel by Saturday. We are going to bring him here for a reunion. Do you approve?"

"It depends on what comes after the reunion."

"That's why we're here," said Ori. "I have the pleasure of telling you your fate."

"Quiet," said Nehori, holding up his hand. "Go on Isreal"

"We want to do this legally" said Director Ballin "So next Wednesday we are going to convene a court martial for the two of you. A five-member board of your peers will gather for a trial. At the conclusion of this trial you both will be found guilty of some very serious charges, charges punishable by death. Once found guilty you will be shot at dawn on Sunday next week, October 24. You could save us the time and aggravation. I could arrange to have poison or a gun given to you. You could be like a warrior of old and fall on your sword." I didn't say a word. I just sat there looking at the three men sitting across from me.

"Evil," I said.

"No, not evil," answered Ezra Nehori, "A necessity for the greater good of our country"

"Do we get to defend ourselves?"

"Of course," said Ballin, smiling. An attorney will be here to meet with you Monday morning. He will stay by your side through the trial. He may even watch you die by firing squad. Of course we will have an attorney present the case against you, possibly some witnesses also. We will keep the entire affair small, internal. No more than 15 or 20 people total. It will be a private affair. Like a mortality play in ancient Greece. I would like to stay longer but we must leave you now. We have important matters to attend to in preparation for the trial of two walking dead men. Until we meet onWednesday." Then they were gone.

CHAPTER 40 ✠ ✠ ✠

I was outside doing push-ups on Sunday morning when an ambulance came up the dirt road trailing a cloud of dust behind. It stopped by the front door of the block house. I jogged over to meet it. Nazim stepped out of the back helped by a burly male nurse. He looked pale, thin, leaning on a cane for support. He was gaunt, drawn, definitely older than the last time I saw him only five weeks ago. I went to hug him.

"Easy bro," he said, holding out his hand to stop me. "I'm still frail and mending."

"You look great", Nazim. "Don't blow smoke up my ass, Alon. I look like shit, still feel that way too." "But thanks for lying to me; makes me think you still love me, though I seem to have vague memories of you trying to do me in."

"What do you mean by that" I asked mystified. "I did all I could to save your life, and it looks like I did."

"You dragged me across the desert when I could hardly breath, tried to drown me, jabbed needles into me. Then tried to make me eat that awful loof. What would you call all that?"

"I'd call it trying to save your black ass." We both laughed at that. "Come inside. It's time for breakfast. Let's try to put some meat back on your bones." "We have a lot to talk about. I got permission for us to sit in the office," the room I called the sanctuary. Once settled in, I told Nazim about the three meetings I had last week. How each differed from the others. The only sympathetic ear I got was from the three military officers since they could relate to our plight.

"Of course, he responded they've probable been in deadly situations themselves".

"In the meantime, our friends at Mossad are throwing us under the bus. They want us dead and buried. Our coming back alive upset all their best laid plans."

"So what do you propose we do?"

"What we always do Nazim – we fight to the end. We don't give up until the fat lady sings and maybe not even then."

"That sounds good, Alon. But you know the deck will be rigged against us. Director Ballin will have five biased judges on the tribunal with him, each with instructions to hang us."

"No, they plan to shoot us at dawn on Sunday; six days and a wake-up away."

There was a knock at the door. It was opened by a minder. "Company," he said, stepping aside.

A youngish-looking Army officer walked into the room smiling sheepishly. "I'm Captain Rosen, David Rosen. I've been appointed your defense attorney."

"Great," I said smiling, "Nice to have you aboard, come join us."

"Not so fast," demanded Nazim. "Rosen, you're a JAG Officer?" What's your background, what is your CV You know your curriculum vitae.

"Yes," I know what you mean. "I graduated law school eight years ago. I joined the IDF with a commission as a captain in the legal department. I was assigned to the Judge Advocate General's office." I've served in that capacity for seven years now.

"So you're about 31."

"Yes, 32 actually. I'll be 33 on December 21st."

"During those seven years, how many capital cases have you tried?"

"Capital cases?" he asked seeming puzzled by Nazim's question.

"Yea, you know major crimes. Where your clients face a death penalty or twenty years or more in a stockade"

"Well none actually."

"How did I know he would say that?" Nazim asked me, shaking his head in dismay.

"Alright then how many serious cases have you tried? You know, like rape of a fellow female trooper, selling drugs or smoking hashish while on duty. Assault of a superior officer desertion in the face of an enemy, cases like that."

"None Sir," He replied glumly.

"Is this getting good yet, Alon? Let's skip to the chase Rosen. How many cases have you tried in your seven years?"

"None Sir. This is my first independent trial as a lead attorney."

"So let me ask you Captain, what have you been doing in the Judge Advocate Corp for seven years?" I see you're still a captain so you didn't distinguish yourself in all that time. Rosen's face turned red at Nazim's inference to his skill. I just sat listening in rapt attention.

"Mostly I prepared briefs for trial Attorneys. I'd sit at the table handing notes and papers to the trial attorney so they had the information they needed when it was needed. I've assisted in at least twenty trials. I was always told the litigators couldn't win without my help. I always got great reviews." I am a proficient researcher and brief writer.

"Good for you Rosen, but that's not what my friend and I need. Now I'm going to ask you a really hard question. Take your time before you answer because I want you to get the answer right. Ready?"

"Sure, let's have it."

"In those twenty cases you assisted in, how many did your team win?"

"Well, he began."

"No, no, Nazim interrupted. "Take your time. Think carefully, how many did you win?"

He looked down at the floor shamefaced. He hesitated before he replied. "I think three or four," he said in a hushed voice.

Nazim looked at me. "Now do you understand what I'm trying to tell you Alon? Can you imagine what our five-member tribunal will be like? What our opposing lawyer will be – I can assure you he will be a tiger out for blood…ours"

"Can we get started," said Captain Rosen. "We have a lot to cover in just two days if we are going to be ready for trial." The Captain may be a push-over in court, but with his papers and books he was right at home. "First, the charges," he began. "They are very serious – all eight of them."

We looked at each other. "Eight charges?" we asked.

"Yes. Four carry the death penalty, three carry a sentence of twenty years in prison, and one calls for a dishonorable discharge."

"Can we just plead to the last one?" I asked.

Rosen actually laughed. "Afraid not. Let's continue."

We did for two days. Our lawyer was smart, a decent guy just out of his depth on this one. But when you go into battle, you go as prepared as possible and make the best of what you have." He was the best we had. There was a large meeting room at the back of the building. It was open, clean and bright. Two armed guards in full dress uniform stood on each side of the double doors to the courtroom. The three of us entered the room taking our seats at the table on the right. Three chairs sat waiting for us. There was a large wooden conference table on a raised dais at the front of the room, six high back arm chairs behind for the judges. The prosecutors table had only two chairs. There was a chair for witnesses on the right side of the judge's table. Three benches were behind us, each capable of holding eight people. Two windows, one on each side wall let in ample light. The wall behind the judge's table was covered by a large Israeli flag. "I hope they don't make us stand to sing *Hatikvah*, the Jewish national anthem," said Nazim,a broad smile on his face. I don't remember all the words." I laughed at his frivolity

"All rise," said my old foe Nestor the head guard. I'd had a run in with him when I first arrived. The animosity still simmered between us. Six people walked into the room coming to stand behind their seats on the platform. "Be seated" Nester called out.

We looked at the six judges in amazement. "I told you," Nazim muttered under his breath, as I sat shaking my head in disbelief. In the center was Israel Ballin on his left, sat Ori. *That's two for death*, I thought. Next to Ori, sat an older white-haired man. The name-plaque before him said, Levy, Collections. A woman wearing a prim black dress and black glasses sat steering at Nazim, loathing Apparent on her face. I could only wonder what falsehoods she had been told. Lohmah Shapiro was from the propaganda and political section. Four people from Mossad. On Ballin's right sat a stern-faced Army officer, a General. His plaque read Yadin, Chief of Staff. But it was the person sitting at the end of the table that made Nazim clutch the arm of his chair so hard his knuckles turned white.

"Easy, you'll break the arm" I whispered. It was Ensign Dovar. The young inexperienced naval officer who was in charge of the mission aboard the Pequad. The same officer who had fucked up our debarkation sending us into the dark night prematurely.

"I told that little cocksucker if he was wrong I'd come back and give him another bris, much shorter this time. Now Ballin has the balls to sit that little prick on our panel." Nazim pointed a finger at the young naval officer, shaking it in a threatening manner. Ensign Dovar turned pale and looked away.

"This Court Martial is called to order," said the army general. I am General Yadin of the Army Staff Corps. I will be lead judge of this duly constituted panel of judges. I' have had experience as a JAG officer and will conduct this trial by rules of military procedure, The uniform code of military justice. This tribunal is now in session with me presiding as chairman and chief arbitrator. Major Russell, as head prosecutor you may begin with the case against these two cowards. Nazim told Rosen to object to the term coward used by the general in reference to us. Rosen stood asking the court to refer to us as the accused or another non-derogatory term. Our staunch defender spoke softly trying not to upset the panel of judges. Point well taken said Ballin. Sit down captain so we can move on. Continue Major Russell, Ballin directed. Rosen didn't appear happy as he took his seat. A smiling smartly dressed Major in full military dress uniform stood at the prosecutors table. "I am Major Russell of the IDF JAG office. I have been given the responsibility to present a series of charges against two defendants, Alon Gold and Nazim, no last name.

Nazim leaned across to Rosen. "Get up and object to that little twerp on the end being part of the panel of judges."

"I can't do that," Rosen replied meekly.

"You do it or I'll rip your heart out right here."

"Is there a problem council?" asked the General.

"A moment please, Mr. Chairman; just a discussion."

"Proceed then, but hurry."

Nazim began again speaking in a stern voice. "Get that prick off the panel now."

"On what grounds?"

"Say he can't be a judge since you intend to call him as a witness for the defense. It would be a conflict of interest."

"I don't know, Nazim. I —"

"If you don't do what I say I'll reach out and strangle you. You'll be dead before anyone could stop me. Trust me when I say this." Nazim's voice was menacing.

Rosen must have believed Nazim because he stood speaking softly. "If it please the court, I move to have Ensign Dovar removed from the panel."

"On what grounds?" demanded Ballin angrily.

"On the grounds I intend to call him to the stand as a witness for the defense. He can't appear in both capacities." Ballin looked at Major Russell, who just shrugged his shoulders.

"Ask who is running this trial," Nazim whispered to our young attorney. Ballin or the General?"

"Don't worry, Nazim. I'll keep my eye on Ballin."

"Very well," said Ballin. "Ensign Davor take a seat in the gallery. I call Navy Captain Harvey Fisher as a replacement Judge."

"Object again," hissed Nazim, "Same reason. He's Davor's superior officer. We want to question him about assigning Davor to the mission." Rosen rose making the same objection. He did so meekly, as if he were afraid he was going to be reprimanded.

"How long do you intend to keep this up, young man?" Ballin asked angrily. Rosen looked at us, than turned to Ballin speaking with more conviction than before. "Until I believe we have an impartial Judge sitting on the panel, Mr. Ballin. And I'm not sure about you yet."

"Good for you, Rosen. Maybe you can shape-up yet whispered Nazim loud enough for the panel to hear.

The prosecutor called three witnesses to the stand on the first day, nothing to damaging. The prosecutor was just laying out the details of the failed mission. Finally, at 4:38, Yadin called a halt to the proceedings. "We continue again tomorrow at 9. A new Judge will be appointed to take the vacant seat."

The door opened on Thursday morning to admit the new judge. I turned to see who the next man up would be. In walked Major Ruben, the paratrooper Major who had come to debrief me last week. How had he managed to get on this council I wondered? He looked smart in his pressed uniform, shirt covered with ribbons, a jump badge and combat awards prominent on his chest. When he took his seat next to the old General they made a sharp contrast.

"Maybe a friend in our corner," I whispered to Nazim.

"You know him?"

"Yes. He was one of the officers who debriefed me last week. He seemed fair, reasonable," Open-minded. It is what we need on the bench. That evening after dinner the three of us sat discussing the strategy for the remainder of the trial. We decided to call three witnesses for our defense. The twerp Ensign, who I'm sure was going to end up a eunuch and knew it; his commanding officer and our final witness, the Captain of the Pequod, captain Golam.

We couldn't think of anyone else to call on our behalf.

Friday morning, the next to last day of our trial everyone was in their seats waiting expectantly to see what this day would portend. Ballin addressed Major Russell. "You next witness, Major."

"Sir, I have an unusual request, which I hope you'll grant."

"What is it, Major? Let's get on with it."

"I would like to call the defendants to the stand."

"What," exclaimed Ballin, "As prosecution witnesses, to testify against themselves?"

Rosen was on his feet. "I protest, these men don't have to testify at all if they don't want to. It's an unfair imposition on the defense."

"Captain Rosen, may I remind you I'm your superior office, said Major Russel in a demeaning tone. In fact I'm your boss. Sit down while I continue," demanded the major curtly.

"You may be my boss in the office, but in this courtroom we are equals. Rosen stood defiantly glaring at his superior officer. I have the same rights and voice you do. Don't tell me to sit down. I no longer follow your orders. Also, if you recall, I'm the one who writes your briefs to make you look good in court. How are you getting on without me he sneered? Stop this cross talk, if you attorneys have anything to say address the bench demanded Ballin. Your Honor, I'd like to confer with my client in private," demanded our counsel.

"Very well, Captain. You may use the study said Ballin. Please hurry since we are running on a strict time table." We have a Sunday morning date with destiny.

"What do you think?" David asked, once we were sequestered. "Is this a trick or an honest request by the prosecution?"

We talked it over then came to a conclusion we could live with.

"We're going to have to take the stand eventually" I said. It's the only way we can tell our story. No one else can tell it but us. Russell will have to treat us like hostile witnesses. We can fight him if we have to. You'll have your chance on redirect to clean-up our testimony if we say something we shouldn't. Let's do it."

"OK" said Rosen, heading for the door.

"Wait a second," said Nazim. "Captain, I just want to tell you your performance with your Commanding Officer in the courtroom was a masterpiece. I'm sorry if we were so hard on you when we first met. You've come a long way in three short days. Just keep it up." You may make a good trial lawyer yet.

"Thanks, Nazim. That means a lot to me. Let's go face the beast."

"Alright mister Chairman, Major Russell. My clients agree to take the witness stand."

"Thank you Captain. I have one further request said Major Russell.

"What now major," demanded Ballin.

"It is unusual I know, but I'd like to question the two defendants together, at the same time."

"Is that proper?" asked General Yadin. "I've never heard that done and I surely don't want to jeopardize this trial. I don't want any questions about fairness when we reach our verdict. These two men are entitled to be found guilty fairly."

I looked at Nazim, we both smiled. The supposed head judge was already saying we were guilty.

"You," Ballen said pointing at Russell's assistant, a young lieutenant who seemed overwhelmed by the proceedings. Look in your computer, see if it says anything about this issue." The young man began typing furiously.

"That was my job before," said a happy Rosen. "Look at me now. I'm in the big time."

"How do you feel about Russell's request David?

"I personally can't see a difference as long as you don't speak over one another. Whoever wants to answer the question do so. The other waits until the speaker is done. Then if the other of you has something to add do it. But speak slowly, calmly. We want to show we are in control of the situation like you were in the field under fire. Got it?"

We nodded. The Lieutenant stood speaking quietly with Major Russell, who turned to face the Judges. "There is no help on the computer council members. It seems this has never been done before. Then I leave it up to the defense. What say you Mister Rosen?" Ballen was even starting to sound like a Judge.

"We will concede to the request, Chairman Ballen."

"Wait, I told you I am not the chairman. I am just a Judge. General Yadin is Chairman of this proceeding."

"Sorry chairman Ballin, I couldn't tell from your actions, you are sure acting like the person in charge." Sorry for the confusion on my part, I will try to remember for the future, said Rosen sarcastically.

"However, he continued, I would like to stress if the procedure gets out of hand, uncontrollable in any way, I will stop it immediately" said our lawyer who was becoming more assertive by the minuet. Rosen was growing into his role.

"Very well, put it into the record. Let's precede instructed Ballin while the general sat by complacently."

Russell was good. He led us through the whole mission from the time it was presented to us by Ori until the disastrous end. Nazim going to the hospital, me to this holding compound. He covered each of the eight charges One-by-one, asking after each: "Do you understand the charge, do you agree?"

We each answered the same to all eight charges. "We understand the charge however we do not agree."

As to the last charge, the most damning charge of all, that of treason, how do you plead. "Nonsense I replied, a complete and horrendous allegation with no basis in fact. Not guilty to that charge or any of the others.

"A despicable lie," said Nazim vehemently. We fought and almost died for the success of our mission. We fought against over whelming odds for the members of our team and for our country. Please tell me how that amounts to treason. Like the rest of this case it is all a lie, a charade, a show meant to cover the real criminals in this room. You two fake Judges

Nazim shouted out pointing at Ballin then Ori. Quiet yelled Ori. Stop that blasphemous speech sputtered a red faced director Ballen.

"That's all, Your Honor said Russell proudly, the Government rests."

"Your turn Captain Rosen. Call your witnesses.

Captain Rosen stood at our table addressing the room. Members of this court, I reserve the right to call either of these defendants at a later time. I call my first witness, Captain Golom to the stand." The old fisherman took his place looking ill at ease. He held his greasy cap clutched in his hand. He told his story slowly in exact detail. He related the salient parts in a calm demeanor telling of our control over the troops, the disagreement with the young Ensign over our time for debarkation, the confrontation where Nazim said he would come back to cut off the Ensign's privates if he was mistaken. That got a laugh from all in the room.

"One last question, Captain. Then you can go. Did you see any fear, nervousness, or hesitation in anyone on the assault team?"

"None," he replied. "These were brave men, intent on fulfilling their mission."

"Thank you."

"I call Ensign Davor to the stand." The young Ensign looked nervous as he took his seat, sweat on his upper lip and brow.

"Ensign, how long have you held your commission?"

"Five months."

"That means when you boarded the Pequod with these fearless men who are being tried here today you had all of three months on active service?"

"Yes."

"Ever served in combat? Seen any first-hand?"

"No Sir."

"Yet, you were given an important task. Put these men on the starting lane for a dangerous mission; maybe a suicide mission."

"I object," said Major Russell jumping to his feet.

"Alright major, objection noted Continue Captain." Instructed Ballen.

"Why do you think you were chosen - a young Ensign with no practical experience?"

"I don't know, Sir."

"Could it be because someone wanted a novice on that bridge, someone who might, under pressure, stress on a dark night, a new officer who might make a mistake? Someone who could cause an error thus making a difficult mission even more difficult than it already was?"

"I don't know, Sir."

"I'm sure you don't, Ensign. One last question. Regardless of the cause, you will admit here and now that your inexperience did in fact result in a major problem in that it caused the men to leave the boat too soon. This error required them to cover a greater distance, putting the entire operation in danger." Not to overlook the precarious landing in the wrong place. Hurtling onto rocks which resulted in the loss of needed equipment and damage to the troops.

He looked down answering quietly: "That is Possibly Sir." "Thank you for your candor Ensign".

"Next witness, Captain Harvey Fisher." The Captain took the stand.

"Only a few questions for you, Captain. By the way I'm sorry I had you removed from the panel yesterday. No reflection on you or your ability to act as a judge but I wanted you on the stand today as a witness for the defense."

"Then don't apologize to me; because we both know you are not sorry."

"You're right, Captain I'm not. I now have you where I want you."

"Tell me Captain, why did you pick young Ensign Davor for so important a job?"

"Because he was the best man for the mission."

"Please Captain; don't expect this room of very astute military minds to believe that bull."

"Watch yourself Captain," said an angry Ballin. "I'm giving you a degree of latitude, don't abuse it."

"Sorry Chairman. Let me rephrase the question. You say the young inexperienced officer was the best man for the mission. Is that still your position? Yes, he was the best person to see it through. Was that mission meant to succeed or fail - because if it was the latter - you may be correct in your choice."

"What are you accusing me of he demanded angrily.

"I'm not accusing you of anything. No accusation by me just a question unless you have a guilty conscience which I would understand under the circumstances. Now Captain, if you wanted your young inexperienced officer, only 3 months removed from the classroom, still wet behind the ears, if you wanted him to get some hands-on training don't you think you could have sent a more experienced officer to be in charge? An officer who had been involved in this sort of thing before. One who could teach young Davor the ropes, so to speak?" Isn't that how we train our inexperienced personnel.

"In retrospect, it's probably what I should have done; it must have escaped me at the time."

"Yes, I suppose that's possible," Rosen continued. "It's also possible that you got a call from someone; let's say someone in a high secure position. This high ranking individual, maybe a director of an organization or head of an important agency could reach out to you possibly put some pressure on you. Maybe this person said, Captain Fisher, do you have a novice who could be inclined to make a mistake on a highly sensitive operation. A young inexperienced novice who has high expectations of himself – much higher than his actual ability. Do you have someone that fits that description? If you do assign him to this operation. Send him as officer in charge even if he doesn't measure up."

Everyone was up screaming at once. "Enough Captain!" that's enough of your slanderous rhetoric. Ori and Ballin were both yelling from the bench while Russell was on his feet objecting to the upstart young defense attorney's pointed remarks.

Rosen just stood hands on hips, smiling. I'm sorry if I offended anyone with my remarks. "No further questions of this witness." Lawyer Rosen took his seat happy with his performance, a smile on his face while others in the room squirmed in discomfort.

CHAPTER 41 ✚ ✚ ✚

That night, we huddled after dinner going over the days' events.

"It wasn't bad today" began Rosen. "But I'm not sure I did enough to swing any votes in your favor. The sad fact is I'm finished, we have no more witnesses to call. So what do I do now throw you to the mercy of the court? There won't be much mercy there, I'm afraid."

"Exactly we agreed."

"Let me tell you how I see it. I can assure you this is one thing I'm very good at, gauging a Judge or jury. There are six people up there who are going to be voting on your future. Two want to hang you both, two others, the old man and the women – both long standing Mossad members – will most likely follow Ballen's lead. The old Army General hasn't a clue about what your operation was really like. He's still fighting the Yom Kippur war with tanks and planes along with massed ground troops. Attack and over run your opponents position to win by conventional means. He has no understanding of special ops. The concept is alien to him. That leaves the Para Major I think he's with you, but is that enough."

"No," I said.

"Right" continued Rosen. "I'm not sure if the General can put any pressure on the Major. Major Ruben is a strong guy; I don't think he can be intimidated. But Yadin is still a General. This is the Army, chain of command you know how that works."

"So what do you suggest?" asked Nazim.

I suggest we get a good night sleep and pray for a miracle. Otherwise, I'll be attending a firing squad execution Sunday morning. And you two will be the targets."

We walked into the court-room taking our places. The tribunal came in taking their seats on the platform. This was the final day, our last chance to make something happen.

"Any other witnesses?" asked Ballin.

"No Sir," said Captain Rosen, standing at his seat. "The defense rests."

"Good, then I suggest the tribunal retire to vote. The doors to the closed court-room were flung open. Five people walked into the court-room. Four were in military uniforms, the fifth in a dark grey suit. The civilian was our old mentor professor Talal, the Hok

"What is the meaning of this?" demanded Ori standing pointing a finger at the five men.

"Sit down and stop pointing," said the rabbi in a stern voice. "Didn't you mother ever tell you it isn't nice to point. Or it's possible you never had a mother."

"You can't speak to me like that." Ori blustered. Who do you think you are busting into a closed session. I can call the guards to have you arrested, all of you.

"Listen to me carefully young man. I can speak to you any way I wish. If I were you I'd sit down and be quiet. It will be better for you in the end, believe me when I tell you."

"Now my good friend Director Ballin. What is the true meaning of this inquisition? What are you trying to hide behind these closed steel doors here in Never-Never Land?"

"This is a legal and just court martial of two cowards; traitors who have disgraced our service – A stain on the people of Mossad."

"Director, you were once a good man but something has corrupted you. I think you've lost your moral compass." What are you hiding in this Star Chamber?

"Don't talk to me like that. What are you accusing me of" he sputtered.

"If not me then who Director? I helped make you. Now I'm going to help destroy you. I have four men here with me who wish to be heard by your tribunal. Are you going to let them speak?

"Can I stop them," demanded Ballin.

"Not if you're smart," said the rabbi.

"Then proceed Ballin said reluctantly."

The navy corpsman was the first to take the stand. He stood proud in his spotless blue uniform.

"Who are you young man?" asked Rosen.

"I am Yosef Holland; Corpsman first-class stationed aboard the Encore, a warship in the INF, the Israeli Navy.

"You have something to say to the court?"

"I do."

"Then say what you wish. I won't question you. I admonish the members of this proceeding to allow these four men the latitude to say what they have come to say without interruption. No objections or attempts to stifle them. Let each man tell their stories as they wish. Rosen directed his gaze and his remarks at Major Russell. Understand." he said for emphasis driving the point home.

Major Russell glared at Captain Rosen. The major wanted to grab him and shake him for talking to him like that in front of everyone. If looks could kill our champion would be dead.

"It looks like our pussycat has grown claws," I said to Nazim.

"Or balls," he replied "tell me who is this one?"

"He's the medic that stabilized you when the ship picked us up. He got some blood and intravenous fluids into you to keep you going for a few more hours until the real veterinarians could get their hands on you."

"I was the first one to climb into the small boat bobbing on the sea." the Corpsman continued. The boat was being held fast by two seamen with boat hooks."

"That man, the Corpsman continued pointing to Alon was standing at the helm of the boat. He was a fearsome sight. His clothes were torn and bloody. He had a pistol in a shoulder holster a knife at his waist. There was also a combat vest on the center console. So to say he was unarmed, or that he had lost or discarded his weapons is a lie. He told me to see to his friend who was lying on the deck of the boat, water sloshing around him I don't think he will last much longer take care of him the man said. Please save him he is my brother. That is what I did. The man I spoke with was very calm in an extremely tense situation. I learned later these men had been in a combat situation which began the night before. They had been fighting and under extreme stress for about eighteen or twenty hours when I saw them, but he acted just as he is now. Calm in the face of death. That was a brave man who would not desert a battle or a companion. That is my opinion." He is no coward.

"Thank you for your testimony. You can step back. Next."

"My name is Eric Levin, Captain of the Encore, a German-built, fast attack corvette. I was contacted by my commanders to go to the aid of a small boat adrift at sea. They suspected those aboard were members of a Mossad Special Ops team that had been intercepted during a mission in Gaza. I went to full speed to reach their position over an hour away. We located them adrift in a small boat taking two men aboard. One was mobile, dehydrated but coherent. The other was gravely wounded. He was unconscious lying in a stretcher. My ship's Medic told me he would die by the time we reached port more than three hours away. He needed immediate help if he were to survive. He needed a trauma team of skilled doctor's immediately. I radioed for a helicopter to come for him. I had the other man relieved of his weapons, then brought to the bridge under armed guard. We spoke for over an hour before he went to clean-up, get some food and a drink. During that hour, he informed me of only a little of what he had gone through.The ordeal of the flight from an overwhelming force of enemy combatants. The fact that he had lost five of his men who he felt responsible for. He also alluded to the fact that it was an ill-conceived mission due to many circumstances that he refused to divulge to me saying they were classified. He stated he now believed the mission may have been meant to fail but he refused to elaborate. I can judge men. I am Captain of a 119-man crew; it is essential to the proper operation of my ship to understand those who serve with me. I can tell you unequivocally that man is no coward. I would say if I had to go into battle he would be a person I would want standing by my side. I think this entire proceeding is a sham." He is taking the fall for someone else's screw up. I told him that when we reached shore.

The Seal Lieutenant came next. "Let's stop this farce," he began. "I'm a trained killer in the defense force of my country as are these two men. We would never desert our mission or our men. We live for each other. These two should get a medal for bravery and devotion to duty. You don't know what it's like in a fire-fight until you've been in one. Once there, you never forget." You sitting here in judgment are not qualified to judge these two warriors. A true jury of their peers would be combat veterans who have fought and bleed while men died around them. Not a bunch of desk jockeys like the five of you. That's all I have to say to you pompous asses.

The fighter pilot spook next standing tall in his Air Force blue uniform. "I spoke with this man for one full day. I have the highest regard for Mossad Special Ops personnel. They are brave, dedicated men who would die to protect you, any of you. This mission was a cluster-fuck from its inception. It could have been achieved successfully by two or three Air Force jets. A clean strike in and out. The Americans showed us how in Iraq in 2001. Why didn't we do the same here? I understand you were in charge, Mr. Chairman? Why wasn't this done right, and why are you trying to crucify these two for your mistakes?"

"Enough," shouted Ballin. "I'm not on trial here."

The rabbi stood walking to the tribunal table stopping in front of the Director. In a low, resonant voice that carried to all corners of the room, he said: "Perhaps you should be on trail here, both you and Quasimodo seated next to you."

"That's it," said Ballin. Enough of this nonsense "We are going to retire to deliberate the fate of these two cowards. Guards watch the prisoners until we return with our guilty verdict."

They were back in eighteen minutes. "We have reached a decision, not unanimous but a majority. Five guilty verdicts for crimes 1 through 8, some of which require the death penalty. There was one vote for acquittal which means it is a majority vote. I declare the sentence by the majority calls for death by firing squad to be carried out at dawn tomorrow."

"I think not," said the rabbi/professor. "I have a get out of jail free card," he said, holding up a sheet of paper.

"What's that, Tal?" inquired Director Ballen quizzically. You are out of order in my courtroom."You have no standing in this proceeding."

"Wrong again, Israel. You see, I received a complete report of this ill-conceived mission over four weeks ago. It was a detailed handwritten report of the entire mission from the planning stage to the catastrophic result. If I remember correctly it was 46 pages long. You could say almost a minute-by-minute timeline of the events. I went over the report with dozens of responsible people. High ranking members of our intelligence services, including Shin Beit,Shabak,Aman and Lekem, Various Government agencies, and all the military branches. It seems they all agree to a person with my student Alon's deduction. This mission was designed to fail from its inception resulting in the subsequent death or capture of all participants. If that is the case, then the planners were the ones who put in the fail option. Tell me Director, did someone tip the Arabs that these seven brave souls were coming to attack at 3:00 a.m.? Did they kill poor Dominus after he sent the information on the meeting by accident or design? And Ori, did you pick the seven who were to die by random selection or were you settling personal scores? In any case, the Prime Minister has given me the power to handle this matter from this point on as I see fit. Do I hear any objections?"

There was silence in the room.

"Good, then this is how we will proceed." Talal turned to the men who had come in with him. "Thank you all for coming today. A letter of commendation will be included in your Service Records."

"You also Major Ruben, he said. "Pointing to the Para-major sitting on the dais."

"I know I shouldn't point. Sorry."

"I wish to thank you for your service Major. That must have been your lone vote for acquittal."

The Para-major stood. "I wish I could do more for both of you. We who have been there and looked death in the eye know what it's like." He left with the others.

"You two continued the Hok addressing the older man and woman. "You are retired from the service effective at once. You will begin receiving your retirement pay in one month. If either of you mention one word of what transpired here your payments will stop immediately. Since you are both members of Mossad you understand we will know if you say anything. So you are warned, now leave to enjoy your retirement."

"This is where it gets interesting Tal smiled. The smile was not one of mirth, more like one of pain. First you General. Israel, the country not director Ballen would like to thank you for your thirty six years of distinguished military service. Go back to your base, get a good night sleep, and then turn in your resignation papers in the morning. I know tomorrow is Sunday, but I have been assured there will be a staff officer in the personnel office to accept your voluntary resignation. Pack your things then go home to your lovely wife. She will be delighted to see you home from the wars at last. She will be happy to have you back full time. I know she misses you, I spoke with her personally two days ago."

"Now, for you two he said looking at the main culprits in this debacle. If I had my way I'd let Nazim have you. He is still hurting thanks to you two. I'd bet Old Black Heart would still take you apart slowly, painfully, however that would be cruel and inhuman on my part. You Ori, go to your room upstairs to wait for the Military Police who will be coming to arrest you."

"Arrest me! For what?"

"Captain Rosen, do you have a list of charge for this man?"

"Not yet, rabbi but if you give me five minutes I'll have a list for you. I think I could come up with eight charges, some might even include the death penalty."

"There you go, Ori – you asked about charges, shall I draw them up for you?"

The rabbi addressed a guard standing nearby, "Take this man to the room I showed you upstairs. Also take ex director Ballin outside, there is a car and driver waiting to take him away. Don't worry, Israel I'm not going to have you shot, but rest assured you're not going to the Hilton."

"Now for you Major Russell. I'm not sure how much you were aware of what was going on here. However I'm told you are an excellent trial lawyer and a very intelligent person. Therefore you had to know something wasn't right with this whole proceeding. A death penalty with execution in one day. No chance for appeal or review. Very strange, don't you think? Yet, not one word from you regarding due process, jurisdiction or authority. I think you should be in another line of work. Maybe a shoe salesman or sanitation worker since this trial was pure garbage. You are hereby summarily discharged from the JAG Department and the military. On Monday you will receive a letter from the Bar Association stating your legal license has been suspended. That means you will no longer be allowed to practice law. You can appeal that decision but it won't do you any good since one of my former students is President of the Bar Association. I'm tired, let's see if we can finish this in the next few minutes."

"Now to you Captain Rosen. I didn't think you had the strength to pull this off, you surprised me."

"Me too," said Nazim.

"Don't steal my show, please."

"Sorry rabbi."

"It seems a vacancy has recently opened in the JAG office. On Monday your promotion to Major will come through. You will be moved to the Trial Division. Take this Lieutenant sitting here with you as your assistant teach him well."

"I don't know what to say, Sir."

"Say thank you and leave," which he did after shaking both our hands. I told you we would need a miracle, said now major Rosen. Looks like we found one in the person of your benefactor, the eminent rabbi. With that he walked out of the room and out of our lives.

Now alone, the three stood looking at each other. "You two were always trouble, the worst of the litter. Why do we always love the worst best? Let's go eat while we figure out what to do with you since as far as your country is concerned your both dead and buried."

CHAPTER 42 ✠ ✠ ✠

We were sitting at the kitchen table, each eating a thick, juicy steak cooked rear.

"This is a meal," said Nazim. "I may even gain some weight after this steak. Don't tell me rabbi, from the Texas Roadhouse, right?

"Exactly Alon. I stopped last night on the way. When I told the cowboy they were for you two, he said he would send his best cut."

We ate in silence just savoring the moment. The rabbi filled three wine glasses with a deep, red wine – a wine from the Negev.

"When it comes to wine, he said - handing each of us a glass – I'm afraid I'm a snob. For me, French is the ultimate. This is a rare Pinot Noir, but from Israel for this occasion. A toast, to a long life."

We raised the glass to drink, when a gunshot shattered the stillness.

"What the hell," said Nazim.

"Nothing," replied the Rabbi nonchalantly. "Someone just cleaning a gun, misfire probably."

"Let's meet for breakfast at 8 in the morning. We still have a lot to talk about. We must decide what to do with the two of you. Now go, enjoy a restful night sleep.

Sitting at the kitchen table at 8 on Sunday morning the Rabbi asked "How does it feel to be alive today? You were supposed to be shot at sunrise."

"Much better to be sitting here with you, rabbi."

"Yes, but now we must get serious since you've been declared dead for over five weeks. We cannot just resurrect you since too many questions would be asked. As far as Israel is concerned you are history, and history is old news. Military records, government records all read Deceased – 9-9-99. That means you can't be seen alive here in Israel. The only viable option for you is to leave Israel forever. You must go to live in another land, another country. Some place where no one knows you. So I ask you, with a whole world to choose from where would you like to go to spend the remainder of your days?"

We sat in silence, each deep in thought, as my mind traveled round the world looking for a convenient place to settle. Finally, I blurted out: "Morocco."

Where the hell did that come from? I wondered.

"Did you say Morocco?" asked the Rabbi.

"Yes I did," I answered.

"Why there?"

"I'm not sure. Let's see if I can find the reason" I said, as Nazim looked at me in wonder.

"I just circled the globe and nothing else fit. Follow me east from here. The Middle East is out. Some Islamic fanatic will find us and hang our testicles on his wall as a trophy. Not interested in the Far East, except for Hong Kong – nice, exotic, a possibility. No Philippines, Australia a maybe. America's great; everyone wants to go to America. But I don't think either Nazim or I would fit in there very well. The U.K. or Europe are nice to visit. I love to visit Paris, but again no. Keep South America and the continent of Africa as a whole defiantly not for us"

"How about the North Pole," said Nazim.

"Better for your cold heart but too cold for me. So, Morocco came to mind. We both speak French and Arabic. It has two coasts, one on the Mediterranean Sea, which I love. It's exotic, dangerous, and a little primitive with the Atlas Mountains and the desert. I think we could fit in there. What do you think my brother?"

Alon was always the smarter one; it makes a strange kind of sense. Also it is only about a thousand miles from home, not too far to travel if we get homesick."

"Don't even think of that," said Tal. "When you go, do not plan on a return trip, you are getting a one-way ticket; so be sure."

Nazim put out his hand grasping mine – "Morocco it is."

"Good, I'll go make the arrangements for your departure. I'll be back for you in the early morning. Be ready to leave by 9:00 a.m." We walked to the front door where a car and driver stood waiting for the rabbi who walked toward the car. The Hok strode to the car standing straight and tall. The old warrior had a regal presence.

"By the way," said Nazim calling out. "Aren't you going to take Ori with you?"

"No," said the rabbi. Ori left last night in a van. Seems he died of something he ate. The coroner is calling it lead poisoning. See you in the morning."

Chapter

Good to his word he sat with us in the closed sanctuary, a briefcase on the table between us. "Ok, here we are He began. A Moroccan Passport for each of you made in the name Alon Gold and Nazim Spirituous Greek for Nazim the spirit, funny, right. A Birth Certificate, one born in Casablanca, the other born in Rabat. Moroccan Driver's License, medical cards, workers permits, military discharge papers along with credit cards from a new bank – Bank Marrakech. Some photos, cell phones, that's about it for paper work. Now for the important stuff," he continued.

"A deposit slip in the amount of $25,000 for each of you. That's $1,000 for each years of your service, $19,000 a 10% bonus, $2,000 more. $4,000 for new clothes, you will need a new wardrobe. That comes to $25,000 in the bank in each of your names, signature cards are on file. Here is a wallet with $3,000 in American hundred dollar bills to carry you for a few weeks, until you get settled. I have 2 Tumi travel bags purchased in Morocco, a little worn you'll notice. Take them to your room and change quickly. You will find appropriate clothes inside the case. Hurry, be back in ten minutes."

We walked into the room wearing clothes with labels from stores in Casablanca. I had on khaki slacks a white Polo shirt and blue blazer, Sperry topsiders on my feet. I looked at Nazim and began to laugh.

"I recognize you now," I said. He stood looking at me wearing black Levi jeans, black crew-neck t-shirt under a black leather motorcycle-type jacket, black leather boots completed his look."

"Cole Haan boots" he smiled "Soft leather."

"Now, the last item," said Talal, handing each of us an Air Moroc flight envelope, your plane tickets. The flight leaves Ben Gurion at 11:45.

I have an escort to take you to your plane. You will not board through the terminal where you may be seen and recognized. Instead I have made arrangements for you to board from the tarmac. The car will let you out at a boarding ramp to the galley compartment of the 737. It has all been arranged. So this is goodbye my students, my friends. I will miss your wild antics, live a good life. Make me proud of you."

"Thank you for all you have done for us" I said, climbing into the back of the black Chevy Impala, Nazim beside me. Our escort got into the front passenger seat. The car accelerated down the dirt road leading to the highway to Tel Aviv. I turned, looking out the back window at the rabbi standing alone before the drab building, a cloud of dust rising around him as he rubbed his eye, dust or a tear, I wondered. It was the last time I saw him.

CHAPTER 43 ✠ ✠ ✠

We caught the Air Moroc flight to Casablanca, and, as they say, the rest is history.

"Some story, Alon."

"Yes, truth is stranger than fiction. But I think I may have said too much. Anyway, it's almost midnight now so you will have to tell me your story on our trip to Rhodes."

"I want to get some sleep since I intend to be under way at 5; see you on deck then."

I was up and dressed, standing on deck in the darkness enjoying the early morning quiet. Alon came onto the deck, holding a cup of steaming coffee.

"I'd offer you some Mark. But I know you don't drink coffee."

"No, but a chocolate milk-shake would be good about now"

"You're a decadent American," he laughed.

The sun was climbing high in a near cloudless sky on what promised to be another beautiful day at sea. Macher moved ahead at an easy twelve knots on a calm western heading, the sun at our backs.

"This is the situation, Mark. The trip at twelve knots is going to take us 28 hours to reach our destination. Twelve knots is this boat's optimum cruising speed for the best fuel economy, especially in these sea conditions. That means we should arrive in Mandraki Harbor around 9 in the morning. We're going to tie-up next to an old Egyptian tramp steamer on the far left side of the harbor about 1,000 yards from shore. Once secured, we are going to transfer our cargo of weapons from our hold to theirs. When the transfer is complete, we cast off and are on our way to places only you know."

"How do we do the transfer," I asked. "Not by hand, I hope."

Alon smiled at me. "No, we use a boom with cargo nets attached. You'll see how I do it, which brings me to your role in the transfer. I'm going to be in the forward hold supervising the loading of the cargo nets. There will be six or eight Arab seamen on-board doing the work in the hold, more looking down from the deck above us. I want you sitting here at the controls holding an automatic rifle while you watch everything and everyone. The slightest sign of trouble you know what to do. We'll be at a distinct disadvantage since well be outnumbered and on lower ground, so you must stay alert."

"Do you expect any trouble?"

"How about these Arabs hate Jews, which we are. If we are dead they don't have to pay us $250k dollars and they can take my boat which is worth a small fortune in Gaza or anywhere else in the world for that matter. No, I don't expect trouble Mark, but like the boy scouts I always like to be prepared. After all these are terrorists we're dealing with, bloody killers."

I was striped to a pair of shorts wearing shades and a baseball cap on my head. The warm sun felt good on my body. A cool breeze was blowing over the bow as the boat moved steadily on toward Rhodes. "I'm going to work on my tan," Alon, I said heading toward the mattress on the forward deck. "Wake me if you want to switch."

It was almost 4 when he came to me. "Your turn at the helm" he said changing places with me. I stood walking to the controls at the helm station. We took turns at the helm during the long night. Alon woke me at 2 to relieve him so he could sleep. "I should be awake by 7" he said, "If not, come get me." Alon walked onto the bridge at 6:45. Like most military men we have built-in alarm clocks in our brains. Just think of a time you want to awake before you close your eyes and they'll open just before that time. It's an acquired trait

"How are we doing helmsman?"

"Fine Captain," I said, carrying out the charade. A dark smudge of land was barely visible on the horizon as a new day dawned.

"Let me check my gauges to be sure its Rhodes and not China." After a few minutes he smiled at me. "Excellent first mate we are right on course. We should be alongside our tramp steamer by 9." Mandraki Harbor was enormous, the entrance almost two miles wide, the inner harbor opened even more.

"Look at all the activity," I said watching ships of all sizes moving over the calm surface of the water causing ripples and waves to spread in every direction.

"Mandraki gets ships from around the world stopping here. Ferries from Greece, Turkey, Lebanon, and Egypt. One ferry used to run from Haifa, I'm not sure it still does. Ships come from around the world – China, Japan, Europe, America, and places in between – all moving freight from one point to another. Then you have cruise ships. Rhodes is a major shore excursion for cruise passengers, thousands come each day. Every line you can think of along with many you never heard of. They all come to call at this gem of a destination. Finally last but not least are pleasure craft of all sizes, both power and sail. You will see some of the world's most exotic vessels in this port. Rhodes rivals the Cote d'Azur for seafarers." Alon was looking through his range-finding Zeiss Binoculars scanning the left side of the inner harbor. After about ten minutes, he said "There she is, anchored right where I told them to. I'll head for that ship sitting alone by the stone breakwater. You go pick out a weapon for show, not the shotgun."

I came back on deck with a Colt M16 five spare clips of ammo in a bandoleer, a Colt 45 1911 in a shoulder holster, and a Remington 810 twelve-gauge shotgun with a box of 25 shot gun shells. Double ought deer slugs.

"You're just breaking my balls with that shotgun, right?"

"Hell Alon, it makes me feel more comfortable. Humor me, ok."

Alon eased his sleek black hulled craft alongside the aged, rusting freighter. The derelict vessel was flying an Egyptian flag from the stern flag-post, a Palestinian black Hamas banner from the tall mast head.

"Brazen cocksuckers with that black flag flying in the breeze. They're just showing off, trying to tell us they aren't afraid of anyone."

"Put out the fenders, than tie us to them when they throw lines over. Leave your guns here. I'll stay at the helm." We touched with hardly a bump as two heavy mooring line dropped from the deck above. I quickly put the loops around cleats fore and aft while crewmen above pulled the lines tight. We weren't going anywhere in a hurry, both vessels now tied together. I lay an axe next to the forward mooring line in case I had to chop us free. I walked back to the helm-station taking a seat in the Captain's leather swivel chair, picking up the M16 as I sat back. I was wearing worn faded denim jeans, white sneakers to give me a grip on the wooden deck if I had to run. No shirt. The warm sun was caressing my back. I wanted to scare the Arabs with my firm well toned body. Don't anyone laugh. I was wearing a pair of Oakley wrap-around sun glasses to protect my eyes from the sun's rays bouncing off water casting a brutal glare.

"Ok Mark its show-time. Keep a sharp eye on the action and your finger on the trigger. Watch my back. Alon walked forward on the polished deck as a boarding ladder was put over the side of the rusting steamer. The ladder was lowered to the deck of our boat, a metal platform on the bottom. Seven men came down the ladder. Six were shirtless wearing ragged trousers, all were barefoot except for the leader who wore canvas Converse high-top sneakers and what could pass for a uniform. He wore navy blue trousers, a white shirt with epaulets, a star pinned to the shoulder board showing his rank, probably first mate. An officers white cap with a black bill completed his air of authority. He walked up to Alon and began speaking in Arabic.

Alon nodded. "Follow me," he said, walking to the forward cargo hatch. He pushed a button; a low-hum came from the electric motors as the deck opened to the large cargo hold below. The leader spoke to the six seamen who climbed down into the opening to the cargo compartment. Alon turned to me, gave a thumbs-up sign, than disappeared after the others leaving the officer alone on deck. I could tell by his posture this guy was ex-military. I could see a slight bulge at the small of his back. He was packing but he'd have a hard time getting that gun out in a hurry. It's just there for comfort. He raised his hand to show me a portable radio then pointed to the ship's deck above. I shook my head *Yes*. Go ahead mate let's get the party started, it was already nearing 10. He spoke into the radio. I could hear a diesel engine on the ships crane engage, the boom swung over the side of the ship above us. A large cargo net attached to a hook hanging from a heavy cable was being lowered toward the open hatch. It disappeared into the hold then stopped as the officer loosened the rings holding the net in place. He spoke into the radio raising his arm over his head, thumb pointed upward. I watched as another empty cargo net dropped to our deck. The officer released it onto the deck at his feet. He then hooked the rings of the loaded net in the hold to the cable raising his hand then watched the bulging net swing up onto the ship disappearing from sight. Once it was clear he kicked the empty net at his feet into the gaping hole in the deck. After fifteen minutes Alon called up to the officer next to the hatch. The officer spoke into the radio raising his left hand in a thumbs-up gesture. The loaded cargo net climbed into the sky to again disappear over the ships side. The precious cargo of weapons now being lowered into the ships hold to be unloaded by the crew above. Another empty net came hurtling down into our cargo hatch to be filled at Alon's direction. I looked up at the ship's bridge high above me where an overweight swarthy man stood looking down at me, a sneer on his face – a White officer's cap on his head, a cap with gold braid on the black visor. I disliked the pompous captain immediately. I moved the barrel of the M16 which was resting in the crook of my left arm slightly, it was now pointing directly at the captains fat belly. My right finger on the trigger as I sneered at his puffy face. The officer on our foredeck had attached the rings of the third net to the hook on the cable. He raised the radio to give the command to hoist away when I yelled "Stop!" in English, khalas in Arabic. One of only about a dozen words in Arabic I knew. He froze, looking at me, as did the captain on the ships bridge along with many other heads peering down at me from the deck above. The officer on our deck looked at me shrugging his shoulder. "What gives," he was asking without saying a word. I looked at the captain now scowling at me, a look of pure contempt on his face. I'm sure he wanted to reach out and strangle his Jewish enemy for defying him while I sat smugly on the puny boat below. I removed my glasses so he could see my eyes looking into his pig face.

"Money," I said, in Arabic. Masari, a word you learn first, that and fuck in all its forms. "Show me the money. Nothing moves till I have the money." I'd now used two of the dozen Arabic words in my limited vocabulary.

Alon's head popped out of the hatch. "What the fuck, Mark. What are you doing, trying to get us killed?"

"Do you want to be paid for your efforts or not," I asked.

"Yes sure."

"Then shut up and put your head down if you're afraid of being shot. I'm a lawyer and a damn good negotiator, especially with a loaded M16 in my hand. Look at that fat Palestinian fucker on the bridge. Do you think he'll pay you once he has all the cargo aboard? Not likely Alon. I get the money now before another load leaves our hands."

"Ok," Mark, "It's your show from here on, he said ducking down into the cargo hold."

"Thanks." I turned back to the captain. "Money Captain, masari I yelled. Money now or no more guns, send me the money." No one spoke, no one moved all eyes were riveted on me. A sailor holding an AK47 stood at the top of the ladder, the gun pointing at me. I could see the man was nervous, his hand shook slightly. I kept my gaze and rifle aimed at the Captain who was beginning to sweat profusely. I could see dark damp spots appear on his shirt. I called out to the officer on our deck speaking softly but firmly, "If that man isn't gone by the time I count to 3 I shoot the Captain first then him, then you before you can get your gun out of its holster." I had his attention now. He yelled up to the deck of the freighter loudly in Arabic, no need for the radio." The man at the head of the ladder disappeared in an instant.

"Ok now tell your men to come out of the hold."

He spoke into the opening. First one man, then another climbed to the deck while the captain and I locked eyes. "Stop!" he yelled in a high-pitched voice. He was so angry he couldn't speak properly he sounded like a girl. We were at a Mexican stand-off. The next move would decide the game. I didn't say a word, just sat with a slight smile on my face waiting as the seconds ticked off. He who speaks first loses. I remained looking relaxed. My entire being was tense from the strain of the deadly confrontation. It was like a freeze-frame. Then I heard the Captain speaking, almost yelling in frustration. Another figure appeared at the top of the boarding ladder. It was a young boy, maybe14 or 15 years-old. He stood there with fear in his eyes visibly shaking, a silver metal Samsonite case clutched in his scrawny hand. The Captain yelled again and the boy began to descend the ladder coming to me. He crossed the deck walking hesitantly toward the white devil sitting with a gun in his hand. The frightened lad approached slowly. He wore tattered slacks too short for his little legs, the pants were frayed at the cuffs. His short sleeve shirt must have been white once but now it was dirty and grease-stained. He probably worked in the kitchen, washed dishes, dumped garbage, scrubbed the floors. He came up to me holding the case before him with skinny arms stretched toward me. He was afraid to come too close to the crazy white devil holding the gun. He kept looking at the knife hanging from my belt. I took the case from his hands snapping the clips lifting the lid. Row after row of neat packs of American hundred-dollar bills sat looking at me; Ben Franklin never looked so good. I could imagine him smiling at me. I closed the case setting it on the deck at my feet. There was a closed pack of gum on the console - Wrigley Juicy Fruit. I took my right hand from the trigger picking up the pack holding it out to the frightened boy, who reached for it hesitantly. "Thank you," I said, in Arabic. "Go." He turned and ran to the ladder not stopping to look back as he disappeared onto the deck of the ship above. I looked at the Captain making a face that I hoped looked like disgust before I turned to the officer standing on the foredeck. I yelled out one word: "Go."

CHAPTER 44 ✛ ✛ ✛

Because of my show-stopping move, the unloading wasn't finished until almost two o'clock. It took a while for everyone to get into the rhythm again. The seven men went up the ladder to their ship, the officer last. He tipped his head at me as he mounted the companion way. That nod could mean anything from good job, big balls, or I'll get you someday partner, some day somewhere. Whatever he was implying we had our money.

Alon walked up to me taking the M16 from my hand. "Cast off the mooring lines, then push us away from that ship. I'm getting us out of here fast, you pissed that captain off, now move!"

I threw off the lines holding the two boats together, then pushed against the rusty hull as hard as I could. Our boat began to drift slowly away from the rusty ship looming above us. Once clear Alon opened the throttle pulling away leaving the Egyptian freighter sitting in our wake.

"Well that was fun, Mark. Did you enjoy yourself?"

"As a matter of fact, I did. I also have that shiny metal case stuffed with American greenbacks. Do you want me to return it, and kiss the fat Captain's ass to make up?"

"No," he said, smiling. "But you sure as hell had us in a tight spot for a while." I thought we were in for a gunfight at the OK coral

"No Alon not true, you had nothing to worry about, I was in complete control of the situation." He looked at me, than we both broke out laughing.

"Ok Mark," he said. When we finally stopped laughing Alon asked "Where to now?"

"How about we head into port for a little R&R."

"What?" asked Alon surprised?

"Well, I'd like to go into Rhodes for the day. After coming all this way I'd like to step ashore so I can actually say I was here. Also, we haven't eaten since breakfast yesterday, over thirty hours ago; remember we finished the last of the Big Al's steak." You told me there are beautiful near nude women waking around this island paradise. I can use a change of scenery after this morning's adventure.

You told me you've been here before so I'm sure you know a good restaurant or two. I'll explain our mission going forward over a leisurely lunch; fill you in on what the Professor told me about the papers in the leather pouch. I will explain the translation he did for me in Jerusalem. We can look around town, get a hotel for the night wake up refreshed in the morning, take a warm shower, and then set sail for Turkey." Turkey exclaimed Alon in surprise.

"Yes, that's our destination."

CHAPTER 45

We ate a superb lunch in an intimate restaurant three blocks up a hill from the waterfront.

"Tourists stick to the restaurants on the promenade they don't know the authentic Greek spots in the side-streets" commented Alon. Lunch finished we sat sipping our cool Argos Greek Beer, as I told Alon the details of Guy de Vaux's manuscript.

"You're telling me these Knights hid a King's Ransom in gold and jewels in an ancient fortress somewhere in Turkey."

"That's what the Professor told me. I have his transcript. You can read it tonight before you go to sleep. We can discuss it over breakfast in the morning. If you agree with me and choose to push on fine, if not we can go back to Israel where you can leave me since I can't go back to Morocco with you."

"Ok Mark, that sounds like a plan. I know an excellent hotel nearby. It's small, but ultra-clean with comfortable beds and plenty of hot water." The owner is an old Greek woman who will take care of us.

The next morning, we sat in a secluded garden behind the hotel eating breakfast prepared by the woman proprietor. She smiled as she served us eggs, sausage, warm croissants with butter, jam, and cheese.

"That is a fascinating story I read last night, Mark. I couldn't put it down."

"Yes, but do you believe it?" I asked.

"You know, if you told me someone gave it to you that way, or someone of lesser stature did the translation I'd be dubious. But you know I have the highest regard for the Professor. He was my teacher at Hebrew University for four years. He saved my life, mine and Nazim's. There is no one I trust or respect more."

"Thanks," I said. "You really know how to hurt a guy."

"Present company excluded," he said laughing. "I didn't realize you were so sensitive."

"Just kidding Alon; go on."

"What I'm saying," he continued, "Is what else we have to do for the next month."

"Or two," I cut in.

"Ok or two. Let's go for it. After all, the notes say there may be as much 92,000 pounds of gold hidden in an old fortress. I did some math. If I got the zeros right, at $1,200 an ounce. That's 14 million, 720 thousand ounces. It comes to $26 billion 496 million dollars. Hell, we might even be able to afford one of those 300 foot luxury yachts tied up on the waterfront. They cost about $500 million each and another mil or two to run a year. That's just for the crew not counting fuel."

We finished breakfast, paid for our stay with four $100-dollar bills – courtesy of Hamas. We were kissed on each cheek by the old woman then walked to our boat tied to the dock at the water front among dozens of other pleasure-craft. With our tanks full of fuel, Alon set a course due east into the bright, round orange sun climbing into another clear robin's egg blue sky.

"My GPS shows 355 miles from Rhodes to Mersin Turkey. Mersin is called the Pearl of the Mediterranean. We sail ninety degrees east for 322 miles, then turn north into Turkish waters. If we sail through the night again it will take us about 29 hours to reach Mersin traveling at twelve knots."

We didn't get underway until 11, which would put us into port there at about 4 or 5 tomorrow afternoon.

"I don't like going into a new port that late in the day. I'd rather go into a new harbor in the morning. Then what do you suggest Alon?"

"We put up here on the Turkish coast at this small port of Makez, sleep the night away, then motor to Mersin in the morning; it should only be about two hours from Makez."

"You're the Captain," I saluted. "That sounds good to me."

CHAPTER 46 ✠ ✠ ✠

After spending a peaceful night tied to a mooring buoy in the quiet harbor of Makez we motored on to the major port of Mersin.

"I looked up Mersin on the computer this morning" said Alon. "It's definitely not the same place our Templar leader came to 800 years ago. Mersin is the largest sea port in Turkey, 45 piers, an area of 194 acres with over 6,000 ships a year stopping there. The city has a population of more than 1 million people and the second tallest building in Turkey – 57 stories high. The major airport is in Adana, 43 miles from center city."

"What are you suggesting?" Mark asked.

"I don't want to motor into the busy port. It will be too crowded and dangerous with all that traffic. There is a yacht club and marina here," he said pointing at the chart on the computer screen. It's about four miles from the main harbor, about six miles from downtown Mersin. I think we could dock there without attracting too much attention. I'll stay with the boat while you go ashore. Find a travel agency or tour company and see if you can make arrangements for a trip to the fortress. You know, say we are just tourist looking to do some sight-seeing. Either that, or find a car rental company that has a 4x4 with a GPS and we can go it alone."

I was walking on a main street into a suburb of Mersin called Erdimli. The yacht club with the moored boat behind me. I walked along a crowed street looking into store windows, watching people stroll by while cars and trucks moved slowly on the crowded street. The smells and sights were intriguing. I had just left a tour office where I had gotten information on the old fortress about fifty miles away. I was walking along happy to be on shore in this exotic city when I felt something moving in my right trouser pocket. *What the hell*, I thought – what's in my pocket, a bug, a snake what could it be. I clamped down with my right hand to squash whatever was moving in my pocket. There was a low gasp as my hand closed around a thin wrist. I turned to see a startled dark face with large brown eyes looking up at me, upper lip quivering, eye's wide with fright.

"What do we have here," I said loudly. "A young pick-pocket caught in the act. What do I do with you now, you little thief? Should I call the police I asked, still holding him firmly by the wrist as he squirmed trying to get free.

A deep voice behind me said: "Excuse me Sir are you having a problem?" The man who spoke to me was tall, maybe 6'2" or 6'3. He had black hair slicked back held in place by gel. The man's eyes were black as coal, his face an olive complexion. The skin tone was not tanned by the sun but a true olive color, his body was trim, not muscular but firm.

"Just a minor problem," I said. "I caught this little thief with his hand in my pocket." The man reached out releasing my grip on the boy's wrist gently but firmly.

"You don't mind if I have a word with him then send him on his way."

I didn't answer. The stranger spoke to the boy in Turkish, patted him on the head, than commanded "Go." The boy turned running off into the crowd of people filling the sidewalk.

"I'm sorry for this unpleasantness. Could I buy you a coffee or aperitif as an apology?"

"No need," I said. "I'll just be on my way."

"No please I insist, come." He led the way to a small café with tables facing the street.

"Please sit. You will be my guest. Would you like Turkish coffee he asked"

"I'm sorry, I don't drink coffee.

"A shame," he said. "Turkish coffee is the best in the world."

The waiter came to our table standing politely while the man ordered for us. There was something familiar about his appearance, It was almost as if I had met him somewhere before. He sat looking at me inquisitively. He was dressed in a stylish black suit, black shirt and tie, black shoes completed his attire. He was a vision in black.

"Allow me to introduce myself. My name is Nawaz, this is my home.

It suddenly dawned on me. The clothes, the name, the man sitting across from me was a twin to my savior in Morocco, they could be brothers, Nazim and Nawaz. The waiter arrived with our drinks

"I ordered hot chocolate for you, not as delicious as my Turkish coffee but I hope you enjoy it." Nawaz reached for his cup as I l studied his hand. There it was the small tattoo between the thumb and first finger, an eye over a dagger – the sign of the assassins.

"I see you are interested in my tattoo. You are familiar with it perhaps? Very few people know of its significance."

"I know it" I replied.

"How so?" he asked.

"I know someone who has the same tattoo."

"Interesting," he said, looking at me closely. "Who is this person? What is his name?"

"It's similar to yours. His name is Nazim."

"Ah yes" he said, a light of recognition in his eyes. "I am aware of him. He is a distant brother. I believe he is living in Morocco these days. However he was taken into the brotherhood when he lived in Israel. He traveled to Syria for a week to meet with the leaders of our tribe. It was then he underwent initiation. I never met him personally but I am aware of some of his exploits. He is an exceptional person I believe. But I asked your name, and the reason you wish to go to the fortress at Zoana."

"My name is Mark. Mark Raden."

"An American," replied Nawaz. From your accent I would guess you are from the north east, yes I'm sure. I would say Connecticut, New York or New Jersey. Am I correct?"

"Yes," I said., a smile on my face "New York and New Jersey."

A smile spread across his face. At least I took it for a smile it could have been a grimace.

"I love to be right," he said. "So why do you wish to go to the old fortress?"

"I am an archaeology student, love to see old ruins, especially castles and forts."

"Yes, once a military man always one, right."

Where does this guy get this stuff from? I wondered.

"Let me ask you, do you have any idea what you are asking?"

"No not really. What are you implying?"

"I have to take you back in time, 800 years back. The fortress, in Zoana, was built to protect pilgrims and caravans traveling from Constantinople to the Holy Land, to Palestine. There is a major cross-road two miles south of the fort. The east-west road came from Syria, and the bad lands of Turkey. Bandits, robbers, killers would swoop down on these caravans to kill, rape and loot. The Knights Templar manned the fort to protect the people and the caravans. They controlled an area in a twenty-mile radius of the fort. When the Templar's were run out of the Levant by the Saracen hoards the Ottomans and Mamalukes, the territory reverted to ruthlessness. It was that way for many years. Then as the story goes, one day ships of the Templar Navy sailed into the harbor at Mersin."

"How many ships were there?" I asked.

"The number varies according to the teller – at least four maybe as many as eight or nine. Whatever the number, the force was formidable. Men mostly but there were some women also. The story said there was a great deal of cargo along with horses and wagons. They say it took over a month to move everything from the port over almost fifty five miles to the fortress"

"I thought it was only about forty miles from the port."

"No, it is closer to 55 miles. Now to modern times 1929 to be exact if you consider that modern. The Turkish Government decided to embark on a major road-building project throughout the country. Make travel easier, allow for the movement of freight from Mersin to Ankara, the capitol, then on to Istanbul. So the civil engineers planned a new route, the most direct route along the best terrain. When the new highway was finished it cut out the old road that went past the fort. We now have a major freeway, a six-lane highway called Route 1, a Federal Highway heading north from Mersin. The new road is 26 miles to the west of the old fort; it is the main North South road used for travel today. While the old route Turkey 301 sits dormant – neglected for the most part. The Macadam is pot-holed and breaking. Some areas are now dirt again. But worst of all there is a section that has fallen under the control of the criminals, the bandits, who rule over that section." It is just like the times 800 years ago.

"Can't someone patrol the area?" Mark asked.

"There are sporadic patrols, always outnumbered, afraid to engage a superior force of ruthless bandits. These bandits control a stretch of about eighteen or twenty mile where occasional acts of lawlessness occur. Now I ask you, is that a journey you want to attempt alone? Just you and your friend who is sitting that beautiful boat at the yacht club?"

I looked at the suave man sitting across from me. "Do you know his name?" I asked.

"If what he registered at the club is his real name, then yes I do. In either case I will know more shortly."

I had a new admiration for the man sitting across from me. I picked up my hot chocolate, which was now cool, taking a sip to give me time to think. He signaled the waiter, who hurried over with a pot in each hand to refill our cups.

"Let me ask you, Nawaz, what would you suggest I do in my present situation?"

"In your position Mark I would hire the best; by best I mean the most experienced guide you could find to lead your expedition into the countryside. I say expedition since you will need support staff to accompany you."

"Would you have any idea where I can find such a person? Can you recommend someone?"

He looked at me over his coffee cup as he took a sip. Then setting the cup onto the table, he said, "Of course, me."

"You," I replied in surprise.

"Yes me. I can promise you won't find anyone better or with the resources I have at my command."

"If I agree we must come to an agreement, set a price then begin to assemble what we will need."

"Alright. Let's get down to details then. First, how long are we speaking of Mark?"

"I think thirty days at the least, maybe forty-five or more. It's hard to say."

He signaled the waiter. "Paper and pen man at once." The waiter came rushing to the table clutching a yellow legal-pad and pen.

"Here Mark, since you are the lawyer. You make notes while I talk."

I looked at Nawaz curiously, did I tell him I was a lawyer. I don't think I did, but there it was.

"Ok, write he instructed. We will need twelve men at twenty dollars per day per man. $240 dollars per day times thirty days, $7,200. We will require three vehicles, a Range Rover for you, your partner, me and a driver. $100 per day, $3,000. Another vehicle, a truck a 2x8 AWD at $200 per day. The truck is to carry our equipment."

"What equipment," I asked.

"Tents, sleeping bags, weapons, communication gear, and anything else I can think of. $10,000 for the truck and gear. Are you writing?"

"Yes."

"Good. Now the third vehicle for my men, for six of them anyway $300 per day."

"Holy shit I exclaimed, what is it a Maybach?"

"Don't concern yourself. When you see it, I believe you will say $300 is a bargain; add $9,000. Now, $50 per day for our driver, another bargain. I was going to charge $500 per day for my leadership capabilities, but I decided $300 will suffice, so add $10,500."

"Are we done yet?"

"Yes, except for miscellaneous."

"What the hell is miscellaneous?"

"I don't know, that is why I call it miscellaneous. Let's say $3,000."

"Let's say $2,000" I responded.

"Alright, I feel generous, $2000, and I'll pay for the hot chocolate."

"You did say to be your guest."

"Yes I did, didn't I?"

"How much is the total?"

"It comes to $41,700."

He slipped his hand into a pouch at his waist, removing a bank deposit slip. "Deposit that sum into this account at any Adana bank branch they are numerous around town. You can take a room at the yacht club for the night, the restaurant there is excellent. Ask for Rashid, he is the maître d. tell him you are my guest he will take good care of you both. Your room will be paid for two nights as will your boat slip for thirty days, more if necessary. Enjoy tomorrow strolling about town. I will make sure no one slips their hand into your pocket again; will you require an attractive Turkish girl to spend the night with. A virgin, I'll bet, I said. But of course what else for my new American benefactor"

"No. But thank you for your concern I'll be fine."

"Then I'll go since I have much to do. We will meet at 9:00 a.m. at the yacht club day after tomorrow. Be ready." We stood shaking hands. To a successful operation" he said, walking away.

CHAPTER 47 ✛ ✛ ✛

We were finishing a light breakfast in the yacht club dining room looking out at the boat's bobbing gently on the rippling water. Our waiter walked to the table. "Masters," "your ride has arrived."

Alon and I walked outside, where a black Land Rover sat idling, a driver behind the wheel, Nawaz standing at the open door, a young boy sitting in the passenger seat. Nawaz was a picture in black from head to toe–black cargo pants, battle jacket, Para-boots and a black beret with the assassin emblem pinned to the front. Alon and I wore tiger-stripe battle fatigues – cargo pants with tight-fitting combat jackets similar to Eisenhower jackets from the Second World War, A pair of brown jungle boots of the Viet Nam era on our feet. The clothes had been on our beds when we returned from dinner last night. We could take the hint.

"This is my adopted son, Kafir. He was found on a garbage heap by one of my brothers who brought him to me. I have raised him and taught him for eleven years, he is 12 now."

"You must teach him to pick pockets better I smiled, looking at the young boy who I caught with his hand in my pocket two days ago"

"I'm working on it," Nawaz smiled. This time a genuine smile.

"What is he doing here? Surely he's not going with us."

"No, he will be living on the dock or deck of your boat for the next thirty days – your 24-hour per day watchman. He will be here to ensure your lovely vessel will be in the same condition thirty days from now as it is at this moment." Nawaz turned to us speaking quietly, "It will also give him a chance to feel important and redeem himself in your eyes Mark, and mine for being caught by you."

"He won't be armed will he?" asked Alon. "I don't want him to hurt himself."

"He won't have a gun if that is what you mean. But he has a long sharp blade which he knows how to use. Remember the primary weapon of the assassins of old was a blade, a dagger. We've had to adopt with the times but a true assassin loves his blade, he is never without it."

He took the boy aside speaking to him softly putting a backpack and bedroll at the boy's feet. Nawaz put the palm of his hand on the boy's head. A few confidential words passed between them. Nawaz turned walking back to us.

"How much is he costing me?" I asked.

"Funny Mark" smiled Nawaz. "He is on my payroll under Miscellaneous. Get in back; It is time for us to be on our way." He climbed into the passenger seat telling the driver to go. The driver's name is Mousa, he doesn't speak much but he is an excellent driver and mechanic."

We sped through Mersin going faster than the speed limit allowed. After half an hour of fighting our way through the city in heavy traffic we came to a roundabout with two signs hanging over head. One pointed left, Federal Route 1 Ankara 317 miles, the other pointed right Route 301, Adana Airport 43 miles Ankara 382 miles, 65 miles longer on the old road.

"The road is decent as far as the airport; from there it's all downhill. The last 22 miles past the airport are a disaster. It will take us 75 minutes to get to the airport. From the airport to the fortress it could take as much as 3 hours or more to reach our destination. As I told you, the road is bad and dangerous once we pass the airport."

We passed the airport cut-off traveling at forty five miles per hour. Two miles past the airport, we were doing thirty. Nawaz didn't exaggerate, the road had turned into a mess of holes, cracks, and broken pavement. A little farther on we came to what once must have been a bypass, – a place slower traffic could ease over to let those behind pass. Now the shoulder was just a mess of grass, weeds and debris. The driver pulled over and stopped.

"We don't have to pee, said Alon why are we stopping here.

"Funny man. We join the rest of the team here."

I looked around at the barren landscape, "I don't see anyone, just empty space, rocks, and shrubs."

The driver let out a loud blast on an air-horn. Two minutes later we saw a cloud of dust rising from the low hills on our right. Two vehicles took shape in the haze driving toward us. They pulled onto the road behind our Range Rover coming to a stop. The first vehicle was a crew-cab Mercedes Benz Unimog which probably cost more than $200,000. Mercedes claimed they could go anywhere over any type of terrain." It was a formidable-looking truck. The second vehicle was even more impressive. An American Army armored Humvee complete with a fifty-caliber machine gun on a ring-mount on the roof of the cab.

"Where did you get that beast?" I asked Nawaz.

"Bought it from the GSA in Washington at public auction. A fifty million-dollar military armored fighting vehicle that I bought for $42,000 US dollars FOB Baltimore Maryland port. There are six men riding in the back in air-condition comfort. Ok Mousa drive."

The remainder of the trip was uneventful, uncomfortable; but uneventful. We saw some peasants, nomads, walking along the road. Some on camels or donkeys but no other vehicles on the road. We bounced along moving at a crawl doing only 20 miles an hour over more of a trail then a road.

"The bad boys know something is up since our three vehicles are unusual traveling on this section of highway. You can be sure we've been reported by to the bandits by now. But they see we are armed so they won't bother us. They like soft targets to attack."

It was almost 4 when Nawaz spoke. "This is the cross-road I told you about. The road to the right leads to Syria that is where the bandits come from to cause trouble here in Turkey. Then run back over the border to hide from the Turkish police. "Look up ahead and you will see the castle rising into the sky."

"I see it, it's a truly awesome sight" exclaimed Alon. "Still in the distance, but its bigger more spectacular than I expected."

"It is three miles from the cross-road, but yes, it sits high in the sky. You can see twenty miles in all directions from the look-out tower. The Templar's could watch and control a vast area from the heights. They could see danger coming hours before it arrive at their feet. Once there, that is usually where it stayed."

"The castle was never attacked, the walls never breached?" Alon asked.

"No never. You'll see why when we arrive."

The three vehicles stopped at the base of a ragged stone mountain whose shear rock face climbed straight up from the plain, the castle towering high overhead.

"Will you look at that," I said in awe.

"Yes, a magnificent sight" agreed Nawaz. "The face is 800 feet of sheer rock wall reaching for the sky. The fortress walls are built upon the flat stone plateau with ramparts, a citadel, large open fields for drill or cavalry to parade. The main building has over 200 rooms for troops and personnel. There are kitchens, store-rooms, meeting-rooms, a church and sanctuary. That room is large enough to hold 400 souls at once. There were gardens, large stables for the Knights war horses, at least three wells and a reservoir for water supply, vast cisterns underground. But most of all since it was a military compound, there were armories for weapons, archers' windows cut into the stone walls, spiral staircases to impede climbing inside the six towers. A stone rampart runs around the outer walls of the enclosure. I believe at one time there were catapults to hurl huge stones down onto any army dumb enough to try to storm that formidable citadel."

"How could anyone get up there?" I asked.

"There is only one way. The ramp that you will have to climb to reach the fortress gates."

"That's it," I exclaimed, looking at a stone ramp rising at a steep angle from the field where we stood. The stone ramp leading upward to the main gate towering high above us. I watched as the twelve men gathered around the truck passing down the gear making neat piles on the ground. These were disciplined men who knew their jobs. They knew what had to be done and did it with being told what to do. Most of the troops had a side-arm, but all had a knife. The size and shape varied, some were carried in their boots, others on web-belts while some had the knife in a shoulder sheath, handle pointed down making it easy to pull in combat. They were all dressed like Nawazi in black combat outfits like British SAS commandoes.

"It's too late to attempt to enter the fort tonight. It will be dark in less than two hours. We'll eat dinner, sleep in our shelters, than attempt to entire the castle tomorrow."

"You say attempt," said Alon. "Is there a problem?"

"Let's wait until morning to see."

A guard roused us at 6:30. It was still dark although a new day was dawning. A fire was burning, food was cooking, coffee bubbled in two large pots.

"I know," I said, smiling at Nawaz. "Good Turkish coffee."

"Not good," my friend he replied, "the best."

After breakfast was finished, he sat with us. "I propose the three of us, along with two of my men, begin the hike up to the top. The men can stay on the ramp to watch our back while we three attempt to enter the grounds. I would like to go in with you, if you permit. It is your expedition after all; you paid for it for which I thank you. My bank called to tell me a sum of $42,000 American hundred-dollar bills was deposited into my account by an Anglo, possibly an American."

"You can join us" I said. "Only this once probably. When we are inside Alon and I are going to stay secluded. We will be examining the castle and grounds. If it is as big as you suggest that may take weeks, possibly a month, maybe more."

"Ah yes, an architect."

"No, I corrected, an archeologist."

"Yes, you're right, a student seeking inspiration." Inspiration and other things I interjected. Like a hidden treasure possibly smiled our benefactor. It was as if Nawaz had some clairvoyant powers since no one had mentioned the Templar's lost treasure.

I slung a rucksack onto my back. It contained an SLR Nikon digital camera with a 1,200-picture card, two extra cards in the pack, 3,600 exposures in all. My transcript of the Templar notes in the embossed leather case still secreted in my IDF bag. Alon's backpack contained some MRE's, military meals ready to eat, our bed rolls and some extra clothing.

"Take a weapon," Nawaz instructed. "Let's go."

After a slow hard climb up a narrow steep ramp we stood on a flat rampart facing a heavy wooden door built into the stone wall twenty yards away. The problem was the gap in front of us. An opening reaching to the ground about 800 feet below the top of the ramp where we stood.

"How do we get across this crevice?" I asked.

"With difficulty, I think," said Alon.

"No one likes a wise guy," I replied, looking at him with a frown.

"I expected something like this" said Nawaz. "These men were extremely smart. I'm sure they had engineers, technicians that had studied

Archimedes with his gears, Lepors, Heron, Philo with his water-pumps and water systems

. Clesibus invented the crane. Then there were Romans with gears, levers, wenches, and pulleys. Looking at that door I think it's hinged to open out and up on a series of gimbals. I'd bet my adopted son could swing that door up with one hand since it will be balanced to open easily by one man. Once out of the way my guess is there will be a draw-bridge that can be lowered across this crevice to allow men and horses to cross,"

"Great," said Alon. "How do we get over there to do what you suggest?"

Nawaz turned to one of his men speaking in Turkish. The man turned trotting slowly down the steep incline leaning back to keep his balance. We sat in the hot sun waiting. It was almost two hours before 5 strong men returned. One carrying a stout cross-bow, two others had heavy coils of rope over their shoulders, while another carried a metal pulley on a heavy stand. Nawaz spoke with the men explaining what he wanted them to do. The cross-bowman took a large arrow from his quiver a small pulley attached to the stout shaft The archer instructed a lineman to thread a very fine piece of nylon line into the pulley holding the end in a gloved hand. The line was on a spool like a fishing reel. The bowman fit the heavy arrow to the bow string, pulled back and let fly. The arrow sailed across the gap thudding into the wooden door with a resounding thump. The line hissed as it played out from the spool, one end still held in the assassin's hand. He began to pull in on the fine nylon line which he attached to a heavier line that was tied to an even heavier one still. Once the heavy line was in place held taught over the deep crevice attached to the metal stand Nawaz addressed us.

"That line should support a man's weight. We can put a canvas bosun chair on the line and pull someone across to open the small door set into the wall next to the massive wooden doors."

"Do you really think that will work?" asked Alon.

"I do," replied Nawaz. "That's my idea unless someone has a better one." No one spoke.

"Who will go?" asked Alon.

"I could go or order one of my men to go in my place." However I am the heaviest of us all.

"No," interrupted Mark. "This is my expedition. It's my place to go."

"You sure?" asked Alon skeptically

"Yes I'm sure. Tie a rope around my body, that way if I fall I'll only fall forty feet into the crevice. I can be pulled back up. Let's go before I change my mind."

The sling supporting me rolled over the deep gorge moving me toward the fortress wall. The line sagged with my weight but held firm. Now flush against the door - the massive arrow just over my head - I lowered myself slowly until my feet were on a narrow stone ledge. I gripped the door-handle – yelled *Open Sesame* - pushing hard on the door. The hinges creaked, as the door swung inward. A smile of triumph spread across my face. I turned to the group on the far bank waving. "We're in" I yelled, stepping through the doorway. It was dark inside, musty, spooky. I followed Nawaz's instructions pulling levers, releasing bolts then pushing against the massive door which swung up and out effortlessly. There was a large wench on the wall with a heavy chain wrapped around the teeth of gears much like an anchor windless on an old sailing ship. I pulled a pin from the cleat allowing the windless to turn. I stood watching the giant bridge lower slowly across the open space touching down gently on the far side. Nawaz and Alon started walking toward me over the sturdy wooden bridge. The three men started back down the steep ramp to the encampment below. Two others stood in position at the head of the bridge atop the ramp. We spent the next two hours walking around the interior grounds of the keep on an open flat plateau that stretched before us.

"Gigantic," said Nawaz. Look at that field. "It's at least a mile square. This place is large enough to hold an army."

"At one time it did" I reminded him.

"I will go back to my people at the foot of the ramp. We will set up our temporary camp there. I will be sure no one bothers you. Sentries will be posted at the bridge around the clock to insure your privacy. I will have food sent to you every few days. If you need any help raise a flag on that pole on the tower. I will come at once or at least as fast as I can." He embraced us both. "Good hunting and good luck."

CHAPTER 48 ✠ ✠ ✠

Alon and I spent the next fifteen days exploring the castle ground which were now our domain.

"Mark, we've been over these grounds ten times, checked on all the hundreds of rooms we've looked everywhere but so far haven't found anything of significance."

"True Alon, but the real search hasn't begun yet. I've been trying to get the feel of the place. What it must have been like for the Knights who were living here. What they would do each day. But mainly where would they hide 90,000 pounds of gold in crates, 100 pounds per crate; more then 900 crates, where would they put it? They would have to have storage underground, like Fort Knox for that amount on treasure."

"I agree. That means they would have had to construct large vaults or chambers to put the hundreds of boxes in. I estimate more than one room, a large space with high ceilings. Each room would be needed to hold a few hundred boxes. That means you would need at least 4 or 5 rooms like that."

"Yes," agreed Alon. They would need a gigantic cavern to hold that much gold." Now all we have to do is figure out where those rooms could be." "I think we should take a day off from our search to clear our heads then come back and start fresh tomorrow" suggested Mark. "Where ever the treasure is it won't be going any place. Beside we can use a break."

"That's ok with me. What do you want to do??"

"I've been looking at the town across the fields alongside the river. I keep thinking of the phrase water and purgatory. There's a river running along the edge of the village and a field now that was once a swampy marshland according to Nawaz; maybe that could be a type of purgatory."

I know that sounds farfetched but who can tell what that crafty knight had in mind.

"Whatever," said Alon. It doesn't make much sense to me but we can use the break, any excuse will do to get me out of here. let's go."

When we reached the bottom of the steep ramp I told Nawaz what we wanted to do.

"Sounds like a good idea he agreed. Mind if I tag along, I always wanted to see Templeton myself but never had the opportunity."

"Templeton?" I asked.

"Yes, that is the name of the town; it's named after the Templar's obviously." He signaled for Mousa his driver and off we went in the clean Range Rover. "I will tell you about the town we are going to, at least what I know." We drove over a smooth hard-packed dirt road. "The local municipal works department of Templeton maintains this portion of roadway, that's why it's in better condition than the lower end toward Adana Airport which is in no man's land. Anyway everyone who came to Mersin in 1311 went to live in the fortress on the mount. Knight's with all their support staff, close to 500 people in all. There were some Hebrews, both men and women, along with the group of Christians from France. Mostly men but there were a few women also. One Hebrew woman, supposedly a Jewish Princess with a court of maids had an advisor who was a scholar. He was a rabbi, along with a bodyguard of Hebrew warriors. The Templar's brought some French women along on their journey, not many – less than a dozen. To round out this group there were Turks who had been pressed into duty as laborers. The Turkmen lived outside the walls of the fort on the plains below. Then of course, there were some Turkish women, companions or whores, probably both who followed the men. That means that there must have been close to 900 or 1,000 people living in or around the castle along with cattle and horses. All had to be housed fed and cared for, a formidable task. Looking out from the castle's ramparts the leader could look down on the fertile land in the bend of a flowing river about nine miles to the north. He sent his men to investigate and report back. The report was positive in all regards but one. The land was firm, the soil good for crops, the river was fresh water fast-flowing stocked with abundant fish of many species. The land would make an excellent site to build a community. The only drawback was a swampy marsh that consisted of dirty stagnant water infested with reptiles and mosquitoes – possibly malaria-bearing. The leader put a large party to work on eradicating the swamp, draining it then carting in clean dirt and sand from the desert wasteland to the east to fill in the damp ground. Once that was complete he sent all the non-military personnel to begin building a city."

"Look," Alon interrupted. "look at those horses in the field alongside the road; they are beautiful."

"Yes, Arabian pure-bred horses. They are some of the best horses in the world. They are bred here on this farm which is renowned the world over."

"Stop," commanded Alon. I want to get out to look at these animal up close."

Standing next to a rail fence we watched about a dozen horses run through the open grass fields.

"They are magnificent," said Alon.

"Yes" agreed Nawaz. "Are you familiar with the Arabian horse?"

"No not really."

"Let me tell you the little I know. The Arabian horse originated in the desert of the Middle East thousands of years ago - maybe 5,000 years. It was bred by the Bedouin tribesmen who used them in place of camels for battle and transport. These horses are intelligent with extreme energy, they can run all day. They have incredible endurance due to a large lung capacity. The Arabian horse has been prized by every ancient warrior from Genghis Khan to Alexander the Great. It is said that even Mohammed the Holy Prophet of Islam had five prized Arabian mares that started a famous blood-line. Here's one for you Mark, during the American Revolution General George Washington's horse was an Arabian stallion. The horses you are looking at could cost several hundred thousand dollars each depending on their blood-line. A million would not be out of the question."

Just then an ATV, an all terrain vehicle, came speeding up to the fence, two men aboard, one armed with an HKMP5. "Help you?" he asked in Turkish.

"Just admiring your animals. "replied Nawaz in Tukish.

"If you'd like to see them or learn more, go to that office building," one said pointing.

"Don't stop here, we get nervous. Bandits are always trying to steal our livestock; we tend to be jumpy. You might just be scoping us out so you can come back in the black of night to ride off in the dark with some of our prized horses."

"I understand," said Nawaz. We meant no harm we'll be on our way." We continued into Templeton.

The town was neat, tidy with wide clean streets lined with glass fronted stores. Well dressed people walked along on cement walkways.

"Seems prosperous enough to me remarked Alon. Look there's, a small café. Let's get some refreshment. I'm thirsty. I could use a lunch break with real food instead of military rations." Alon and Mark sipped Perrier with real ice and lemon, Nawaz had his Turkish coffee as did Mousa, who sat quietly at the table not speaking. When we finished we made a circuit around town. There was a post office a police station some warehouses or industrial buildings. A red brick building I took to be a school near a city hall with a gold dome on top. A residential area with street after street of one and two-story houses all nicely landscaped. The city of Templeton seemed prosperous, a nice place to live. We drove to the wide flowing river." Park on the bank near the bridge Mousa, we can get out there."

"It's wide and clean said Nawaz, standing on the bank at the side of the wide swift running river. "Look at the bridge spanning the river to the far side."

"Strong and well-constructed," said Alon. "The river must be at least 150 feet across at that point. Wonder when it was built and by whom."

A car pulled up behind our Land Rover. A plain black American Ford Crown Victoria.

"The police, I said, same the world over."

A very big young man wearing a crisp blue uniform no hat walked up to us. "Good day can I help you?"

"I don't think we need any help," I said rudely. *Sometime Police bother me.* He colored slightly at my remark.

"I didn't mean to intrude; it's just that you aren't from around here. I wanted to know if there was anything I could help you with. You know like directions or information on our city."

"No, we were just passing through, so to speak. We want to see Templeton while we are here."

"This is a very friendly town; friendly people. We live a healthy, happy carefree life. We are not normally bothered by the outside world. It's been like this for 800 years. It is how we like it."

"Excuse me for asking," said Alon. "But your accent – are you Israeli?"

The man smiled. "Yes I am, can't seem to get rid of the inflection. I'm A Sabra from a kibbutz near Galilee. Some people from Templeton came to my kibbutz to study our water purification and-bottling plant. One was a young woman, an extremely pretty young woman. We were attracted to each other during her stay in my kibbutz. When she left I vowed to come to her as soon as my military service was finished; that was six years ago. Now I'm married to that beauty. We have a young son and an equally beautiful daughter. I am also Chief of Police."

"How many men on your force, Chief?" I asked, trying to make amends for my earlier out of character remark.

"Two. He laughed, but I'm Chief."

Back at the base of the ramp we said goodbye to Nawaz then started the long steep climb to the castle high in the sky. A guard stood waiting for us at the draw-bridge, he saluted as we passed. I spent the next day and a half going over the transcript from Professor Tal, looking for a hint – anything to help in our search for the treasure.

"Could it be a hoax?" asked Alon. "The treasure is a fabrication of some old men in Paris." A myth as transparent as a pane of glass.

"You mean a taunt to King Philip and Pope Clement?"

"Yes. The Templar's knew they were going to die so they let the King think they hid a vast treasure in a secret hiding place. They then went to their deaths keeping the story alive to cause the King untold anguish. It was their way of seeking revenge. The truth would be known only to them. People have been looking for this supposed treasure for 800 years. Has even one gold coin been found?"

"No," I answered. "Think about that Mark." People have searched around the world, Ireland, Scotland, Nova Scotia. The search has gone on for an eternity yet nothing has ever been found.

Our hand-held radio beeped, the red light blinking steadily.

"Now what," I said, as I put the receiver to my ear.

"Mark its Nawaz. You have company down here. Three people want to come up to see you."

"I don't know anyone here. Who wants to see me?"

"It's the Police Chief; he has a most beautiful creature with him. She brings you food from Templeton. A Turk servant is carrying a large box that smells good. If you don't want it I will be glad to accept it on your behalf."

"Food," screamed Alon. "Send them up at once, I need a good meal."

We walked onto the draw-bridge to wait for our surprise visitors. The big Police Chief helped the girl along the steep incline while a stocky dark skinned man walked behind carrying a large cardboard box.

"Good to see you both again. I hope you are in a better mood today than when we first met," smiled the chief of police.

Now it was my turn to color slightly. "Let's forget that, Chief. We'll start fresh."

"Good idea" he said, a bright smile showing strong white teeth. This guy could make a ton of money as a male model for the Ford Agency in New York.

"Let me introduce Ms. Roberta Bourn a citizen of Templeton." I couldn't speak. I was looking at a canvas by Botticelli, Bernini, or DaVinci. The girl was exquisite. Tall, at least 5'8, slender; a clinging cloth dress reaching to the ground hugged her frame showing her well-rounded breasts; flat stomach with prominent hips, child-bearing hips. She had long blonde hair braided into a ponytail that hung down her back reaching to her waist. But it was her face that held my gaze. No makeup, clear smooth skin, full lush lips, eyes so cool and pale they looked almost transparent.

"Why have you come?" I asked, addressing the Chief. But it was Roberta who answered.

"Benjamin told my sister and me about your meeting by the river. He told us you'd been working on an archeological survey for almost three weeks sitting alone night and day without a good warm meal. So we decided we would bring you some hearty food to keep you going, to keep your spirit up. I was interested in meeting the two of you since nothing very exciting happens in Templeton. Also, it gives Benjamin a chance to check you out some more."

"Come in, we can talk while we eat. My partner is salivating at the smell emanating from the box, let me lead the way." We started across the bridge into the castle, the man servant, if that's what he was, following behind.

"Stop! I ordered. "Alon you carry the care-package, while you I said, pointing at the swarthy man, you wait outside on the ramp. Don't step foot onto the bridge or come into the castle."

"What was that all about?" asked the Chief.

"I am a lawyer by trade. In my profession I have to evaluate people in a few seconds – clients, opponents of clients, other lawyers and of course jurors. That man is shady. No worse, he is not trustworthy he could be dangerous."

"Nonsense," said Roberta. "He has lived among us since he was a small child. He worked for my father on the ranch. I've known him my entire life. I can assure you Gozani is harmless."

"We'll see," was all I said. Let's sit in the portico and eat. "The meal was delicious." That's the best meal I have had in three weeks Alon sighed. I'm glad you liked it since I cooked it myself." said Roberta, who wished to be called Beth "I'm glad you enjoyed it."

"Like it, we loved it beamed Alon. I feel like a new man ready to go back to work. You can cook for me anytime Beth." That's all he had to say. Beth came with food every day, always in the company of the same shifty Turk. On the fifth day, she came with her older sister Rachel. I was amazed when they came over the bridge together since they were total opposites. Where Beth was fair, Rachel was dark with long black hair, an olive complexion, almost black eyes. Rachel was at least three inches shorter then her sister. Yet for all the difference you could see an uncanny resemblance. Rachel was a feisty woman, two years older than her sister yet just as beautiful in her own way.

"I'm 23" she told us as we ate. A candle flickered in the center of the table. The day was grey, ominous – a storm was coming, a strong wind blowing from the desert. While we sat enjoying our meal and the company of the two comely women we were interrupted by a loud commotion outside the castle.

"Wait here I said, I'll be right back." The Turk Gozani was grappling with one of the assassins who were guarding the draw-bridge. The assassin was reaching for the knife in the sash at his waist. The argument was about to end for Gozani, and end badly.

I pulled the Colt 45 from my shoulder holster, walked up to the two men putting the barrel of the gun into Gozani's right ear. In a low sinister voice, I said: "Stop or I will pull the trigger." He was afraid to turn his head, but he shifted his eyes looking into mine. Then he slowly sank to his knees, fear evident on his face. "Tell me Omar what is happening here?

"Afendi," he begun. "This pig of a half-breed wanted to go into the castle. I told him *no*, it is forbidden. He pushed me aside rushing for the entrance when I grabbed him from behind to stop him. He turned on me angrily grappling with me. That is when the fighting began."

"So Gozani, you want to go into the castle even after I told you to remain outside. What do you think is in there? What do you want to see so badly? There is nothing but stone nothing for you to steal." He remained on his knees looking up at me, eyes pleading the barrel of the gun pressing against his forehead. "You know Omar, I'm going to break one of my own rules. I'm going to take this snake into the castle. On your feet, follow me."

"No, no Master, I don't want to go, leave me here please." I reached down, grabbing him by the ear, twisting as he howled in pain.

"Follow me," I repeated. We crossed the bridge into the castle. I turned right walking along the inside stone wall. Whoever had planned and built this place was a visionary. They saw the need for cells to hold prisoners near the gated entrance. There were six stone cells, 8x10 feet with heavy wooden doors that were held in place by shafts of hard wood. I pushed Gozani into one of the cells slamming the door closed with a loud bang.

"No Master, please I'll go. I promise not to return," he pleaded. His muffled voice called out from behind the heavy door.

"No, you stay until I let you go. You are now my guest, you belong to me." I walked back to my meal with the two interesting sisters.

Before they left, I took Beth aside: "Beth, I would like to ask you an important question. Alon and I are going to be finished with our exploration in 10 days maybe two weeks. We will be going to Israel to settle some business there. We have been meeting here with you each day for what eight or nine days. I have been impressed with your intelligence, and knowledge, both you and your sister'. You have indicated your options here in Templeton are limited. Am I correct so far?"

"Yes Mark. What you say is true."

"So this is my proposal to you and your sister. Go with us to Tel Aviv.

I have friends there who will help you apply for admission to university, either in Tel Aviv, Jerusalem or Haifa. You can continue your education, live in a thriving economy and who knows what your options will be after graduation."

Her eyes sparkled a broad smile lit her gorgeous face. "Don't tease me Mark."

"I'm not. I mean what I say. Your education will be paid for I will see to that for both you and Rachel if you will come with me."

She put her arms around me, kissing me on the cheek. "Thank you Mark. I'll talk to Rachel."

"Good," said Mark. "Remember, we leave in about two weeks; decide by then."

No one came the next day. We examined the cellars of the cattle pens looking for an entrance to a chamber or passageway which would lead us to the treasure. Nothing. After a restless night with little sleep, we were walking on the parade grounds in bright sunshine when the radio beeped. "What is it, Nawaz?"

"We have a problem down here Mark."

"Don't tell me about problems" I answered briskly "I have enough problems of my own. We are running out of time with less than a week to go to 30 days. One week to go and no progress in sight. You take care of the problem I don't have time."

"I can't," he replied. "This problem is all yours."

"Alright, tell me, what is this big problem. What's so damn important?"

"There is a woman here who wants to see you, No - who demands to see you."

"I don't have time for this Nawaz. Send her away, whoever she is."

"She said I would have to kill her since she is not leaving until she sees you."

"Who the hell is it?! I don't know anyone here."

"She said her name is Rose, mother of Rachel and Roberta."

"Oh shit," said Alon, as I looked at the radio in horror.

"Say something, Mark."

"Ah… I stammered… Nawaz, send her up." The woman who walked into our temporary office was a composite of her two daughters. Her complexion favored Rachel in that she had dark hair a tawny olive complexion and dark intense eyes. She was of average height for a woman, about 5'5, with clear skin, highlighted by a few freckles over her nose. The most striking thing was the set of her jaw and the look on her face. Determination, anger, maybe defiance probably all three.

"Which one of you is Mark," she demanded, hands on hips, legs spread firmly apart, wearing beige jodhpurs, polished brown knee-high riding boots. She was an imposing figure of a woman.

"I am," I answered. "What's wrong? What's the problem?"

"You're the problem, you dirty old man!"

"Whoa," I said. "What are you talking about? I've never been called a dirty old man before. What have I done to offend you?"

"I'm talking about your offer to run off with my daughters." "He wants to take us to Israel" Beth tells me all expenses paid. I guess that's one way to get into a girls pants!"

"That wasn't my intention," I said in my defense. "Let me explain."

"Go ahead, and it better be good or I'll set Ben on you."

I tried to explain my proposal. "I offered it because I could see the vast untapped potential the girls had. They speak three languages, are conversant in philosophy, psychology and history. I only wanted to offer them an advantage to continue to grow intellectually."

"Truly," said Rose skeptically. "You have no designs on their bodies?"

"Rose, I'm almost old enough to be their father. They are both singular beauties, different but similar in many ways. Any man would be happy, no fortunate to have either of them. However I can assure you my only intent was with their well-being." I could see her visibly relax.

"Then let me ask you, why not take this up with me, their mother and protector?"

I sat, not knowing what to say when Alon stepped in as my savior. "May I call you Rose he asked pleasantly?"

"Yes," she replied. "You can call me Rivka, Rose in Hebrew."

"Ok, Rivka then. My friend is not a parent. Also, he has been under a strain for the past few months which means he wasn't thinking clearly when he spoke with your daughters. I can assure you he meant no disrespect by not approaching you first. As you can see he now regrets it. Of course as the mother of the two women in question your decision should be considered. So speaking for my friend go talk with your daughters, make a decision everyone can live with then let us know. The offer is a valid one meant in good faith." Now that the hostility was out of the way, the conversation turned civil.

"I have a question for you Rose. Your daughters are so beautiful yet so different why is that?"

"They are only different in physical appearance. Under the skin they are very similar, both smart, vibrant, intelligent women. I raised them that way. Would you like to know the story?"

"If we are going to take them to another country, put ourselves on the line so to speak, yes we would said Mark"

"Before I start, I must ask, have you seen Gozani the Turkish horse-groom? He's been missing for four days. My daughter told me the last time she saw him he was waiting outside the castle by the draw-bridge."

"I'm afraid we haven't seen him," said Mark thinking *I'll let him out of the cell once I've heard the story. Maybe maybe not.*"

CHAPTER 49

ROSE STORY

I was born in Templeton. I was educated here through high school. Then attended Marmara University in Istanbul where I majored in political science and foreign languages; I speak six fluently. After I graduated with honors I came back to teach in the high school called Delhawal High, which is where I met my husband; but I'm getting ahead of myself. Eric, my husband, was born in Iceland. His father was a Norwegian Jew, a doctor who escaped from Norway in 1943 when it was occupied by the Germans. At that time the Nazi's began rounding-up Jews for deportation to concentration camps. The Doctor was smuggled to Iceland aboard a fishing boat after paying the Captain 20,000 Norwegian Krone. It took the man years to get a license to practice in Reykjavík. In 1951, he met his wife, Eric's mother a native Icelander. So you have two Vikings, or at least two Norse people uniting. Both were tall, strong and fair. The language is Icelandic – a north German language. Iceland became independent from Denmark in 1944. There were only about 100 Jews in Iceland living amid a lot of anti-Semitism. Unfortunately it's the same all over the world. When Eric was three years-old, his mother and father were killed walking home from synagogue one Friday night. No one was ever convicted of the murders. An American professor who was in Iceland to give a lecture heard about the attack which left a poor boy, a poor Jewish boy, an orphan. The Professor went to the Government and asked to become guardian of the child. The Government of Iceland wanted to keep the incident quiet so they agreed to let the Professor take the child. The Professor was a bachelor which meant he couldn't keep the boy or raise him properly. But this collage professor had a married sister living on a ranch in Texas. She lived with her husband who owned one of the largest cattle ranches in the State of Texas. The ranch was called the Tule Ranch in Briscoe County Texas. Margret and Martin Borne had been happily married for 20 years but had no children. She couldn't have any so they were overjoyed when her brother came to the ranch with a three year-old infant for them to care for. It was a gift from heaven for the couple and for Eric also. He grew up in the outdoors learning his adopted father's business. He learned to ride horses; herd cattle manage hundreds of workers. He was a hands-on manager like his father who took pride in teaching the boy as he grew into manhood. He treated Eric as his real son and heir. Eric mastered all the details necessary to run a major working ranch. His mother made sure he became educated the old way, home-schooling, she was his teacher. They also made sure he knew he was Jewish by bringing a rabbi to the ranch twice a week for three years to educate him in the Torah. He was a bar mitzvh at thirteen in a temple in Waco Texas by the rabbi who had educated Eric in the basics of Judaism. When he was sixteen he learned about Birthright in Israel. Do you know what that is?"

Alon said "Yes." Mark said "No."

"Tell him Alon," Rose said.

"Birthright is an organization in Israel that sponsors free ten-day trips to Israel for Jews from around the world. The trips are all-expense-paid junkets for young Jews, 18 to 26 years-old to come to see the country. It is called Taglit, which means discovery. The trip is meant to help these young visitors connect with Judaism through a close association with Israelis, both civilian and military peers."

"Yes," agreed Rose, It is an awaking of the Jewish spirit. Eric, at the age of sixteen, wanted to go on this adventure."

"Wait," said Mark. "I thought Alon said eighteen was the minimum age."

"He did and it is. But Eric was the adopted son of a prominent, powerful and well-connected family who had sent others to Birthright some years before. One phone call to a wealthy philanthropist in Philadelphia who supported Birthright along with a hefty donation cleared the way for Eric to go at sixteen. He went for a ten-day visit and never returned to Texas on a permanent basis. He would only return for short visits. Once when his mother died then again when his father died. His father's will pasted ownership and control of the Tule Ranch to Eric. He arranged to give operational control to Robert Morse the Manager who had worked on the ranch for over 20 years. Eric put Robert in charge of the operation of the ranch then went back to Israel, the land he had come to love. He would go back to Texas every year for a few weeks to look over the ranch, check on the operation with Robert, than come back to his interest here in Turkey. I will explain. After we married I went to Texas with him once before my children were born. It was quite an experience for a small-town girl from Templeton. Anyway, Eric fell in love with Israel - the people, religion. But most of all the energy of this country to succeed. When the Birthright trip was over he went to live on a kibbutz. The kibbutz in Israel are mainly agricultural. They grew fruit and vegetables which are sold in the produce markets of the big cities. Eric decided he would introduce animal husbandry to the kibbutz where he was living. First, he got a bull from his Arab neighbors. The kibbutz already had some goats, and a few dairy cows. Eric set out to find a beef cow to mate with the bull. Within a year he had three calves running around the fields of the kibbutz. Next, he bought two horses from a Bedouin tribesman which he began to train. Soon his reputation spread to other kibbutz'. The word traveled from one kibbutz to another – there is an American Jew at Kibbutz Tovah who is good with animals. He will help anyone with advice about setting-up a corral.

One day a car drove up to the office of Kibbutz Tovah, an expensive sedan with a driver. An older man got out of the back, walked up to the old Jew who was the head of the kibbutz, like a mayor of a city. "I have come to see a kibbutznik who lives here, Eric Borne."

The old Jew looked at the man with disgust on his face. "Don't corrupt the young man. He is a good worker, a devoted socialist."

"You mean communist," said the man. "I know how this kibbutz is run, like all 400 others in Israel. Everyone lives free here, housing, food, clothing, all free. But Kibbutz Tovah gets to keep any income raised by its inhabitants for the good of the whole. I'm sure you take your share."

"How dare you!" said the old man.

"I dare because I'm a capitalist, an entrepreneur. That's why I dress well, live well; drive in a shiny new car. It's why I have a fat bank account.

My money isn't dirty I work hard to earn it. I also employ hundreds of people who can afford to live well because of my efforts."

"I understand you don't like me or the capitalist system, but we try to co-exist with your Draconian ways. Now get this young man so I can speak with him."

Eric came into the office tall and proud. He was only nineteen, still growing; but he was almost at full adulthood.

"Talk," said the old Jew.

Alone was the reply: "Leave us alone. When they were alone the man began his spiel. Eric my name is Moshe Mandel. I don't expect that means anything to you so let me tell you, I am one of the wealthiest men in Israel."

"What do you want with me?" asked Eric. I'm just a poor goat herder."

"You belittle yourself young man. I have been led to believe you are an expert in the breeding, raising, training and riding of horses. Am I correct?" The two spoke for hours, everything from Texas quarter horses to thoroughbreds. Finally, the man said: "Eric, I'm satisfied you are the man for the job I have in mind."

"What job," replied Eric. "I'm happy where I am."

"You are wasting your time and talent, my boy. I'm going to give you a chance to expand your horizons. I have Polo ponies and race horses. I want to have a stable of Arabian beauties, the oldest and best breed in the world. I want to hire you to go find me six of the best Arabians you can find, two stallions and four mares. I want you to purchase them then bring them to my farm in the Valley of Elah. There you will breed them to give me strong colts that will grow into a magnificent herd."

"I know horses but I don't know a great deal about Arabians," Eric replied.

"Then learn. I will pay you while you learn and employ you to search for horses for me. Not just any Arabians but the best you can find. I will employ you and pay you well to give me a special herd. You will be my head groom, trainer or whatever you want to be called." The two shook hands, the deal was sealed.

Eric spent months to learn about Arabians. Once he was satisfied he traveled throughout the Middle East looking for good animals to mate. He went to Syria, Iraq, Iran and Turkey. That's when we first met here in Templeton. I was at the Knight's stable exercising one of their stallions.

A large, jet black Arabian named *Ace of Spades*. I came back to the stable my horse-running hard lathered with sweat and foam. When I neared the corral I saw this tall, handsome man speaking with the stable owner, Ibrahim Aminos. I thought *The young man was bald*. Until, I walked up to them, leading the horse by the reins, letting him walk out to cool down.

"Come here," called Ibrahim. "I want you to meet a young man from Israel. He is here in Templeton looking to buy some Arabians. What do you think of that Rivka?"

"I think he came to the right place," I said, smiling at the tall handsome young man.

"His name is Eric, this is Rose" said Ibrahim, by way of introduction. Eric reached out to shake my hand. His large hand engulfed mine in a tender grasp.

"Careful," smiled Ibrahim "This Rose has thorns. He is staying with me for a few days while I show him some of our livestock. Care to join us for dinner?" Ibrahim asked.

Turning to Eric, he continued "This young lady knows a great deal about horses. You saw how she rides. The conversation over dinner was lively the company pleasant." I didn't see Eric for the next few days since I was teaching in the high school while Eric spent his days looking at horses.

On Saturday he found me reading on my porch. "I've come to say goodbye. I will be leaving this afternoon to return to Israel. I bought two horses from Ibrahim; that completes my quota of six horses. My work in the field is done. Now I go home to breed them."

"Good for you, Eric. It was nice meeting you I hope we meet again."

"Yes, thank you," he said. "I hope we meet again also." He began to walk away when he stopped turning back to me.

"By the way Rose one of the horses I bought was *Ace of Spades*, a magnificent animal. Each time I see him I will think of you riding him. You both looked majestic." I colored slightly then he was gone. I didn't see him again for three years. I was 24 now still teaching school. I came into the parking lot at the end of the day walking to my bicycle for my ride home when I saw Eric standing next to a car, one red rose in his hand, a smile on his face.

"Eric," I exclaimed happily. "What a surprise. Are you here to buy more horses?"

"Well yes and no" he said. "Can I take you to dinner tonight? I'll explain then. I may even ask for your help."

"Sure," I said, both interested and curious. When Eric returned to Israel after his first trip abroad he prepared the stable for the arrival of the six horses he had purchased. The day they arrived, Moshe-Pipik, that's what Eric called the wealthy industrialist, Moshe loved the horses Eric had purchased. But he swooned over *Ace of Spades*. Moshe claimed the horse was the finest beast he had ever seen and made it a point to ride the horse himself whenever he had a chance even though he was not a good horseman. Moshe opened a bank account for Eric in Bank Leumi. The first deposit was $50,000, as a bonus for the months Eric spent searching for the first six horses. After that, Eric earned $800 per week also deposited into his Leumi account. Eric told me he was allowed to purchase a few horses for himself for re-sale using Moshe's money. The profit made on these horses was split 50/50 with Moshe. By the time Eric left to come to Templeton, he had accumulated $188,000 in Bank Leumi, which he transferred to a branch in Mersin.

"First I want to tell you how lovely you look tonight. I will always remember the first time I saw you on *Ace of Spades* running hard across the field, you standing tall in the saddle."

"Yes," Rose answered smiling as she recalled that day.

"You'll be happy to know he is on his way here by steamer. He will be my prime stud."

"You mean you are going to bring a horse farm to Templeton?"

"Yes, that's exactly what I mean to do, and I want your help to do it."

"What do you need from me?" I asked.

"First, I don't know the area well. I need a piece of flat grazing land, at least forty acres with good road access. I want to open a horse-breeding operation. If the property has a house or a barn that would be a plus."

"Give me a few days," Rose replied. "I'll come up with something for you. Where are you staying?"

"At the B&B on the side-street called the Gien."

"Mrs. Schwarz, excellent choice she is a nice woman. She will mother you."

We met after school two days later. "I think I have what you want," I told Eric.

"I know you do Rose" he replied, a mischievous smile lighting his handsome tanned face.

Rose blushed. "I mean the property you wanted."

"I knew that's what you meant he smiled a boyish twinkle in his eyes. Hop into my pick-up and point the way." After driving about six miles from town on a dry dirt road I told him to stop by a low rail fence before an open pasture.

"This is the property I had in mind for you. Its 63 acres of flat farm land with good grass. There was a house on the property but it burned down three years ago. The owner was so depressed he just up and left. The farm has lain vacant ever since. The town took possession of the property for back taxes since it was abandoned. There's an old wooden barn, it's kind of rickety so it will need to be repaired. I know the parcel is for sale. The town would be happy to get it back on the tax roll. Let's drive in so I can show you the barn."

That night at dinner Eric asked "What do we do now? I liked what we saw today he continued. The barn can be repaired easily while the foundation and basement of the burned house are solid. I can have a new house built to my specifications on the old foundation."

"We can go to the City Planning Commissioner tomorrow," said Rose. "I'll get a substitute to cover my class for me."

The next day we sat with Dennis Osman, in his office in the municipal building. The sign on his door announced property and land department manger. "I'm very happy someone finally wants that property. It's an ideal place for a horse farm." The two men negotiated for an hour to reach a price that was agreed upon. "Good luck you two" Osman said. "You have a nice young man here Rose; keep him happy."

Eric hired five farm-hands who set to work fixing fences, repairing the barn, tending the grounds. They worked from sun up until dark, Eric working at their side. The hired hands slept on cots in the barn while Eric stayed at the inn as construction began on his house. "What should I name our new enterprise?" he asked me one night over dinner. He began to rattle-off names one after another.

"Stop," Rose said. An Arabian horse farm can have only one name. He looked at me, a perplexed frown on his face.

"And you have the answer? The one fitting name for my farm?"

"Yes I do," Rose replied. "There is only fitting name. One that every Arab horseman will know immediately, one every Islamist will love. Your farm will be famous around the world."

"And you have this magical name," he asked again.

"I would say more mystical than magical. But yes, I do."

"Then please tell me."

"First, I must ask you Eric, are you familiar with Mohammed the Prophet and his ascension, his night journey."

"No, I'm not," said Eric. "Tell me."

"Mohammed was asleep in Mecca when he was awakened by the Angel Jibril-Gabriel."

"Come with me Mohammed, Allah your God is beckoning you." Jibril led Mohammed outside where a winged white horse stood prancing. "Mount the steed," commanded Gabriel "And we will be off." Mohammed jumped onto the horses' back as they flew over the land to Jerusalem, to the Al Aqsa Mosque. From there the horse ascended into the heavens where Mohammed met Allah. After their discussion the horse took Mohammed back to the mosque; then returned him to Mecca in Saudi Arabia, all in one night. It was said the strides of the horse were the limits of his eyesight."

"Don't keep me in suspense, girl. What was this creature's name?"

"The horse was called Al Buraq. That will be the name of your farm, Buraq Farm."

"That was the beginning of the most famous Arabian horse farm in the Arab world. You can visit it today though it has grown greatly. The original 63 acres in Templeton only keep horses ready for sale or sold awaiting shipment. There are an additional 198 acres run by Eric's partner Mehdi. Then there are two more parcels some miles north of Templeton. One parcel is 834 acres for horses, the other 765 acres is used to raise cattle - mainly Texas Longhorns, along with Angus and Brahmin bulls. Cattle that Eric breeds for beef for the tables of Turkey. The Angus comes from Scotland. Eric was fond of Angus cattle. He would breed them with Herefords originally imported from the UK."

"So you're telling me what started as a small horse operation grew into a major animal empire."

"Eric was a good businessman, but a better horse and cattleman. The partnership he entered into with Mehdi proves that. Mehdi was a few years older than Eric, A native of Templeton, a Turkish Jew whose parents came here from Istanbul. In the beginning, they were friendly competitors. Mehdi ran old man Ibrahim's farm after he passed. The two got along well even though they were competing for the same clients. One day over drinks Eric said: "Mehdi, you're a better businessman than I am but I can run circles around you when it comes to animal husbandry."

"True enough," replied Mehdi.

"So why don't we join forces" continued Eric. "You can handle the books, money, contracts while I run the farms. We join your farm with mine to create one enterprise under my name."

"But my farm is twice the size of yours."

"True," said Eric. "You have close to 180 acres to my 63, but who has the better bred stock? Whose animals command more money on the open market? It will even out in the long run. We'll both be better off and make more money."

"So they had another drink, shook hands, and joined forces under the Buraq banner. One stormy evening I was home grading papers when there was a loud banging on my door. I opened it to see Eric standing there soaked from the rain, a puddle forming at his feet. What is it Eric what's the matter.

"Get a jacket Rose, come quick, I need your help."

"What is it?" Rose asked. "One of my Arabians, she's giving birth but the foal breached. I tried to get Mustafa the vet, but he's stuck out in the county somewhere. You've got to help me or I'll lose both mother and foal."

"This was in the early stages of his operation; to lose both animals would put a strain on Eric's operating budget. So I grabbed a jacket and ran with him."

"Slow down Eric or you'll kill us." The pick-up was sliding from side-to-side as we sped down the slick dirt road. We were splashing through puddles, spray flying while lightening flashed lighting the black angry sky like a strobe light. The truck came to a sliding stop near the barn. We jumped from the truck running through the slashing rain to the open entrance of the barn. A light was burning overhead showing us the way to the stall where the poor horse was whining in pain. The mare lay on her side taking short painful breaths between cries of agony. I saw the problem immediately. The colt's backside was extending from the mother's womb;

but its hind legs were stuck in the opening. Eric and I worked to push the colt around until we could free its legs. I pulled gently as Eric worked with the mother to push the baby back into the mare then turn the body to extract the hind legs first. It was rough going but we finally succeeded in helping free the colt from the mother's womb. The baby popped free of the mother who lay shacking on the bloody hay moaning feebly. Eric wiped the colt down with a damp cloth. I did the same to the mother who raised her head looking at me with big brown eyes as if to say thank you. We stood together looking at mother and new born colt when Eric's hand found mine. He gave a little squeeze to let me know he was there with me.

"Thank you, Rose I don't think I could have managed without you." But we are a sight he remarked. He was right. Aside from being covered in blood and gore we were both soaked to the skin from the rain. I began to shake, my body trembling uncontrollably. It is either the damp chill or the drop in adrenaline level Eric told me.

"Probably both," said Alon.

"Yes, you are probably correct."

"Come into the house" said Eric leading me by the hand. "The shower is hot; I'll get some dry clothes for you and a shot of vodka or bourbon. There is a fire burning in the fireplace, if it hasn't gone out. It will warm you. Sitting on the couch in front of the fire, a glass of Wiser Canadian Whiskey in my hand I felt relaxed after the hot shower. I'm not sure if I seduced Eric or if he came on to me all I know is I was in his strong arms our lips locked together. We'd been together constantly for nine months by this time, yet up to this moment had never kissed or made physical contact. Although I had thought about what it would be like to make love with Eric it was an unfulfilled fantasy.

I had imagined what our love-making would be like many nights as I drifted off to sleep. Now here I was in his strong arms. This was our first embrace, our first kiss, our first romantic contact. Our first kiss seemed to last a lifetime. I won't bore you with the details but the reality was even better than the fantasy. I guess it was for Eric also since he asked me to marry him two weeks later. We were married in the local synagogue in Templeton then went to Israel for a two week honeymoon and business trip. It was a beautiful time for us both, a memorable honeymoon filled with gayety and love. After two weeks we came back to Templeton to build the farm into a powerhouse. It was Eric's dream to create an empire, a dynasty, which Eric did. And now you want me to let my daughters move to Israel with a man I don't even know."

"Rose, I tell you again, I meant no disrespect to you." My intentions were honorable. I was only thinking of your daughter's welfare.

"Speaking with you now Mark I realize that is the case. You are just another dumb man who needs a woman to help him see clearly. I'll leave you to your studies now." With that, she got up walking out of the castle over the draw-bridge to return to her life in Templeton.

"Some women," said Alon.

I just shook my head in agreement.

CHAPTER 50

That night we were asleep in our sleeping bags when I bolted upright in the dark chamber. The answer to de Vaux's riddle blinking like a neon sign before my eyes.

"What is it?" asked Alon. "What's going on?" he murmured, still groggy with sleep.

"I finally solved the puzzle. I understand what deVaux was telling us.

"You mean the purgatory thing?"

"Yes, it's suddenly clear to me. I must admit that Templar leader was a shrewd knight. If I'm right we will discover the treasure today, if I'm wrong, it will be time to fold our tents like the Arabs and steal away into the night."

"Good" said Alon. "Then we can go back to smuggling or arms running instead of being cooped up in this mausoleum for a month with nothing to show for our efforts. Now do you want to tell me your brilliant deduction so we can get on with our search now that I'm awake and curious."

"Yes but it may seem far-fetched, so try to follow my thinking. First the reference to purgatory, do you know what Purgatory is, Alon?"

"Yes, it is hell. A hot place below ground where the damned are sent for eternity." "They are condemned to shovel coal to keep the fires burning. You know, like Dante's Inferno.

"you are partially correct." Mark laughed.

"What do you mean partially," Alon demanded.

"Purgatory is not hell. It is an intermediary space below heaven but above hell. It is like a holding space where people who are not good enough for heaven but not bad enough for hell are sent. While there they can work at becoming a better soul. If they succeed, they can then rise to heaven, if not they are committed to the depths, to hell. So the first fact and the important one for us is that purgatory is a holding area, a storage place. Secondly, Purgatory has been described as a space in a deep dark mountain. What is our castle sitting on?" I asked.

"We are on top of a mountain of solid rock rising from the flat land below up to a height of 900 or 1,000 feet.

"Correct, we are sitting on solid rock. But I believe that solid rock has been carved out about 100 or 200 feet below us. I'd wager there is a man-made cavern that is full of a priceless treasure sitting under our feet. What we have to do is find the entrance to the chamber. We just have to find the way in."

"How are you going to do that, Mark? We've been looking for an entrance for 28 days with no success."

"Yes Alon. We've been looking, but in all the wrong places. We have to look in water."

"There isn't a great deal of it up here" Alon pointed out. "Just the large catch basin on the plain at the edge of the parade-ground."

"That's not it," Mark said firmly.

"Then what water are you speaking of?" asked Alon, mystified.

"Where else do we have water?" asked Mark. "Think."

"The only other water is in the fountains or the large well by the kitchens. The decorative fountain in the courtyard and the other well by the barracks building for drinking water for the populous."

"That's it, I can't think of any other water. Hell Mark, we've been over these grounds a hundred times, that's all the water I can think of."

"No," said Mark. "There's one more well, the smallest one in the castle. You have overlooked the well outside the sanctuary in the loggia."

"That's right; I didn't think of it. That well is almost invisible, because your eye is drawn to the sanctuary on one side and the great hall on the other." Two splendid rooms that occupy your vision.

"Exactly what deVaux intended."

"You're saying the entrance to purgatory is through the water in that well."

"That's my guess," said Mark.

"How do we travel through the water?"

"We don't. We make the water disappear."

"How the hell do you intend to do that, Mark?"

"I'm not sure yet, but there will be a way; we just have to find it."

We walked to the small well in the loggia.

"The stairway to paradise," I said, as I began to remove my clothes.

"What are you doing, Mark?"

"I'm going for a swim. There must be a clue in the well." I dropped into the water of the well, where the surface was about three feet below the rim, level with the floor. I ran my hands over the bricks.

"What are you looking for?" asked Alon, peering over the side, a bright light shining in his hand.

"I'm not sure, but I'll know it when I find it. I'm going down." I took a lung full of air, than dove below the surface. The water was cold and dark, no light down here. I swam deeper about ten or twelve feet below the surface feeling along the walls as I went. All I felt was smooth stone, nothing unusual. I surfaced for air.

"Anything?" asked Alon.

"No, just stone walls, maybe I didn't go deep enough. I'm going to swim down 25 or 30 feet then work my way up." This reminded me of my SEAL training in the deep-dive tank at the sub-base in New London, Connecticut. The dive tower is 120-feet deep. Its primary use is to train submariners in escape procedure, presumably from a sunken submarine to the surface above. But for the SEALS it was used for dive-training. We would dive from the surface to the bottom, 120-feet away; then swim back to the surface. Scary stuff until you got used to it then it was fun. There were escape chambers every 25 feet with air above the opening. You could duck into one if you had a problem. The difference between this cramped well and the sub-tower was enormous. The tower was light and bright with quadrants and markings on the walls to insure you always knew where you were. Also the tank was big – 25' feet across. Here I was in a three-foot pitch-black shaft. I started swimming slowly toward the surface, thirty feet above me, hands extended onto the walls as I rose upward. My head broke the surface where I sucked air into my lungs in huge gulps.

"Anything?" asked Alon.

"Nothing yet but I'll try again once I catch my breath." This time I dove down until I felt the solid bottom of the well. I guessed I musts be forty feet below the surface. I started up slowly, my hands running over the stone walls as I rose toward the light from Alon's torch shining dimly above me. My hand encountered a recess in the side of the stone wall. I stopped running my hand into the cavity. Then I felt it. Just as I thought it would be. I hovered in place trying to picture what I was feeling. My lungs began to burn as I took a thin piece of nylon line from the knife-handle at my waist. I tied one end of the line to a metal lever in the recessed space swimming for the surface the other end of line in my hand. I broke the surface gasping for air sucking huge breaths into my lungs.

"Well?" Alon asked calmly watching me trying to breathe normally.

"I think I've found what we are looking for, I managed to say while breathing hard. Hold this line while I go back down one more time."

"You need to rest, Mark. You look blue to me." plus your breathing is erratic.

I realized I was shaking; the water was cold. "One more dive, then I'll come out." Back at the depression I ran my hand into the cavity trying to determine what was there. I felt a metal lever about a foot-high alongside a spooked metal wheel. I climbed out of the well with Alon's help. He wrapped a blanket around me as I stood shaking uncontrollably, a puddle of water forming at my feet.

"This is it Alon the entry point to the underground vaults I'm sure of it. We have found the way in; all I have to do now is figure out how it works. I'm going to go into the well again once I stop shaking. I'll move the lever, than try to turn the wheel. After several minuets I climbed into the well swimming into the dark following the line to the lever. I grabbed it with both my hands moving it in the groove until it came to a stop. I gripped the wheel and began to turn it. I expected resistance since this well must have been full of water for over 700 years. To my surprise, the wheel turned easily. I could hear a low swish in my ears like the sound of a bath-tub drain with the water rushing out. I swam upward for the surface and much needed air. My lungs were burning. I realized the rim of the well was further away. Alon reached for my hand but couldn't reach me. I was slipping away from him.

"What's going on!" he yelled down to me. What's happening?"

"The water level is dropping I yelled up to him, I must have opened a vent or drain. Somewhere below me water must be escaping in a vent from the mountain. I kept dropping with the water level. I was now a good thirty feet below the lip of the well and still going lower. The rope and bucket came flying down to me.

"Hold the rope, Mark I don't want to lose you. I'll pull you up if I have to."

Suddenly my feet touched bottom or at least something solid, under me. The water continued to drain away, the level dropping on my body, neck, chest, waist, thighs, calves, ankles, until I was standing in a small puddle of water on the stone floor of the well. I looked up at Alon some distance above me.

"Drop my clothes and shoes to me. Find a heavy rope, secure it on top, than slid down to join me. Bring two good lights with you but raise the draw-bridge before you come to me, I don't want any unexpected company, male or female. With Alon squeezed into the narrow space beside me we stood looking at an opening carved into the side of the well wall.

"That's the entrance to Purgatory we've been looking for," I said.

"But how is it that the space didn't fill with water from the well?"

"A problem in psychics; our friend Archimedes again. Water seeks its own level. Duck into that opening and there will be another tube of stone, similar to this one. It will be the same height as this stone well. The water in that tube and this well would be the same depth due to water pressure and air density. The old Greeks knew what they were doing, and so did the Templar's. Follow me we have to climb out of here." There was a metal ladder built into the inner tube which I climbed, Alon coming behind me. Once over the top we stood on a solid stone platform. The platform was only five feet square, a stone stairway leading down into a dark chamber from one edge. I shined my lantern around the dark space where I could see the steps descending to the room below. It appeared to be a cavernous room stretching away into the darkness at the end of my beam of light. We walked down the carved stone steps beneath our feet.

"We're going down even deeper into the mountain" said Alon.

"Yes, we must be almost a hundred feet below the floor of the castle above and still going down." After what I estimated was another fifty foot descent the floor leveled out.

"We are definitely deep into the mountain now." We walked a hundred feet through a long tunnel whose ceiling was just above our heads. At the end of the tunnel we stepped into a huge open room. The ceiling was at least thirty feet high. We stood in awe looking into a tremendous open space.

"This chamber must be 50 feet long, by at least 40 feet wide."

"Yes, and it's stacked with wooden boxes. I'll bet about 300 boxes filled with ten gold bars. Each bar weighing ten pounds, one hundred pounds of gold per box."

"Shall we walk around the room and check it out." That's what we came for Alon, lets see what the crates hold. We walked up to the first row of wooden crates which were stacked in neat rows 3 boxes high.

"Help me set one box on the floor." We struggled to lower one wooden crate to the stone floor, it weighed 100 pounds. Alon took his K-bar knife from its sheath at his waist and began to loosen one of the planks of wood of the cover prying out the hand-made nails. It was difficult getting the board loose.

"We could use a pry-bar better than my knife."

"Yes, but we have to make do with what we have" Finally after much effort the board creaked then gave way. The reflection from our lamps was dazzling as the light bounced back at us from the orderly row of gold bars inside the box. Alon shook with emotion while I stood speechless looking at a ten-pound gold bar. Each bar was worth over $200,000 at current market price and there were over 9,000 bars down here. I picked up one bar looking at it closely.

"Beautiful isn't it?" asked Alon.

"Yes Alon, it is beautiful," I said, setting it back into the box "Come, let's explore what else de Vaux left for us to find." We walked around the rows of wooden crates, stacked in precise rows each three boxes high. At the far end of the vast chamber we came to a passageway leading away into the darkness the ceiling was low only about seven feet high, narrow, similar to the entrance tunnel to the main chamber. We walked into another chamber similar to the first.I think there will be one more like this holding the last of the 900 odd boxes. We came to another tunnel leading off the main vault.

"You go in," said Alon "I'll stay here in case you run into trouble." I began down the passageway coming to a gated opening on one side.

"A small chamber," I called back. "Like a cave really, just stone walls full of boxes and chests I'm going in." Opening the boxes I was dazzled by the contents. There were all sorts of gemstones inside. Some were set into rings, bracelets or necklaces, others just sitting in piles of loose stones. Some chests contained bejeweled statues, figurines, or other precious objects of art. I continued down the passage, walking past barred gates to more rooms built into the stone walls. Each room filled with an assortment of boxes creates or chests of various sizes and shapes. Once back in the main room I told Alon what I'd found. It is too much for the mind to absorb. The magnitude of the riches contained in these rooms is staggering.

"Amazing," was all he could say.

While you were gone I found another passageway on the opposite side of the main chamber, it's similar to the passage you described. There are many small rooms carved into the stone walls. The rooms on that wing were all filled with armor and weapons. There were swords of all types, lances, helmets, shields, full suits of body armor, room after room." We sat together on a stone bench built into the side of the ramp contemplating what we had discovered, wondering what to do next.

"You did it, Mark you solved the puzzle. Now you possess the wealth of a kingdom. My God Mark, you will be the wealthiest man in the world. You will posses more wealth than many third world countries."

After a few minutes of silence while we sat looking at our surroundings I stood. "Let's go, I've seen enough for one day."

It was 2:30 in the afternoon. We were sitting at the table in the makeshift study when Alon asked, "Have you decided what you are going to do now Mark?"

"I think so. I'm still working out the details in my mind. Put the draw-bridge down Alon I'm going to call Nawaz to come up and join us." Nawaz sat with Mark and Alon as Mark explained what needed to be done.

"This is what I need from you Nawaz, if all goes well we can be done in Templeton in three or four days."

"Tell me what you need, Mark I will see to it?"

"I need a mason one that can be trusted. I want him here as soon as possible. One of your men must bring him to me blind-folded. He is to bring five bags of ready-mix cement, twenty cinderblocks and 4 individual-6 foot lengths of ½" rebar. I will show him what must be done when he stands here before me. I will take off his hood and blindfold myself and replace it when it is time for him to leave. Next, I need another vehicle to take the two girls with me if they decide to go; I will speak with their mother again today. I want two military rucksacks with a back support, heavy duty rucksacks capable of carrying at least 100 pounds. That's it for now."

"I will have the mason here tomorrow by 1:00 p.m.," said Nawaz. "One of my assassins will leave in the Range Rover at once. He will return with the mason and the supplies you require in the morning. When you are finished with him my man will take the mason back to Mersin. If you wish to kill him to keep your secret safe let me know. The drivers will return with the vehicles you require on Saturday; That way we can leave for Mersin early Sunday morning."

"Very good, thank you Nawaz. No interruptions until the mason arrives."

"What are you up to Mark," asked Alon when we were alone. I told him my plan in all its detail.

CHAPTER 51 ✛ ✛ ✛

Nawaz brought the mason to me himself while his men transported the cement cinderblocks and rebar into the courtyard loaded on four mules. They unloaded the items onto the ground then left with the mules. The mason stood before me, black hood over his head, Nawaz at his side. I removed the hood from the man's head then the blindfold covering his eyes. He squinted in the light shading his eyes with his hand. Nawaz spoke to him in Turkish then turned to me.

"He does understand some English Mark. Explain what you want done. He is very competent at his trade; I wouldn't dear get you an inferior tradesman. With that Nawaz left to join his men in camp at the base of the ramp. I took the skilled mason to the top of the deep well sliding down the rope to the bottom below. I told him what I wanted done by words and gestures. He looked at me in surprise but seemed to understand my meaning. Alon passed down the supplies we would need in a large bucket tied to a heavy rope. The mason looked at me with wide brown eyes.

"Close hole?" he asked.

"Yes I nodded. Close the hole in the side wall. After the cinder blocks were in place he put a layer of cement over the entire wall covering the place where the opening had been. Back on top, I pointed at the well mouth.

"I want to make a ledge at the six-foot level, then cut rebar to cross over the well opening. Rest the rebar on the ledge that would now protrude from the side-wall. Once the rebar is in place I want you to close the opening with heavy chicken wire, cinderblocks and cement."

He said: "Crazy," in Turkish. "Alright, maybe I am crazy, just do as I say."

Once the ledge was in place I told him to stop.

"I'm going down to fill the well with water up to the level of the ledge. Alon when the water is at the right height pull the rope tied to me. I'll close the fill pipe trapping the water inside the well"

That done, I climbed from the well, the water just below the opening at the six-foot level from the top of the well. The mason was now closing the opening with cinder blocks

When he finished, it was 9 o'clock at night all was dark outside. The 3 of us sat down to eat an MRE dinner. When we finished eating I took a sleeping bag leading the mason to a cell in the outer wall, a cell next to where I had kept Gozani. Early the next morning I walked down the ramp leading the mason by the arm his eyes again blindfolded, the black hood over his head.

"I am sending three men to Mersin this morning, said Nawaz. One to bring back our Land Rover, the other two will bring two other vehicles to us"

"Why two?" I asked. "I just need one for the girls,that is if they decide to go with me."

"You will see why I want two, call it Nawaz-cunning he said smiling."

We stood watching the pick-up drive away. The mason alive in the passenger seat on his way back to Mersin after a harrowing two days with a crazy American.

I'm glad you didn't have me kill poor Ismail. He was frightened he was about to die. When I told him he could go but to forget everything that had transpired here he kissed my hand and blessed me. I believe he truly thought he would die by your hand or mine. Rest assured he will never speak of this incident to any one on fear of death.

"I'm going to Templeton to speak with the mother. It's Friday, time is running out on our enterprise here at the Gidian Crossroad." It is time to leave this place.

"Yes," agreed Nawaz. "It is time for us to go since I have observed someone watching us for two nights now – from that hilltop, to the east of us."

"Do you know who they are or why they are watching us?" I asked.

"No. I have let them live for now but we will move at first light in two days, Sunday morning at 8 sharp." We will leave the Templar's castle behind.

"I'm going to Templeton to speak with Rose. I must see if she has made up her mind regarding her daughters"

"Do you want Mousa to drive you?" asked Nawaz.

"No, I think I'll run to the village. I've been cooped-up in that castle for the last month with little chance to exercise. I could use a brisk run, beside It's only about eight miles to town. I should be able to cover that distance in a bit more than an hour. I remember when I could cover eight miles in less than fifty minutes."

"Yes Mark, but the hands of time catch all of us. I can remember when I could make love all night long with two or three partners."

"Didn't the sheep get tired?" I asked.

"Very funny, Mark. Maybe I'll let you run all the way to Mersin." Before I left I instructed Alon to fill the well to the brim with water from the pond. That way the well would look natural. No one could see the shelf I had the mason construct six feet below the floor.

I was jogging along the road at a steady pace hardly breathing hard. After spending yesterday morning moving some treasure with Alon, my body felt good, firm and strong; physical activity always made me feel better. As I came around a bend in the road I saw a black Ford pulled onto the shoulder, Benjamin stood leaning against the front fender. "What are you running from Mark, is someone chasing you?"

"No Officer. I'm just working up an appetite."

"Come, hop in, I'll drive you the rest of the way. Seated in the front passenger seat the police chief asked politely, why you are going to Templeton this morning?"

"Is that an official inquiry or social discourse?"

He laughed aloud. "No, just making small talk since I know you offend easily"

"I'm going to see Rose."

"To find out about her girls?" he asked.

"So you know about my offer then."

"I know you offered to take them to Israel, put them into university; even offered to pay for their education"

"That's true, Ben but how do you know all this?"

"Rose came to see me a few days ago to ask my opinion. She is godmother to my wife who is the daughter of her best friend. She values my opinion as a male figure ever since her husband was killed just over two years ago."

"What!" I yelled, startling Benjamin. "Pull over and stop now!" My head was spinning. "I spoke with Rose for nearly four hours. She told me her life story but never mentioned that Eric was dead. I had no idea. No wonder she was pissed at me for trying to take her girls away. Tell me the story Ben tell me what happened to Erik, how did he die? Rose led me to believe he was an exceptional man, a true Norseman. I had no idea he was dead,"

"He was both those things Mark, and more. Tall, blonde, strong as his bulls. He was bigger than me and accomplished at many tasks. A great father and husband. His two daughters meant the world to him as did his wife. He built a multimillion dollar international business right here in the town he loved. You see just a small part of his vast holdings in and around Templeton. Buraq Farms has 2,000 additional acres of land thirty miles north of here with over 5,000 head of the best beef cattle in all Turkey. Buraq beef is renowned in the Middle East, hell maybe the world. I can guarantee it is superior to Australian, Brazilian, or even Japanese Kobe beef. Each day some 200 head of cattle are sent to slaughter in Istanbul. Anyway what you want to know is what happened to Eric two years ago. Mehdi, Eric's partner had sold two stunning Arabian pure-breed white stallions to a buyer in America. The buyer was paying $350,000 each for the animals. Eric was going to drive the horses to Mersin to be loaded on a freighter for the trip to America. They left in the GMC Denali crew cab pick-up, the horses in a trailer behind, three Turk men, ranch hands accompanied Eric in the crew-cab. Eric and Mehdi talked into the night about the money Eric was going to receive on delivery of the horses to the ship. They decided to bring the money back to Tempelton in cash. The next morning when Eric was leaving, Mehdi, who was the businessman of the organization, changed his mind regarding the $700,000 dollars.

"I don't want you driving back with that much cash he told Eric, it's too dangerous. Deposit $680,000 into our account at Bank Leumi, just bring $20,000 back with you."

"Do you know if anyone listened to their conversation? Either that night when they spoke of the $700,000, or in the morning when they changed their plans?"

Ben was silent for a few minutes while he racked his brain to remember. "It's possible someone could have overheard the conversation the night before Eric left since they were talking in the office which is open to anyone standing near. But no one could hear their conversation in the morning. When they spoke in the morning they spoke next to the trailer holding the horses. They were alone in the dark; no one was close to them. Eric delivered the horses at the port with the help of the three grooms. He received the stamped bills of lading from a ships officer to present to the bank to collect the funds. When the documents were presented to the bank it triggered the letter of credit. We know Eric left the bank with $20,000 in a green zipper-bag, a pouch with Bank Leumi printed on it. The four men started back for home at 5:30 in the afternoon. Everyone believes they should have slept over night in Mersin and left to return in the morning."

"Why?" asked Mark.

"Because they were driving into the bad lands at dusk, a dangerous time to be there. Had they left Mersin after breakfast the whole trip would have been in day light. As they drove north into the dangerous section of roadway both front tires on the pick-up blow out at the same time. Eric stopped the truck ordering everyone out to see what happened. A spike-board had been placed in the road meant to stop the pick-up at that precise spot."

"Do you think Eric's truck was targeted?"

"I think so, but that's a suspicious Police Officer talking. A one-time military detective in the IDF, but one with a nose for quirky events. The bandits came swarming from the brush. The leader took the Bank Leumi case opened it, taking out the $20,000."

"Where is the rest of the money?" he demanded.

"That's all there is," replied Eric.

"Don't lie to me, or I will kill you."

"I'm telling you the truth, that's all the cash there is."

"No Infidel with the light hair, there is $700,000 dollars, I want it now! Do not try to deceive me or you will die, no more beautiful wife, no more young virgin daughters!"

"I'm telling you the truth that is all the cash I have. The balance is in the bank in Mersin." The Turkish bandit shot Eric in the right knee. Eric fell to the ground, he was in pain but bit it back.

"Tell me where the money is and you can live. Otherwise, you die like these Turk dogs with you." The bandit shot both grooms dead in front of Eric to make his point. He then shot Eric in the left knee.

"You can kill me now since I've told you the truth, that is all the cash I have."

"The man walked up to Eric, straddled his body, lowered the pistol to his head and shot him. He then proceeded to shoot the last groom.

"How do you know the details of this horrendous crime. It's almost as if you were reading an official police report."

"Your good Mark. All that information is in the official government report on the events that day. I was able to get a copy of it."

"Who gave the details to the police inspectors if everyone was shot, all four men dead."

"When Eric failed to arrive home by midnight, Mehdi went out to find him. I followed in my police car. After driving over two hours, we came upon the terrible scene – three dead men lying in the road, one badly wounded sitting in the truck. It was the wounded man who told the story about the events. Mehdi called the Federal Police in Mersin on his cell phone while I examined the scene by flashlight. I also lit some flares placing them in the road. After that I proceeded to tended to Gozani's wounds. He had been–"

"Stop," I said. "Gozani was the wounded survivor, the one who made the report?"

"Yes. He had been shot at close range under three feet I'd say since there were powder burns on his shirt and skin around the wound."

"Tell me Ben how were the three men killed?"

"Eric was shot in both knees, then the forehead between the eyes. Each of the grooms was shot once in the forehead between the eyes."

"And Gozani" I asked, where was he shot"?

"The wound was in the left shoulder just below the collarbone. The bullet passed right through, it was a clean wound."

"The kind of wound we'd call a million-dollar wound in the military."
"Bad enough to get you removed from battle, but not lethal; no chance of dying unless you bled to death. He was shot at close range, but in the shoulder, not between the eyes like the others. Don't you find that a bit strange Mr. Detective?" He looked at me, a quizzical expression of his face."

"What are you saying?" he asked me.

"I'm not sure," I replied. "But if you kill the other three, why let one live?"

"To tell the story?" he replied

"I don't think so. Those bandits don't want to leave anyone alive to tell their story. They don't need publicity since they aren't governed by the Geneva convention. They don't operate like civilized people because they are cold blooded killers The shooter could have moved the barrel of the gun six or eight inches and blown Gozani away like the others. But he didn't do that, why. As a smart police officer I'd say it's something to think about."

"Now, back to Rose," I said. "Why didn't she tell me Eric was dead? Why keep it from me?"

"You have to give her some leeway here, Mark. When Eric was killed it was devastating to Rose. She and Eric were more than just husband and wife. They were friends and close companions. They rode horses together, looked after the livestock together, and went everywhere together. Eric treated her like one of the guys, his equal in all things. I don't think he ever made a major decision without discussing it with Rose first. He worshipped her and respected her business sense. After his death she took his body to Mersin to be buried in the Mersin Interfaith Cemetery. It is one of the only cemeteries in the world where the three major faiths – Christian, Muslim and Jew – are buried side-by-side. Rose had Eric buried with the two Muslim Turk men beside him."

My thinking continued. "Ben explained even now, two years since Eric's death, she has a hard time accepting the fact he is gone. Eric is still a part of her, she keeps his memory close. So my suggestion to you is to broach the subject delicately. Let her come out with the story her way; try to be diplomatic."

The Police Chief gave Mark his card as he let Mark out in front of the café. "Call me if you need a ride back to your camp, I'll come for you."

"Thanks Ben," Mark said, as the black Ford drove away.

Mark entered the café. Is Rose Bourne here he asked the waitress?

"You're in luck, Sir. She just came in; she's sitting in the courtyard behind the restaurant." Rose was sitting alone at a table under an open beach-umbrella.

"Mind if I join you?" I asked.

"Please do," she said. I can use the company. What brings you into town?"

"Actually, you do," said Mark. My work is almost finished. Another day to wrap things up and we'll be leaving for Israel."

"Good for you. I hope your trip was a success."

"I won't know until I have time to study my notes and the thousands of pictures I've taken. I will consider my journey a success if you tell me you will go back to Israel with me and your two daughters."

"Oh, so now you want me to join you on this magic flying carpet-ride?"

"Rose, I've already told you I meant to be proper in my offer. I would have included you had I known your true situation. I was surprised to learn Eric is dead. The way you explained things to me a few days ago at the castle, it seemed he was alive living with you. I couldn't see you going with me then. But now, since the situation is different, I want to take you and your girls with me. The three of you can be together in a new location. A change of scenery could be good for the three of you."

"That's kind of you Mark. But for me Eric is still alive; he's alive here; this is his domain. It's where we lived, loved, and grew together. I was twenty when I met him, only 24 when we married. We were together 25 years, raised our daughters here, grew a multi-million dollar business here, and now you – a stranger – sit with me and ask me to leave him and all my memories behind."

"I'm not asking you to leave him. He will be with you wherever you go forever. He will be with you for all time. What I'm asking you to do is move on with your life. It's time to stop mourning, time to wake from a bad dream and start to live life again."

She became angry, tense. "Who are you to tell me that? What gives you the right to give me directions regarding love, life and death? What makes you an authority?" she demanded angrily.

"Do you think you're the only one who experienced the loss of someone you loved, someone you cherished," Mark asked. "You're not unique in that regard. Do you want to know what makes me an authority?"

"Yes, tell me," she demanded.

"I was deeply in love with a wonderful woman. We were not married but just as attached as you were with Eric. We lived together for nearly two years in New York City. Katherine was a Vice President with

Intercontinental Airline. Her duties were varied. She traveled a lot. On one extended trip we decided to meet in Paris for a week, then go on to London for four days, a business and vacation trip. We were due to fly back to New York the next day but went to have dinner in a famous restaurant with another executive from Intercontinental, a lawyer for the airline and a close friend of mine. I was paying the cab at the curb as the two of them crossed the street to the restaurant. I looked up to see a man, a suicide bomber detonate a suicide vest filled with explosives, ball bearings and nails. This martyr stood in the entrance of the restaurant when he detonated the bomb. My friend and my lover were both killed instantly. I was severely injured but survived. It took me months to be able to come to grips with the loss. I think about Kat daily; I'm sure I always will. I also blame myself each day for their deaths. I should have been able to save them. I saw the bomber, realized what was happening; but I was too late. I couldn't go back to work as a lawyer in my old firm. I tried, but couldn't cope. So I moved on; I left New York. My life in New York was a good one. I lived in a Penthouse apartment, which is beautiful. I had women chase after me but with Kat dead I wasn't interested. I think that gives me the right to give you advice; since I had to endure that horror just like you." It is hard to lose someone you love, someone you long for, but trust me Rose, life goes on and so must you.

"I'm sorry Mark. I had no idea."

"Of course you didn't. Neither did I know of your situation until an hour ago. I came to see what you had decided about your daughters. Now I want you to make a decision about yourself as well. I'm asking you to come with me." "The three of you."

"Why is this so important to you, Mark?"

"Rose, people are important to me; you are important, your two daughters are important. Think about what I've told you. If you decide to come, be at the foot of the ramp at the fortress at 7:30 Sunday morning. I have transportation already arranged for you. Please don't disappoint me." I stood, taking her hand in mine. "Your choice, Rose. Shiva is over, throw the black torn ribbon away; It's time to move on with your life. If Eric where able to speak he would agree with me."

CHAPTER 52

We stood by the vehicles at 7:40 on a clear Sunday morning in Turkey. Alon, Nawaz and me, talking together while the men loaded the vehicles in preparation for our departure

"Will the women show?" asked Nawaz.

"I don't know, "I replied. "I did my best. Now we will wait to see if it was good enough."

7:50 came and went and still no sign of Rose or her two beauties. Nawaz had the vehicles lined up on the road ready to depart. Our Land Rover first, then a black Hummer – meant for the women; the Mercedes truck next in line, the armed Humvee at the end.

"It's 5 of 8," advised Nawaz. We leave at 8 on the dot with or without them"

I looked at the second Hummer sitting off to the side of the road. It was an exact mate of the one in line.

"Was there a fire-sale on Hummers?" I asked, to keep my mind from worrying about Rose.

Nawaz laughed. "No not really. I bought five of them last year. General Motors makes a good off-road truck. I have a car dealer I work with in New Jersey. He is a used car specialist but he has connections to get any make or model of new car or truck I want. So I contact my friend Gary Glaser at Gary Motors in Lodi New Jersey via e-mail. Tell him what I want and presto he quotes me a price. I wire the money and he does the rest. He arranges to get the vehicles to Port Newark, files the shipping documents and about six or seven weeks later I have my vehicle in Mersin. I sold three of the Hummers to buyers in Istanbul for a handsome profit. The money

I received for the three paid for all five. So in effect these two were free, they cost me nothing, zero."

"Now what are you doing with the second one?" I asked again.

"I called Benji, the Police Chief. He should be here to see me shortly. He doesn't know it yet, but I am giving one to him – a gift."

"But you said you could sell it for a lot of money. Why give it away?"

Alon cut in. "A token of friendship, of cooperation. What Nawaz is saying is you never know when you might need a friend."

"Exactly, Alon. As a smuggler, or someone outside the law, you know you need all the friends you can get; especially ones with power."

We heard the roar of the Crown Vic's interceptor engine as the car sped toward us then screeched to a halt in a cloud of dust. Ben got out from behind the wheel, another Police Officer exiting the passenger door. Nawaz walked up to Ben pulling him aside as the rear doors of the car opened. Rose, Rachel and Roberta stepped out. I walked over to them.

"Glad you decided to join our party."

"I'm Termil" said the officer. "Where do you want their luggage? It's in the trunk."

"Put it in the back of the black Hummer, the one that's in line on the road."

Benjamin and Nawaz came up to join us. "Sorry I'm late, said Ben. The girls had to get in some last minute goodbyes, but at least we made it in time."

"You did with only minutes to spare. We move at 8." We shook hands all around.

"Thanks for my new car Mark." Nawaz told me "you and Alon had a hand in arranging it for me. I'll think of you every time I drive it. And Mark thanks for talking Rose into going. You did a masterful job."

I was going to say: I didn't do anything, but decided to keep my mouth shut. I walked Rose to the black Hummer, the girls were already settled inside.

"Say all your farewells?" I asked.

"Yes, by the way, something unusual happened two nights ago."

"Friday night?" I asked.

"Yes. There was a knock at my door. Strange I thought, who could be banging at my door at 10:30 on a Friday night? I opened the door to see

Gozani standing on my porch. He looked awful – disheveled, dirty and he smelled horrible.

"Gozani, where have you been? I asked, I've been worried about you. No one has seen you for over a week. Mehdi said you didn't come to work, he wants to fire you. Gozani mumbled something about a religious retreat which seemed strange to me." He was never a religious person. Maybe he converted in my cell I thought.

"Ms. Eric," that's what he calls me. "Ms. Eric, I hear you go away. Leave Turkey, leave Gozani."

"Yes, I have decided to go away for a bit."

"When you go?" he asked. With the American and the others?"

"Yes," I replied, I am going with Mark, the American.

"Did you tell him when we were leaving?"

"Yes, this morning at 8 – driving to Mersin."

"Ok, in you go," I said, helping her into the passenger seat of the Hummer. I walked to Nawaz, who was standing with Alon next to the Range Rover.

"We have a problem," I said, telling him the story of Eric's death and my suspicions, then repeating Rose's story.

"What are you suggesting?" asked Alon.

"I'm not suggesting anything. I'm telling you I think Gozani was part of the group that killed Eric two years ago. I think he is with the same group now somewhere down the road waiting for us with his henchmen. I think he is waiting to kill us – me especially – then take the women hostage to extract a fat ransom from Mehdi for their return, we know that will never happen. They will be tortured, sexually abused then killed."

"I agree with you said Nawaz," "As one warrior to another, I trust your instincts. Better to be safe than sorry. Our instincts, our gut feelings are what keep us alive."

"If we get to Mersin without incident, I will laugh at you over a drink. If we are attacked, I will commend you over a drink. So we get to drink either way."

Nawaz called his men together speaking to them in Turkish. They seemed to grasp the importance of what he was saying since the attitude of the troops became serious.

"I'm changing the order of the vehicles. The Humvee with the 50 caliber machine gun will go first. I'm taking two men from the truck putting them in the Humvee. The Humvee will now have the driver and machine-gunner in front, four armed men in back. We go behind the Humvee, the Hummer with the girls behind us, then the truck with eight fighters last in line."

A black-clad assassin came to us carrying two AK-47's. "These are for you and Alon. There are four extra clips of thirty rounds, plus the clip in the weapon. That's 150 shots each."

"I have my Colt pistol," said Mark. "Alon has a nine-millimeter Beretta."

"Good, both Mousa and I have HK-5 MPS automatics— lethal at close range. You know we will be out-gunned and out-numbered I said."

"Of course," agreed Nawaz with a laugh. They know how many we are. Aside from the low-life traitor Gozani, I told you we were being watched. That's where Gozani probably was when no one saw him for all those days. He wants to kill you himself Mark. You embarrassed him, in front of my men. Then you locked him away in a windowless cell and made him crawl in front of you only to beg for forgiveness. I'd hold onto my balls if I were you since I'm sure he has designs on them. Let's get underway. My men know what to expect and what to do if we are attacked."

We drove for over an hours without incident.

"Maybe I was wrong, "I announced aloud.

"Do you believe that?" asked Nawaz.

"No," I replied. "Then we must be vigilant. If an attack is coming it will be in the next twenty minutes this is the danger zone." There was a tremendous explosion in the road ahead. The lead Humvee shuddered, shook then pulled to the left side of the road coming to a stop, smoke pouring from the damaged vehicle. Mousa reacted immediately turning the wheel hard right bringing the Land Rover to a stop on the shoulder of the road next to an open culvert.

"Move!" commanded Nawaz, dropping to the ground crawling into the culvert as bullets smashed into the Range Rover, glass shattering. More bullets were hitting the smoking armored humvee but were unable to penetrate the heavy armor

Alon was panting beside me lying in the ditch bullets whizzing by overhead, fun and game time, Mark."

I peered over the edge of the culvert looking for something to shoot at as bullets sprayed around us. I could see the black Hummer pulled up alongside the Humvee as the driver helped the three females into the safety of the armored hull. The machine-gun was blazing away from the top-hatch sending a steady stream of fifty caliber bullets into the brush. The truck was stopped further back on the road. There were two men prone on the ground under the truck firing into the heavy vegetation across the road. Where were the rest of the men from the truck? There should have been eight, but I only saw the two lying on the ground under the truck.

"Nawaz," I yelled above the noise. "Where are the other men?"

"Don't worry, Mark. They are around." An RPG round hit the Humvee, bouncing into the air to explode harmlessly. "Let's head down this culvert. Maybe we can hit them on the flank before they know we moved."

"Alon, stay here with Mousa. Keep up a steady rate of fire while I go hunting with Mark." I gave Alon two of my clips. "Ninety rounds will be enough for me, you take the rest try to hit someone" After crawling about one hundred feet, we raised our heads to see if we could locate the enemy. Some of the bandits were just across the road from us still firing at Alon's position where they thought we were.

"On three we charge across the road at them ready." I shook my head Yes.

"Three!" Nawaz yelled, jumping up running toward the brush on the far side of the road. The HK-5 machine gun chattering in his hand. I was up running beside him my finger pressed on the trigger until the bolt clicked. Thirty rounds fired in a matter of 3 seconds. I dropped next to two dead bandits, scarves wrapped around their heads and face.

"Reload, we push on," said Nawaz smiling. I stood to move when I saw three more dead men. We were a little behind the front-line as we continued to move and shot. Another click, two mags used, as I pushed the last one into place. Maybe I should have kept all five instead of giving two to Alon. Bullet continued to snap over our heads.

"Keep low. Friendly fire."

Suddenly, there was a barrage of gun-fire further to our left.

"That's the other troops you were worried about. They came in from the opposite side. We now have the bandits in a vice caught between us, It will be over soon. Keep your eyes open some may be heading our way."

As if by magic a group of about a dozen men came running straight toward us. They were running from Nawaz, men who were chasing them to us. When they were forty feet away, we stood up shooting into them. It was like shooting ducks in a pond, the line of men staggered, stopped then fell over dead. All was quiet except for the moans from some wounded. My AK was empty. I dropped it pulling my 45 Colt from the shoulder holster as Nawaz slung his HK over his shoulder. We walked back to the road where Alon came to join us. Mousa, our driver was standing next to the Range Rover checking the damage.

"Everyone alright?" I asked.

"Still checking," said Alon.

Three of Nawaz's assassins came out of the brush pushing five men before them.

"Looks like we captured a few alive. Look," said Alon pointing "Your friend, Gozani, is one of them." The five men stopped in front of us.

"On your knees," ordered Nawaz. "Who is the leader here?" No one spoke. Nawaz pulled a large revolver from his belt, raised the barrel, pointing it at one of the bandits. Without another word he pulled the trigger. The revolver roared as one of the five men crumpled to the ground, his head blown apart. I didn't know the caliber of that handgun, but it was powerful.

"Now who is next?" Nawaz asked quietly. "I want the leader. Who is it?" Two of the men stood trembling pointing to one wearing black riding boots with jodhpur slacks. "So it's you" said Nawaz pointing the gun at him. I should have guessed dressed in that fancy outfit. "Your name," he demanded.

"I am Jibril, the leader of the Farakech peoples' army."

"Yes, I've heard of you. – The killer of children, the rapist of women, young or old, the coward who is afraid to fight like a true warrior. What made you attack us? What made you think you could beat us?"

"Him," he said pointing at Gozani. "That fool told me you were a small party, only ten or 12 men. He led me to believe your people were weak; they had been sitting idle for a month. There were two pale-skinned westerners who would run at the first sounds of gun-fire. He told me you had excellent cars and trucks worth much money. I should have known better than to listen to that one. The last time he had me attack the blond horse man for $700,000, all I got was a measly $20,000."

The hair on the back of my neck stood up. I was right about Gozani but I had to push. "He gave you the information about the money and the blond horseman?"

"Yes it was him. He was supposed to get $10,000 from me as a reward, what is it called, ah yes, find fee. Finders fee said Nazam. Yes that's it. But instead of the money I let him live. I only shot him in the shoulder so the Police would not suspect him. I should have shot him in the head like I did the others. Now enough of this nonsense," Jibril said. "Let me leave to go back to my village to recruit more warriors since most of those who came with me are now dead."

"How will you go?" I asked.

"The horses of my men are behind those hills. I will take one and ride to my camp."

"I don't think so," said Nawaz.

"I am Jibril the Mighty. I will go to form another band of men." I turned to face the treasonous wretch who was responsible for the death of Eric and the two Turk grooms.

"Gozani, we meet again. Do you remember what I told you when I let you out of the cell in the castle? I warned you if I ever saw you again I would kill you. I told you that standing on the draw bridge after I let you out of the cell. Do you remember?" Mark held the Colt 45 in his right hand. "For Eric, for his wife and children and for all man-kind, you must die. You are evil, like the serpent in the Garden of Eden." You must die for your wicked ways.

"Wait," a voice called out from behind us. It was Rose.

"How long have you been standing there?" I asked.

"Long enough to hear all that Gozani said. To hear him admit he set Eric up to die, a man who took him from the gutter - gave him a job, a home. A man that treated him like one of the family; only to turn on Eric like a scorpion. You killed my husband as surely as if you pulled the trigger!"

"No, Ms. Eric. I never meant for him to die. I have regretted it every day of my life."

She held her hand out to Mark. "Your gun, Mark. Give it to me."

"Careful girl, it has a hair-trigger."

"I'm familiar with guns Mark. Eric and I were excellent shots." She took the gun from Marks hand walking to stand in front of Gozani. "You won't have to regret Eric's death any longer since this is the last day of your life. Mark told you if he ever saw you again you would die. The man is like Mohammad, a Prophet." With that she raised the gun to his face and pulled the trigger blowing his head apart. A 45-caliber hollow-point bullet will do that.

CHAPTER 53 ✠ ✠ ✠

The six of us were sitting at a table in the Mersin Yacht Club dining room enjoying a delicious dinner.

"So," said Nawaz. "Our last dinner together on this Monday night in Turkey."

"Yes, "agreed Alon. "I spent the day going over the boat in preparation for our departure for Israel."

"We leave at 7:00 a.m.," said Mark. "Everything has been stowed. The women have the forward cabin to themselves. Alon and I will be in the sea-cabin taking turns sleeping in the watch-crew bunk. It has been an interesting month gentlemen,said Nawaz beaming. I wouldn't have missed it for a bundle of money. I must congratulate you both on your military skill. I'm not sure how our encounter with the Arab fighters would have turned out if not for your expertise in battle." I commend you both, a navy seal and an ex Mossad special operator. You two make a formidable pair.

"What happened after we drove off?" asked Alon.

"My men cleaned-up the area. They placed all the dead men's weapons on our truck, moved the bodies about a mile from the road, and laid them out on the ground for the native creatures to dispose of."

"You mean eat?" asked Rose.

"Yes," replied Nawaz. "That is exactly what I mean. The laws of nature survive. I also instructed Berat, the most senior of my men, to cut the heads of Jibril and Gozani from their bodies, then drive ten miles on the road toward Syria, which is where the bandits came from. Mount the heads on stakes driven into the ground as a warning to any others who might think it's a good idea to come commit a crime in Turkey. Berat placed the assassin sign on the stakes so any bandits would know who would be waiting."

As dessert was served, Mark took the silver metal briefcase from under the table. "Nawaz, this is for you. Alon and I wish you to have it for all you have done for us."

"Do I dear open it here at the table?"

"You can."

He popped the two catches then lifted the lid looking at the rows of money stacked in neat bundles inside the case. "What is this?" he asked. "You have already paid me."

"Yes, we paid you to lead our expedition, to act as a tour guide. But you did much more, including save our lives in a dangerous situation. Three of your men were killed in the fighting. You can give some money to the families of those men. We also wanted to give you money toward the Hummer you gave to the Police Chief."

"Thank you both. It is most generous of you, but I think excessive. How much is in this case?"

"We didn't count it. But my calculated estimate is close to $180,000."

Nawaz took seven bundles of ten thousand dollars each from the case, then snapping the case shut he handed it back to Mark. "You take the case with $110,000 Mark. Seventy is more than enough for me. Use the money for the women in Israel." "I wish you all God speed and safe passage tomorrow, and for the rest of your lives."

The next morning we stood on the dock by the boat. Everyone had gone aboard except Mark and Nawaz who stood face to face.

"So this is goodbye my friend. I doubt we will meet again on this side."

"I agree," replied Mark but in life one should never say never." Very true" agreed Nawaz holding Marks hand in his grasp.

"It was a good meeting my brother. We had an exciting month together. I'm happy to have known you. I wish you a good trip Mark. I will always be here if you need me."

"Just one more thing before I leave you," said Mark. "Your adopted son, our security guard on the boat for the last month, he is still sitting on the aft deck. He refuses to leave until ordered by you Nawaz."

"An obedient soldier, I will call him now."

"Before you do, and with your permission, I would like to give him my

Colt 45 pistol and shoulder holster as a token of friendship for the job he did. Also to show I have no hard feelings about his trying to lift my wallet. If it wasn't for him we wouldn't have met. So I owe him my gratitude."

"You may give him the weapon. I will keep it for him until he is big enough to use it." Nawaz called out: "Kafir, come to me." The boy came on cats feet, quietly – almost floating above the concrete dock. He stood before us while Nawaz spoke to him in Turkish.

I handed him the holster and pistol. "For your exceptional vigilance watching my boat, I reward you with this pistol." His eyes opened wide, as I handed him the gun.

"For me?" he asked in halting English.

"Yes, for you, and the man you will become." He looked at his father who shook his head yes. Only then did the boy reach for the gun, a broad smile on his young face. We embraced, the boy first, then Nawaz. They walked to the black Toyota tj waiting at the head of the pier, Mousa behind the wheel.

CHAPTER 54 ✠ ✠ ✠

It was late afternoon as the boat cruised slowly along the Israel coast, Tel Aviv rising in the distance.

"Well, I guess this is the end of the line for us, Mark. I can't enter Israel and you can't go back to Morocco with a murder rap hanging over your head. What will you do now?"

"I'm a Jew, Alon. That means at least one of us can enter the country." "Don't rub it in Mark, it is difficult enough for me to be so close to home yet not be able to go ashore." "Well I have a right of return on my side. I'll speak with the Professor; see if I can stay in Tel Aviv. I plan on getting my license to practice law. I'll pass the Israel bar and open an office here in Tel Aviv. Israel will be my temporary home until Lawyer Daoud gets the murder charge against me in Morocco dropped."

"Don't hold your breath waiting for that my friend. The wheels of justice turn slowly in Morocco."

"It's the same all over the world, Alon." "The criminal justice system is a bureaucratic quagmire everywhere; it moves at a snail-pace while people rot in jail suspended in limbo on pre or post-trial probation." "I'm taking the two rucksacks with me," said Mark. "I removed five gold bars from one of the backpacks last night while you were asleep. That pack only weighs fifty pounds now. Rose can carry that one while I carry the heavier one. I put five gold bars under the central floor hatch in the galley. Three bars are for you Alon, for all you've done for me on our journey. Give two bars to Nazim. One for him for saving the boy and me over seven months ago. The other bar is for Lawyer Daoud. Have Nazim tell him it is from me. Maybe he will work harder to obtain my release. Don't use the gold bars.

Give them to Nazim to convert into cash. Each one should be worth about $250,000. Nazim will know where to exchange them."

Alon smiled. "If anyone can do that and do it clandestinely, it will be Nazim."

The boat entered the Marina Leonardo. The marina was a well-laid-out boat yard for pleasure craft in the center of Tel Aviv. It was adjacent to the Leonardo Hotel for which it was named. The boat touched the dock gently being held in place by two young dock works. The two sisters climbed to the dock first followed by Rose who stood looking back at me. Mark passed over three suitcases then the two rucksacks. Rose easily swung the lighter one onto the dock but both girls had to help her with the other one since it weighed 100 pounds.

"Mark, what do you have in this backpack? Rocks?" asked Rachel.

"Just some stone from the castle for the Professor." I crossed to the dock looking back to face Alon watching as the boat move slowly away from the dock. I snapped a smart military salute at my departing brother.

He smiled at me. "I'll take care of those items for you," he called across the widening gap as the boat pointed its nose out to the wide blue Mediterranean Sea stretching away to the distant horizon.

I was sorry to see him leave. We had become closer than brothers during our time together. We lived and nearly died side by side on many occasions. Nothing brings men closer than facing death side-by-side; it forges an unbreakable bond. A Chevrolet Tahoe SUV was waiting for us in front of the Leonardo Hotel, a driver standing by the open rear-hatch. The girls climbed into the back bench-seat, while the driver loaded our gear into the rear compartment. The driver grabbed my backpack.

"Let me help," I said.

"No, I've got it," he replied as he went to swing it into the open hatch.

"On second thought, you'd better give me a hand this damn thing is heavy "What's in there rocks?" I I smiled "something like that." The Chevy Tahoe pulled up in front of the Rabbi's house in old Jerusalem. "Here we are girls. This will be our temporary home until we sort things out." I went to pay the driver.

"No need mate, all taken care of."

The rabbi stood just inside the open door, an attractive young girl at his side.

"So we meet again, Anna. It seems you are always around."

"Yes, it seems so. The rabbi needed help after the sudden departure of his last companion. I volunteered to stay to help him during that difficult time."

"So these are the lovely ladies coming to stay with me," smiled rabbi Talal. I introduced everyone.

"Anna," said the rabbi. "Take our guests up to their rooms. Let them wash-up and get comfortable while I spend some time with Mark in my study." We walked into the comfortable study where I stopped to look up at the ceiling. The rabbi caught me looking.

"Nice job right can't tell where the hole from the bullet was. This room was cleaned, the ceiling fixed within an hour of your walking out my front door. Mossad cleaning crew is very efficient." We sat looking at each other across the rabbi's large, wooden desk, neither of us speaking.

"So tell me, my boy, what have you been doing for the last 48 days? What do you have to tell me?

"Tal, it has been a fascinating time. I was traveling in the company of a former disciple of yours Alon Gold. He told me he is your nephew along with many other fascinating stories. After all we were together for five months, plenty of time to exchange war stories. First we went to Rhodes on a mission of Alon's. We had to deliver some cargo to… yes I know Tal interrupted. We, that is Mossad received an anonymous radio transmission which we traced to the waters off the coast of Rhodes. The message alerted us to the fact a ship registered in Egypt, a freighter loaded with illegal weapons was sailing for Gaza. A tracking device had been inserted into the cargo which made it relatively easy to locate the ship. A Special Forces commando unit boarded the ship at sea diverting it to the naval base in Haifa. We now have the weapons in our possession, not the Hamas terrorist in Gaza." My respect for Alon increased immeasurably. After everything that had happened to him he was still a protector of his native country. "To continue my story I found the castle in Turkey which was the easy part. Alon and I spent a month living in the old drafty grounds searching for the treasure with no luck. Then one dark night the answer came to me out of a dream. I saw everything clear as day. It was as if Guy de Vaux was speaking to me. He was telling me where the treasure was waiting to be discovered allowing me to finally solve the puzzle."

"What puzzle?" Asked the old wise man.

"Remember Tal, you translated it for me. The treasure is in Purgatory but you must travel through water to reach it."

"Yes, yes. I do remember," said the rabbi excitedly.

"It took me 28 days to figure out what De Vaux meant. But I finally figure it out."

"Then you found the Templar treasure, the treasure that has been lost for 800 years."

"Yes," said Mark. "I found it. I sat looking at the enormous wealth of a kingdom stacked in boxes in gigantic stone chambers carved out of solid stone in the heart of the mountain. Try to picture it Tal. Row after row of neat lines of crates, three crates high, 180 stacks. 900 boxes, each box containing ten bars of gold weighing ten pounds each. 100 pounds of gold in each box, 1,600 ounces per bar 16000 ounces per box. That means there was a total of over 14 million ounces of gold in the underground vault. At today's market price of $1,200 per ounce I was looking at a vast sum."

Talal shook his head in wonder. "Mark, that's over 16 billion dollars, billon with a B."

"Yes, and that's just the gold. There was room upon room built in passageways off the main chamber, rooms of varying sizes, some 10x9, others 9x12 a total of thirty rooms in all. Each filled with the most amazing collection of valuable treasure imaginable. Gemstones set into crowns or tiaras, necklaces, bracelets, rings. They were sitting in chests, crates, boxes of every sort, along with hundreds, maybe thousands of loose gemstones. There were rooms with armor of all types, swords, lances, daggers, shields, helmets and suits of armour, room after room. Other rooms with statues, ivory, marble bronze, some of the most beautiful figures I've ever seen – museum quality work."

"How could you see it all?"

"I didn't Tal. It would take months, maybe years to go through it all. I just gazed at it in awe, and then I made a decision."

"What was your decision, my boy?"

Mark looked at the old man, a man of knowledge, wisdom with a clear understanding of the workings of the world. "rabbi I thought of the all the conflict in the world, the greed, hatred and strife between countries and people. I reasoned if I were to announce this find I would bring chaos between countries, friends would become rivals, enemies even. Such wealth could cause disastrous economic upheaval. The world financial structure would collapse. There would be turmoil throughout the land. So I decided the enormous amount of treasure should remain where it is, where it's been all these years – it should be left undisturbed."

"What did you do?" Talah asked.

"Like the Red Sea that Moses parted, then closed after his people fled Egypt so the waters I parted closed again. I took special pains to hide the way to the treasure vault. I feel confident, with your help, the treasure will never be discovered, at least not for another 700 years."

"What do you mean with my help?"

Mark walked to his old trusty IDF back pack resting against a wall of the study. He opened a flap removing the leather pouch containing the original manuscript with the translation Talal had made. Returning to his seat he placed the pouch on the professor's desk.

"Look familiar?" asked Mark.

"Of course," replied the Professor. Remember my bright Hebrew Bocher, I spent a month with these papers by my side day and night while you spent your days relaxing in the library.

"When I left you more than a month ago –"

"Nearly two," interrupted the Professor.

"Yes," agreed Mark. "Nearly two," I told you, when I left this room these papers might yet be yours one day."

"I recall that," said Talal. "Well that day has arrived," "I will give these papers to you now on one condition."

"You must be a lawyer," said the old rabbi laughing. "Always one condition with you. So alright already, let me hear your condition."

"You can do what you wish with this manuscript; it is yours unconditionally." "You can say you found it or a courier brought it to you, which is almost the truth. Say whatever you want, the decision is yours and yours alone"

"Ok, but what is the condition already?"

"You must delete any reference to a treasure. You can say the treasure was in the castle in France but when the Knights Templar were rounded-up and killed, Guy de Vaux and his men ran for their lives leaving the treasure behind in their haste to save themselves. Reduce the number of ships in the armada to three. The warship and two cargo ships – one for the horses of the knights, the last for the remainder of the knights' party, the grooms, workers, cooks and the like, with the leader of the knights on the warship. They renounced the knighthood and became a band of independent warriors living in a castle somewhere in Turkey or Syria. Be unsure of its exact location. Dispel the notion of the existence of any treasure ever leaving France."

"That may be difficult," said the wise rabbi.

"Maybe difficult but not impossible. You are the only one who can decipher the manuscript. You may remove the offending pages, those making any reference to the treasure. It wouldn't be unusual for a document this old to have some pages missing. It's that or the bag and its contents will be burned tonight removing any mention of the Templar's during this period. The choice is yours professor; choose wisely."

"You are a hard man Mark, a tough negotiator. You know how much I want these pages, this historic document to release to the academic world, to the world at large."

"Then I repeat my terms for the release of the templar's manuscript. I don't think my demand is extreme. Just delete any reference to the treasure leaving France or arriving in Turkey. I think that is a small price to pay. I'm giving these documents to you and the world at large."

Professor Tal sat quietly for several minutes deep in thought, looking contemplative. Mark sat not saying anything to break the mood. He knew that in situations like this the one who speaks first loses. Finally, after what seemed an eternity, the old wise man spoke. "You drive a hard bargain my young friend. You know how much I want the ancient manuscript. I see your point in not mentioning the treasure. If I did, people would flock to the site from around the world – treasure hunters, adventurers, people of dubious character, all intent upon enriching themselves with no regard for the impact it would have on mankind as you did." "It would also destroy the tranquility and life for the people of Templeton. I believe your action with regard to the treasure, its enormous wealth, is an act of one person in a hundred, maybe a thousand, more likely one in a million. If you could walk away from that amount of wealth I can accede to your wishes and delete any mention of the treasure. I will comply with your demand and say the treasure, if it ever existed, was left behind in the castle in France when the Templar's fled for their lives. They ran with nothing but their horses in order to save themselves from the treacherous King and his hoards."

"Good," said Mark, pushing the leather case across the desk to Tal. 'That is a wise decision." "These papers are yours to do with as you wish. Now to the next topic. I'm not as altruistic as you think. I did help myself to some of the Templar gold. I have a backpack by the wall with ten, ten-pound bars of gold. It's worth a bit more than 2 million dollars at today's price." I purposely didn't mention the other five bars in the backpack Rose had. "Is there anyone you know that can convert the gold into cash for me quietly so no one will know?"

"Yes," said the rabbi "Of course." He wrote something on a slip of paper handing it to Mark. "Go see this man; he is an old Arab, old like me. He has a stall in the Souk near the Jaffa Gate. Go to him, tell him I sent you or he will not speak with you." "These money lenders must be extremely careful in their line of work. He will assist you in your efforts. Now, what other surprises do you have for me?"

"Just the three women I've brought you."

"If I were forty years younger I'd thank you for such a splendid gift. However at my age I can only look and remember."

Anna called us to dinner. We sat around the dining room table as Tal and the three women got acquainted.

The days passed quickly as everyone worked on their respective futures. The rabbi reverted to his role as a university professor spending long hours with Rachel and Beth discussing schools and admissions procedures; Rose spent her time wondering about the city as a tourist taking in the sights of Jerusalem. I went to find the Arab money-changer. The old man sat in a small stall in the crowded market. He sat alone waiting for customers to approach him. *I was here to make his day week or maybe his month with my proposal.* When I told him the purpose of my visit and that the Jewish rabbi Talal sent me, he became instantly interested.

"Can you handle this amount of gold?"

"100 pounds you say?"

"Yes, ten bars, ten pounds each, about three million dollars."

"That is a lot of gold. Ten bars. Where did you get such a large hoard of gold bars? It is a significant quantity to possess at one time." Most of my business in gold is a few coins at a time, maybe ten or twenty coins, a gold chain or bracelet. Ten pound bars of gold is very unusual and ten bars is even stranger.

"I don't ask you what you do with the bars, that's your business. Where or how I got them is mine."

"I didn't mean to offend you by my question. Just my curiosity. You realize the quantity is unusual."

"Can you handle the transaction for me or not?

"The rabbi has many contacts. He sent you to me because I am the best person to fulfill your need. I will have to see a sample of the gold to determine its content, purity and type before we can proceed."

"I anticipated that," said Mark holding the IDF canvas back pack on his lap. "I have one bar in this bag."

"You must leave it with me. Come back tomorrow, we will talk further then."

Mark hesitated handing the bag over. "After all he estimated the bar was worth $250,000 dollars. Men killed for a lot less."

"I see you are hesitant to give me the bag. I must inform you a man like me lives by his reputation. You don't know me we only just met. If you wish to consult with your benefactor before turning the bar over to me please do so." However, be assured I have been conducting sensitive financial transactions at this location for more the 60 years. My word is my bond. Any dealings we have will remain between us; you can be assured of that

After a brief second Mark nodded in agreement: "No need to consult with anyone else, he concluded. We must have mutual trust if we are going to move ahead. The rabbi trusts you I will also. Here is the bag. I will see you tomorrow morning"

Mark arrived at the stall at 10 the next morning. "Please sit," said Zafer Giul, the money lender. "My assayer told me this is the purist gold he has ever encountered. No flaws at all, 100% gold of the highest quality."

"What does that mean to me?" Mark asked.

"It means," continued Zafer, "That I can offer you $1,546 per ounce. That's $247,360 Per bar, or $2millon473 thousand for the ten bars. Since you are giving me 10 bars in one transaction I will offer you 2.5 millon dollars for the lot. Is that satisfactory?"

"Can you handle the entire lot?" asked Mark.

"Yes, but it will take a week to assemble that amount of cash."

"That's not a problem for me," said Mark. "I want the money to be in United States dollars, 100-dollar denominations."

"That can be arranged," replied Zafer.

"When do you want the merchandise? We can make the exchange here a week from today." You will give me the gold; I will give you the money. Is that satisfactory?

"Very good," said Mark. "Tell me Zafer, can you handle another transaction of five additional bars in two or three weeks?"

"I think; yes. However, I will let you know when we meet next week to conclude this transaction."

The days went by slowly for Mark. He had told the rabbi his plans to go to Tel Aviv to study Hebrew and law in order to take the Bar Exam that was given in July. If he passed he planned to open a law office in Tel Aviv to earn a living while he built a law firm in Israel to go with his firms in New York and Casablanca. Now that he had the money from Zafer packed in two large leather salesman sample cases – 250 packs of $100-dollar bills, $10,000 dollars per package, he was ready to move on with his life in exile. We had been staying at the rabbi's house for three weeks. On this Friday night we sat comfortably around the dining room table preparing to enjoy the Friday night Sabbath meal. All was serene in the happy household.

"Roberta, you say the blessing over the candles," instructed the rabbi, and you Rachel the blessing over the challah. Mark, you do the blessing for the wine. So children, your applications for college have been submitted. It will be at least a month or two before you hear from the schools you applied to. In order to prepare for college I took the liberty of enrolling you both in the Crest Academy. It is an excellent prep-school which will make entry into college classes easier. If you agree you will attend classes beginning in two weeks, May 15th."

"How often do we have to attend?" asked Rachel.

"The classes are four days a week from 9 until 1; that shouldn't be too difficult. The term is eight weeks long, it ends on July 15. You don't have to show up to college until August 25 or later depending on where you are accepted and decide to attend." They both agreed happily. With that out of the way, the rabbi turned to Mark: "what are your plans *boychik*?"

"I'm going to Tel Aviv Tal. I'm going to study Hebrew so I can become fluent in the language. I've also contacted the Bar Association in Tel Aviv. I've applied to take the exam being given on July 8th and 9th. They recommended a school that gives a review course which I will take beginning on May 18th; it is a six-week course." It ends a week before the exam.

"Sounds like you will have a busy schedule."

"I'm going to Tel Aviv to find a place to stay on Tuesday."

"Let me see what I can do for you Mark. After all I am indebted to you for your magnanimous gift to me said the rabbi smiling, indicating the manuscript in the leather pouch resting on his desk in the study. And you my lovely Rose what are your plans?"

"At this moment Rabbi, I don't have any. After three weeks I've had my fill of Jerusalem."

"Then just relax and enjoy yourself life is good here."

At dinner Monday night, Tal spoke to the people gathered at his table as Anna served a delicious brisket of beef with noodles. "Mark, I think I have solved your accommodation problem in Tel Aviv."

"I didn't realize I had a problem. I was going to find an apartment to rent."

"Nice apartments are scarce in Tel Aviv if you are lucky enough to find one. They are extremely expensive – at least $3,000 or $4,000 per month with first, last and two months security for a yearly lease."

"I think I can afford that rabbi."

"Yes, I know you can. But I'd just as soon see you keep your money in the bank. Anyway, I know a high-ranking diplomat in our government. He has gone to take a post as UN Ambassador in New York. He will be staying at Israel's Embassy Guest House with free accommodations for at least the next year. His apartment in Tel Aviv will be sitting empty while he is away. I had a mutual friend at the agency contact him in New York yesterday. This friend of mine told Mr. Herzel a friend of the agency needs a home in Tel Aviv. After a few minutes conversation, Herzel said since it was an agency matter he would be happy to let his apartment be used by a member, better than sitting vacant for a year."

"What agency" asked Rachel?

"The agency," replied the rabbi. "There is only one organization known as the agency in Israel. So Mark that means you now have a three bedroom, four bathroom penthouse apartment in one of the most exclusive buildings in all of Israel, the Crystal Tower. I'm not sure of the decorations since Herzel is a 52 year-old bachelor and a bit of a bon vivant. I can assure you this apartment would rent for $9,000 per month, maybe more in today's hot real estate market. It's yours for just over ten months since Herzel left five weeks ago. He may decide to stay on for a second year at his option. By the way it is free to you, the agency will provide for the Ambassador. So my boy, what do you say?"

"I'd be crazy to turn it down. It seems you are my benefactor once again."

"Just enjoy the view from the top floor. Here is a card to a Yeshiva not far from the Crystal Tower. The head of the school is Rabbi Gabi Hirschman - some name for a Rabbi, Gabi, Tal laughed. "He will be expecting you. He was a student of mine at University. I had him when he was in rabbinical school. He was kind of slow. He will be glad to help you."

"Thank you again Tal."

"Mark, rabbi," said Rose excitedly "I have nothing to hold me here. My girls will be studying in prep school during the day. I've spent weeks touring Jerusalem. I'd like to go to Tel Aviv also. You said the apartment had three bedrooms rabbi?"

"Yes. 4,300 square feet I'm told. Quite palatial with large balconies looking out over the city."

"Mark," Rose began "if you let me join you I promise I will leave you to your studies. As a matter of fact, I can help you with your Hebrew since I speak it fluently. What do you say; can I join you in Tel Aviv?"

Mark thought a moment. This could have some pluses, also some drawbacks. "I'll tell you what Rose; we can give it a try. If it works fine. If not I'll help you find a place of your own but you must agree to go if that's what I decide."

"You have my word, Mark. I will abide by your decision"

"Ok then, we leave tomorrow at 10 in the morning, a car will be here to take us to our home away from home"

CHAPTER 55 ✚ ✚ ✚

The Cadillac limo stopped at the front entrance to the Crystal Tower apartment building on a wide street in a new section of Tel Aviv. I carried the two sample cases while, Rose carried our two suitcase, the IDF backpack hung on my shoulder We walked up to the front desk being tended by a uniformed desk clerk.

"Good afternoon," he said. "How can I help you?"

"My name is Mark Radin. I'm staying in Mr. Herzel's apartment while he's away."

"Yes Sir Mr. Radin. Mr. Herzel called me from America early this morning. It was only 2a.m. in New York when he called. You must be a good friend for him to get up that early."

"You know diplomats never sleep" I said,

"Here are the keys to the apartment; 14th floor. I'm sure you will enjoy it the view is outstanding."

"Thank you. This is Rose Borne. She will be staying with me. What's your name?"

"Hayim I'm the day concierge on duty from 7 to 4. Issac comes in from 4 to midnight, then Avi works from midnight to 7. When I come on"

"Good, we'll meet them each. Thank you Hayim." There was an express elevator for floors 12 and 14, no 13. I had to insert a plastic card into a slot for the 14th floor or the doors wouldn't open. When they did open I could see why a card was needed. The elevator opened directly into the vestibule foyer of the apartment which stretched away before us. We walked from room to room inspecting our sumptuous surroundings. I was impressed at the spaciousness and decoration of the apartment.

"Some spread" said Rose. "I could get used to this fast. Look at the view from those windows, and a wrap around balcony to sit on outside"

I dropped the bags to the saturnia travertine tile floor, the elevator doors closed behind us. "Let's go check out the bedrooms said Rose eagerly." There were three bedrooms, each with its own en suite bathroom. The master bedroom was massive, about 20x30 with a desk in a sitting area in an L-shaped corner of the room. The bathroom was huge. A stall-shower, tub with Jacuzzi jets, a toilet alongside a bidet, dual sink with a marble counter top, a wall of mirrors behind the sinks. Two other bedrooms were down a long hallway, one on each side.

"Come in here Mark check out this bedroom." Another large room with a king-size bed, dresser, a large walk in closet, a chaise lounge in front of sliding glass doors opening to the balcony. Another door opened to a marble bathroom with a stall-shower, counter with a sink and built-in make-up table. "Not bad Mark I can be comfortable in this room. It's far enough from the master suite so I won't bother you." The third bedroom across the hall was smaller, but functional with two twin beds and its own bathroom. "This will be great if my girls want to sleep over; their room just across the hall from mine."

We went out to dinner each night enjoying the many restaurants along the waterfront, all just two blocks from our apartment. Sunday night we ate in and relaxed since I was starting my continuing Hebrew education early Monday morning followed by law review classes in the afternoon.

"Tell me Mark, what's your schedule like?" It's a full one I'm afraid.

"I'll be starting Yeshiva at 7:30. Yeshiva Torah Yisroel on Elat Street. Rabbi Gabi Hirschman will meet me to get me started. He was a student of Tal's at Hebrew University. I'll study there until 11:30. Then it's off to the Kaplin Institute on Ha Yarkon Street. The law review class starts at 1 until 5 each day for seven weeks. I'll be home by 6 or so. We can have dinner together. After dinner I'll study until bed-time." Lights out about 11.

"I will help you with your Hebrew lessons," said Rose, happy to be of some assistance to pay her way.

We settled into a routine: dinner at 7, practice Hebrew for an hour, then study some law review if I was up to it. Then to bed since I had to be up at 6 to prepare for another long day.

After the third week Rose made an announcement at dinner: "Starting today Mark no more English. We speak only Hebrew from now on. That way you will learn faster."

I found the law academy library at Tel Aviv University a perfect place to study on Saturday and Sunday. I would go to the law library both days leaving Rose alone. Her girls would come to Tel Aviv by bus to spend the weekends with her. They had happy times together while they waited to hear from their respective universities regarding acceptance for the fall semester. I was sitting at a table in the library when a female voice startled me from my concentration on a case in a legal journal.

"Excuse me," she said. "You aren't a student at the law school are you?"

"No," I replied, looking at the young woman standing before me.

"I didn't think so," she continued. "I just graduated a few weeks ago, I don't remember seeing you in any of my classes. Are you studying for the bar exam?"

"Yes," Mark replied. "I'm a bit out of practice. It's been fifteen years since I've been in school. I'm taking a review course during the week then spending weekends here to bone-up for the exam."

"My friends and I are studying for the exam also," she said indicating a table where four men sat nearby watching. "We do a three-hour review on Sunday afternoons in a small conference room. We study another topic each week - torts, property, contracts, criminal law. You can join us tomorrow if you wish."

"That's kind of you, but I don't want to intrude."

"No, it would be no intrusion. We would like to have you join our group; we all agreed."

"Thank you for the invitation. I'll take you up on it."

"Good. My name is Myria. We will see you here tomorrow."

Mark settled into an easy routine. He went to Yeshiva in the morning, Kaplan law review in the afternoon, home for dinner, then a few hours of study. More studying at the law library on the weekends. On Sundays the small group would meet to go over a legal subject. It was an intense emergence into each subject just as Myria had indicated. After the last Sunday session Mark addressed the group of 5 eager prospective future lawyers: "If I pass the bar exam it will be in part to the help you've given me each Sunday. I'd like to thank each of you."

As usual, Myria spoke for the group. "It was our pleasure to have you.

Your insight has helped us see the law in a more practical, a realistic way. Don't worry Mark we will all pass the exam; I guarantee it."

The exam was intense. It was broken into two parts, a morning session then a one hour break for lunch followed by an afternoon session. I explained the procedure to Rose on Monday night at dinner. "Tomorrow morning I must report to the ballroom at the Hilton Hotel only a few blocks away. All those taking the exam must check in at 8 in the morning, the exam starts punctually at 9."

"Do you know how many people are taking the exam?" she asked.

"I think about 600. Approximately 400 will pass the exam. The morning consists of true false or multiple choice questions. We break for lunch at noon, return at 1 for the afternoon session which is the hardest part of the test; this is where most people fail. There will be three essay questions that count for sixty percent of the exam. From my experience the questions will be difficult with subtle trickery on the part of the examiners requiring concentration and knowledge of the main issue. The trick is to figure out what the primary issue is since there will be many secondary issues put in to lead you in the wrong direction." It is a mind puzzle in the law.

"I will get up to make you breakfast, help your brain get going so it will function clearly"

After breakfast the next morning, Rose leaned in to kiss Mark on the cheek. "*B'hatzlacha* (good luck)," she said in Hebrew.

Mark walked into the ballroom showing his identification to the proctor. "Here is your number, Mr. Radin. You will find a spot at a table with your number on it take that seat." Mark settled into his chair laying four No. 2 pencils by his right hand. The long table sat twenty; everyone in his row was male.

"Hi," said the man next to him. "My name is Max. Good luck on the test"

"You also," replied Mark.

The day flew by. Mark had a light lunch with Myria, who was at a table toward the rear of the ballroom.

"How did you find the morning session?"

"Not too bad," she said. "But it's the essays that will be difficult."

"Don't let them fool you, Myria. There will be all sorts of actions in each question. Take your time, read the questions two or three times before you start to write. Then pick the main issue, that's what it's all about."

"Thanks Mark, good luck."

"You can leave as soon as you complete the test announced the proctor. Turn your papers in to me, and then go. Do not hang around the building. The results will be announced September 4th they will be published in the paper."

Some people began to leave at the end of two hours. Mark was still on the second essay question. The room was more than half-empty when Mark walked up to the Chancellor. "Here you are," said Mark handing over the papers.

"How did you find the exam?" the man asked.

"I found it to be a bit difficult for me. It's been many years since I've taken an exam, especially one in Hebrew."

"You look familiar to me," the man said looking at me quizzically. "Do I know you?" he asked, looking at the number on Mark's paper. No names were used. "What is your name?" he asked. "I can tell from your Hebrew you're not an Israeli. At least not a native, not a Sabra."

"My name is Mark Radin, I'm American."

"Now I have it. You're the lawyer from New York, the Intercontinental case, right."

"Yes," replied Mark that's me.

"Let me shake your hand and give you my card. I'm an attorney with Lansky and Geller, a major law firm in town. Call me when you get the results." Maybe I can help you my name is Ezra Goldberg'

"Thanks," Mark said, slipping the card into his pocket.

When he got home, Rose was waiting. "How'd it go, Mark?"

"About what I expected. No telling how I did until the results are announced."

"I made reservations for us for dinner since I didn't feel like cooking tonight. Also, I thought after being locked up in a room with 600 people all day you could use some fresh air and conversation to clear your mind."

"Good thinking, Rose. Just let me shower and change then we can go.

Sitting at Danny's on the beach promenade north of hotel strip we sat looking across the road toward the black Mediterranean Sea. I began to relax, a tall glass of Perrier with lemon by my hand.

"I brought you here since I know you enjoy the food and atmosphere Mark. Also because Shlomo treats you like a celebrity, like a famous movie star"

"Yes," Mark smiled at the statement.

I have some important news to tell you," continued Rose. Mark perked-up, all attention focused on his roommate.

"I've made this decision a few weeks ago," she began. "But I wanted to wait until you finished your exam before I told you." I didn't want it to be a distraction before your exam.

"What is it, Rose?" he asked, as a dark cloud settled over him.

"I want to return to Templeton Mark. I've made up my mind. I'm going home; it's where I belong." Mark just sat looking at his attractive companion unable to speak.

"Tel Aviv is beautiful, exciting. But after three months I've come to the conclusion I'm just a small-town girl at heart. I love my life in Templeton, the farm, the animals; its mine and it's where I belong. It's also where Eric is. I know his partner Medhi, has always admired me, I knew he was attracted to me but kept his distance because of Eric. When Eric died he tried to console me. He tried to take Eric's place but I rejected him, I pushed him away. I became a recluse, standoffish. I had no interest in another man. My feelings were similar to your experience with women when Kat was killed. I think I might be able to rekindle that interest, and who knows, maybe we can consummate a union. It won't be like my love affair with Eric, nothing will ever be able to replace what we felt for each other. But maybe we can become close, share a life together. After all, we own ranches together. A profitable sprawling enterprise. The largest business of its kind in the Middle East. Just think Baraq will be one entity." I could help Medhi run it; he has been doing it alone while I lived a care free life here in Israel.

"That's a lot for me to absorb at once, Rose. I'll miss you immensely, I mean that. You've come to mean a lot to me over these months together." I'll be sorry you won't be part of my new life her in Israel.

"Thank you, Mark. I give you full credit for caring for me, for helping me find my way, setting me free from Eric's grip. I'll always love you for that."

"What about your daughters?"

"I've already spoken with them over the last two weekends while they were here with me. You were off studying at law school. Rachel is still waiting to hear from Tel Aviv University. Roberta has already been accepted to Haifa and Hebrew University. My guess is she will enroll in Hebrew University for the fall term to be close to Tal. He has become a surrogate father; maybe grandfather would be more accurate. He dotes on her. Both girls will be sad to see me leave but happy for me when I explained my reasons. They look forward to coming home to spend the summers with me in Templeton since it is their home too."

"So it's all decided then?" Mark asked.

"Yes it is."

"When do you intend to leave?"

"Now that I've told you, and my children agree with my thinking, I plan to leave next week. I'll spend the weekend with my girls in the apartment, we will say goodbye when they return to Jerusalem. Then I'll be ready to go."

"I'll make flight arrangements for you. Arkia Israeli Airline has one flight a day into Adana Airport. I'll make a reservation for Tuesday's flight that will give me Monday to spend with you before you leave."

"Thank you, Mark."

They stood in the small terminal building at Dov Hoz Airport. Dov Hoz was a small field in Tel Aviv proper on the Mediterranean Sea just north of the sprawling city. It reminded Mark of Love Field in the center of Dallas or Midway in Chicago which was in downtown Chicago right on the lake.

"Rose, I contacted Nawaz last night. He is going to have two men and a car meet you at the airport. You will know the driver Abdel. He drove you from Templeton to Mersin. They will take you home, make sure you are safe."

Rose put her hands on Mark's shoulders, looking into his eyes. "I'm glad we got to know each other Mark. Our first meeting was a bit contentious to say the least. But coming to know you as I have I feel good knowing you will look after my daughters in my absence. I love you Mark, not as lovers but as two attached people. Keep well my friend I look forward to seeing you in the future. You will always be dear to me." They announced boarding for flight 143 to Adana, Turkey. Rose reached up, pulling Mark's head to hers kissing him gently. "Shalom."

He watched her walk out of the small terminal to the twin engine Embraer jet sitting on the tarmac. *Goodbye Rose*, he muttered to himself turning his back walking from the building to get a cab to the Crystal Tower.

CHAPTER 56

It was the last day of August, a warm day in Tel Aviv. Mark sat on the balcony looking out at the sparkling Mediterranean Sea watching the sun, a bright orange orb sink slowly on the horizon when his phone rang.

"Hello." I was glad to hear Tal on the other end of the line "To what do I owe this honor rabbi? Is it Friday already and I forgot to light the *Shabbat* candles?"

"No," said Tal laughing at Marks attempt at humor, "Even better. I want to be the first to congratulate you on passing the bar exam."

"Wait Tal. How could you know that today? The results aren't made public until next week, the 4th or 5th of September."

"Yes, that's true my young lawyer. But I know the President of the Bar Association. He was a student of mine some twenty years ago. So I called him and asked if you passed the bar exam."

"That's unethical. As a rabbi, you should know that," Mark exclaimed.

"I do, and evidently so does Gideon Gantz. He answered me the same as you. I can't do that rabbi; it's not ethical. I'm the President of the Bar, elected in insure the practice of law runs on ethics; the bar association is a sacrosanct order. My board of governors would censure me if I gave out that information before it becomes public knowledge."

"Yes, I understand Tal replied. "I was just checking to insure I taught you well."

"You see you did." Then Let me rephrase my question as you lawyers like to say.

"Please tell me how many people took the exam?"

"Only 579 this year."

"How many passed?"

"397."

"That means 176 failed," said Tal.

"Yes, that's about right, about 30% Fail each year."

"So I ask you my old student please tell me Giddy, do you see the name Radin on the list of people who failed?" There was a pause. Tal could hear the rustle of papers as he waited patently

"No rabbi. I don't see that name on the list of students that failed"

"Thank you, Gideon. I'll stop by to see you one day soon."

"I doubt it, rabbi; but thanks for remembering me."

"So there you have it, Mark you didn't fail the exam."

Mark laughed loudly. "Rabbi you are one sneaky devil, you bear watching at all times."

"By the way, he continued you know Rachel was accepted to Tel Aviv University. She begins on Monday. If you have time next week make plans to take her to dinner. I know she would appreciate the gesture. Find out how she is adjusting, how she is getting along in school, if she needs anything." She is very fond of you for all you have done for and her sister.

"Thanks Tal, I'll do that and I'll let you know."

The next week the results of the bar exam were published in *Haaretz*, the leading newspaper in Israel. Mark saw his name among 397 others. He was happy to see Myria, along with the other men of the study group had *all passed*. He was busy the entire week so he didn't have a chance to call Rachel until the following week.

"Hello Mark, it's good to hear from you. Yes, I'm fine; studying a lot for my classes but all is going well."

"Can you have dinner with me tonight Rachel?"

"Sure Mark I'd love to, where and when?"

"How about Danny's on the promenade? Your mother and I used to eat there often, I'm sure you'll like it. I'll come for you."

"No need Mark. I know the place I can get there. What time?"

Seven if that's ok with you."

"Seven is fine I'll see you at the restaurant."

Mark arrived early as he did for all appointments. He didn't like to keep anyone waiting for him. It was a trait he picked up in the Navy that had just stayed with him. He asked Schlmo the maître d', who he was on a first-name basis with, having dined in the restaurant so often. "I need a table for two, Schlmo, near the back since the young lady and I will be talking over dinner."

"Sure Mark, no problem, Follow me."

I sat facing the open front of the restaurant where a row of tables lined the street. I had learned to dress like a local that meant very informal in Tel Aviv. No one dressed in this country. If you wore a jacket, the joke was are you going to a funeral or court? I wore a black t-shirt with khaki slacks, a pair of Cole Haan burgundy loafers on my feet, no socks. I sat sipping a bottle of Dancing Camel Beer from a heavy glass mug when Rachel walked into the restaurant. I hadn't seen her in months, almost four months since I'd left her in Jerusalem with Tal. I couldn't believe the woman I was looking at as she walked toward me, a wide smile on her tanned face. She put her arms around me, kissed me on each cheek European style.

"It's so good to see you, Mark. You look wonderful."

"Not as good as you, Rachel. You look radiant – the tan, your hair is lighter, your brown eyes have gold specs flashing in the depths"

"Yes, my tan and hair are from the sun at the beach." I didn't want to mention her figure stuffed into a clinging pink t-shirt, which did nothing to hide the fact she wasn't wearing a bra, tight white jeans showing her thin waste and well-rounded ass. The young woman standing before me was a knock-out.

"Please sit," I smiled pulling out her chair. "It looks as if life at school in the busy city agrees with you, Rachel."

"I've never been happier, Mark. I have a dorm-room with a super roommate from Galilee. She's so smart; we get along great." They talked for the next hour as the food was consumed. When they were finishing the meal there was a loud explosion nearby, strong enough to cause the water in the glasses to shake the plates to jump

"What was that?" asked Rachel, her eyes growing wider. Mark knew the answer as soon as he heard it. A bomb had exploded close by. He looked at the street where people were running in panic, all except for one young man standing at the curb in front of the café, an AK-47 in his hand. The Russian made AK-47 was the favorite weapon of terrorist the world over. Mark didn't hesitate. He tipped the heavy granite-topped table over causing everything to crash unto the floor. He reached out pulling the frightened girl to the ground behind the table. The AK-47 began to chatter sending out a spray of bullets. The magazine on the AK 47 holds thirty rounds of ammunition which can fire at the rate of 750 rounds per minute, thirteen shots per second. On full automatic, the magazine would empty in less than three seconds.

"Stay put keep your head down," Mark whispered into Rachel's ear. When the firing stopped Mark stood sprinting for the sidewalk, the heavy glass beer mug in his right hand. The shooter was standing in the road about 45 feet away. An average soldier could change a clip in an AK-47 in about eight seconds. A good soldier in five while a nervous terrorist might take ten seconds or more. Those thoughts passed through Marks mind as he ran toward the Arab killer struggling to get the new magazine into the grove of the automatic rifle. The terrorist stood facing down the roadway, the gun pointing ninety degrees away from Mark as the man struggled to insert the loaded clip into the rifle. Mark ran toward the killer as fast as he could sprint. He lowered his shoulder like a football player going for the opposing quarterback with the game on the line. He was aiming for the shooter's body. The man sensed Mark running toward him at the last split second before impact. He looked at this crazed Jew who should be cowering in fear in the devastated café. He turned toward the body hurtling at him but it was too late. Mark hit him low at the waist driving the terrorist into the road behind them where they landed hard on the pavement. Mark on top of the shooter, the AK-47 flying through the air. Mark straddled the body under him holding the man down with his left hand as he punched him in the face with the heavy glass mug in his right hand – once, twice, three times smashing the man's face while he screamed in fury. He raised his right arm to deliver another blow when a hand grabbed his wrist.

"That's enough," said a voice in his ear. "We want him alive to answer questions. We have him now. Stop or you will kill him." Mark turned to see two uniformed security officers along with a few soldiers in military uniforms, rifles at the ready surrounding him. One of the officers held Marks arm in a tight grip, the bloody mug clutched in Marks bleeding hand. Slowly, Mark stood to survey the carnage around him. Tables and chairs were overturned, bodies lying on the stone floor, blood everywhere. Medical personnel rushed into the restaurant to help the wounded. Others checked people lying still on the cold blood drenched floor to see if they were dead or unconscious. Mark walked through the chaotic scene to the overturned table where Rachel still cowered behind the thick garnet top table that had acted like a shield to protect her.

"Come Rachel, it's over, we can go now. Just follow me, take my hand, and try not to look at the dead bodies on the blood-soaked floor." They walked out the front of the restaurant to the crowed street now swarming with first responders and dazed civilians. Mark saw Shlomo lying in a pool of blood, his face blown away, his once white shirt red with his blood. There were roadblocks set up on either end of the street halting all traffic. The barriers watched over by armed military personnel both men and women. They walked pasted the roadblock manned by armed soldiers, police cars with lights flashing blocked the street.

"Are you alright, Mark, asked a pale Rachel. It was obvious she was badly shaken by her ordeal. Your shirt is ripped and the knees are torn out of your khaki slacks. You have blood on your hands a cut over your eye dripping blood down your check. Are you sure your ok." Do you need a doctor?"

"I'm good, Rachel just a little shaken. That Arab killer sure messed up our dinner date. We will have to do this again soon. Let me get you a cab to take you back to the campus. It's more important that you're alright. If anything had happened to you while you were with me your mother would come down here to kill me herself."

Rachel laughed a hearty laugh. "Is that why you went and tackled that murderer? You're more afraid of my mother than an Arab fanatic with an automatic rifle?" We both laughed at that remark. I put her into a cab.

"The University," I told the driver, handing him money. "And don't stop for anything on the way. Rachel – call me when you get to your room. I want to know you're safe." I stood watching the cab pull away, then turned walking up to the barricade blocking entry to the shattered street.

"Sorry Sir, no one allowed past this point." Mark shrugged his shoulders. "It's ok," he said to the policeman. "There is nothing more I can do here." The adrenaline rush was wearing off. Mark could feel the pain in his knees and right hand from pummeling the Arab's face with the mug. His knuckles were skinned, his hand sore. He walked two blocks until he found another empty cab "the Hilton Hotel," he told the driver.

Mark didn't normally drink in a bar but he felt the need for a stiff drink now. The bartender looked at him when he sat on a high bar stool. "Have you been in a fight mister? Your clothes are ripped your hands and face are bloody. Are the police looking for you, do I have to call them.

"You could say I've been in a fight but there is no need to call the police since they already know. Let me have a shot of vodka, Belvedere, chilled but straight up with a twist." "Make it a double."

"Are you going to tell me shaken but not stirred."

"Looks like I don't have to tell you since you already know." While the bartender was making his drink the television above the bar showed a picture of a scene of devastation – a smoldering restaurant blown apart, the news camera panning around the interior.

"Breaking news," the female reporter began. "There was a terror attack at two restaurants on the promenade on north beach tonight. A suicide bomber walked into one restaurant where he detonated his bomb in the crowed dining room. It is estimated at this time that eighteen people have been killed in the ensuing explosion, many more wounded. Some of the injured are in critical condition and are not expected to live. At the same time another terrorist was subdued at a second restaurant two doors away. We have pictures from a video-camera in the restaurant showing this attack."

The bartender set the drink before Mark turning to the T.V. The screen showed the killer raising the gun to his shoulder as he began to fire into the crowded room. People screamed, some ran, others fell to the ground dead, one of those was Shlomo. The gun stopped chattering as the attacker dropped the empty magazine to the ground pulling another from his jacket pocket and attempted to insert it into the breach. There was a blur as a body hurtled into the picture heading straight for the shooter.

"Look at that idiot," said the bartender. "He must have a death wish."

The collision was violent. Both bodies smashed onto the road bed the gun flying into the air clattering to the ground some feet away. The picture showed the backs of the security guards pulling one of the people away, an unconscious gunman lying in the street, blood covering his battered face. When the man turned to walk back into the restaurant there was a clear picture of his face, blood running down one cheek from a cut over his right eye. Then he disappeared out of the camera view only to appear a few seconds later leading a woman by the hand.

The female reporter continued: "The authorities are trying to determine the identity of the individual who knocked the assailant to the ground and held him until the authorities arrived. The shooter is being detained in a secret location where he is receiving medical attention prior to being questioned. More news to follow."

"That was you," said the bartender watching Mark drink his vodka. "You were the crazy bastard that tackled that killer. Tell me, was that you?"

"How much do I owe you" asked Mark?

"Nothing If that was you the drink is on Conrad Hilton. Tell me was that you?"

Mark laid a ten-dollar bill on the bar next to his empty glass. "Thanks for the drink," he said, as he walked out into the street.

The night concierge was at the desk when Mark entered the building. "Good evening, Mr. Radin. Good to see you're alive." Mark rode the elevator up to the penthouse floor. He realized some observers recognized him from the T.V. story of the attack. He was sure his picture would be on the front-page of the morning papers. Not a good way to start the day. He entered his apartment directly from the elevator when he saw a dim light on in the great-room. The T.V. was flickering but there was no sound; it was on mute. Mark wished he had a gun as he moved cautiously into the large room looking out at the Mediterranean through the floor-to-ceiling windows. He caught a reflection in a window, someone sitting in the easy chair.

"Don't move. I have a gun pointed at your head."

"Don't make me laugh. You're not armed or you would have shot the terrorist instead of tackling him then trying to beat him to death with a beer mug. Hell, If security officers hadn't stopped you, our Arab killer would be a dead martyr now." Couldn't you find a better weapon.

"Talal, what are you doing in my apartment, how did you get in.?"

"I saw the television footage of the take-down of the terrorist. Once I realized it was you I decided to come pay you a visit. We can talk about your situation since you're the most sought after man in Tel Aviv tonight. At least the most sought after who isn't a terrorist."

"How did you get here so fast from Jerusalem?"

"I wasn't in Jerusalem. I was in Tel Aviv at the office when we got the news of the attack. We had a live feed of the video-footage before anyone else. We also had an agent on site within minutes. No matter, since I recognized you immediately. When I saw you leaving with Rachel I was sure it was you. What you did was very brave Mark. You saved many lives by your quick response. That killer was going to reload and spray the restaurant with thirty more rounds of nine-millimeter bullets."

"But I'm afraid due to your actions you have to leave Israel tonight since everyone is looking for the hero who tackled the terrorist. The office wants to protect you. We think Hamas or al- Qaeda thugs will be searching for the promenade hero also. They are not happy you spoiled their deadly attack. Come with me, we must leave at once I have a car waiting outside."

The black Chevy Impala, an office driver behind the wheel drove through the dark streets of Tel Aviv going north on Dizengoff to Nemal where he turned right on the main road leading to the port. The car stopped at the security gate where two armed sentries stood beside a guard-house one raised his hand. Stop. A third man watched from inside through bulletproof glass.

"Not like the port in Alexandria," said Mark.

The driver rolled down his window, showing his Government I.D. to the guard. They stood aside to let the car pass, fingers on the trigger of their Uzis.

"Are they jumpy because of the attack tonight?" asked Mark.

"No, they are always like this. You never know when the Arabs will attack so we must be ready, vigilant at all times."" Unfortunately that is life in Israel today."

"Why are we here at the port, are we meeting someone?" Mark asked.

"It was decided by our council members the best place for you would be on one of our new S-Class Corvettes. The Hanit is tied-up at Pier 8, the INF pier. It's going to set sail ten minutes after you clear the gang-way. You are going for a two-week Mediterranean cruise; The ship is to set sail from here to Tiarco on the Lebanese coast, then west to Cyprus, Rhodes Malta and Spain, Barcelona I beleive before turning back to Egypt, then home. You will return to this same dock in sixteen days. I will have a car waiting for you at 10 a.m. on September 30th. And Mark, try to grow a beard will you, something to change your features since we are sure the terrorist have your description and are looking for you to extract revenge for your brave act tonight."

"Will a dark tan do?"

"I doubt it," said Tal good naturally as we stood on the cement pier at the foot of the gang-way leading to the ship's deck. A naval officer, two seamen at his side stood waiting.

"So this is my reward for a brave act," said Mark. "Exiled at sea."

"Be happy my boy, it's better than Elba. Just think how much a sixteen-day Mediterranean cruise would cost on your own private yacht." They both laughed at that. Tal hugged Mark tightly, then pushed him away: "Go my boy. They are waiting for you."

The gang-plank was lowered as soon as Mark stepped onto the ship's deck. He heard the Captain yell down from the bridge: "Single-up all lines." Followed by another command a minute later by the words: "Cast off." The ship shuddered beneath his feet as they got underway. Mark looked at the pier slowly drifting away in the dark night. Tal was still-standing in place watching the ship carry Mark out to sea, to safety. No vengeful terrorist could get their hands on him now. He would be safe for at least sixteen days.

The next two weeks passed quickly for Mark who loved being at sea, especially on a Navy warship, a fast attack-vessel. The *Hanit*, meaning spear in Hebrew, was a late model Corvette with a compliment of nine officers and crew of 120 men. At 291 feet in length, it was one of the largest ships in the Israeli Navy, along with its two sister ships. Mark quickly made friends with the nine officers. He ate with them daily in the officer's wardroom. He was bunked with the gunnery officer in a comfortable two-man cabin. The Captain, Mordichi Stern, had the Quartermaster issue Mark two white officers dress shirts, two pair of navy blue slacks and two white t-shirts with the ship's name and emblem on the left breast. He was also given a navy baseball cap with the ships name embossed in gold, a red spear through the name.

"You know Mark this ship was built in the United States for our Navy explained the captain. It was built to Israeli design and specifications in a place called Pascagoula Mississippi. The shipyard built three, all to the same specs – one in 1998, another in '99 and this one in 2001" I went to inspect her with various engineers before we took delivery; I spent 3 weeks ashore in Mississippi.

"No wonder I feel at home Mordi it's like being in America." They both laughed at the poor joke.

The 16 days flew by sailing over the vast Mediterranean Sea from one point to another but never touching land. Now on a brilliant clear morning the Hanit made her way toward Tel Aviv growing closer in the distance. Mark stood on the bridge-wing as the round red ball of the sun rose slowly into the clear blue sky over his adopted country.

"Right on time," said the executive officer. "We'll have you at the pier a few minutes before 10." Mark, wearing the white officer shirt with epilates and navy uniform trousers,the ball cap on his head walked down the gang-plank to a waiting black Chevrolet Impala. An army driver in fatigues, a holstered pistol on his hip stood by the open rear-door.

"Welcome home Sir, he said as Mark climbed into the rear-seat a small canvas sea-bag in his hand which contained his few possessions. The car took off immediately leaving the Port behind as it entered Tel Aviv traffic.

"Are we going to my apartment?" Mark asked.

"Eventually I think. But I've been instructed to take you to one of our annex buildings since the main office buildings may still be under surveillance. The media has been trying to unidentified the man from the video in the hope he might still show up. The speculation is that he is an agent of the agency. A Mossad operator who is in hiding. Reporters are still searching for you. Not many people know of this annex, it's a closely guarded secret" The car came to a stop on a narrow street flanked by grey stone buildings on either side. Mark got out of the car standing on the sidewalk. The driver walked up to him, his right hand extended. "I'd like to shake your hand Sir. That was a very brave thing you did. I'm proud to have met you. Just go through the front door, someone inside will help you." Mark walked into the grey stone building. Everything about the building seemed to be shades of grey. The front façade of the building outside was grey, the steps leading to the doorway were a dirty grey. Inside the lobby the stone floors were grey marble with a mosaic pattern in darker grey a gold emblem embossed in the center of the floor, Mark didn't recognize the emblem. The ceiling overhead and the columns in the large entry were all a shade of grey. How many shades of grey were there? Maybe fifty he wondered.

A young man in a grey suit was standing inside the door. "Please come with me, Mr. Radin." An elevator took them up to the fifth floor. At least it was light and bright up here he thought as he walked from the elevator into the open corridor. The atmosphere was different, the surroundings pleasant. The walls were painted tan, carpet on the floor a soft shade of beige with a deep olive pattern running through it. Bright lights added to the sunshine spilling from the windows at the end of the hall. My escort knocked on a door then opened it ushering me into a large well-lit room where sunlight poured through glass windows on two walls. There were six men in the room. Two I recognized. One was my good friend and mentor, rabbi Talal the other was Benjamin Netanyahu, the Prime Minister of Israel who walked across the carpet to greet me.

"Welcome home my friend. Did you enjoy your sea voyage?"

"Yes I did Mr. Prime Minister; I enjoyed sailing on one of your warships very much. I would have liked to have been able to go ashore in one of the many exotic ports we sailed past, but that was not to to be."

"Sorry for the inconvenience but we had your safety in mind. Sit down please Mark so we can talk. May I call you Mark?"

"Mr. Prime Minister, as the leader of the country, you can call me anything you would like." Everyone laughed politely as we all sat.

"I'm sure you would like to go home to your apartment so I'll be brief. The other men at this table have a great interest in keeping Israel safe from terrorists. The kind of fanatical terrorist you encountered two weeks ago. We are here to thank you for your unselfish act on that day. You took action at the risk of your own life. We all applaud you for that." And they did; the four men in uniform clapped their hands in unison. "I believe we have done all we can to try to make your face disappear from public scrutiny." "You will have a Mossad agent, or two, following you for a while to make sure you are safe." "I know you are used to stalking and killing." At my request, my some time friend President Obama had your records – both military and FBI's private file – sent to me." "From what I read you are an exceptional human being." "I also received the information on your affair in Morocco." "I want to reassure you no one from that country has asked for your repatriation." "But if they do our Legal Department will block them for many years to come." "You are free to go and pursue your life here for as long as you wish to remain an Israeli citizen." "Which brings me to ask: What do you intend to do with yourself?""I just passed the bar exam, Sir. I'm going to start a law firm here in Tel Aviv. I hope to be in operation by the first of the year." "That is if I can forego any more extended ocean voyages." Everyone smiled again.

"Good luck then, Mr. Radin." Each man came and shook Mark's hand.

Then rabbi Talal said "Come, Mark, I'll see you out." The car and driver were waiting at the curb. "Goodbye Mark. The driver will take you home. Try to keep a low profile, no more pictures in the papers or on T.V."

CHAPTER 57 ✦ ✦ ✦

During the month of October Mark set out to find office space for his law firm.

"Sharri, you've shown me more than six offices in the past week and I don't like any of them," Mark said to his real estate agent. "They are all glass and chrome, no warmth, no personality. I want stone and wood." "I want my clients to see a sturdy structure not modern glitz."

"You're a tough customer Mark. I've shown you the best space on the market, yet nothing agrees with you."

"Sharri, what you've shown me is adequate, but all the same. Kind of dull really, glass and chrome when I want wood and stone."

"I don't know what to tell you Mark. Especially since you want to be in by January first. That doesn't leave us much time since it's already October 21st."

"Just keep looking, Sharri. My phone is always on. Call me when you find something suitable, something warm, something inviting and substantial."

Mark was working his way into fighting shape going to the gym three or four mornings a week and running three or four miles on alternate days. He was usually up and out by 5:30 each morning. On this particular morning he decided a good hard run along the beach was in order. He rose from his comfortable bed slipped on a t-shirt, runners shorts and Adidas running shoes. He stepped into the elevator pushing the button for the lobby. The elevator stopped at the fourth floor. *Unusual* thought Mark. It's only 5:30. Not many people in this classy building were up at this time of morning. The door opened to reveal a young disheveled woman who staggered into the elevator almost falling. Mark caught her in his arms holding her gently to support her. She was barely able to stand. Her light-brown hair was a tousled mess, her blouse torn buttons missing revealing her bare breast. She had no shoes and she was sobbing quietly. Mark could see she had a split lower lip and a bruise on her left cheek. The doors closed, the elevator continued down to the lobby. Mark asked in a hushed voice, "Are you alright miss can I help you?"

She seemed to come out of a trance noticing him for the first time. "I'll be al…al.. alright," she stuttered, looking at him through bleary eyes. The split lip was still oozing blood and the bruise on here cheek was beginning to color slightly it would be a rainbow of color tomorrow.

"What happened to you? Where are your shoes?" The doors opened to the lobby.

"Let me help you," said Mark, leading the woman to a chair. Avi stood behind the desk gazing at the pair.

"Get me some water Avi," Mark commanded "be quick man." Standing next to them he told Mark "That's the girl that came in with Charles just after midnight. What happened, to you Miss?"

"Go back to the desk; I'll take care of to this young lady"

"Please tell me what happened?" Mark asked softly as he gave the frazzeled woman some water to drink. She had stopped sobbing; now hesitantly she told him the story.

"Charles Goodman is a client of the law firm I work for. My boss gave me some papers for Mr. Goodman to sign, papers I could then notarize. My boss made arrangements for me to bring them to Goodman for his signature. I came to his apartment at 8 last night because I had to wait for the paralegal department to finish them. Goodman had to read the documents before he would sign them which took over two hours. When we were done it was after ten. Mr. Goodman asked if he could buy me dinner since it was late and he felt responsible for making me wait so long. I was famished, hadn't eaten since breakfast, so I said yes. We had a nice dinner in a cozy restaurant close by. Goodman was very polite, charming, a real raconteur. I had left my briefcase with the documents in his apartment when we went out. Once we finished dinner I went with him to retrieve my case then head for home. When we entered his apartment his whole personality changed from an affable, friendly, gentleman to a villain, a horrible brute. He locked and bolted the door, then poured two glasses of vodka, handing one to me.

"I don't want this," I said, putting the glass down on the counter. I picked up my briefcase walking to the locked door to leave.

"Where do you think you're going you cheap slut" he snarled at me menacingly

"I'm going home," I replied. I'm tired and my bed is waiting".

"Like hell you are! You're going to spend the night in my bed satisfying me. If you try to leave I'll beat the shit out of you then drag you to my bed."

"Look Mr. Goodman, I replied, trying to remain calm. I'm not going to bed with you and I'm surly not having sex with you. I'm an attorney, an associate at Howell. So I suggest you open the door and let me leave now." I started for the door when he grabbed my arm, spun me around and threw me to the floor. He was on me in a flash. Slapped me in the face, punched me in my mouth. He pulled my skirt up sliding his hand between my legs. I fought with him but he is bigger than me and much stronger. He ripped open my blouse pulled down my underpants and mounted me. That was the how it started she sobbed. It went on for four hours.

"Did he rape you?" She started to cry again her body shaking.

"He dragged me to his bedroom, ripped my clothes off and had his way with me. I fought back but he punched me in the face and stomach. I didn't want to die so I just gave in. When he was done with me he threw me out into the hall and locked the door."

"Are all your things still in his apartment?" Mark asked.

"Yes, my briefcase, my handbag with my wallet and credit cards and my shoes. Unless he threw them into the hallway when he was done with me."

"I think we should go pay Mr. Charles Goodman a visit. Come with me," said Mark, reaching for the girl's hand. He noticed she had two broken fingernails.

"Mr. Radin, be careful advised Avi. I know that Mr. Goodman, he is not such a good man. Nasty, cruel, does drugs; and I think he has a gun in his apartment."

"Thanks *Netzhawk*. I'll keep it in mind." We got on the elevator together. I pushed the button for 4 holding her arm to support her.

"I don't want any more trouble," she pleaded. Please let it go. He is a sadistic bastard.

"What's your name?" Mark asked gently so as not to upset her.

"Kimberly. Kimberly Fried."

"You just stay behind me Kimberly. I promise he won't hurt you anymore."

The floor was quiet when we stepped off the elevator standing silently in the hallway.

"Which apartment?" Mark asked. Kimberly pointed at a door marked 401. Mark walked up to the door knocking lightly. There was no answer so he knocked again, harder this time. Still no answer. After waiting fifteen seconds Mark banged sharply on the door with the palm of his hand. The door swung open to reveal a big well-muscled man in his late thirties standing naked except for a white terry towel wrapped round his waist.

"Who the hell are you and what do you want, he snarled?"

"What we want, said Mark in a calm voice stepping aside so Charles could see Kimberly, are the items that belong to this young woman. It seems she misplaced them in your apartment."

"I don't know what the hell you're talking about, and I don't know who that tramp is with you. She looks like a drugged out whore. I suggest you get out of here before I lose my temper and hurt you badly, both of you."

"Look Charles, I'm trying very hard to be civil. Let her in to get her things and we'll be on our way."

"You must be deaf" he said grabbing the door to slam it shut in our face. Mark waited until the door was almost closed, then raised his leg and kicked hard as he was taught 20 years ago in a Marit Kev training class-training in Israel. The door swung open, the edge catching Goodman in the shoulder driving him back into the room. Mark followed quickly. Goodman steadied himself taking a swing at Mark with a tightly clenched fist but he was off balance. Mark blocked the punch easily with his left arm, then delivered a sharp blow with the palm of his right hand to Goodman's solar plexus causing an out-rush of air from the preditor's lungs. In one swift motion Mark ripped the towel from around Goodman's waist leaving him standing there completely naked. Before Goodman could react Mark reached out with his left hand cupping the big man's testicles in a tight grip. Goodman cried out in pain as Mark squeezed and pulled down forcing Goodman to follow his balls until he was on his knees facing Mark who had also dropped to his knees. The two were face-to-face, only eighteen inches apart.

"Kimberly close the door and come here to me," Mark said over his shoulder.

When she was standing over them Mark asked: "Is this the big, bad wolf that attacked you?"

"Yes," she said.

"Those scratches on his chest and neck, they from you?"

"Yes," she said again as Mark squeezed the man's balls harder.

"Please," he gasped, tears running from his eyes. Please, you're hurting me."

"Listen to me you low-life piece of shit. I'd like to kill you for what you did to this girl. I hate men who abuse women. I'd like to rip your balls from your body, and I can."

"No, no, please," he begged in pain.

"Kimberly, get your things. If you see Mr. Smarty's wallet, take that too. Then come back to me. Look at me Goodman and listen closely. I could call the Police and have you taken away. The list of charges would be a mile long – rape, kidnapping, assault and battery, robbery. Maybe even attempted murder in the second degree enough for thirty years to life in prison."

Kimberly was back with her things in her hand Goodman's wallet in her other hand. She had her shoes on, one had a broken heel. "Take the money from the wallet then throw it to the floor. I think you earned it however much it is." "Listen to me you creep."

"I could kill you and claim self-defense or we could leave and no one ever mention this night again. What do you say Kimberly, what do you want to do with this low-life animal?"

"Let's get out of here and leave this prick alone. I've had enough of him to last a life time."

"Listen to me carefully Goodman. I understand you think you're a heavyweight who can get away with the shit you pull. If I had to guess I'd say this isn't the first time you played this game on an innocent woman. You think you're connected to the right people. You think you can do anything and get away with it. I want you to know I've got you trumped, do you understand me."

"Yes, yes. I understand," he gasped; as I increased the pressure squeeze with my left hand.

"I don't ever want to hear your name again. If I do you'll regret it. Also, if I were you, I'd move out of this building, maybe even out of Israel." I let him go standing next to Kimberly as he slumped over on the floor drawing his knees up to his chest in a fetal position. He slid his hands between his legs to soothe the extreme discomfort I'd caused.

"Let's go. We're done here." We got onto the elevator. Mark pushed the button for 16th floor.

"Where are we going?" Kimberly demanded in a near panic as the elevator rose.

"To my apartment. Don't worry; I'm not going to molest you." "But it's obvious you can't leave in your present condition. Your blouse is ripped open revealing your breast, your skirt has a big tear by the zipper. One heel is broken on your shoe, and your face and hair are a mess." The elevator doors opened to the foyer of Marks spacious apartment. "You can use the shower in the second bedroom. Lock the door behind you so you will feel safe. You'll find a closet full of women's clothes. There is a dresser with various accessories, panties, bras, everything you will need to leave here presentably dressed. Help yourself take whatever you want."

"Whose clothes are they?" asked Kimberly.

"I'm not sure," said Mark. "Various girlfriends of my bachelor friend who owns this apartment. They stayed over and left the clothes behind thinking they would be retuning. Maybe they thought they would come back but never did. I don't know. But if it fits and you like it help yourself. I'll be waiting in the living room, take your time. Mark went into his bathroom to shower and change. He never did get to run but did manage to get in some exercise. He was sitting in the great-room when Kimberly came to join him.

"You look much better now" said Mark. Her lip was still split but partly hidden behind faint, pink gloss. Her brown hair was washed and brushed back; it had a shine to it. A slight coloring about her right eye was still visible behind some blush. It would be a multi color shiner by tomorrow.

"That suit looks good on you," said Mark. "A nice fit." It was a beige pant suit with a coral blouse under the jacket. Leave your torn clothes in the bath room. I'll get rid of them for you.

"I feel strange taking clothes that belong to someone else."

"Don't let it worry you. I doubt anyone will miss them. Enjoy them since, they are yours now."

"Now what?" asked Kimberly?

"I'll see you out," said Mark. "Get you a cab. Are you going to work?"

"Yes," she replied. "I'll be in my office by 8. I can give Jed the papers he sent me to get from Goodman."

"Come then, let's go." Out On the street, Mark held the door of a cab as Kimberly climbed in. She opened her purse removing a business card handing it to Mark.

"Thanks for your help Mark. I'm not sure what I would have done without you. Take my card. If there is anything I can ever do for you just call me. I'm in your debt."

"Thanks Kim. Just be well." He stood watching the cab pull away.

CHAPTER 58 ✝ ✝ ✝

Mark's phone rang. "Hello."

"Mark, its Sharri. I have news for you."

"Sharri, I haven't heard from you in weeks. I thought you'd given up trying finding an office for me."

"To tell you the truth Mark, I did. You are one tough customer." "This morning I was speaking with an associate who told me his accounting firm closed." It seems the senior partner died which caused a big shake-up in the office. The owner's death forced the company to close. We should meet at once so I can show you this space before it becomes public knowledge."

"Fine with me, when can we see it?"

"Are you at the Crystal?"

"Yes, I'm at home."

"Pick you up downstairs in ten minutes." Mark stood at the curb as Sharri pulled up in her old silver Hyundai Omega. Mark climbed into the passenger seat as Sharri accelerated into traffic.

"Where are we going?" Mark asked.

"South of here, toward Old Yafa. The space I'm taking you to see is on the corner of Prof. Yehezkel Kaufman Street and Shanker Street. It's across from Charles Clor Beach and Park. Do you know it?"

"I'm afraid it wasn't on my must-see list."

"I think you'll like the area. Anyway, here's the story the way it was explained to me. The space is 9,000 square feet on the sixth floor of a six story office building, the top floor. The office occupies the entire floor. It was home to an accounting firm, Adler, Roth for over twenty years. Roth died three years ago. Adler continued to run the firm which employed about 35 accounts and an office staff of 20 assistants."

"That's a pretty big firm," said Mark.

"Yes, it's one of the top three in Tel Aviv. It had an excellent reputation. Five month ago Adler died." "An office manager was trying to run the firm, but it was too much for him." "So Marsha Adler, the dead owner's wife, walked into the office yesterday and announced she was closing the doors. She told everyone to take their personal possessions and leave at once." "Then she locked the door for the last time." I understand she collected two or three million on her husband's life insurance policy. Her attorneys sold the accounts of the firm to the largest accounting firm in Israel for $100,000 up-front with additional payments at the end of a year based on how many accounts stayed with the new firm."

"That's a normal arrangement" said Mark, as the car sped south from Ha Yarkan Street onto Elezer Pari Street.

"It's a nice ride, Mark. The same road all the way. It just keeps changing names." Buildings on the left-side, and hotels, beach and sparkling emerald water on the right. "Anyway, old lady Adler locked the door and hasn't paid the rent since her husband died. The landlord is suing for the money owed $9,000 a month for five months, $45,000." "But Marsha Adler is a stubborn woman." "She told her lawyer to screw the landlord." "She isn't paying a dime, since there is no more firm now that her husband is dead." "Adler and Roth signed a new ten-year lease four years ago which means it still has six years remaining." They were driving on Herbert Samuel Street.

"Almost there now," said Sharri, as she made her way through traffic.

"Do you know where Mrs. Adler lives"? Mark asked. "I'd like to see that lease and find out if it has an assignment clause in it."

"No, I don't, but I know who her attorney is." "He probably has the lease, since he is handling her affairs." The street-name changed again. Now they were on Professor Yehezekel Kaufman Street. "The building is on this street just a few blocks farther" said Sharri.

"What are those buildings on the left?" asked Mark.

"The modern one is the Dan Panorama Hotel, and the other is Hassan Bek Mosque." Sharri made a left turn onto Shanker Street. She pulled to the curb and stopped the car. "That's the building on your right, Mark. There's a parking-lot just behind the building," she said as she pulled into the lot and parked the car. They walked around the side of an impressive brown stone building.

"It is the only structure on this side of the street. It fronts on Kaufman. This side is on Shanker while the back and the parking-lot are on Migali." Across Shanker were new, high-rise glass office buildings, the kind of buildings Mark didn't like. They walked into the spacious lobby through double glass doors, with a revolving door to one side. The lobby was all stone in various shades of brown with marble floors and walls in an attractive sand stone color. Two banks of elevators with shiny brass doors stood in an alcove to the side of the lobby.

"I have a key card that will open the doors on the sixth floor, let's go." They exited the elevator directly into a bright waiting area, with a large window to the right looking out to the park across the way. A reception area was to the left of the elevator. The walls were dark wood, and the floor was light beige granite. Two doorways stood on either side wall, one on the left, the other to the right of the reception desk.

"Come this way" said Sharri, leading Mark to the door on the left which she opened with a key. "These doors are locked so no one can enter without an escort. The receptionist has a button to open either door." Once through the door, they faced a row of offices that ran down the entire front of the building, with a corridor going all the way around the space.

"These are the executive offices; the windows look out over Kaufman Street to the park and the beach beyond with a spectacular view of the Mediterranean Sea." We could see boats darting across the flat azure surface of the sea, people lying on the sand or strolling along the promenade.

"The furniture," said Mark looking around the luxurious space, "It's all still here."

"Yes. Mrs Adler left everything in place. The desks, chairs, file-cabinets were all sitting untouched. She had no use for any of it. The office is just as it was the day she locked the door."

"How do you like the space?"

"Like it? I love it," replied Mark. "Rich, just the right atmosphere I was looking for. Exclusive and elegant, but not showy. Low-keyed elegance, exactly the feel I was looking for." They walked down the corridor, where four Executive offices were on the left side of the space. A glass-fronted conference room occupied the right interior wall next to a large open secretary station with four wooden desks.

"This is some fancy conference room," said Sharri. There was a heavy wooden table with eleven chairs, five on each side with one at the head. They turned right at the end continuing down the corridor walking by a series of smaller offices on the interior wall, with windows on the wall facing Shanker Street and glass towers on the far side. Continuing around the corridor, there were more offices and a large room with cubicles that held white Formica modular desks.

"This is where the bulk of the accountants worked." We continued along the corridor opening a door to the reception area from the opposite side, having completed a full circle around the office space. The corridor was like a horse-shoe with the reception area at the open end.

"What do you think?" asked Sharri

"I want it," replied Mark. The space is perfect. It is exactly what I envisioned. "Now we have to figure out how to get it," replied Sharri.

"That will be my job," said Mark. "You've done yours by finding it for me."

Once Mark was back in his apartment, he called the attorney Sharri had told him represented Mrs. Adler.

The phone was answered by a man with a pleasant sounding voice "Fred Metelnikow, how can I help you?"

"My name is Mark Radin. I'm an attorney looking to lease the vacant Adler office for my firm. I understand you represent Marsha Adler. I'd like to talk to you about the lease for the Adler space."

"Come to my office Mr. Radin. We can talk then. I'm in the Aloki office building, 34th floor. It's in the Azrieli Center."

Mark walked into Metelnikow's office located in a modern glass and chrome skyscraper, the type building Mark disliked.

Metelnikow was a well-dressed man in his fifties who was tending toward obesity. He was already heavy-set from years of a sedentary lifestyle.

"How can I help you, Mr. Radin?"

"I'm interested in the lease for the Adler office. I would like to know if the lease has an assignment clause in it."

"It does," said Fred. "What do you have in mind?"

"If she assigns the lease to me I will get your client, Mrs. Adler, out of the lease. I'll get the landlord to drop the lawsuit for the $45,000 in past rent, which will be $54,000 in another week and counting, plus get her $25,000 to assign the lease to me."

"Good luck, Mark. You don't know who you're dealing with." "The landlord is a very wealthy man. He owns property all over the country." "His properties include Office buildings, hotels, apartment's warehouses, and huge amounts of vacant land." "You name it, he owns it. They call him the Donald Trump of Israel." "He's a tough customer to deal with. An old time self -made billionaire."

"You let me worry about him," said Mark. "If I can do what I say, do we have a deal? We have a deal," said Fred, extending his hand for Mark to shake.

"Please advise Mrs. Adler of my intensions so we can move ahead quickly."

"Here is Zuckerberg's phone number." "Keep me informed of your progress, I wish you luck, you're going to need it." You'll need all your skill dealing with old man Zuckerberg, he's a real mumser."

Back in his apartment, Mark dialed the number Fred had given him. A gruff voice answered with one word, "Zuckerberg," that was all he said. Mark introduced himself. "I'm calling about the vacant Adler office space; I would like to talk with you about that lease." Zuckerberg began a rant spiced with some colorful language ending with the phrase, "screw that old dried up bitch, I'll get even with her yet."

"If you'll meet me tomorrow, I may be able to solve your dilemma."

"Come to my office at 7 in the morning. I start early. The address is 21 Kikar Street. It's just a few doors in from the corner of Dizengoff."

"I'll find it," I replied. "See you at 7." The cab dropped me off at 10 minutes of 7 in front of a one-story cinderblock building painted battleship grey. There was colorful graffiti painted on a side wall next to a vacant lot. I stood looking at the building wondering if I was in the right place: What is a multi-millionaire, no a billionaire doing in a building like this. It looked like a derelict property. Mark climbed the three steps to a small porch, a scuffed brown wooden door as the only entrance. A dirty glass window was next to the door. Mark opened the door, and walked into a good-sized square room.

"You must be the hot-shot that called me yesterday about the Adler's space, right?" An older grey haired man sat behind a large wooden desk that had seen better days.

"Yes, Mr. Zuckerberg, that's me". "Sit down, Radin, Let's talk." "I'd like to know what you can say that would convince me to assign that lease to you." "I'd have to be crazy to do that when I already have a firm contract in place." "But I'll listen before I throw you out and, I may not open the door when I do it." The man my have been old, but he had a large frame with broad shoulders and a lean body. I had no doubt he could handle himself in a scuffle. This was a man of the streets used to hard physical work not some fancy board room type.

"I like your office Mr. Zuckerberg," said Mark, looking around the plain drab room. He didn't see any desk for a secretary or assistant, just an old, scared table with papers in neat piles scatter over the top along with maps and diagrams.

"First stop calling me Mr. Zuckerberg, the name's Nathan." "You can call me Nat, while I call you Radin." "I looked you up on Google last night to find out a little about you." I must admit I was impressed by what I read." "I have a real American hero, an ex-Navy Seal with plenty of medals and ribbons earned in combat." "Then law school moving on to specialize in aviation law." "There was an article in the New York Times that said you won the largest airline settlement in history, a crash of an Intercontinental Airlines flight a few years ago." "It said the total settlement was in the billions. Your share must have been huge."

"Let's just say it was sufficient," replied Mark.

"Modest and humble too; I like that." "But it didn't say what you were doing in Israel or what you want my office for." I thought the offices were Adlers?" "I own that building and when I'm finished with that old hag the space will be mine again." "Now why do you want the office?"

"I just passed the Israeli bar exam." "I'm going to open a law office here in Tel Aviv, hopefully in the old Adler space"

"Why not go back to New York? You already are a partner in a firm there."

"I have a small problem, I can't go back to America yet."

"If we are going to do business together I want to know why you can't go back to New York."

"What I tell you is in strict confidence, Nat. No one, or at least very few people know the story and I intend to keep it that way." "I'm wanted in Casablanca, Morocco for murder, which is why I came to Israel." "There is no extradition treaty between the two countries, but there is with Israel and the United States. Does that answer your question?"

"Did you kill someone? Are you a murderer?" Mark looked into Zuckerberg's eyes.

"The answer is complicated. "I did kill a man but it wasn't murder." Mark related the story to the billionaire landlord.

"Thanks for telling me Mark. It shows some trust in me on your part." "I appreciate your honesty but you still haven't showed me why I should assign the lease to you."

"I'll give you the reasons."

"You mean there's more than one."

"Hear me out," said Mark. "The first is money, it usually is." "From what I've been told you have enough money already actually more than enough if that is possible." "like my court award let's say its substantial." "Yet, you continue to do what you do." "Why I ask myself." I'll tell you the answer," continued Mark. "It's the challenge, the competition, at this point in your life it's a game." "You're a winner and you like to keep winning it's what motivates you, what gets you up every morning." "More money is always nice, but it's more the contest, am I right, Nat?"

"Keep talking Sonny, I'm listening. I haven't thrown you out yet."

"Look at it this way," continued Mark. "Mrs. Adler's lawyers are pretty good. I've met them." "They could keep you tied up in court for at least two years." "If they don't know how, I could show them." "I understand you're out five months' rent already,that's $45,000 shekels, not small change." "It's going to be $54,000 in another week and climbing." "I have a copy of the lease, which I read four times last night." "It's mostly boilerplate, a standard lease in the name of Adler and Roth, with personal guarantees signed by both." "The only problem is, they are both dead." "That means you can't get money from their estates or from Mrs. Adler because she isn't on the lease." "That means you're stuck with a non-performing piece of real estate. I'm sure the monetary loss won't hurt you too much." However, it pisses you off that your stymied by the situation." "I could have Mrs. Adler assign the lease to me." "The wording in the contract says you will approve the new lessee if you find the tenant financially solvent." "I'm sure you will find I am." "The lease has just over six years remaining." "I could be your tenant until June of 2023, but then what?" "You'd be so pissed off at me I'd be out on my ear." Either that or you would raise the rent to such a prohibitive figure; I'll have no choice but to leave."

Zuckerberg smiled at me. "You're pretty smart hot-shot so what do you propose?"

"I say tear-up the lease if you can get it back, and then sign a new lease with me." "I want a five-year lease at $10,000 per month. That's $1,000 more than Adler was paying." I want a five-year option. The sixth year at $11,000, the seventh and eighth and ninth years at $12,000, with the tenth year at $14,000." "That helps cover the five months of no rent which will be six months and counting." "As I said earlier, this vendetta with that old dried up bitch, to use your words, could drag on for a long time, if you let it."

"You're an interesting guy, Mr. Hot-Shot. So what's your alternative to this imbroglio?"

"There are a few other provisions," I added. "You drop the lawsuit and give Mrs. Adler a check for $25,000 with a full release."

"You've got some *cajones, Radin*!" "It's a simple fact Nat; you just have to face it." "The $25,000 is what you make in two years on the increase in rent so, in effect, I'm paying the widow." "That still gives you $100,000 more over five years than you have now." "Also, as far as the release of the past-due rent goes, I told you, you will never see it, which I know you know." "You just don't like losing." "If you agree to this deal and we are both winners, which is always a good thing." "And who knows, ten years from now when it's time to talk about a new lease, we can sit down as friends, or at least respected business associates."

"You know Hot-Shot, when you came in here I told myself, I'll listen for five minutes, then throw the conniving bum out." "I expected you to come in to try and squeeze me for concessions like most people would do." "But instead, you give me my lease back with the opportunity to make a new lease for more money." "I see why the jury voted in your favor in that crash case." He reached across the table grabbing Mark's hand in a very firm grip. "You have a deal, Sonny. I'll call my lawyer; tell him to contact you to come up with a new lease." I'll also have him call that prick

Metelnikow and tell him a check for $25k from Zuckerberg Real Estate is coming his way." "Are we done?" he asked

"Unless you want to go to breakfast."

"No, I'm good. But I'll be in touch, I like your style"

Mark caught a cab to his apartment, where he called Sharri immediately to give her the news.

"That's fantastic Mark. I'm happy for you."

"Thanks Sharri. But you were the prime mover in getting this deal done." "Without you, I wouldn't have ever known about the space." So tell me what do you earn what's your commission on a 5 year lease?"

"Nothing, I'm afraid, since I don't have a listing agreement." "There is no contract in place. I didn't negotiate the deal for you so no one has to pay me."

"What would your fee have been?"

"It would be 3% of the lease amount. $120,000 a year for five years is $600,000. At 3% it would be $18,000."

"Thanks again Sharri, I'll be in touch." The phone rang ten minutes later.

"Hi Tal," said Mark. "What's happening?"

"That's what I called to ask you Mark. Are you keeping a low profile?"

"Yes rabbi, at least I think so." "It's good you called, because there is something I want to ask you." "I'm very close to signing a lease for new office space for my law firm but I need a name."

"Good, my boy what is the name to be?"

"I want to use your name."

"Talah," he said incredulously.

"No rabbi, your last name. I want to call the firm: Aksimon & Associates, if it's alright with you."

"It's fine with me Mark. Although, it might not be as widely accepted as you think if it's associated with me."

"I'll take my chances, rabbi."

"So now you have a name and an office but what about a staff? "Or, are you going to go it alone?"

"Rabbi, I have 9,000 square feet of office space. I'm going to have to find some people to fill it."

"That's why I'm calling," said the rabbi. "I gave a lecture last week called Religion and the Law. It was well-attended; about 75 lawyers came to hear my lecture." "After the lecture I was meeting and greeting, you know, we Jews call it schmoozing." "A lawyer who was a student of mine at the university, which to Tal meant Hebrew University, came over to talk to me." "I haven't seen him in fifteen years. He left Hebrew University as a sophomore transferring to Haifa." "I only taught two classes for him: Ethics and Philosophy, I remember him being an astute student." "Anyway, during our conversation he told me he has been working for a firm in Tel Aviv – Stein and Schwartz, a midsize law firm with a reputation as shysters." "They are not very ethical or employee-friendly." "They earned that reputation because of the way they treat associates, they have a high turnover rate." "Lawyers stay for two or three years to gain experience then move on which is what the partners want since they replace them with newbie's who work for less money." "Well Teddy, that's his name, Theodore Levine, but everyone calls him Teddy, has been there ten years, a record I think, except for the partners." "During our conversation, I got the impression he was disillusioned and maybe looking to jump ship. Give him a call. See what happens."

"Thanks Tal. I'll speak with you soon." I called the number Tal gave me. A strong male voice answered.

"Is this Teddy Levine?"

"Yes, who's calling?"

"My name is Mark Radin; Rabbi Talal Aksimon gave me your number. I'd like to speak with you in person, if you have some time."

"When and what's this about?"

"Don't worry Ted. I'm not going to sue you. How about tomorrow morning?"

"Let me check my calendar," said Teddy. "Looks like tomorrow's good. We're getting toward the end of the year so the pressure has eased somewhat."

"Good," said Mark. "Meet me at my apartment at 10:30. No one will bother us here. It is The Crystal Tower on Sderot Nordan and Dizengoff. Do you know it?"

"Yes I do – the high-rent district."

"Yes, well just tell the concierge you're here to see me, Mark Radin. I'll let him know to expect you."

The next morning at 10:30, Mark's intercom buzzed.

"Mark, this is Hayim at the front desk. You have a visitor, Mr. Teddy Levine."

"Thanks Hayim, Send him up."

The elevator door opened to admit a tall well-dressed man who stepped into the apartment walking toward me, his right hand extended. "I'm Teddy," he said in a melodious voice with an American accent.

"Good to meet you Teddy, Mark Radin. Just call me Mark."

Teddy was dressed in a navy blue suit, light blue shirt open at the neck in typical Israeli style with brown oxford shoes.

"Come, we can sit on the balcony, it's cool out this morning. We can be comfortable while we talk." They sat across from each other. Ted was a bit shorter than Mark's height about 5'10" with a trim athletic build. He had a nice complexion, large brown eyes and brown hair combed back, no part. His hand was firm when they shook. Mark noticed he had long fingers. Could have been a piano player, Mark thought to himself.

"So, what's all the mystery? You said you weren't going to sue me. I never met you before so I can't owe you money. Please tell me what this meeting is about?"

"I told you, Rabbi Tal gave me your number saying he thought we should meet. I listen to Tal's advice; it's been excellent in the past."

"He is a brilliant man" agreed Teddy. "I took a few classes with him when I attended Hebrew University. That was before I transferred to Haifa."

"Why did you do that?" I asked.

"Transfer you mean?" "My mother got sick. She was dying, so I went back to Haifa to be close to her." "She had cancer, died seven months after I came to be with her." After she died, I just stayed on to finish my studies rather than move to another school again." After graduation, I went to law school there." "When I finished law school I came to Tel Aviv to get a job, since I felt the opportunities were better here in Tel Aviv." "I got a good job with a big firm, over thirty associate attorneys, two senior partners and two junior partners." Stein & Schwartz founded the firm, the two junior partners are Simon and Shapiro." "I've been with the firm almost ten years; I'm the longest tenured associate." "No one else has stayed for more than four years."

"I don't know much about the firm," said Mark. "I'm kind of the new kid on the block, but what I've been able to find out doesn't give Stein and Schwartz stellar reviews."

"I know all the stories" continued Teddy. "Some are true, others exaggerations. The joke around town is the name should be Stein and Schlock, Sleaze, or even Stein & Skeevy. I know them all," said Teddy. "But I told myself when I got out of law school I wanted to be a partner in a law firm inside of ten years. I thought my best chance would be to work hard with one firm and I would be invited to be a partner." Well, I've worked hard for nine soon to be ten years." I'm the lead litigator in my firm but each year the partners tell me the same story: We are sorry, Teddy. You've done an excellent job for us again this year; but the partners have decided we are not adding any new partners at this time, maybe next year." "Then I get a measly $3,000 increase in pay plus a $5,000 bonus and we move on. You know that is a paltry $155 dollar a week increase and it's insulting, contemptible on the part of my bosses."

"Then why do you stay?" asked Mark.

"If I move to a new firm now I'll have to begin to prove my bona fides all over again." "It could another six years until I can even hope to be offered a partnership." I'm 36 now, almost 37, but I've finally decided it is time to move on." "I'll start looking at new firms at the beginning of the year." "That's only five weeks away." "No one moves firms in December since everyone is holding out for a year end bonus."

"What are you looking for in a new firm?" asked Mark.

"Is this a job interview?" replied Teddy, eyeing Mark with a quizzical expression.

"No," laughed Mark. "I'm Just making conversation."

"I don't know about that since I seem to be doing all the talking while you're asking all the questions."

"Speaking of talking, you sound like an American. If I had to guess I'd say from the Midwest."

"Good guess" replied Teddy. "I was born in Rockford, Illinois not far from Chicago. I went to high school in Rockford and lettered in wrestling." "My dad was an engineer in Chicago when an Israeli firm offered him a job in Haifa." "They offered him a large salary to move." "I was sixteen when I came to Israel; I finished high school in Haifa, and then went to

Hebrew University. I wanted to be a philosopher, but couldn't see much opportunity in that field other than as a teacher, so I went to law school instead."

"Its 12:45 Teddy, We've been talking for two hours. Do you want to go to lunch with me?" "Don't worry, I'll buy."

"Sure," said Teddy. "Let's go."

Sitting on the promenade at a restaurant a few doors down from Danny's, where Mark had been having dinner with Rachel on that eventful night two months ago, they continued the conversation. Over dessert Mark asked: "Teddy, how are your relations with other firms here in the city; other lawyers?"

"I know many other lawyers. The litigators, the good litigators all know each other, since we are always in court facing off against one another." "The judges get to know you, also." "They know those lawyers who prepare well, who know the case and what their strategy is." "When you win a case, the opposing attorneys and firms make note of you, so they can be ready to oppose you the next time you meet." "To answer your question, I know my way around in this town and people know me." I've been practicing in the courts of this city for ten years." "I'm a proven commodity." "Now level with me Mark, what's this all about?"

"Before I answer you, let me ask you one more question." "How important is it for you to be a partner in a law firm? Or better yet, what would you be willing to do to be one?"

"I think I've already told you Mark." "A partnership is what I've wanted and worked toward for ten years." "As far as what I'll do to achieve that goal, I would do anything necessary as long as it was legal." "Now, let's stop fencing and get down to the real meaning for this meeting."

"Alright," said Mark. "I've been an attorney over 15 years. I have two partners in a firm in New York City. I just passed the bar here in Israel and I'm going to be opening a new law firm. I just took office space by Charles Clor Park. Do you know it?"

"Yes, it's a trendy section of town. It's becoming a popular business center."

"Yes, well," continued Mark, "I've just rented a 9,000 square foot office completely furnished with just me to fill it. I'm looking for a staff to join me."

"Are offering me a job" asked Teddy.

"No," replied Mark. "I'm offering you a partnership in the new firm, an equal partnership, you and me."

"Mark – I don't know what to say. You don't even know me. We just met"

"I'm a pretty good judge of character Teddy. I can usually get the feel of someone quickly, sometime within the first five minutes." "We've been together five hours now; I feel comfortable with you and think we can work well together." "You came highly recommended by my rabbi." "I'm offering you what you say you've always wanted and what you worked toward for ten years." "It's not with the four S's, I don't care that your last name starts with an L. Do you want the partnership or not?"

"What do I have to bring to the table?" asked Teddy. "I've got some money saved. You can have it."

"I don't want your money. I want your experience, your know-how, and your contacts in the legal profession in Tel Aviv." "I told you I was new here, but you're established, you've already made a name for yourself in this town." "That's what I need, your guidance." "I'll depend on you to show me the way since I'm a novice in Tel Aviv.

"Do I have to tell you now?"

"Yes, Teddy you do." "I want to be open for business on January 4th. That's only five weeks away and I still have much work to do before we will be ready to open." "You know what prosecutors say to a defense attorney, – This is the deal. It's on the table for ten minutes, and then I retract it so take it or leave it."

"Mark, is there anything I have to know about you before I say yes?"

"I'm a member in good standing of the Bar in New York, New Jersey, Illinois and Florida and now Isreal." "I am also wanted for murder in Morocco; I killed an evil person there, someone who deserved to die, the world is a better place without him in it." "Other than that I don't see anything to stop us joining forces."

I have a sufficient amount of money to carry the firm until we have clients producing income for us."

"There are so many issues to consider," said Teddy. Most of all you said you are wanted for murder." "Yes, that's true, however, I'm innocent, I killed a man but it was in self-defense." "Most murderers say that, Mark."

"Well, in my case it's true." "You'll just have to take my word for it." "As for other issues, we will face them when they arise, together if you say yes." "You know the saying, we'll cross that bridge when we come to it."

"We just go about our business and take care of items as they come up." "Now, as they say in Rockford, Illinois, Haifa, or Tel Aviv, the ball is in your court Teddy." "Are you going to serve or retire?"

"All I can say is if you conduct all your business this way, it should be an interesting partnership."

"Does that mean you're in?" asked Mark.

"I'm in," Teddy replied, shaking Mark's hand." "Thanks to you partner, I'm a partner in less than ten years."

The next few weeks were hectic. The office was being renovated. New computers, printers, and other equipment along with supplies needed to run a busy law firm were arriving daily. On December 12th, Mark took a business card from his desk and dialed the number on the card. A female voice answered the phone.

"Hello," she said.

"Kimberly, this is Mark Radin. Do you remember me?"

"Mark, it's good to hear from you. Remember you, I'll never forget you. What can I do for you?"

"Could we meet for dinner tomorrow night? Are you free?"

"Yes, I am. What do you have in mind?"

"I'll explain over dinner. Do you mind if I bring a friend along?"

"Male or female, Mark? I'm not into *ménage à trios*."

"No," Mark laughed, a social dinner with a little business thrown in. Meet you at Hatraklin Bistro on Herchal Hatalmud Street. Take a cab there. I'll get you home after dinner."

Mark and Teddy were sitting at a table in the corner of the outdoor patio behind the restaurant. It was a cool night in December. Mark had requested a table set apart so the three could talk in relative privacy. Kimberly walked in following the head-waiter to the table where both men stood to greet her. She kissed Mark on both cheeks then shook hands with Teddy. Mark made the introductions as the three sat down.

"I've never been here, before" said Kimberly. "It's a nice place."

"Yes, the food is very good, also. There is a reason for this meeting other than the food. I have a plan in mind. A plan that involves you".

"What would that be?" she asked.

"Speak with my associate. He is a fellow attorney. He worked; I should say, works for Stein and Shapiro."

"I know the firm," replied Kimberly. "A high out-put organization. They charge fancy fees to clients who operate just this side of the line, sometime over the line. What do you do for them Teddy?"

"I'm head litigator, the firm's trial attorney. I'm their go to guy."

"How about you," Teddy asked.

"I work for one of the partners of my firm. I do all the grunt work; write briefs file motions, that sort of thing." "I'd like to try cases in court or have my own clients with cases to pursue, but my chauvinistic boss won't give me any leeway." He has been holding me back for three years." Maybe he is afraid of the competition from a woman." Teddy kept questioning Kim about her work, education, and what she wanted in the future while the food was served. At the end of the meal Mark turned to Teddy and spoke as if they were alone while Kimberly watched in silence.

"What do you think, Teddy? Will she do?"

"In my estimation Mark, I think you picked a winner. She is just what we need. A budding star waiting for a chance to shine."

"Very good, I heartily agree." Mark turned to face Kimberly. "How would you like to come to work for a new law firm? I that is we will hire you for $20,000 a year more than you are making at Howell." "Plus, I guarantee you will have plenty of cases to work on of your own." "If my partner is so inclined, you may even get to go to court with him as he tries a case."

"Is this some sort of joke?" Kimberly asked looking from one man to the other.

"No," said Teddy. Mark operates at warp speed." "He made me his partner in just 6 hours after I'd been waiting 10 years to become a partner at my old firm." "We are offering you an opportunity to work with us in a new start-up law firm." "You will get paid more money, have more opportunities to spread your wings and a chance to be your own person." "All you have to do is say, yes like I did" "How much notice do you have to give Jed, your boss?" asked Mark.

"Two weeks would be more than enough. But, when I tell him I'm leaving he will probably tell me to pack my bags and leave immediately."

"You know how that works, he'll be worried about what I'll be doing before I leave."

"So is that a yes then?" asked Teddy.

"A definite yes," replied Kimberly. I can't believe I have a new job, more money and more responsibility all during a delicious two-hour dinner." "You are one amazing man Mark, that's all I can say."

"Waiter," called Mark. "Three glasses of Slivovitz, we have a toast to make." They stood at the curb waiting for a cab to take Kimberly home. "So it's just the three of us?"

"For now that's it. Although I'm still trying to fill out a staff."

"Do you mind if I ask someone in my office to come aboard. She's a paralegal who is being worked to death by the partners."

"Is she good?" asked Teddy.

"Yes, very competent. I've worked on some briefs with her in the past. She has good work habits, sharp instincts, is very knowledgeable when it comes to research and the law."

"Then, by all means ask her to come with you, we'll meet her salary."

CHAPTER 59 ✚ ✚ ✚

Mark had decided to have a New Year's Eve party to welcome in 2014 and celebrate the opening of his new law firm, Aksimon and Associates. He sent written invitations to each of those he was inviting, but also called each by phone to extend the invitation in person. It took Mark most of the morning contacting the invited guests. He was inviting twenty-eight people from four countries. It was a demanding task, but by early afternoon he had contacted most of them. He had one more job to do. He spent an hour trying to find a phone number for the person he wanted to reach but to no avail. Then he had an idea and called Rabbi Tal explaining what he needed. Tal was back on the line within ten minutes.

"Here is the number you want. My friend, Gideon at the Israeli Bar Association had it on file as you suspected. Good luck. I look forward to seeing you at your gala celebration New Year's Eve."

Mark dialed the number Tal had given him. A female voice answered.

"Myria, this is Mark Radin from the study group, remember me?"

"How could I forget a handsome Hebrew speaking sexy American? It's good to hear from you Mark, to what do I owe this call."

"I'd like to know if you'd gotten a job yet."

"I had a job at an old-time law firm; I was the first female associate ever." "All I did was spend three months filing papers." "One of the male associates told me the only reason I was hired was because I was a female." "The joke in the office is I was the show-broad." "I was there to prove the old-boy network was progressive, forward thinking." "To show They were all for diversity and equality when in truth they were intent on keeping the status quo." "I was just window-dressing." "I'm too independent to put up with that crap so I resigned last week." "I'll look for a new job in three weeks after the new year."

"You won't have to look for a job if you want to come to work with me."

"What do you mean, Mark?"

"I've formed a new firm. We'll be starting from scratch but I'm confident we'll be successful. We can grow quickly with the talent I've assembled."

"How many talented people are we talking about, Mark?"

"I have two experienced, competent attorneys and me." "You will be number four if you say, yes." "I'm trying to convince one more person to join us, but it may take some time." "You won't be the show broad in this firm since one of the attorneys you will be working with is a smart independent woman. I'm sure you'll fit right in."

"I trust you, Mark, you just hired your forth lawyer. When do I start?"

"Great, Myria. Come to the Zucker Building on Monday morning to meet the others. Our paralegal and receptionist will be here along with Ted and Kimberly, a nice happy group."

Now that the staff was complete Mark had a few more items to take care of. He placed a call to Nawaz in Mersin, Turkey. "I'm happy to hear your voice, my friend it has been awhile what can I do for you?"

"Two things," said Mark. "Call your car dealer in New Jersey." "I want a car delivered to Tel Aviv as soon as possible, a Hyundai Genesis, black with cream leather interior." "Get the better model, whatever that is." "The second thing is, I want you to attend my New Year's Eve party." "I've invited Rose and her business partner who may be her partner-partner by now." "Contact them and make arrangements to come together." "I've invited twenty-eight people to attend." "I'm sure you'll find more than a few to be interesting, including my other assassin Nasim, and my friend Alon." "They will be coming under assumed names, since they aren't allowed in Israel." "They are coming from Morocco with my attorney and partner." "It should prove interesting when they see the old rabbi, their benefactor protector and friend." "He will be surprised to see them since I haven't told him they are coming."

"I'll come for the festivities then, since it should prove interesting. As they say, I wouldn't miss it for the world"

"Good, I'll pay you for the car when I see you In Tel Aviv. By the way,

all expenses are taken care of except those that fall under miscellaneous."
"And what would they be," asked Nazam.

"How do I know? That's why it's called miscellaneous." That got a boisterous laugh from the Turk assassin. Mark's two partners were coming from New York bringing Stacy with them. He also invited Eric his rescuer on the failed mission in Gaza and Mordici the Captain of the *Hanit*. He told Eric to bring the medical corpsman who saved Nazims life. Sharri was coming along with Rabbi Tal and the Trump of Israel, Nathan Zuckerberg. The two college girls were happy to attend when Mark told them their mother would be there. Rachel asked if she could bring a school-mate, Uri Richland. I said, fine. Mark walked into the Hilton Hotel on the beach to make room reservations for his guests

"I want to reserve ten rooms for December 30-31 and January 1, High floors with water views," he informed the manger.

"Very good, Mr. Radin I'll see to it personally. I will get you a special corporate rate. What is the name of your company?"

"The name is Aksimon & Associates, a law firm in the Yafo district to the south. I passed a dozen hotels to come to you so I want my guests to get the royal treatment."

"Very good, Mr. Radin. I'm on duty those days. I'll make sure your guests are well taken care of, I am the general manager, my name is Isaac, you can call on me at any time." Mark handed Isaac a crisp hundered dollar bill. "There will be more if my guests are well cared for."

Mark entered the lobby of the Crystal Towers apartment after a long day's work to be stopped by the concierge at the front desk.

"I have some news for you, Mr. Radin. You remember that creep no one liked, Mr. Goodman on four?"

"Yes," replied Mark. "What about him?"

"He left this morning with two suitcases. I'm moving to Spain, he said. My lawyer will be disposing of my apartment and all the furnishings." With that he drove off in a cab. Didn't even say goodbye, no tip nothing."

Mark smiled as he rode the elevator to his luxurious apartment. He walked to the phone to dial Kimberly.

"Hello Mark, what's up." she asked.

"Hi Kim, I have a question for you: What is your ex-boss's name?"

"It's Jed Fishman, why?"

"I just got some good news that I think you'll appreciate." "Your rapist friend Goodman has moved from the building." "I'm told he's heading for Spain, guess my message to him that morning sunk-in after all. So you needn't concern yourself with him anymore."

"What's that have to do with my boss?"

"I'm going to try to repay a friend with a favor. I'll see you at the office Monday morning Kim, thanks."

The next call was to Sharri. "I have a lead for you," Mark began. "I just found out an apartment in my building is vacant, Apartment 401." "It belongs to a jerk named Charles Goodman who moved to Spain today." I believe his attorney is Jed Fishman." "Jed is trying to sell the apartment and all its contents." "Call him, here's his number, see if you can get the exclusive listing."

"Thanks Mark. I appreciate the call."

Twenty minutes later the phone rang. "Shalom," said Mark.

"I owe you big-time Mark."

"What happened, Sharri?"

"Fishman said I was the answer to his prayers. He doesn't have time to sell real estate." "He told me he's a lawyer not a real estate salesman and a busy one since his assistant just upped and quit." "Left him burdened with a lot of extra work." "He turned the deal over to me, and has already faxed me a contract." He told me to contact him with any offers which he'll send on to Goodman who is most anxious to get rid of the apartment?" "In the real estate business, we call that a motivated seller."

"Good for you Sharri. I hope you make a score."

"I'll thank you in-person at the party Mark."

"I look forward to it, Sharri. See you then."

On Monday morning, December 21, the staff of the new law firm gathered in the sixth floor conference room. Teddy and Mark had been to the office on numerous occasions since their agreement. This morning there was a lot of activity as new phone lines were being installed and tested. Other men worked running wires in the ceiling for the computers and closed-circuit security cameras. Mark showed Kimberly and Myria their offices which were next to Mark and Teddy. Each had an office with a view of the park, beach and Mediterranean Sea. Teddy's was first, than Kim, next was Myria while Mark had the corner office with windows on two walls. They were all impressed with the large glass fronted wood-paneled conference room. Kimberly took Adrian, the Paralegal, to her office on the inside wall next to the conference room, just across the corridor from the four attorneys.

"This is your work-station" Kimberly told her. "You are just across the corridor from our offices, so you'll be nearby when we need you." "Let me know if there is anything you need, otherwise, make yourself at home." Mark is going to hire another paralegal to assist you when the workload grows; it's up to you to tell us when that is." The four attorneys were sitting in comfortable leather chairs in the conference room when a tall attractive red-haired woman knocked on the door frame, the door was open to the corridor. Mark stood walking to the alluring well groomed woman standing in the doorway. A smile lit Mark's face as he looked her over. Taking her hand he drew her into the room.

"People, this is Caitlyn Harrington, we can call her Lyn"

"Lyn, this is Teddy, Kimberly and Myria. Lyn is our receptionist." "She is from England, Manchester, now living in Tel Aviv." "I hired her for three reasons." "She is smart, street-smartand well educated." "She is extremely charming well-dressed and appealing which will impress our clients.She speaks English and Hebrew with a delightful English accent." Our clients will be impressed with her."

"When we have some clients to impress," said Teddy.

"Yes," I agree Mark smiled, "When we have some clients." "Lyn will be at the front desk in the lobby, the first person anyone will see." "She will set the tone for the firm."

Mark didn't tell his people he met Caitlyn standing outside a coffee shop a week ago, a battered suitcase in one hand and a scuffed purse in the other. The wallet in the purse was empty.

"I hate to ask you Mister," she said. "But I'm flat broke sitting on my bum in the street with no place to go ormoney for a meal." "I haven't eaten in three days." "Could you give me a fiver so I can get some food?"

"Come with me," said Mark, "I'll buy you breakfast." They sat in a booth in a local coffee shop eating breakfast. Mark sat nibbling at his food while he watched Caitlyn wolfing hers down. "You really are hungry," said Mark, as the waitress poured another cup of tea for Caitlyn. "How did you come to be on the street broke?"

"How do you think?" she sneered. "It's always because of a man." "My boyfriend, I should say my ex-boyfriend, he just picked up and left me stranded."

"Why would he do that to you?"

"Because his success means more to him than I do, I guess." "He's from back home, Manchester England." "He played minor league soccer for the Manchester Spartans for a few years until a team in Tel Aviv hired him to come play for them there. So my handsome prince picked up and moved to Tel Aviv." "Got to follow my dream" he told me. "But come with me girl. I'll take you to Israel with me. I'm getting paid good money to play for the Macabes come with me it could be fun plus you can keep my bed warm." "We can live the good life you and me." It will be grand adventure surrounded by Hebs." "He played the full season here in Tel Aviv." "He did good, no, he was better than good." "He was the star player on the team. His name was in all the papers and soccer magazines around the world." "He got some write-ups in the sports pages, pictures and such." "He Scored 46 goals in 49 games." "We lived in a small cozy apartment, everything was fine until last week. That's when the walls came crashing down on me." "What happened last week?" asked Mark?

I came home and Greg, that's his name, Greg Kingston, was packing his grip. "Where are we going?" I asked.

"We ain't goin nowhere, girl'." he said sarcastically. "I'm off to Dusseldorf."

"You mean Germany?"

"You got that right. I've just been signed to a fat contract. I have to report to the club day after tomorrow. So this is *Adios*."

"What do you mean, Greg? What am I supposed to do?"

"Whatever you want," he says. "Stay here or go back to Manchester. I don't care. I'm done with you." "It was fun while it lasted but I don't want you anymore." "You're a decent piece, I'll say that for you, but it's the big-time for me." "As a star on the Wolfburg team I can get all the groupies I want, young sweet meat." "I don't need you to hold me back." "Then he ups and walks out the door. No kiss, no goodbye, just bloody well fuck-off." "The creep didn't even pay the last month rent, so I was thrown out the next day." "He didn't leave me a cent not one shekkil. I had 230 dollars I'd managed to put aside but that didn't last long." "I needed a place to stay at night and some food to eat. I ran out of funds a few days ago." "Now you know my sad story," Caitlyn said, trying to smile.

"What do you do?" Mark asked.

"I can do a lot of things." "I was a store-clerk, an administrative assistant in a travel office." "Many years ago I was a Phys-Ed instructor in a gym. Why do you want to know?"

"I'm a sucker for a pretty face, especially one in distress, which I believe you are; so I want to help you."

"Don't get cute with me, Gov'ner. I appreciate the meal, but don't think that gives you a right to get into my knickers."

"No, Caitlyn you've got me wrong. I want to offer you a job."

"Doing what?" she said, looking at me skeptically.

"I'm a lawyer opening a law firm a few blocks from here." "I need a receptionist." Someone who is smart and someone who can take care of herself and an office of first rate attorneys. Do you think you can do that?"

"You mean a 9 to 5 ere, a real job?"

"Maybe 8:30 to 5:30 or 6, but yes, a real job in an office with four lawyers and a paralegal."

"When does this job start?"

"Opening day is January 4th, Monday. But we'll start putting some time in beginning December 21. We have to get the office in shape and begin to work together, so we can be an effective team when the curtain goes up." "Today is the 18th. What do I do until then?" she asked. "Where do I stay, and how do I feed myself until we start work in three days."

"From today til Monday I'll put you up in a hotel." "I have room in my apartment, but that wouldn't look kosher; especially if you are going to be working for me." "I'll check you into the Hilton for the time being, I have a friend who may have an apartment in this area." "That way you'll be able to walk to work since you have no car." I don't think you have a suitable wardrobe in that tattered case do you?"

"No, just some jeans and tops; a skirt with two blouses."

"I'll pay you $18 dollars an hour to start. You'll make between $720 and $800 per week." Mark reached into his pocket taking out three hundred dollar bills which he handed to Caitlyn. "This is pocket-money for you until January 4; that's two weeks from now, so make it last. The hotel room will be paid for; you can charge your meals to the room so you don't have to worry about that. This is my credit card, Mark said, handing over his Bank Leumi blue-card."

"What is this for?" she asked, looking at Mark with wide eyes. I want you to go clothes shopping over the next few days to get a basic wardrobe of clothes suitable for an office environment, a wardrobe you can wear to work each day. You can spend up to $1,500 dollars, so shop wisely."

Caitlyn sat looking at mark sobbing quietly, a tear running down her cheek that she wiped away with the back of her sleeve. "I don't know what to say to you, Mark." I've never met a man who would do a fraction of this without trying to get me in bed on the floor or in the back of a car."

"It's not a gift Catlyn, you can pay me back a little each week from your salary, whatever you can afford will be fine." "Plus, I expect you to be the best receptionist in all of Israel." Mark paid the check walking into the street with the tall slender woman at his side. "Let's take a cab to the Hilton. I'll check you in and leave you to get cleaned-up and relax for the day. Get some rest. I want you at your best when you walk into the office to meet your co- workers on Monday. I'm taking a chance on you so don't let me down."

Now she stood next to Mark looking radiant. Red hair cut short in a boyish style, a black-sheath dress with red high heels showing off her shapely legs. The begger of a few days ago was a stunning princess. The transformation was amazing. Mark was happy to see he still had an eye when it came to picking an exceptional woman. Greg would eat his heart out if he could see Caitlyn now. It was like a scene from My Fair Lady.

"Welcome aboard," said Teddy, smiling approvingly as he introduced the other members of the team. Everyone went to their respective offices to began preparing for the opening just two weeks away. Mark sat at his desk and placed a call to Nat Zuckerberg.

"Zuckerberg" said the gruff voice on the other end.

"Hello, Mr. Zuckerberg, its Mark."

"I told you, Nat. No Mr. Zuckerberg; makes me feel old like your father."

"Ok, then Nat it is."

"I got the invitation to your New Year's Eve party and the luncheon the day before. Showing off for the good people of my city?"

"Yes, you could say that Nat. But I'm calling you for another reason, a favor."

"Is it going to cost me money this favor of yours?"

"Maybe, maybe not."

"What is it, *boychik*? What do you need?"

"I need an apartment Nat. Preferably within walking distance of your office building here on Shanker Street."

"You have a place at the Chrystal Mark. Why another? For a *Chorva*?"

"Not quite. It's for one of my employees. My receptionist had to move out of her present apartment. I need something nearby for her, since she has no car." "I thought with all your buildings you might have something available"

"As a matter of fact I do." "A punk druggy was living in an apartment at 20 Deyanga Street, one of my buildings." "He didn't pay rent for two months, so I had my property manager throw him out a week ago." "The place was a mess; A real disaster." "We had to throw everything out including the carpet." "The flat has been repainted, new carpet put down, I even had it disinfected." "Leon, he's my property manager, is going to buy new furniturefor the place." "I rent it furnished for $680 per month it's yours if you want it." "Tell your receptionist to call Leon she can go with him to pick out the furniture." "The apartment is on the fourth floor of a four-story building." "It's a walk-up but since it's on the top floor it has a balcony overlooking the street."

"Thanks, Nat. I have something else I want to propose to you."

"Not going to cost me is it?"

"No, I'm going to save you money."

"This I want to hear, you always surprise me."

"I want you to hire my firm to represent you in –"

"Whoa," he said. "I have a top-notch law firm that I've been with for thirty years. I'm not about to change."

"I know that Nat, and I'm not asking you to change. But, your firm is handling all your work including the small nuisance work like evictions, collections, minor insurance claims." "You know, slip-and-fall, that kind of thing. Your high-priced firm is charging you partner-rates, probably around $400 or $500 per hour that an associate is doing for $200 an hour. I want that work and I'll do it for a flat-fee of $1,200 per month for twelve months whether you have one case or 100." "That way your fancy high-priced firm won't miss you as a client." "Hell Nat they may even be happy to be relieved of that dirty-work and it will save you money."

"I will say one thing for you, you've got *Chutzpah*. I'll think about it."

Mark told Lyn about her new apartment. "Call Leon at this number. He'll show you the apartment." "If you like it, if you want it you can go with Leon to pick out the furniture." Let me know what you think when you get back." "If you want the apartment it's yours for $680 a month." No first and last month rent, no security deposit, just 680 dollars on the first of the month." "I have a connection with the landlord who will accept my guarantee for your rent."

Mark had the workers clear out the large common accountants' room, and then set it with small round cocktail tables and chairs adding two long tables along the walls, a bar in one corner. He was going to have a buffet luncheon at noon on December 30th for select guests, prospective clients and other lawyers that his people were inviting. It will be an opportunity to show off the new offices and staff of the Aksimon law firm, sort of an open-house reception. Mark hoped that seventy-five to one hundred people would show for the event which would be a prelude to the closed party for twenty-eight people at his Crystal Tower apartment the next night. Teddy invited a dozen lawyers to the luncheon along with two judges. Kimberly asked her ex boss Jed along with a dozen lawyers from other firms she had been in contact with while working at her old firm

"I'm not sure the judges will show up, but they thanked me for the invitation." Teddy informed me.

Kimberly's old boss, Jed, was coming with his partner, and Myria asked some of her law school friends to come along with the old boy network from her chauvinistic firm where she worked for three months. When they heard there would be free food and drink, they all said yes.

Lyn came into my office at 3:30 all smiles. "I love you Mark," she began. "The apartment is beautiful. It's on a quiet street only eight blocks from our office so I can walk to work." "The apartment is bright and spacious and since it's on the top floor, there are two skylights." "Leon was a dear." "He let me pick out all the furniture for the two bedrooms, a living room, eat-in-kitchen, plus two lounge-chairs for the balcony." "It's a fourth-floor walk-up, but that's ok, it will keep me in shape climbing those stairs." "Everything will be delivered this week, Leon told me I can move in Saturday, the 26th. I can't wait. I'll have a place of my own; I won't have to depend on anyone again." "I'll be an independent woman at last all thanks to you." "You'd better stop being good to me Mark, I'll never be able to repay you."

"If you're happy Lyn you will do a better job for me, for the firm. That will be repayment enough."

Mark was looking forward to the activities of Thursday the 31st – the last day of the year. Then to Monday, the 4th of January, the start of a New Year, 2014, a *year to shine*, thought Mark, as he put his arm around Teddy's shoulder. "What do you think partner?"

"To success" Teddy said enthusiastically.

THE END

J.